BOBBY'S GIRL

America, 1968. Everyone has one special summer. For British students Penny and Kate, and Americans Bobby and Sandy, it was that summer on Cape Cod. Warm, languid days filled with love, laughter and music. Until the night Bobby's car crashed and burst into flames, and a bitter old woman took control, changing the survivors' lives for ever.

BOBBY'S GIRL

BOBBY'S GIRL

by

Catrin Collier

Magna Large Print Books
Long Preston, North Yorkshire,
BD23 4ND, England.

British Library Cataloguing in Publication Data.

Collier, Catrin
    Bobby's girl.

    A catalogue record of this book is
    available from the British Library

    ISBN   978-0-7505-3557-1

First published in Great Britain in 2011 by Allison & Busby Ltd.

Copyright © 2011 by Catrin Collier

Cover illustration © Susan Fox by arrangement with
Arcangel Images

The moral right of the author has been asserted

Published in Large Print 2012 by arrangement with
Allison & Busby Ltd.

Magna Large Print is an imprint of Library Magna Books Ltd.

Printed and bound in Great Britain by
T.J. (International) Ltd., Cornwall, PL28 8RW

*For my beautiful new American
daughter-in-law Qita Iseley Watkins.
Welcome to the family.
Ross is a very lucky man.*

CHAPTER ONE

CAPE COD STANDARD
MONDAY, 2ND SEPT 1968

In the early hours of Sunday morning a custom-built, imported, European automobile left the approach road to the Brosna Estate, crashed and burst into flames. At the time of going to press a spokesman at the local hospital refused to comment on the condition of the passengers or confirm the driver had been fatally injured.

Eyewitnesses reported seeing the vehicle, with four people inside, being driven erratically before the incident. The vehicle is registered to Robert 'Bobby' Brosna, heir to the multimillion-dollar Brosna Empire. Rumours he was at the wheel remain unconfirmed.

Hyannisport Cape Cod, May 1987

The press cutting was yellowed by age and spotted with brown blotches. Robert Brosna closed the scrapbook and opened the desk drawer intending to replace it. A photograph frame lay face down in the bottom. He picked it up and turned it over. Two young men wearing white shorts and two young girls in bikinis stood on the deck of a custom-built wooden 1930s schooner. The name was painted on the side. The *Day Dream*.

Images, real and tangible, flooded his mind carrying with them a rush of scents and sounds. He heard the cry of the gulls circling overhead, smelt the salt tang of the sea softened by the heady orange-based perfume both girls had worn. *'We share everything – life's cheaper that way.'*

He recalled the way heads had turned their way in the marina, to look at the girls. Both slim, long-legged and beautiful in the way only the young can be. Their bodies firm, smooth, displayed to male heart-stopping effect in tiny black and white geometric-designed scraps of cloth. Neither had needed their British accent to attract attention. Their swimsuits had been enough. Penny's black circles on a white background, Kate's white squares on a black background, so Carnaby Street – or so they'd assured him; bought on a shopping splurge funded by an unexpected wind-fall.

And now – so passé. What had been stylish two decades ago belonged in a ragbag. He wished he could relegate his memories into a trunk of obscurity like discarded clothes.

Penny's auburn hair fell in a curtain to her elbows. The fringe that covered her forehead was thick, heavy, the eyes beneath it sparkling, tawny brown. One of the waiters at the restaurant where they'd both worked had described them as 'come to bed eyes'. He'd been punched for saying it. Kate's blonde hair was cropped in an urchin cut. Her eyes were the softest of light greys; Penny had called them 'dreamer's eyes'.

He prised the back from the frame and removed the picture. The frame had hidden an inscription,

12

scribbled carelessly in the right-hand corner in a heartbreakingly familiar hand.

Bobby, Sandy and their girls, August 1968.

He ran his fingers over the outlines of the four people in the group. Had this really been him? Had he ever been that good-looking?

Nineteen lonely, pain-ridden years had failed to help him overcome the tragedy of the night that had ended that summer. The passage of time had done little to heal his physical injuries and nothing to soothe his emotional wounds. Four lives ruined and still the repercussions echoed, damning, damaging and destructive.

He binned the frame, slid the photograph into the scrapbook, dropped it into the drawer and closed it. Leaning heavily on his stick he limped to his chair.

It was angled to receive the warmth of the log fire that burnt in the hearth, or more accurately the warmth his Irish wolfhound Czar allowed him to receive. A whisky glass stood on the table at his elbow, his favourite guitar music played softly in the background; a file of Brosna Enterprises financial year-end accounts awaited his attention. And, when he was finished with business, a new thriller by an author he admired had been delivered that morning.

His house was his universe. He'd lived out every moment of the last nineteen years that he hadn't been forced to spend in hospital behind its mirrored glass windows. He could see out, no one could see in. The manufacturer's assurance that not even the sophisticated camera lenses of the most persistent paparazzi could penetrate the glazing had proved correct. Either that or the threat of litigation had deterred photographers from trying.

The house held memories. Happy ones he occasionally succeeded in recalling. He had learnt to take pleasure in solitary occupations: music, books, films, good food, wine. He indulged himself, furnished the house with the luxuries that came with wealth. He had everything a man could want. Except human warmth, companionship and...

The past burnt again as hot and horrific as the fire that had scorched and scarred his body. The cruellest words in the English language – 'if only'.

'If only' he could turn back the clock to the early evening of that September night. 'If only' they hadn't quarrelled. 'If only' they hadn't all climbed into the car. How different would their lives have been?

He left his chair and paced to the window. There were no curtains. They would have been superfluous as no one could see in. Lights shone from the veranda of the main house. Above and behind them every lamp in every room of the mansion that faced the sea was switched on – except one. And that one emitted an eerie, cold, blue-tinged glow. He stared at the telephone.

'How much longer can a hundred-and-four-year-old woman with pneumonia and kidney cancer hold out?'

He realised he'd spoken aloud when Czar opened one eye and looked at him.

'Sorry, boy.' He stood next to the dog and

14

scratched his ear gently with his stick. 'I'm on edge.'

The dog grunted, closed his eyes and rolled over to toast his other side before the fire.

Robert glanced at the file that held the account statements. Charlotte Brosna's hectoring voice lectured in his mind.

'Duty before pleasure, boy – always.'

The first Robert Brosna had made money. The second had partied most of it away before marrying Charlotte. She'd salvaged what she could to create Brosna Enterprises. One of the many things he'd learnt since he'd taken control from her was he couldn't afford to relax his vigilance for an instant. Not if the Brosna Empire was to continue to thrive under his direction as it had done when she'd been at the helm.

He returned to his chair, sipped his whisky, took a calculator from his pocket and opened the file. He hadn't finished inputting the first figure when the telephone rang. He picked up the receiver before it rang a second time.

One of his grandmother's many Hispanic maids whispered down the line. 'Miss Buttons asked me to call you, sir. Mrs Brosna is asking for you. The doctor says it's very close and–'

Robert cut her short. 'Thank you.' He ended the call then rang an internal number. 'Tim, can you bring the car around right away?'

'I'll be with you in a few minutes, sir.' Tim was the one who'd suggested the use of the 'sir' because it didn't raise eyebrows on the rare occasions Robert ventured out in public.

Robert took a white silk hood from his pocket

15

and slipped it on. Apart from holes for his eyes and mouth, it covered his head and neck. He heard the car arrive when he was putting on his hat and jacket. Although the sun had set hours ago, out of habit he pulled his hat low on his forehead before picking up his walking stick and leaving the house. He locked the door and clambered into the back of the car. Tim drove to the main house in silence.

'There's no need to wait, Tim. I'll ring when I want you.'

'No trouble. I'll be in the kitchen.'

'Thank you.' Robert went into the mansion. Leaning on the banister he climbed the stairs slowly and awkwardly. He tapped the door of his grandmother's suite before entering. The enormous room that had served as Charlotte Brosna's study and sitting room for over eighty years looked as though it had been cleared in preparation for a realtor's valuation. He had never seen it as devoid of her personal possessions, not even when she'd been travelling to or from one of the other Brosna houses.

The polished leather top of Charlotte's eighteenth-century mahogany desk was bare. The table beneath the window had been swept clear of silver-framed photographs. There was no sign of Charlotte's eighteenth-century French porcelain clock and ornaments. Considering their value, he trusted they'd been carefully packed away.

Charlotte Brosna had made preparations for leaving life as meticulously as she'd prepared for every other journey she'd taken.

The door to her bedroom was ajar. Robert

16

looked inside. The main lights were switched off, the stained-glass sidelights shaded by silk scarves, which explained the muted glow. The doors to the second-floor veranda were open and the white muslin drapes moved delicately, twin pale translucent ghosts in the sea breeze.

The nurse and doctor stood side by side at the foot of the bed. Charlotte's housekeeper, Harriet Buttons, sat in a chair drawn close, but not too close to the bed. Harriet's hand lay beside her employer's on the lace bedspread but they did not touch and Robert realised, even now, the housekeeper lacked the courage to offer physical comfort to her employer.

'Your grandson has arrived, Mrs Brosna.' Harriet's voice was thick, clotted with unshed tears.

'Perhaps now you'll finally allow me to give you a shot of morphine, Mrs Brosna.' The doctor didn't attempt to conceal his irritation.

Charlotte opened one eye and glared at him. 'You never could understand the word "no", James. It's a blessing at my age to feel something, even pain. Get out, all of you. I want to speak to my grandson.' Her voice wavered but it was stronger than Robert had heard it for some time.

The doctor and nurse left the room. Harriet followed and closed the door softly behind them.

'The file. Bureau, top drawer. Get it. We're alone, so take off that damned hood.'

Robert unmasked and returned the hood to his pocket. He caught sight of himself in the mirror above the dresser and turned aside quickly. He needed no reminder that he was monstrously

17

scarred, or that his lips, nose and ears were un-
natural appendages to what was left of his face.
His skin was thick, blotched and reddened by
numerous transplants, some of which had 'taken'
better than others. Only his eyes remained un-
blemished. Blue crystals in the shadowy gloom.

He went to the bureau, glad of an excuse to
move away from his grandmother. Charlotte had
been old ever since he could remember. Her skin
hung loose in folds around her neck like a ragged
sail on a ship in a breaker's yard. Her thin, blood-
less lips were pulled back, exposing teeth that
appeared too large for her mouth and her white
hair hung loose, fanning out on the pillow behind
her head. But her eyes still had the power to
intimidate. Even now, visiting her deathbed, he
was finding it difficult to imagine them permanently dimmed.

He picked up the file and stared at the photograph pasted on the outside.

'Surprised?' she muttered when he returned to
her bedside. 'I paid your detective to duplicate
his reports. It's all there. The complete history of
the heir to the Brosna Empire. Don't try to
contest my will...'

'I won't.'

'Not so quick. You don't know what's in it.'

'I've never asked you for anything.' He was
bitter.

'Your fine feelings didn't stop you from taking
what I offered.'

'Damn you...'

'My grandson,' she mocked. 'Who doesn't flinch
from cursing an old woman on her deathbed.'

'I am what you made me.'

She moved her arm as though she wanted to wave him away. But the effort sapped her remaining strength. Silence reigned in the room for five long minutes while she fought to remain conscious.

'My will,' she wheezed. 'The lawyers assure me it's litigation-proof. You'll have two million dollars, your house and annuity for your lifetime and the use of all the Brosna assets, including the houses, cars, yachts and jet. But you cannot dispose of anything because the entire estate ... all the companies, money and assets...' Charlotte laboured to draw breath. 'It goes to him.' She pointed to the file. 'Robert Brosna the Fifth. The lawyers will inform him after my funeral. If you want to tell him before...' Her voice faded.

'His name is Andrew John not Robert Brosna,' Robert contradicted.

'The photograph. He's a Brosna...'

'If you read my detective's reports you'll know Andrew wants to be a doctor. He could refuse the inheritance.'

'He won't. Business is in Brosna blood. It will out in him as it did in you.' She closed her claw-like hand over his. 'Robert Brosna the Fifth. My great-grandson. You'll guide him, help him... Promise...'

'I promise I'll try to see him. Nothing more. There's Penny—'

'Stupid girl! How dare she refuse me! How dare she—' Charlotte shuddered and cried out. Her fingernails, horn-like, yellow, dug painfully into his wrist.

'Doctor!' Robert shouted.

Charlotte's piercing screech deepened to a guttural rattle.

'Doctor!' Robert failed to free his arm from Charlotte's grip. Scrabbling in his pocket for his hood with his other hand, he called to the doctor again.

The door burst open. The doctor ran into the room followed by the nurse as Robert pulled his hood, one-handed, over his head.

The nurse reached for Charlotte's wrist to take her pulse. It took her a few moments to prise Charlotte's dead hand from Robert's arm. 'It's a reflex, sir. She wouldn't have meant anything by it.'

'I know.' Free from his grandmother's grasp Robert looked down at her. Her sightless eyes stared blindly up at him.

'She's gone,' the nurse declared superfluously.

The doctor checked his watch and noted the time.

Robert leant against the wall for support. Charlotte Brosna had died as she'd lived. Thinking only of the Brosna business empire; treating her family and the people around her as puppets, whose only purpose was to serve and amuse.

'Would you like me to call the undertaker, sir?' Harriet asked Robert from the doorway.

'Please, Harriet. Did Charlotte leave directives regarding her funeral arrangements?'

'Her solicitor has her written instructions, sir.'

'That's Charlotte. She trusted no one to carry out her wishes and left nothing to chance.'

'She was one of the old school. The last of a

20

kind.' The doctor picked up his bag. 'We won't see her like again.'

Robert refrained from saying 'I hope not'. After all, what had Charlotte done to him that was so terrible?

Neither he nor his friends had been in a fit state to pick up the pieces after the crash in 1968. Charlotte had simply done what she always did in a time of crisis. Rearranged the jigsaw as she'd seen fit, and to her own advantage.

None of them, especially him, had been in a condition to confront or challenge her. And, it could be argued that, despite his devastating injuries, he'd gained the most of the four.

CHAPTER TWO

Tim was waiting for Robert in the hall. 'The maids said it's over.'

'Yes.' Robert continued to limp down the long staircase.

Tim knew better than to offer insincere condolences. 'Home?'

'Please.' Robert looked down and saw the file in his hand. He hadn't realised he'd taken it.

Tim went ahead and opened the car door. Robert climbed in and they drove the short distance to his house.

'Do you want me to come in or would you rather be alone?' Tim asked.

'Alone. But thank you for asking.' Robert left

21

the car, opened his front door, and stepped inside. Czar left the Persian rug in front of the fire and came, tail wagging, to greet him.

'Good boy.' He took a treat from his jacket pocket and fed it to the dog before locking the door. His glass of whisky still stood, untouched, on the table next to his chair. He went to the drinks cabinet and moved a full bottle and ice bucket next to it. He set aside the accounts, sat down and studied the photograph on the outside of the file he'd taken from Charlotte's bureau.

Charlotte was right.

'The photograph. He's a Brosna.'

There was no mistaking the black, tousled, curly hair, deep-blue eyes and well-built frame. They added up to rugged handsome good looks. Andrew John was a Brosna all right. But it remained to be seen whether or not he would become a Brosna in name. And if he did, how would Penny cope with the defection of her only child?

He turned the page.

Andrew Robert John, born 2nd May 1969.

Weight 7lb 11oz.

Status illegitimate.

Mother, Penelope Maud John, born 20th October 1948.

Occupation, student teacher.

Illegitimate – more of a stigma in 1969 than it was now. He flicked through the pages. The file provided a comprehensive overview of Penny and Andrew's life over the last eighteen years. He didn't need to reread the reports that had been sent monthly to know that Andrew 'Andy' John

22

was a much loved son, grandson, nephew, cousin and friend.

Bright, intelligent, academic, athletic, the captain of his school rugby and swimming teams, who'd represented his country in golf and fencing tournaments, and won several cups in local gymkhanas.

He looked closely at the last photograph in the file. It had been taken at Andrew's grandparents' golden wedding celebrations. He was handing his grandmother a bunch of fifty golden roses.

'What are you really like, Andrew John?' he questioned softly. 'The Robert Brosna the Fifth your great-grandmother wanted, or the Andy John your grandparents and mother brought up?'

Robert looked at the photograph for a long time. But no answer came.

As she'd stipulated in her will, Charlotte Brosna's funeral was conducted three days after her death. She was buried with minimum ceremony in the Brosna family plot alongside her husband who'd predeceased her by seventy-eight years.

The minister had received his orders on his last visit to Charlotte. There was one hymn and the bare rites. Enough to satisfy social proprietary and not a word more. Less than twenty minutes after arriving at the cemetery, the funeral procession began the journey back to the Brosna compound for the wake.

Tim Garber slowed the car when he approached the estate. The guard at the entrance operated the switch that opened the gates. Tim pressed the intercom that connected with the back of the limousine.

'The main house or yours, sir?'

'The main house, but I won't be leaving the car,' Robert qualified. 'Fetch Harriet. I'll speak to her here. Afterwards you can drive me home.'

Tim touched his cap to the security guard and drove the limousine through. The procession of funeral and private cars followed them up the incline to the white clapboard mansion, but only Tim parked in front of the entrance. The others made their way to the car park at the side. Tim switched off the ignition, opened the window that connected with the back and faced Robert.

Anyone attending Charlotte Brosna's funeral in the hope of catching a glimpse of the face Robert Brosna had kept hidden from the world for nineteen years would have been disappointed. Charlotte's funeral had been public but Robert had worn the white silk hood that had become synonymous with his persona. As always, outside his house, it was anchored by dark glasses that concealed his eyes, and his hat was pulled low over his forehead.

'Admiring the invisible man effect, Tim?' Robert enquired dryly.

'I was offered three hundred thousand dollars for a photograph of you without the hood,' Tim revealed laconically.

'By anyone I know?'

'Steve Mercer. He has a cousin who works for a newspaper syndicate.'

'Do I know Mr Mercer?' Robert asked.

'He was recently promoted third assistant to the head of Brosna marketing.'

'Remind me to ask Bill James to sack him.' Bill was head of marketing.

'You won't need reminding.' Tim opened the car door. 'I'll get Harriet.'

Grateful for the limousine's blacked-out windows that enabled him to see without being seen, Robert studied the distant Brosna cousins and staff who'd gathered for the wake. There were no friends. Charlotte had none living. Everyone she knew had either loathed her or been terrified of her, the depth of their emotion dependent on their status within the Brosna hierarchy.

Was it his imagination or had the cloying scent of the sickly sweet spring funeral flowers permeated his car? He turned his back on the guests entering the house and looked out over the estate. Built on a headland, the twenty acres of grounds that swept down to the sea were relatively private, thickly wooded around the landward perimeters. But the high fences Charlotte had erected after the accident couldn't screen the grounds from the seaward side.

The last photograph taken of him that had appeared in the press had been snapped by a freelancer when he'd been carried out of a Boston hospital in December 1968. His face had been swathed in bandages. No one could have identified him from it, but Charlotte hadn't taken any chances. After engaging the best lawyers she could find, she'd taken the freelancer to court and sued him for invasion of privacy.

The Brosna name, coupled with the tragedy of that summer night, had gained the judge's sympathy. The compensation the photographer had been ordered to pay had plunged him into bankruptcy and ended his career. Charlotte had achieved what she'd set out to do. The judgement had deterred others from venturing too close.

The house overlooked tennis courts, cultivated gardens and a winding lane that led to a dozen guest houses clustered around a swimming pool. Tim lived in one. The others hadn't been occupied in decades. Two hundred yards behind them, bordering the private beach, was the summer house that had become his home and haven.

He'd had to fight Charlotte for the privilege of solitude. It had taken a year of angry exchanges before she'd capitulated and allowed him to move in during the autumn of 1969. After that, she'd respected his request that neither she, nor the household staff, go near the place; its care and cleaning had been left to him and Tim. Not that Charlotte had approved of Tim Garber.

A Vietnam vet who'd lost his right leg to a landmine and been badly disfigured by shrapnel injuries, Tim had written to Robert in the summer of 1969. Claiming acquaintance with a mutual friend, he'd asked Robert for help in finding work. To Charlotte's annoyance Robert made Tim his personal assistant. The title was window dressing. Tim was more than Robert's assistant and chauffeur. He was his confidant, closest and only friend, knew all there was to know about him and could sense how he felt in any given situation. Robert had wondered if it was an empathy born of common physical disabilities. Tim's facial injuries and scars were not as extensive or hideous as his, but enough to

26

know what it was like when heads turned and people stared.

Harriet tapped the car window. 'You wanted to see me, sir?'

'Please, step inside.' Robert opened the door and she climbed into the back of the car, sitting on one of the pull-down seats opposite him.

Harriet had spent thirty-two of her fifty-six years working for Charlotte. Despite Charlotte's domineering personality and insistence on fastidiousness in all things domestic, Harriet had attracted staff of the highest calibre and succeeded in keeping them. Robert had attributed her success to the high wages Charlotte paid. But when he'd assumed control of Charlotte's personal finances three years ago, he'd discovered his grandmother was out of step with inflation.

He'd doubled and in some cases trebled the wages of his grandmother's staff. They graciously accepted their rises and back pay but none voiced a complaint against Charlotte. It was then he'd realised they served her because their respect for her outweighed their dislike.

'Tim said you won't be coming in for the wake, sir.' Harriet glanced through the window at the guests streaming through the door.

'I won't.'

'Would you like me to send dinner down to the summer house, sir?'

'No, thank you. If I want anything I'll ring the kitchen.'

'As you wish, sir.' Her eyes were cast down. Like all the staff, she had been trained by Charlotte never to look at his hooded face.

27

'I've spoken to the lawyers. She left a few staff bequests. You've received notification of them.'

'We have, sir. Thank you. Mrs Brosna was generous.'

'Please inform the staff I won't be making any changes. Although I'm not my grandmother's heir, I'll do all I can to ensure they'll have a home and job here for as long as they wish. I won't be moving into the main house.'

'You won't be closing it up, sir?'

'Not at the moment, Harriet. I may visit from time to time but I won't be checking for dust on the picture and door frames,' he added.

Realising she was dismissed, Harriet opened the car door. 'Thank you for keeping me informed, sir.'

'Tell Tim I'm ready to be driven down to my house.'

'Yes, sir.'

Robert saw the guests watching his car from the veranda as Tim drove away.

'Your ears burning, sir?'

'From more than the scars, Tim,' Robert concurred.

Tim parked at the side of the summer house and opened the car door. Robert reached for his stick and made his way to the front door. Czar was outside in his run. He whistled to him and the dog ran through the flap that opened into the den.

'I'll be in my house if you need me, sir.'

Robert nodded. He unlocked the door and walked through the living room, which he only used in the evening, into the shabby sun-bleached den. The first Robert Brosna had made millions in the gold rushes which he'd invested in railroads and the motor industry. When the investments began to pay off around the time of the First World War he'd bought land and built the Brosna Estate on the proceeds. No Brosna had made any major changes since, other than to update the decor.

The white-painted floorboards were partially covered by an antique Persian rug that had been deemed too faded for the living room of the beach house thirty years ago. The desk was European, of obscure vintage. Robert loved the pine pedestal with its high top that contained numerous drawers – some secret, which he'd enjoyed discovering over the years. To his disappointment they'd all been empty. Generations of Brosnas had been renowned for the skeletons in their closets, but they'd been too cautious to leave written records of their indiscretions.

The bamboo-framed sofa and easy chairs with their huge feather-filled cushions were as old as the house. As were the chests of drawers. His only contributions to the room were a telephone, fax, computer, printer, television and home movie and audio systems.

A door to the left led to two bedrooms and a single bathroom with tub, shower, washbasin and toilet. The bedroom furniture was pine, the linen, white cotton. The bedroom and bathroom in the main house Charlotte had prepared for his use after the accident were the epitome of masculine luxury. She'd never understood his taste for simplicity in all things except electronic. No one had except…

He pushed the memory from his mind before it paralysed him, opened a desk drawer and lifted out a sheet of headed notepaper.

BROSNA ESTATE

Should he write the letter on the computer and print it out?

No! This was one letter that should be handwritten. But writing pained what was left of his right hand. Would it tempt Penny to reply?

He sprang one of the secret drawers and withdrew the bundle of letters it contained. He removed the topmost one and reread it, wincing at the rejection. It was couched politely enough; he wouldn't have expected anything else from her, but cold civility failed to soothe the sting. He set it aside, unscrewed the top from his fountain pen, gripped it in his fleshless claw and began to form letters, slowly and meticulously.

11th May 1987

Dearest Penny,

As you see from the date, I'm writing this nine days after Andrew's eighteenth birthday. On the desk is the letter you sent me after he was born, together with my cheque which you'd torn in two and the letters I've written you since that you returned.

You insisted in 1969 you didn't want Brosna money, or your son to claim his father's name or any part of the Brosna inheritance. I believe Charlotte was an important enough figure for you to have heard of her death, even in Wales.

You met her; you know what she was like. She never

changed. She was alert, tyrannical, self-centred and domineering to the last.

But, now she is dead and Andrew an adult, the situation has changed. Charlotte has willed the entire Brosna Estate to Andrew. Her lawyers will soon be contacting you. That's if they haven't already.

I know you've never been interested in the Brosna money either for yourself or Andrew, but you've no right to keep the knowledge of the Brosna family and fortune from Andrew any longer.

Logic dictates your son is not wholly yours. Hasn't he inherited a single Brosna characteristic to remind you of that summer we shared?

The telephone number and address below are those of my English lawyer. Speak to his office and they will arrange flights to the States for you and Andrew, or if you prefer, I will come to you.

There is nothing I wouldn't do for you, or Andrew. But you've known that for eighteen years.

Love, as always.

Should he sign it? He couldn't bear to – not to Penny. He initialled it *RB* then reread what he had written before flicking through the file again. There were so many photographs; images that recorded Andrew John's journey from babyhood, through childhood, to young adult. Money really could buy anything. Given enough dollars he had acquired photographs he had no right to claim.

He left the room, went into the living room and opened the drawer that held the scrapbook. He removed the photograph of the two couples standing on the yacht, placed it between pieces of card and folded it into the letter he'd written.

31

Taking an envelope from a cubbyhole in the desk he pushed the letter inside and sealed it. He didn't need to look up the address.

When he finished, he lifted the telephone and dialled an internal number.

'Tim. I have a letter that needs to be posted right away. Send it tracked, signature required. It will be on the desk. If you or Harriet need me, I'll be on the beach.'

Robert whistled for Czar, lifted the dog's lead from its hook, left the house and locked the door. Tim had a duplicate key. He headed for the beach and the fence that separated the Brosna section from its neighbours. When he reached it, he leant against it and looked along the coast.

Few people arrived this early to summer on the Cape, so most of the fences that prevented people wandering from the public beaches on to the private hadn't been replaced after the winter storms.

In the distance he could see the masts of the boats in the dry dock. Somewhere among them was the *Day Dream*. The Robert Brosna who'd ordered the schooner to be custom-built in the Thirties had more money than imagination, christening it after Percy Blakeney's yacht in *The Scarlet Pimpernel*.

He had to admit the name suited the vessel. Looking back that's how he remembered that summer of 1968. An idyllic daydream. Life as it should be lived, until death had intruded and shattered the illusion.

If only the four of them had known that it couldn't last ... they could have ... what?

Prepared for the tragedy?

If they had, would they have lived out those months any differently? And, would the outcome have hurt any the less?

CHAPTER THREE

Penycoedcae Pontypridd, May 1987

Penny John heard a footstep on the gravel path outside her window and turned away from the canvas she'd been studying. Brian knocked on the door and walked straight in. It was the Pontypridd way. He sniffed the air and dropped his postman's bag.

'You're a lifesaver, Pen. I'd never finish my round without a dose of your coffee to send me on my way.'

'So, it's my coffee you love, not me.' She filled a mug and added sugar and milk to his taste. 'You're early today.'

'Mondays generally bring a lighter load.' He sat on a cane chair that faced the french doors that opened into the garden. 'You've one to sign for today. From America. You selling to New York publishers and galleries now?' he fished.

She stirred his coffee and handed it to him. 'I wish.'

'Could be someone who's seen your work and wants to offer you a commission?'

Penny glanced out of the window. 'There's a

red dragon flying towards Beddau.'

'Very funny.'

'Want a biscuit?' She offered him a tin.

'Don't I always after I've walked up Penycoedcae Hill? I swear it's getting longer and steeper. Either that or my legs are getting shorter.'

'It's your legs getting shorter. Old age does that to you,' she teased.

Penny and Brian had begun their education in the same babies' class in Maesycoed Primary School and had been good, if not close friends ever since the teacher made Penny say 'sorry' to him for painting his face blue. 'Miss' had refused to take into account the fact that Brian had been willing and sat still while Penny wielded the brush.

'If you're talking about old age you can speak for yourself,' he countered.

'You can't escape it, Brian. The big four-O is looming for both of us.'

'Not for another year.' He opened the biscuit tin and made a face. 'Ginger nuts. Haven't you any chocolate?'

'Andy ate the last of them yesterday.'

'Tell Andy from me, he's a greedy boy.'

'Growing boy more like.' Penny glanced through the window across the lawn and into her parents' conservatory. Her eighteen-year-old son was breakfasting with her father as he did most mornings. The newspaper was spread on the table around them and they were laughing.

Penny refilled her own coffee mug and sat next to Brian. He usually turned up between seven and half past and she rarely began any serious work until after he left. Determined not to become a financial burden on her parents and make a success of single motherhood and self-employment, she'd vowed to be in her studio every morning by six-thirty. Nine days out of ten she was, but the first hour was rarely productive. She'd tried to fool herself and anyone who asked by pretending she used the time to look over her previous day's output and plan her work. The truth was she usually wasted the hour drinking coffee, nibbling biscuits, and listening to the radio.

Brian pulled her mail from his bag. 'Sign this now, before I forget.' He handed her a form and pen along with her letters.

She scribbled a signature and flicked through the envelopes. There was an electricity bill, a gas bill, a new cheque book from her bank, a royalty statement from her artists' agency; and the recorded delivery from the States. She turned it over and read the return address.

'Someone you know?' Brian asked.

She struggled to remain impassive. If Brian had a fault, it was his addiction to gossip. He also told his wife, Betty, everything he heard and she was even fonder of tittle-tattle.

'Mmm,' she mumbled, not trusting herself to speak.

'Someone you met when you were in America?'

'A casual acquaintance,' she lied. She had only been to the States once, nineteen years ago, but she was aware people in Pontypridd still speculated about her trip, principally because she'd returned with the ultimate Sixties souvenir – a pregnancy. 'So tell me.' She feigned interest. 'What's happening in town?'

'Peter Raschenko's talking about retiring again.'

'And ... you believe him?'

'Everyone knows he'll be running that garage when he's eighty, never mind sixty. How are your mother and father?'

'My father's well, my mother isn't so good.' It was Penny's automatic reply to any enquiry about her parents' health. Her mother suffered from osteoarthritis, a condition that had worsened over the past couple of years.

'Sorry to hear it. But it's this damp weather. Old Mrs Harris down the hill was complaining about her rheumatism...'

Penny didn't want to hear about Mrs Harris's rheumatism. She wanted Brian to leave her in peace so she could open and read her letter.

'You all right, Pen?'

'Pardon?' She realised she'd stopped listening to Brian.

'Nothing wrong, is there? Andy's A levels–'

'Andy has only just finished sitting his mock examinations.' She knew she'd snapped when Brian looked at her even more oddly.

'He's expected to do well, though, isn't he? I mean he has a place lined up in university.'

'Medical college,' she corrected, still terse. 'But he won't be going unless he gets the A-level results they want.' She crossed her fingers behind her back. Andy was bright, but the college place was by no means certain. Although he was the grandson and nephew of doctors he wasn't getting any special consideration. Nor did he

36

expect any. He had to achieve two As and a B grade. His teachers had assured Penny he was on course to get them but that hadn't stopped her from worrying he wouldn't. He could have a cold on the day – or a headache...

'He'll follow in his great-grandfather's, grandfather's and uncle's footsteps. The fourth generation Doctor John in Ponty surgery,' Brian observed.

'If he returns to Pontypridd and goes into general practice after he qualifies.' Penny was irritated by the general assumption that her son would join the medical practice her father had inherited and her brother ran, with occasional help from their father who insisted he had only 'semi-retired'.

'Well, must be on my way. Can't keep the farmers waiting for their circulars from the feed companies.' Brian carried his mug to the sink and turned on the tap to rinse it.

Penny had to stop herself from shouting, 'Leave it. Just go.' When he turned and she saw the expression on his face, she was ashamed. She gestured towards the canvas on her easel.

'Sorry,' she apologised. 'It's not going well.'

Brian squinted at the half-finished painting, a jacket for a romance novel. 'Looks good to me. Mam and Betty always say your book covers stand out a mile in Smith's. They're streets ahead of the others. The only complaint Betty makes is about what's inside. According to her, the best bit of the books she reads these days is what you've put on the outside.'

Penny knew Brian was trying to make her feel

better but she still wanted him gone. She went to the door and opened it. 'Give my love to Betty and your mother.'

'I will.' He left the mug on the draining board and picked up his bag.

Feeling guilty she called after him. 'See you tomorrow. If I finish the painting, you can give me your verdict. And I'll remember to buy chocolate biscuits.'

He waved back at her on his way to her parents' letter box. She closed the door, took a clean paintbrush and slid the wooden stem into the corner of the envelope. Mouth dry, heart beating erratically, she unfolded the letter, removed the cards and studied the photograph.

She hadn't seen it before, of that much she was certain. She couldn't even remember it being taken. But there was no mistaking the four people pictured. Two young couples smiled directly into the camera lens from the deck of a yacht. Their arms were so tightly entwined it was difficult to work out which limb belonged to which body. Given the boys' long hair and the cut of her and Kate's bikinis it could have been a vintage advertisement aimed at luring holidaymakers to Cape Cod. Scrawled across the corner in a familiar hand was *Bobby, Sandy and their girls*.

Penny couldn't bear to look at it.

She opened the drawer she kept her stationery in, pushed the photograph beneath a pile of envelopes and slammed it shut. Then she checked the name and address on the back of the envelope. Not that she needed to. She knew exactly who'd sent it, although there were only initials on the handwritten sheet. It had been optimistic of her to think he'd allow Andy's eighteenth birthday to pass without attempting to get in touch with her...

She read the letter and reread it, until it was imprinted on her mind.

There is nothing I wouldn't do for you, or Andrew. But you've known that for eighteen years.
Love, as always.

Penny slipped the letter into the back pocket of her jeans, opened the french doors, and breathed in the aromas of spring. Damp acidic earth, rosemary and bluebells, the light perfume of apple and cherry blossom; and, overlaying everything, the lingering fragrance of woodsmoke from the cold embers of the bonfire her father and Andy had fed yesterday evening with winter's dead wood.

It was peculiar how a scent could conjure the past even more effectively than a photograph. It demolished the floodgates she'd built to hold memories she couldn't bear to dwell on. And, as her defences crumbled, the intervening years washed away. She was back in that summer of 1968.

So many memories. Not all of them painful. Late evening after darkness had fallen, thick and fast. Without light pollution from street lamps, the moon and stars had shone brighter than the neon glares of Broadway. A circle of young people sitting around a campfire in a yard, roasting potatoes and melting cheese, and marshmallows that dripped from the sticks into the flames. Eating – talking – arguing – laughing – demolishing the hidebound institutions of the world and rebuilding them in fairer, more honest modes while watching smoke drift upwards in the still, humid air. Lulls in the conversation, when Bobby or Sandy, or both, played their guitars, and they sang – sang what?

The anthem of the Sixties, immortalised by Joan Baez, 'We Shall Overcome'? Because everyone under twenty-one fervently and sincerely believed that they could create a better world to replace the corrupt one they'd inherited. Or had they sung the signature tune that had become hers for a season – 'Bobby's Girl'?

In 1968 she *was* Bobby's girl. All her dreams and aspirations had been centred on Bobby. She'd loved him with her whole heart. Simply being close to him had made her happier than she'd ever been before – or since.

When that magical once-in-a-lifetime summer was drawing to an end on Cape Cod, she'd thought nothing could change between them. That she would go on loving him until the end of her days.

She found herself smiling, despite what had happened afterwards. Nineteen years later, some memories still had the power to warm.

'You all right, Pen?'

Her father had left the conservatory and walked to the door of her studio and she hadn't noticed.

She felt her lips stiffen. 'Fine.'

Her father shook his head. 'You never could tell a lie, not even a white one, as well as your

40

brothers and sisters.'

Realising she was trembling, she sat down abruptly. Her father went to the table, refilled her coffee mug, and poured another for himself.

'Thank you.' She took the coffee mug from him. Her father had always been a constant in her life. There for her, ready and willing to try to solve her problems, large and small. For the first time she noticed his broad back was bowed and his auburn hair had turned iron grey. It couldn't have lost its colour overnight. The father she adored had become an old man. And she hadn't noticed.

He sat next to her and reached for her hand. 'Anything I can help with, sweetheart?'

'Where's Andy?'

'Picking up his rugby kit and bags. He told me he's already said goodbye to you.'

'He has.' Andy, like Penny, hated drawn-out goodbyes. Penny had brought up her son to be self-reliant and independent. But, close as they were, she hadn't been able to prevent him from adopting some of her foibles. A dislike of salad cream, bottled tomato sauce, eggs with runny yolks and slugs and snails. He'd also inherited her abhorrence of cruelty to all living things and an aversion to prolonged goodbyes.

Using the excuse of taking his clean washing to his room, Penny had said goodbye to Andy first thing. And, mindful of the antics the school's senior rugby team had indulged in on past tours and the town had talked about for months, she'd delivered a lecture of dos and don'ts. Andy had mocked her gently by reminding her he was no

41

longer six years old.

She watched Andy reverse the car his grandfather had bought him for his eighteenth birthday out of the garage. He hit the horn, wound down his window and shouted, 'See you next week, Mam.'

'Wait.' Penny ran out and kissed his cheek through the open car window.

'I'm only going for a week,' he reminded her irritably.

'Sorry, impulse,' she apologised.

He gave her a sheepish smile. 'I love you too, Mam. Bye, Granddad.'

Penny watched him drive through the gates and on to the lane that led down the hill into the town.

'Will his car be safe left at the school?' She returned to her chair.

'Safer than here I should think,' her father reassured. 'They lock up at night.'

Penny thought about the letter.

Hasn't he inherited a single characteristic of his father's?

The answer was too many for her to forget for an instant the man who had fathered him. Thick, black, curly hair, deep-blue eyes that usually sparkled with mischief; a six-foot-six well-built frame, taller than any of her brothers' or sisters' children. Her son – and Bobby's.

She waited until the sound of Andy's car engine died away, before taking the letter from her pocket and handing it to her father.

Her father read the letter before returning it to her. 'Do you remember what you said to your mother and me when we brought you back from America?'

'I remember confessing I was pregnant and being terrified of your reaction. I expected a scene. But all Mam said was, "A grandchild, how lovely." And you said, "We'll do whatever we can to help. It's your decision but I think you should finish college."'

'Which you did,' he smiled. 'It took courage for you to finish your course in Swansea, Pen. Some people were still petty-minded about illegitimacy at the end of the Sixties. But to answer my question, what you actually said was, "Better I bring my child up alone than go begging to a man who doesn't want me or his baby." But this,' he tapped the letter in her hand, 'wasn't written by a man who didn't want you. What was it, Pen? I know his disfigurement wouldn't have stopped you from marrying him. Was it his money?'

'It's not what it seems, Dad.'

'Did he make things difficult for you? I've treated men who've been horribly maimed in the pits. Some did all they could to push their wives and girlfriends away lest love turn to pity,' he suggested astutely.

'If that had been the problem, I believe, given time, I could have overcome it.'

'Was it his grandmother? Charlotte Brosna certainly didn't want you to see him after the accident. She couldn't wait to get you out of the States. Even bought you a flight ticket home.'

'Which you refused to take.' She finished her coffee and set her mug on the floor.

'I didn't like the way the woman tried to

assume control, not only of her grandson's life but my daughter's.' He wrapped his arm around her shoulders. 'But bullying has its own reward. Charlotte Brosna reached a ripe old age.'

'After Bobby recovered as much as he's ever going to, I doubt Charlotte could have stopped us from seeing one another – if we'd wanted to.'

'She wanted Andy when she found out you were pregnant.'

'She couldn't do anything legally without Bobby's permission. I have him to thank for respecting my decision to bring him up alone.'

'Pen, those letters you wrote to your mother and me from America, you were besotted with Bobby Brosna. If you really meant that much to one another, I can't understand why you wouldn't let him help you to bring up Andy. Tell me, if it wasn't the accident, what really happened to separate you two?'

She couldn't answer him because the secret wasn't hers to tell.

'Do you want to talk about it, sweetheart?'

She shook her head, buying time to fight the tears pricking the back of her eyes. She didn't give herself long enough. Her voice wavered when she finally answered. 'The choices I made seemed right at the time.'

'But not now?'

'I don't know what I feel now, Dad.'

'You do know you have to tell Andy about his father – and this legacy.'

'Not until after he's sat his exams.'

'There I agree with you. I've seen how a little money can unhinge a teenager. But billions? Even

I, at my advanced age, can't comprehend wealth on that scale.' Her father rose to his feet. 'I'll leave you in peace, Pen. If you want to talk, you know where to find me. Whatever you decide, your mother and I will be behind you as we've always been. Just one word of advice.'

She looked up at him.

'For the first time in eighteen years and almost two weeks think about someone besides Andy. Think about yourself, Pen. Then do what's best for both of you.'

CHAPTER FOUR

Penny couldn't settle after her father left. She picked up her paintbrush and looked critically at the unfinished canvas on her easel. She'd never aspired to be Andy Warhol, but long hours and hard work had eventually paid off. For the last seventeen years she'd made a reasonable living painting book jackets for crime and romance novels. It helped that she'd never had to buy a house or pay rent. Her parents had converted an old barn at the back of the family home into self-contained accommodation for her and her baby before Andy was born.

They'd refused to allow her to pay rent but she'd insisted on paying her own bills from the outset and, as soon as she could afford to, she'd set money aside to repay them. Before Andy's sixth birthday she'd cleared the debt. Two years later she'd made enough to rebuild the derelict stables adjoining her barn conversion and turned them into a studio. Since then, she'd brought in enough money to meet her own and Andy's needs and most of Andy's wants, as well as set aside savings for Andy's college fund.

The background on the jacket of the bodice-ripper she was working on was exotic eastern – the scene tropically garish but the heroine didn't look right. The publishers had asked for sultry, but the girl she'd painted looked sulky. Penny wondered if it was her fault or that of the model she'd hired to pose in harem dress. She studied the photographs she'd taken at the shoot and couldn't decide.

She busied herself mixing fresh paint but even as she lightened and darkened shades on the palette, she knew she was about to make a bad job worse. After scrubbing off a couple of daubs and smudging the canvas, she accepted she wouldn't do anything worthwhile in her present mood.

She packed away her paints, cleaned her brushes, hung her smock behind the door, threw a poncho over her shirt and jeans, and left the studio. She'd intended to head for the open mountain, her own and her brothers' and sisters' playground when they'd been children. And her sanctuary since the birth of Andy had forced her to accept that she'd 'grown up'. But something held her back and she found herself standing at her front door.

She ran up the stairs past the bedrooms and headed for the attic stairs. There were skylights in the roof. It had been boarded out as a playroom-cum-study for Andy. But during the conversion she'd asked the builder to erect a partition wall at the far end. The result was a storage area six feet deep by twenty feet wide. A 'glory hole' she and Andy used to house things they no longer needed but couldn't bear to part with.

Andy's study area was unnaturally tidy. His BBC computer unplugged, and his videos stacked in a neat pile next to his video player and TV. A sure sign he'd be away for a few days.

Penny crossed the room and unlatched the door to the cupboard, fumbling for the light switch because there was no window or loft light in the area. Three of the walls were shelved. As she'd made a point of labelling everything before storing it, and insisted Andy do the same, the labels read like a history of their lives.

Andy's high chair, cot, pushchair and baby walker, shrouded in plastic sheeting. Andy's early Fisher Price toys. Why had she kept them when she could have passed them on to nieces and nephews who were younger than Andy? A desire to bring them out some day, show them to her grandchildren and say 'your father loved this toy when he was your age'?

Had she dreamt of a family life for Andy with a wife and children because circumstances had made her a single mother? She turned her back on Andy's toys and found what she was looking for under a pile of boxes that held Andy's early paintings and schoolwork.

It was a battered canvas holdall in green tartan with vinyl handles. She'd bought it on a stall on

47

Pontypridd market for her trip to America. She could even remember the banter she'd exchanged with the good-looking young stallholder.

'Going somewhere nice, love?'

She'd tried not to boast, but it had been difficult. *'America.'*

'Ooh, get you. Well there's enough room in that bag for me. When do you want to pack me in it?'

She set the boxes aside, picked up the bag and shook the dust from it. It was heavy. She switched off the light, closed the door and carried it down the stairs to her bedroom. She set the bag on the cream crewel work rug beside her bed, instantly regretting it when she saw the dust smudges it made. The zip was stiff, rusted with age, the vinyl cracked. She persevered and broke two finger-nails before she finally managed to open it.

On top was a photograph album. The plastic cover she remembered as white had yellowed. She opened it and was faced with a photograph of herself and Richard 'Rich' Evans taken on their first day at Swansea Training College. Under-neath, she'd written *Two head teachers in the making*. She'd meant it ironically. Neither of them had the slightest intention – then – of pursuing a career in teaching.

Rich was going to be an actor. The only question was whether his career would progress along the Royal Shakespeare Company, classic theatrical route, or the film star path that led to Hollywood. She was going to be a groundbreaking artist who would create 'true art' – or what she at eighteen believed 'true art' to be.

Both Rich's parents and her own had insisted

they have 'qualifications to fall back on' because their chosen professions were notoriously precarious. They'd picked Swansea because it had been one of the first colleges to offer a Bachelor of Education degree. It was also the only college to offer them both a place. And, as they, but not their parents, considered themselves engaged to be married, they'd refused to be separated. Rich had opted to study English; she, art.

Penny turned the page. Her with Kate Burgess, her best friend since their first day in Pontypridd Girls' Grammar School in 1959, and her travelling companion on that fateful 1968 trip to the States.

She leant back against the bed, thought of the letter she'd received, pictured the disfigured recluse who'd written it, closed her eyes – and the years tumbled away.

Swansea, January 1968

If she hadn't cut her moral philosophy class to play chess with Rich in the common room, she might never have gone to America. Within an hour of the announcement being posted on the noticeboard, all the flight tickets had been reserved and deposits paid. A fist fight broke out in the union offices over the last two. But thanks to Kate, she'd booked hers before the trip had been advertised.

She and Rich had tucked themselves into a corner and were in the closing stages of a game. The room was unpleasantly warm. The college

49

could never get it right. In winter, the students either froze or baked. The atmosphere was dense, blue with cigarette smoke, and heavy with the mixed odours of coffee, sweat, cheap aftershave and scent. She was about to checkmate Rich in six or ten moves, depending on whether or not he'd seen through her strategy, when Kate burst in.

Everyone turned when Kate slammed the door back on its hinges. She looked as though she'd been under a shower. Her nylon mac dripped puddles on the vinyl tiled floor; her white tights were grey with mud splashes, her short blonde hair was plastered to her head but her cheeks glowed with excitement.

Kate shouted but she couldn't hear her above the political arguments raging against a background of Jimmy Ruffin's 'What Becomes of the Broken Hearted' being belted out on the record player. She shook her head and pointed to her ears.

Kate charged across the room. Oblivious to their game her overflowing bag hit their chessboard. A yoghurt and monster bar of chocolate spilt out knocking over half a dozen pieces.

'Pen, you'll never guess—'

'Thanks for killing our game and so much for your diet, Kate,' Rich griped. He and Kate had hated one another for years. Neither of them bothered to disguise their mutual loathing. She'd told both of them it wasn't easy having the love of her life and best friend at constant loggerheads but her protests hadn't had the slightest effect.

'I'm talking to Pen, not you,' Kate snapped.

'That's my rook you sent flying across the room. And I was winning,' Rich carped, when Kate swept the board again with the edge of her mac.

'No you weren't. Pen had a cunning plan to checkmate you in three moves. She always does.' Kate picked up the rook and turned her back on Rich. 'The union's chartered a plane. It's leaving for New York the first week of June and returning mid September. Forty-eight pounds return and they'll help any student who wants to go to find a job.'

'Forty-eight pounds! You sure?' She abandoned the game.

'Where are you two going to find forty-eight pounds?' Rich scoffed. 'It's two weeks into term but everyone I know has an overdraft.'

'Not me. After watching my mother struggle with the tallyman for years I know how to hold on to my money.' Kate had been brought up by a widowed mother on a council estate. The poorest and roughest in Pontypridd.

'Do you have forty-eight pounds?' she asked Kate.

'I handed in my cheque ten minutes ago.'

'Rob a bank or gone on the game, Kate?' Rich goaded.

Kate ignored him. 'I met Joe Hunt in town. He was on his way back from a meeting at the university union. The notice won't be on the board until tomorrow morning. There's bound to be a rush for seats because the offer's open to all Swansea students in the Uni, Tech and Art

51

colleges.' Kate gave Rich a mocking smile. 'As for the forty-eight pounds, the Dragon Hotel was advertising for a waitress. All day Saturday and Sunday and two week-night evenings. Five pounds a week plus tips and a free ride back here at the end of the shift.'

'You've taken it?'

Penny didn't know why Rich had asked. It was obvious from the triumphant look on Kate's face she had.

'It gives me four months to replace what I've taken from my grant cheque and save spending money.' Kate wrinkled her nose. 'Not that we're going to be allowed to take more than fifty pounds out of the country. Stupid government and their stupid penny-pinching rules to stop the rich spending abroad; if we don't find jobs within a day or two in the States, we'll be sleeping in the street.'

'Do the union want all the money upfront?' Penny'd tried to calculate how much was left of her grant cheque in her bank account. She'd a massive overdraft before Christmas and spent more than she should have on presents for her family.

'Do you think I would have handed my cheque into the union office if they didn't? I'm still living off what I made working in the Post Office at Christmas. I haven't touched my grant. I won't need any extra cash for a few weeks and, when I do, I'll have my Dragon wages to fall back on.'

'You're going to wear yourself out, waiting tables two days and four nights a week as well as studying. Most people who flunk out do so after the second-year finals.' Rich couldn't resist the opportunity to forecast doom for Kate.

'You're thinking of students of low intelligence and no stamina, like yourself,' Kate bit back.

Rich ignored Kate and glared at Penny. 'You can't seriously be considering going, Pen?'

'It's America.'

'It's not like the TV shows.' Rich was always teasing her and Kate about their addiction to American westerns, like *Bonanza* and the *High Chaparral*. 'The cowboy films you watch are their idea of serious history. And Hollywood is a right dump. Worse than the council estates around Ponty.'

'Been there, have you, Rich? The council estates as well as Hollywood?' Kate sniped.

Rich remained unabashed. 'Face it, Kate, you live on an estate. You know what I mean.'

'No, I don't. Would you care to explain?' Kate demanded.

Penny'd stepped in. 'Stop quarrelling.'

'Kate started it.'

'No she didn't. You're being childish. We've moved on since Victorian times. No one gives a damn where people come from these days.'

Even then she'd occasionally wondered why she stayed with Rich. It wasn't as though she hadn't had offers from boys just as attractive. But whenever she came close to moving on, Rich would say or do something heart-meltingly sweet, like drive her down the Gower so she could photograph and sketch the landscape while he stood around freezing. Or produce tickets for a Royal Shakespeare production in the Aldwych they were both desperate to see. Or escort her to an art exhibition that bored him witless just so she wouldn't have to go on her own.

'Coming with us, Rich?' Kate taunted, knowing Rich's teacher father insisted both his sons work on their grandfather's farm every holiday 'to keep their feet on the ground'.

'I suppose I could ask my old man if he'd let me off herding sheep, milking cows and mucking out horses this summer.'

'Don't bother. You'd cramp our style.' Kate wasn't joking and Rich knew it.

Tired of listening to Kate and Rich fence words, Penny'd left her chair. 'You going to the hostel, Kate?'

Kate stuffed the yoghurt and chocolate back into her bag. 'Yes, before I get any more gibes about my diet.' She waved the bar of chocolate under Rich's nose. 'Alison asked me to get this when I said I was going into town.' She bent close to Rich's ear. 'It's for her little brother's birthday,' she shouted, making him jump.

'What about our game, Pen?' Rich questioned petulantly.

'Kate's right. You were losing.'

'I wasn't. And, you said you wanted to see *The Magic Roundabout*.'

The only time the common room was full was the ten minutes when the cartoon was shown on television before the evening news.

It was Rich's remark that made her decide, no matter what, she was going to the States. If for no other reason than it would prove her independence.

She'd picked up her bag. 'I need to phone home about America. If I plead poverty, my father may cough up the fare. He's always telling us travel broadens the mind.'

'Travel in Europe maybe,' Rich declared. 'But I fail to see how travel in America will do anything of the kind. There's no culture...'

'See you at supper.' She'd pretended not to hear Rich when he called after her but she noticed Kate turning and poking her tongue out at him.

CHAPTER FIVE

'America, darling, what a marvellous opportunity. For four months you said?'

'June to September.' Penny knew her mother would be pleased at the thought of her travelling with other students.

'Is Rich going?'

'He's thinking about it.' Her parents had made it clear they felt she and Rich had become too serious about one another too young. 'Kate's going.'

'That's wonderful, Penny, darling. I'll get your father to transfer forty-eight pounds into your account tonight.'

'It would be better if he sent me a cheque made out to the student's union, Mam.'

'You're overdrawn again.'

'Not by much,' she lied.

'How much is not much?'

'I'm not sure.' She reflected that that, at least, was the truth.

'Sort it, darling, and tell me how much you need. And if Kate needs help...'

'She wouldn't take it, Mam. You know how independent she is.' She glanced over her shoulder into the foyer where Kate was waiting for her.

'You could try, but be tactful.'

'I'll ring you again when I know more. Love to you, Dad, and everyone.'

'I'll pass on the message. You're eating properly and taking care of yourself?'

'Of course, Mam.'

'You'd better do some clothes shopping. Depending on where you go in America it could be hot. Shall I ask your father to put a hundred pounds into your account? Or won't that be enough?'

'I'll make it enough.' She wondered if the Dragon needed another waitress. 'And, if he does stretch to a hundred pounds, tell him I won't need another sub until the autumn and I won't then, if I get a halfway decent job in America.'

'Seeing is believing, darling.'

'You're not cross about the overdraft?'

'Resigned. You're no worse than Rachel, Ned and Evan.'

'The advantage of being the youngest is your parents have seen it all before. That's the pips, Mam. I haven't any more money. Love you.' She hoped her mother heard her last words before the line went dead.

'Well?' Kate asked.

'My mother's going to ask my father to send me the money.'

'Lucky you.' There wasn't a trace of envy in Kate's voice. She wasn't sure there wouldn't have been in hers, if their situations had been reversed.

'We'd better talk to someone about work permits.'

'And jobs,' Kate echoed.

'You're really going?'

Rich's question irritated her as much as his attitude towards Kate. 'I dropped a post-dated cheque into the union office an hour ago.'

They were facing one another across the supper table. The dining room was almost empty. It was Wednesday, the one weekday evening when visits from the opposite sex were officially allowed in the hostels from seven until ten o'clock. Not that the privilege affected the boys' hostel. Their wardens treated them as adults and allowed them to have visitors for as long as they wanted, at any hour of the day or night – and all night if the mood took them. Unlike the elderly female warden the girls had nicknamed 'Fanny', who supervised the girls' hostel.

Fanny spent her evenings and nights creeping up and down the corridors in soft-soled bedroom slippers, listening at their doors for a masculine voice. If she heard one, the punishment was swift and severe. The visitor's hostess was exiled to selected 'digs' where the landlady's rules were even stricter than Fanny's.

'What about me?' Rich asked.

'What about you?' She dipped a spoon into a bowl of apple pie and custard, decided she wasn't hungry enough to eat it, and pushed it aside.

'I can't believe you're going to leave me for four months.'

'We're not married.'

'We agreed to marry after we qualified. I wanted to buy you an engagement ring for Christmas. You wouldn't let me.'

'I'm not in the mood to argue with you.' She left the table.

'Pen,' he followed her into the car park. 'I'm only upset at the thought of not seeing you for months on end. Come to my room and wait for me while I phone home,' he begged.

'You're going to ask your father if he'll let you off working on your grandfather's farm this summer,' she guessed.

'After I've spoken to my brother.'

'Clever move. Get Jack to argue your case for you.'

Rich's elder brother was a postgraduate research student in London. Much to their geography teacher father's disgust he'd chosen to study philosophy. Jack, too, helped out on their grandfather's farm. When it came to family arguments, Jack always fought in their mother's best interests as she was self-effacing and their father overbearing. Jack also did his best to protect his younger brother from their father's volatile temper and arrogance, traits she was beginning to suspect Rich had inherited.

Rich held out his hand. 'I'm sorry.'

She capitulated and took it.

'Forgiven?'

'I'll think about it while I wait for you.'

They crossed the lawn. Rich went to the payphone in the foyer and she took the lift to his top floor room. Even the corridors in the boys' hostel smelt differently from the girls'. Mixed odours of male sweat, stale beer and burnt toast hung unpleasantly in the air, and Rich's room had a distinct 'dirty sports socks, gym changing room' atmosphere. She opened the window. Shivering, she gazed out at the view of Swansea Bay.

The curve of the shore was highlighted by street lamps that burnt golden in the misty twilight. Boats bobbed on their moorings at the Mumbles end of the bay but all she could think about was America.

She'd plenty of time to dream of New York and art galleries. As the minutes ticked past she stopped looking at her watch. She'd seen Joe Hunt when she'd dropped her cheque off at the union office. He'd given her a photocopied list of summer camps that employed students as counsellors but she'd set her sights elsewhere. She intended to find a job in the city. Waiting tables or working in a bar in Greenwich Village in the evenings so she could spend her days visiting the centres of culture she had read about. The Guggenheim, the Metropolitan, the Museum of Modern Art...

Penny heard the lift whirr upwards. The doors opened, footsteps echoed down the corridor and Rich strode in. She asked the question, although she already knew the answer from the expression on his face.

'What did your brother and father say?'

'Jack was great. He always is. He phoned my father for me but the brute wouldn't even consider it. He said Granddad needs all the help he can get this summer. The old man says he wants to sell the farm in a year or two and needs to get it in good shape. That means repairing and repainting the farmhouse, all the outbuildings, and rebuilding the drystone walls. He can afford to get in professionals. But his grandsons are cheaper. Never mind that they have their own lives to live. And I don't believe for one minute he's serious about selling. They'll carry him out of that farmhouse, feet first. I tried phoning my father after I talked to Jack but...'

'But?' she prompted when he hesitated.

'I never want to see or speak to the bastard again.' Rich threw himself on the bed and crossed his arms behind his head.

'That's your father you're talking about.'

'He's an unreasonable sod. I wish I had yours.'

'I'm lucky.' She kept her relief in check. Ever since Kate had suggested that Rich would 'cramp our style' she'd been imagining the two of them wandering around America, sharing experiences, making new friends – and without Rich's watchful and jealous eye – of both sexes. 'I'm sorry.'

'No, you're not. You couldn't wait to rush off with Kate to phone your mother earlier.'

'I phoned my mother because I didn't want to miss out on a seat on the plane. I doubt I'll have the chance to go to America again at that price.'

'You want to go to America so you can spend the summer hunting boys with Kate.'

Her temper rose. 'Where's that coming from?'

'I saw the look on your faces when you left the common room. And I suppose you'll stay on the pill when you're there, so you can sleep with anyone who takes your fancy.'

'How dare you!'

He confronted her. 'But you will stay on the pill?'

'You know damn well you can't just stop taking it without risking a pregnancy. You'd have to start using condoms now if I did, and you'd have to use condoms when I came back for at least a month, if not two. You're the one who hates them. But that's not the point. The point is – you don't trust me. That hurts.'

'Does it?' he challenged.

'Yes, it does. You know you're the only boy I've ever slept with.' She went to the door.

Rich blocked her path. 'I do trust you, Pen. Can't you see this stupid argument isn't about trust or me and you or the pill? It's Kate. She's always creating trouble between us and you always take her side.'

'If I "take sides", it's the side of common sense. And you're wrong. This argument *is* about us. Being my boyfriend doesn't give you the right to tell me when I can and can't take the pill. The next thing you're going to say is you're sorry the pill was invented because it gives women too much freedom.'

'You're never going to let me forget my father said that, are you?'

61

'No, because there are times when you behave just like him.'

'I'm sorry. I do trust you, Pen, except when you're with Kate. She needles me...'

'And you needle her. You know how sensitive she is about her background.'

He shrugged. 'She did well to get into grammar school.'

She finally erupted. 'Don't you *dare* patronise her. Kate's my closest friend and she's where she is because she's intelligent, works hard, gets a full grant and is willing to do any job she can get to supplement it. Your constant sniping at her is wearing me down.'

'Kate enjoys annoying me and you know it.'

'Only because you harp on about her living on a council estate. Given that her father died when she was two, it's not as though her mother had a choice. And Kate *did* do well. Do you know how many girls attended the girls' grammar school from that estate? Two; that's not in our year, that's in the entire school of five hundred and something. And the teachers were foul to both. Is it any wonder Kate's sensitive?'

Rich capitulated but only because Penny's anger could smoulder for days. 'You win, Pen, I'll try to be nice to Kate, but it's not easy when she takes everything I say the wrong way.'

'She wouldn't if you spoke to her with respect.'

He changed the subject, as he always did when he was in danger of losing an argument. 'Pontypridd won't be the same without you this summer. We always have fun together, don't we?'

'Yes,' she conceded abruptly.

'It would have been our last summer before getting married.'

'I haven't said yes to an engagement ring yet. And marriage is the last thing I want to think about before my finals.'

'When I asked you to marry me, you agreed we'd set the date after we left college.'

'That was when we were still at school.'

'So now you don't want to marry me?' he challenged.

'I don't want to *know* you when you're in this mood, let alone marry you.'

He pulled the sad clown face that usually amused her. 'I don't want to lose you.'

She didn't move from the window. 'You will if you carry on like this.'

'You're talking about going away for four months.'

'To work and see a new country.' As Rich had made the first apologetic move, she felt she had to give him something in return. 'I may appreciate you all the more when I return.'

'Is that a promise?'

'We may have gone to separate schools–'

'Only because they wouldn't let me into the girls' grammar school.'

It was a poor attempt at humour and Penny ignored it. 'But we haven't spent more than a couple of hours apart since we came to college. I'd have been happy if you could have come with us, but thinking about it, perhaps it's not a bad idea to take a break after living in one another's pockets for the last eighteen months. If only to be absolutely sure of our feelings.'

'I know what I'm feeling is the real thing. All I want is a chance to persuade you that you can trust your feelings too.'

He left the bed and kissed her slowly, thoroughly and hungrily. They'd come a long way since their first fumbling attempts at lovemaking on her fifteenth birthday.

'Is the door locked?' The boys had a disconcerting habit of walking in and out of one another's rooms at all hours.

He stepped back and turned the key. 'It is now.'

She pulled off her cardigan and tugged her sleeveless black polo neck skinny-rib over her head.

'You have such a beautiful body.' He watched her step out of her tights and grey miniskirt. 'You can't blame me for being jealous.'

'Who else should I blame?' She unclipped his belt and unzipped his jeans.

'I'm sorry for being an idiot,' he nuzzled her neck.

'Show me how sorry.'

She fell backwards on to the bed and he entered her.

But even during the shattering climax of orgasm, when she dug her fingernails into his back and he breathed heady protestations of love, she found herself wondering if there was more in store for her in America than Rich could give.

Later, with hindsight, she suspected a part of her she'd never allowed to surface hoped there was.

CHAPTER SIX

Pontypridd, May 1987

Penny shifted slightly on the floor, padding the base of the bed with her duvet. When she'd made herself comfortable, she turned to the next photograph, a black and white snap taken with a box Brownie. She and Kate were on the pavement outside the college dressed in jeans, suede boots, thick sweaters and second-hand combat jackets. Their college scarves were draped around their necks. She had a duffel bag and Kate was clutching her 'haggis'. A sure sign they were about to hitch-hike.

That was something she couldn't bear the thought of Andy doing.

The standard ironic parental advice: 'Don't do as I did, it's dangerous and you could get hurt.'

It was why she'd allowed her father to buy Andy a car. Her parents and Kate's mother would have locked them up if they'd known how often she and Kate had disregarded their stern warnings and stood, thumbs extended, at the side of the road.

Given the number of certifiable lunatics in the world, they'd been lucky. The worst that had happened to them in Britain was a Rolls-Royce they'd been given a lift in had broken down on the road outside London.

But that had been before they'd reached America.

London, May 1968

'We'll never get through. It's bedlam.' Kate dropped her bulging 'haggis', a kitbag she'd knitted from odd ends of wool to a bizarre pattern created by her overactive imagination. She was careful to hold on to the drawstring that fastened the top.

They were on the fringe of Grosvenor Square. Mounted police ringed an enormous mob of students who'd linked arms to prove they were in possession of the area and intended to keep it that way. Half the protesters were standing, half sitting and lying on the grass. Their shouts filled the air.

'Ho! Ho! Ho Chi Minh! We shall fight and we shall win!'

There must have been an American contingent because *'Hell no, we won't go'* had a strong eastern seaboard accent. Just as *'Make love, not war'* was shouted in very English tones.

Fired by the atmosphere and camaraderie, Penny grabbed Kate's arm. 'Let's join them.'

'Are you mad?' Kate, the ever sensible asked. 'We're here to get work permits. If we're arrested for protesting against the Vietnam War and the embassy staff see us, they'll never give them to us.'

'Everyone knows the Americans are fighting the entire Vietnamese population,' she argued. 'My brother Evan says Communism is the fairest

66

way for the feudal medieval societies of Russia and China to progress to the modern age.'

'Say that any louder and we definitely won't get work permits,' Kate warned.

'None of the American conscripts want to be there. That's why so many American boys are in Europe. Evan met dozens of them in music college. They would have preferred to have studied in the States, but if they'd remained they'd have been drafted. They didn't see why they should die for a cause they don't understand. It's not as though the Vietnamese are threatening to invade the States. So what are the Americans doing in Vietnam? Thousands of American boys have been killed. Some of them younger than us. Think, Kate, how would you feel if we were being shipped off to face death–?'

'We won't help American conscripts by fighting the police in London,' Kate broke in. 'But, if we don't get our documents we'll lose forty-eight pounds and can kiss goodbye to a summer in America. You don't want to work another season in Barry Butlin's do you?'

'Not if I can help it.'

The protesters on the outside of the circle linked arms and surged in slow motion towards the mounted police, who began to move just as unhurriedly towards them.

'This is hopeless. The police will never let us reach the embassy,' Kate complained.

There was a tap on Penny's shoulder and she found herself staring up into the cold brown eyes of a grim-faced constable.

She instantly felt dishevelled, grubby and unaccountably guilty. She and Kate had left Swansea that morning at six o'clock and most of the lifts they'd cadged had been in lorries with filthy cabs. Their jeans were crumpled and stained, their army surplus combat jackets had seen better days and they were wearing the instantly recognisable student 'badge', a college scarf. An essential accessory for hitch-hiking, but one that wouldn't endear them to the police.

'What you got in there, miss?' The officer eyed her duffle bag.

Penny opened it and he rifled through the contents. Thankfully they were innocuous enough. Her purse, make-up bag, toilet bag with soap and toothbrush, scent, comb, hairbrush, and a bag of mint imperials. When he finished, he turned his attention to Kate's haggis. It was lumpy and stretched to capacity, over three and a half feet long and eighteen inches wide. Even she'd wondered what Kate was carrying.

'And you, Miss. What you got in that thing?' he demanded of Kate.

'Personal things,' Kate answered.

Kate might appear calm to someone who didn't know her but Penny could read the tell-tale signs of stress.

Kate's lips were compressed, her knuckles white. Just as they'd been every time they'd been sent to the headmistress's study for a dressing-down – usually over trouble she'd instigated.

'Show me,' the officer ordered.

Kate opened the drawstring. The officer peered into the sack. 'Take out those bags.'

Kate lifted out her toilet and make-up bags and

purse and handed them to her friend to hold.

'And the rest.'

Kate piled her hairbrush, a rolled-up sweater, spare set of underclothes, jeans, socks and a towel into her outstretched arms. Penny wondered what emergency Kate had been preparing for.

'What's in the paper bags?'

'Pasties and sausage rolls,' Kate answered.

He didn't ask her to open them, presumably because they were grease-stained and emblazoned with the logo of the Swansea Uplands baker's shop.

'The file?'

'Personal papers.'

A roaring filled the square. A mounted officer cantered along the clear strip of 'no-man's-land' that divided the protesters from the police. He headed for half a dozen students lying flat on the ground.

Realising trouble was about to erupt, the constable didn't ask Kate to open the file. 'You two look quiet enough girls,' he allowed grudgingly. 'I'd hate to have to arrest you.'

'You don't have reason to. We haven't done anything,' Kate protested.

'Yet,' he qualified. 'Why are you here?'

'We're trying to get into the embassy,' Penny answered feeling the entire conversation shouldn't be left to Kate.

The officer stared at them in exasperation. 'Isn't there enough trouble for you out here without you two taking it inside?'

'We need work permits and visas. To work in America. Our college has chartered a plane for a student exchange. We've bought our tickets.' Penny pulled her passport and the forms she'd completed from her duffel bag.

He flicked through them. 'Given what's going on here, why didn't you post them?'

'We were afraid our passports would get lost in the mail. We're supposed to leave in four weeks. We tried phoning the embassy but were put on hold or sent around in circles. They kept telling us we couldn't get a work permit without a visa or a visa without a work permit. It cost us a fortune in calls. So we decided to come here in person,' she explained.

'Where you girls from?'

'Swansea,' Kate answered. 'And we're hoping to get back there tonight.'

'Follow me.' He escorted them around the protesters to the embassy door.

Two hours later they were back in the square, their work permits and visas tucked into their bags.

'That was almost too easy,' Penny commented.

'The constable who took us to the door is watching us,' Kate warned.

'I know.' She made a 'thumbs up' to let him know they'd been successful, followed by a friendly wave, but he didn't wave back. 'Pity he's watching, I'd like to have joined the protesters; it would have been something to tell my grandchildren.'

'You ever thought what your and Rich's kids will be like?'

'Why do I know you're about to say something horrid about Rich?'

'I wasn't.'

Feeling slightly guilty about leaving Rich for four months, she changed the subject. 'Let's find somewhere to eat before we head out.'

'We have pasties and sausage rolls,' Kate reminded her.

'Bought yesterday. They'll be stale. Stand you egg and chips in a café,' she offered.

'I can't afford egg and chips and I refuse to sponge off you.'

'It wouldn't be sponging. It would be a thank you for hitch-hiking with me. You know my parents hate me doing it.'

'They hate you doing it with or without anyone. Almost as much as my mother hates the thought of me getting into a stranger's car.'

High-pitched shrieks, screams and a roar accompanied by the thunder of horses' hooves filled the square. Without warning, the mounted police charged the protesters. A tide of students swirled, changing direction before surging towards them at speed. Kate flattened herself against a wall. Penny wasn't so lucky.

A punch between her shoulder blades sent her flying sideways out of the path of a police horse. She stretched out her hands to save herself and landed on concrete, skinning her palms and, by the feel of it, her knees. Before she could catch her breath she was hauled unceremoniously to her feet by the collar of her combat jacket and dragged to the edge of the crowd.

Furious, she looked up into a pair of deep-blue eyes. 'You pushed me over.'

'To save your ass.' The blue eyes were topped

by unfashionably curly black hair and accompanied by the most seductive American accent she'd heard away from a TV screen. In fact, the first American accent she'd heard in reality. But she was in no mood to be seduced.

'If I hadn't pushed you, you'd have been squished.'

'What kind of a word is "squished"?'

'A New England one.' The American gave her a broad toothpaste advert smile. She noticed he was tall – very tall. Her two brothers and father were all over six feet and he was a couple of inches above them.

A police officer moved in behind the American. He grabbed both his arms and twisted them high behind his back. 'You knocked off my helmet, son. Where is it?'

'Not me, sir. I haven't touched anyone's helmet.' When the policeman didn't say anything in response, he added, 'You must have mixed me up with someone else, sir.'

The officer twisted the American's arms higher until he winced. 'Assaulting a police officer is a serious charge, son.'

'I didn't assault anyone.'

She noticed two officers closing in on her. One pushed his face a scant couple of inches from hers. 'Why did you throw yourself in front of that horse, miss?'

'I didn't.' Even as she declared her innocence she felt colour flooding her cheeks.

'You all right, Pen?' Kate ran up to her, saw her hands were bloody and offered her a handkerchief.

'You know these two, miss?' the officer who'd spoken to Penny asked Kate.

'Penny and I travelled up from Swansea together today.' Kate tried to pass her the handkerchief but the policeman closed his fist over Penny's upper arm and yanked her back, out of Kate's reach.

'You were protesting with them?' the officer who was holding Penny asked Kate.

'The girls weren't protesting. They were just standing outside the embassy,' the American interrupted.

'This isn't the first time I've picked you up, is it, son?' The officer holding the American eyed him suspiciously.

'The girls aren't with me.'

'That's not what I asked you.'

'Yes, you've picked me up before,' the American answered irritably. 'And no, these girls aren't with me.'

'If they're not with you, why are you talking to them?'

'One of you maniacs almost trampled one of them under his horse. I pushed her out of the way.'

'Proper Sir Galahad, aren't you, son?' the officer questioned caustically. 'Saving a damsel in distress from a maniac on horseback. You see any maniacs riding horses around here, Sam?'

'No maniacs,' his colleague replied. 'Only officers trying to do their duty while dodging missiles thrown by young idiots who think it's fun to assault police officers.'

'I think it's time we had some of the fun, don't you, Sam?'

The two officers hauled the American behind a

73

line of buses marked POLICE. They pushed him face forward against the side of a vehicle. One of the officers pulled his truncheon from his belt and slammed it across the American's shoulders. He continued to beat him even when the boy had dropped to his knees.

Appalled, Penny shouted, 'You can't do that! This is Britain! He wasn't hurting anyone...'

'Know that, do you, miss?' The policeman holding her propelled her rapidly towards the bus. The officer who'd beaten the American hooked his truncheon back on to his belt. He hauled out her hands and snapped handcuffs on her wrists before shoving her towards his colleagues who were loading protesters on to one of the buses.

'Obstruction?' an officer holding a clipboard and pen asked.

'Affray, assaulting an officer and obstruction,' the officer who'd handcuffed her shouted over his shoulder as he walked away.

Rough hands bundled her inside the bus. The American was slumped, dazed and disorientated in a double seat behind the driver. She stood in the central aisle, ducked down and looked out of the window, searching for Kate. She couldn't see her but she could hear her.

'Where are you taking my friend?'

The driver started the engine and drowned out a reply – if there was one.

The bus moved and she fell sideways against the back of a seat. An officer grabbed her painfully by the neck and pushed her down beside the American.

Terrified, she looked up at him. 'Where are you

taking us?'

'Not on a tour of London, miss. That's for sure,' an officer with a bloody nose who was standing with his back to the windscreen answered.

'I have to go–'

'The only place you're going is Bow Street police station. You broke the law, miss.'

She summoned what was left of her courage. 'I didn't–'

'Down from Wales for the day, by your accent?' an officer sitting in the seat across the aisle from her asked. His left eye was swollen, closed by bruising.

'Yes,' she answered, trying to look braver than she felt.

His voice hardened. 'And decided to make trouble for the authorities while you were here?'

She tried telling him about needing visas and work permits, but he was too engrossed in cleaning the cuts on his hands to listen. She looked around and realised all the officers on the bus were injured.

'You were protesting, miss,' the policeman with the bloody nose said. 'And when you come up before the magistrates in Marlborough Street tomorrow–'

'Tomorrow! I have to be back in Swansea tonight! If I'm not in my hostel by eleven o'clock–'

The officers laughed. 'You won't be back in Wales tonight.'

'You don't understand. I'll be thrown out of my room...'

'You should have thought of that before you went to Grosvenor Square.'

75

The American struggled to sit upright. 'They're taking us to the police station so they can formally arrest us,' he mumbled, his voice thick with pain.

'But I haven't done anything,' she insisted.

'None of us have!' a girl shrieked, shrill and angry from the back of the bus. 'But this is a fascist state run by fascist pigs. Innocent or guilty, it makes no difference to them or the bloody magistrates who'll send us down.'

Penny felt as though the bus was spinning around her. 'Magistrates...? Court...? Sent down...?'

'Take a tip from me, love,' an officer advised. 'Plead guilty. If you've a clean record ... you do *have* a clean record?' he questioned pointedly.

'Of course,' she answered eagerly.

'Plead guilty. Throw yourself on the mercy of the court and if, as you say, it's your first offence, you'll get off with a caution.'

'Don't believe him,' the girl contradicted. 'My brother pleaded guilty and he got two months for affray.'

'Shut your mouth, bitch.'

The sound of a slap resounded from the back of the bus. Penny turned her head.

'Don't,' the American boy warned.

'But–'

'This the first time you've been arrested?'

'Yes.' She felt as though she was trapped in an *Alice in Wonderland* world where no one understood her. Either that or they didn't believe a word she said.

'Stick close to me. If they allow us our free

76

phone call, I'll try to get us out of this mess.'

'How?'

'I know people.'

'Is that supposed to impress me?'

'It's an offer to help by way of an apology.'

'First you mix me up in your protest and get me arrested; then you offer to help. Thank you *very* much.' Even as she snapped, Penny knew she wasn't being fair. He *had* saved her from being trampled. And she would have joined the protesters if Kate hadn't stopped her. But sitting on a police bus listening to talk of guilty pleas, magistrates and courts had unnerved her.

'I'm sorry for the trouble I've caused you. I'm Bobby by the way. Forgive me?' Despite his obvious pain, he managed a crooked smile.

'Penny.' She took the hand he offered.

He didn't shake it. Just squeezed it lightly and hung on to it. *'Come live with me and be my love, and we will all the pleasures prove.'*

'That chat-up line was old when Marlowe wrote it.'

'Wonderful. You're a lover of literature too. But I don't think we should tell people we met at an anti-war protest that turned into a riot. Or exchanged names on a police bus after we'd been arrested.'

'That's an even worse chat-up line.'

'It made you smile.'

'If my lips moved it was a grimace.' She pulled her hand away. 'You're mad.'

'Possibly.' He frowned. 'If you weren't protesting at the embassy what were you doing there?'

'Getting visas and work permits. We – that's me

77

and Kate, the girl who tried to give me a hand-kerchief – are going to America for the summer. If they'll let me in after this.'

'What are you going to do there?'

'Work, see something of the country. Our students' union has chartered a plane.'

'That's great! I'll show you around.'

'You're here.'

'I won't be for the summer. Which union?'

'Pardon?'

'Which students' union has chartered the plane?'

'Swansea.'

'How long you going for?'

'Four months.'

'You got a job yet?'

'No.'

'I'll help you get one...'

'Bow Street, lover boy.' The officer with the bloody nose grabbed Bobby's arm and yanked him past her and out of the seat. 'Move, every-one!'

CHAPTER SEVEN

London, May 1968

She wasn't able to stick close to Bobby. Officers lined the route from the bus to the station door. They studied the faces of the students as they passed. More than half, Bobby among them, were picked out and led away.

A group of girls, including her, were shepherded down a corridor by female police officers who confiscated their bags, coats, shoelaces, belts, cigarettes, matches, lighters, money and the entire contents of their pockets.

When all the girls' possessions had been collected, bagged and tagged, they were led into a room by the officers, who closed the door and stood in a line facing them.

'Strip!'

She stared at the female officers in disbelief.

One officer stepped forward. 'Are you deaf or stupid? Strip!'

She recognised the shrill voice of the girl on the bus. 'And if we refuse, fascist sow?'

'We'll send for the men.'

One look at the female officers' faces convinced her they weren't joking. The girl standing alongside her started to unbutton her blouse.

'Hurry up! We haven't all day.'

Slowly, reluctantly, Penny pulled her sweater over her head and looked around for somewhere to leave it.

'On the floor,' the officer barked.

She took her time over folding it, hoping for a respite. She simply couldn't believe what was happening. The first girl to remove all her clothes was pulled forward. One of the officers snapped on a pair of rubber gloves and subjected her to a rough, intimate and public body search. The entire time the officer's fingers prodded and poked, the girl kept her eyes tightly closed.

She'd never felt more embarrassed or humiliated in her life. She was the sixth in line to get the treatment. Although she'd avoided watching the other girls being searched she thought she knew what to expect. But her imagination hadn't prepared her for the sense of violation she felt when the most intimate and private areas of her body were invaded by brutal and insensitive fingers. As soon as the officer had finished, she wiped the tears of humiliation from her eyes, stumbled back to her clothes and pulled them on as quickly as she could.

'Satisfied, now you've mauled us about? Were you expecting to find anything up there, or did you want a lesbian thrill?' The girl with the shrill voice had her face slapped for the gibe.

After they'd all been searched, the officers marched the girls into a corridor studded with metal doors. They were pushed in through the open doors, four to a cell intended for one.

She found herself in the company of two painfully thin blondes who sank to the floor, wrapped their arms around one another and started sobbing as soon as the door slammed. She steeled herself for the sound of the key turning in the lock, but the reality made her blood run cold.

'Not like watching a film, is it?'

Swallowing her tears Penny looked at her fourth cellmate with gratitude simply because she appeared calm. 'Penny John.'

'Rose Meyer. You been arrested before?'

'No. You?' If Rose had, the fact she'd survived gave her hope.

'No. I only went to the stupid demonstration to be with my boyfriend. He's into politics. I'm not, and I won't be anymore after this. You were with Bobby.'

'I'd only just met him.'

'On the bus?'

'In the square. He pushed me out of the path of a police horse.'

'That's our Bobby. Save the world and anyone in trouble.'

'Your Bobby?' She felt unaccountably disappointed, not that she'd believed the fast-talking American had been sincere.

'He's a friend of my boyfriend's. They're draft dodgers, prepared to risk England with all its dangers of bad plumbing and warm beer as an alternative to fighting in Vietnam. We're at Oxford. Mike – that's my boyfriend – is reading Classics, I'm French. Bobby's graduating this year but he's returning to do a masters in medieval history in the autumn.' She looked around the cell. 'It's bloody freezing in here.'

'Icy.' A single naked bulb illuminated yellow painted brickwork. The clothes she'd thought warm that morning did little to keep out the cold without the top layer of her combat jacket.

'I suppose this is where we wait for someone to open the door while hoping those two eventually stop howling.' Rose curled up on one end of the bare metal bunk and closed her eyes.

She took the other end, wrapped her arms around her knees and curled into a ball to conserve what little warmth remained in her shivering body. She'd never felt so abandoned or afraid. And it didn't help that the two blondes were still sobbing.

'Penelope John?'

She opened her eyes with a start, what could have been one or ten hours later. She glanced instinctively at her wrist, but her watch had been taken along with the rest of her personal possessions. Not that it would have made any difference. It was impossible to determine if it was day or night in a windowless cell with a naked burning light bulb. She'd lost track of time and wondered if she'd dreamt someone calling her name. The silence was so absolute it seemed to buzz.

Her muscles were stiff, frozen. The right side of her body where she'd leant against the cell wall was numb from the cold and lack of circulation. When she touched the fingers of her right hand with her left they felt odd, as though they belonged to someone else.

Disorientated, she looked around. Any hopes she'd nurtured of her arrest being a nightmare shattered in the face of the painted brick walls. And, as if the cell wasn't proof enough, her hands and knees were throbbing with pain from her fall.

The blonde girls were still hunched on the floor, their eyes closed. It was impossible to tell whether or not they were sleeping. She didn't disturb them. She was grateful they were silent.

Then she heard footsteps outside the cell accompanied by the jangle of keys.

'Penelope John! Penelope John!'

It was the same harsh female voice that had woken her.

Rose opened her eyes. 'That you?'

She nodded, shivering from more than cold. She called out, 'Here.'

Rose whispered. 'The protesters who'd been arrested before warned Mike not to sign anything or admit he was guilty of any charge, no matter what the police did or said to him. Apparently, everyone who takes the officers' advice to plead guilty ends up in court and prison.'

'Thanks for the warning.' After seeing officers beat Bobby, she knew she was too cowardly to stand the threat of police 'questioning' for any length of time.

A key turned in the metal door. It swung open. A woman officer stood framed in the doorway.

'Penelope John?'

She clambered awkwardly to her feet.

'Why didn't you answer when I first called?'

'I'm sorry. I was asleep.'

'Follow me.'

'Good luck,' Rose shouted after her.

'Straight ahead to the end of the corridor.' The policewoman walked behind her.

She clamped her hand on the waistband of her jeans. They'd stretched since she'd last washed them and without a belt were in danger of falling down.

'Into reception,' the officer barked.

She walked through the door. Kate was standing pale-faced in front of the desk. Next to her was a handsome, middle-aged, tall, slim, blond man wearing a camel-haired coat. He exuded authority and a confidence born of good looks, expensive clothes and wealth. Penny froze, too weakened by relief to take another step. The man turned and held out his arms. She fell into them.

'Is this your niece, Mr Powell?' the officer behind the desk asked.

Haydn Powell lifted his head above hers and rested his chin on the crown of her head. 'Can't you see the family resemblance, Super-intendent?'

Given that her Uncle Haydn had blonde hair and blue eyes and she'd inherited her father's auburn hair and tawny-gold eyes, her uncle was stretching a point, but she was too happy to see a familiar face to contradict anything he said.

'We have to give her a formal caution, Mr Powell.'

'Do you think you'll survive that indignity?' Haydn held her away from him and winked at her.

'We'll also need to complete our paperwork and return her personal possessions.'

Haydn gave the superintendent and the room in general the full benefit of the professional smile that had charmed international audiences for over thirty years, and five women into marry-ing him. 'I would be grateful if you could do it quickly, Superintendent. I have to fly to the States tonight and I would like to spend some time with my niece before I leave.'

'Time you'll spend lecturing her on acceptable behaviour, I hope, Mr Powell.'

'Naturally.'

'Ten minutes, Mr Powell.'

'Thank you so much.' Haydn looked into her eyes. 'You all right, Penny Piece?'

It had been his nickname for her ever since she

could remember and it helped her to finally find her voice. 'Now I am.'

He turned her hands over and examined her grazes. 'You're hurt?'

'It's nothing. I fell in the square before they brought me here.'

'They treated you well?'

She was too keen to leave the police station to make a complaint that could delay her one second longer than necessary. 'Yes.'

'Thank you for taking care of my niece, Superintendent.' If Haydn intended the comment caustically, she didn't pick up on it. 'My office will be in touch in the morning about those tickets.'

The next ten minutes passed in a blur. She was still threading her belt through the loops in her jeans when Haydn escorted her and Kate to his car. Haydn's chauffeur opened the back door and she and Kate piled in, dragging their bags behind them. Haydn sat alongside her on the bench seat. Kate took the pull-down seat opposite.

'How did you find me?' she asked Kate as soon as the chauffeur closed the door.

'One of the officers in the square said they were taking you to Bow Street police station. I looked for a phone box and rang your mother,' Kate confessed.

'You what!'

'It had to be your mother. Mine's not on the telephone; besides, I knew she'd be at work. They hate her getting personal calls at the factory and there was nothing she could do to help.'

'You told my mother I'd been arrested?' She

was panic-stricken at the thought of her parents finding out she'd been locked up in a police station. And that was without bringing up hitch-hiking.

'I told her you'd been taken in a mass arrest of protesters outside the American embassy when we went there to get visas. I emphasised that the police had made a mistake because neither of us had been protesting. Then she put me on to your father.'

Haydn continued the story. 'Your father knew I was in London. As it would have taken him half a day to get here, he telephoned my office to see if there was anything I could do.' Haydn tapped a cigar from a gold case and lit it.

'Your uncle was fantastic, Pen.' Kate looked shyly at Haydn. 'He ordered a taxi to pick me up in the square, paid for it to take me to his office, made some calls–'

'All I did was explain the situation to the police calmly and sensibly. Once they were in possession of the facts they admitted they'd made a mistake,' Haydn interrupted.

'They actually said they'd made a mistake?' She thought about Bobby, Rose and the others still in the station and felt guilty for leaving them. But not guilty enough to want to return.

'They did when I offered them two dozen tickets to see my next London show.' Haydn smiled, and that time the smile reached his eyes.

'There were other people with me...'

'Pen, darling, it was as much as I could do to get *you* out of the cells. Have you any idea how many police officers have been hurt in Grosvenor

86

Square since the anti-war protests started?'

'Those others – the ones arrested with me – they will be all right, won't they?' She didn't know why she was asking. Bruised and battered after the fall and brutal and humiliating body search, shivering after her incarceration in the cells, and witnessing first hand the treatment that had been meted out to Bobby and the girl who had shouted from the back of the bus, she knew they'd be anything but all right.

'I doubt the police will line them up against a wall and shoot them. But that's not to say that they won't be roughed up on their way to court and, if they're unlucky, prison. Do me and the family a favour, Pen. Give the anti-war protests a wide berth from now on,' Haydn advised.

Haydn was her mother's younger brother. An exotic, glamorous, fabulously wealthy show business figure by Pontypridd – and international – standards, he'd made occasional fleeting appearances in the flesh during her childhood. She and her brothers and sisters had frequently been taken to the County Cinema to see him on screen, and once, sometimes twice a year to see him perform in a matinee in the West End. Generous to a fault, he showered the entire family with presents whenever he saw them. Everyone adored him, although she'd sensed from odd remarks of her mother's that Bethan was concerned about the lifestyle her younger brother had chosen to follow.

'How are Aunt Poppy and Maud?' she asked.

Poppy was Haydn's current wife. Twenty-five years younger than him, she'd been a dancer in one of his London shows, but she'd abandoned her career after the birth of their first child, Maud, who was Haydn's fourth daughter. Poppy was also Welsh, from Cardiff, and to quote Penny's father, after he'd met her for the first time, 'had her head screwed on the right way.' She recalled her mother saying Poppy's head couldn't be that well screwed on because she'd married Haydn.

'They're fine. Poppy's just bought a house for us in Las Vegas. I have a six-month contract there with a casino. My show's opening the day after tomorrow. So if there's such a thing as a good day to get arrested, Pen, you chose it,' Haydn declared. 'I only arrived in London three days ago. I would have liked to have stayed longer and visited your mother but I have to fly out tonight.'

'It must be marvellous to travel as much as you, Mr Powell,' Kate said enviously.

'Not really. Have you ever thought how much time I spend alone in hotel rooms or talking to strangers? And two days out of the three I've been here I've been working, filming a TV special. But Vegas won't be too bad. Poppy hates hotels even more than me, especially with Maud. They're never geared for kids. But when I've finished in Vegas, I've a short season in the West End followed by a couple of months filming just outside London. So your mother can brace herself for our long-threatened visit. But she'd better put away her best china. Maud's at the terrible-two marauding age. She put one of my golf clubs through the window of the Californian house last week.'

'I can't wait to see her again,' Penny enthused.

'She couldn't talk when I last saw her.'

'And you'll be wishing she couldn't the next time you see her. Maud's never quiet, not even when she's sleeping. Here we are, home sweet home.'

CHAPTER EIGHT

'Home sweet home' was the Savoy.

Penny knew her uncle kept a permanent suite in the hotel. He'd written to her mother years ago inviting the family to make free use of it whenever they were in London; as if they made a habit of visiting the city. The only times she could recall the entire family travelling there was to see Haydn onstage and, more often than not, even then they all returned home to Pontypridd on the milk train rather than stay overnight.

Haydn greeted the doorman who opened the car door. Kate took one look at the man's grey morning suit and top hat and froze. 'I can't go in there.'

'Why ever not?' Haydn asked.

'Not like this, in jeans and a tatty coat.'

He laughed. 'Some people may be better dressed than you two in there but they're only people, Kate. They have two arms, two legs and, in view of what you did for Pen today, a lot less brains.'

'But they look like millionaires,' Kate whispered as a glamorous blonde girl about her age strolled into the foyer of the garden entrance as if she owned the place. She was dressed in a silver chain-and-plate miniskirt and vest that left little to the imagination. White tights that showed off her long – very long – slim legs, a silver diamante-studded feather boa and silver leather boots that skirted the top of her thighs completed the ensemble.

Kate coveted those boots. She'd priced similar black ones in David Evans in Swansea but they'd been way out of her budget at three quarters of her annual grant.

'If you're thinking of her, she's not a millionaire. She's out to catch one. What do you say, Brian?' Haydn offered the doorman his cigar case.

'Whatever you say, Mr Powell, sir.' The door-man took a cigar and slipped it into his top pocket.

'Brian, meet my niece and her friend.'

'Pleased to meet you, ladies.'

She thought the doorman looked sceptical, then realised how the situation could be reported in the tabloid newspapers.

Star picks up girls young enough to be his daughters from police station and takes them to his private suite in the Savoy.

'Ask Anna or one of the girls on duty to go up to my suite, will you please, Brian. The girls will be staying the night, so they'll need some things. Tell Anna to buy whatever they want and put it on my account. And ask the bellboy to collect my cases.' He turned to his chauffeur. 'You've an hour before you have to take me to the airport, Phil. Grab a meal and a cup of coffee and put it

90

on my bill.'

'Thank you, Mr Powell.' Unlike the doorman, the chauffeur smiled at her and Kate.

'Don't forget to be here at nine tomorrow to take the girls shopping. Their train leaves Paddington at two o'clock. See them on to it, please.'

'You can rely on me, sir.'

'We'll make our own way back to college.' Feeling like a stray dog, she walked at her uncle's heels when he strode into the hotel.

'Your own way is hitch-hiking out of London because although your parents give you the money to buy train tickets you'd prefer to spend it on other things?' he guessed.

'We got here by hitch-hiking,' she replied defensively.

'The next thing you'll be telling me is that your mother approved.'

'Kate and I've never had any trouble.'

'I don't have many nieces, so I'd rather not lose one. The train tickets should have been delivered to the suite by now. You can sleep and breakfast here, do some shopping in Carnaby Street, where I'm told all bright young things shop, and catch the early afternoon train back to Swansea. First class, on me.' He lifted his eyebrows at Kate. 'And don't say you can't accept the ticket, young woman. Not after rescuing Penny. I may not see my nieces and nephews often but I'm fond of them. I wouldn't have known she was in a cell if it hadn't been for you.'

They followed him into the lift. When they reached the top floor he pulled a key from his pocket and unlocked a door.

91

'Room service menus are on the table. Ring down and order whatever you want. You'll be more comfortable here than in the restaurant,' he suggested tactfully. 'There's a well-stocked bar, but if you don't see anything you fancy, order something else, but no more than one bottle of wine between you or two pints of whatever young people drink these days each. Please don't get drunk. Your father I can cope with, but if your mother finds out she'll string me up. As for food, please, eat the kitchen empty. You could both do with fattening up. Door to guest bedroom and bathroom. There are twin beds and it's yours for the night.' He pointed to a door on the left. 'If you'll excuse me, I have to change for the flight. Order smoked salmon sandwiches for me, please, Pen.' He disappeared into the bedroom.

Her parents had taken her to hotels, but she'd never seen anything as sumptuous as her uncle's suite in the Savoy. Not even in the upmarket hotels her father had insisted on splashing out on in France. And, although Kate was doing her best to conceal it, she could see she was over-whelmed.

She opened the door to the 'guest bedroom'. It was enormous, far larger than the common room in college, and the en suite bathroom with its gold taps, sunken bath and Italian tiles wouldn't have looked out of place in a Hollywood film.

'I can visualise Doris Day lying in that bath covered in suds.' Kate eyed a basket on the shelf. 'Look at all those toiletries. Soap, shampoo, bath oil, there's even body lotion.' She picked up the bottle, unscrewed the top and sniffed the contents.

'It smells heavenly.'

'I've never seen so many complimentary toil-etries, or towels so thick and fluffy.' She fingered the flannels.

'If one of us snores in the night the other can always sleep in the bath,' Kate joked.

'And use the bath mat as an eiderdown.'

'Talk about how the other half live.'

It was the first time she'd ever detected envy in Kate's voice.

'We didn't have a bathroom until we were re-housed by the council when I was eleven.' Kate glanced at her watch. 'As we're not expected back in Swansea tonight, I intend to make the most of this.'

'Did you ring the college?' Penny asked.

'Your father volunteered. He said he'd let them know that we've been delayed and won't get back until tomorrow.'

'Delayed as in me being arrested?' She was alarmed by the thought.

'Delayed as in we came here to get visas and had problems with transport. He did say he wouldn't tell the college any more than he had to.'

'He's never met Fanny. I think she was an inter-rogator for the KGB in her youth.'

'She's too true-blue British to be KGB. She could have worked for MI5 but I refuse to believe she was ever young,' Kate countered.

'I'd better order Uncle Haydn's sandwiches.' Penny returned to the sitting room. 'What do you want?'

'Nothing, thank you,' Kate refused. 'My

93

stomach's in knots. When you were driven away in that bus I was terrified they wouldn't release you. I'm not sure what I was dreading the most, hitch-hiking back to Wales on my own, or facing Fanny and the principal when I arrived at college. As for your parents and my mother...'

'What would you have said to them?'

'I've no idea,' Kate admitted.

'You have to eat,' she lectured. 'I'm not hungry either but all we've had today is a couple of sausage rolls and a cup of coffee on the road. We'll be ill if we starve ourselves. How about cheese sandwiches and a bottle of wine?'

'I couldn't. Not on your uncle's bill.'

'Yes, you could.' Haydn left his bedroom. 'It's not often I have the chance to treat my niece. I take it you haven't ordered yet?'

'No. We were debating what to have.'

'As I have to leave shortly let me make the decision for you.' He was dressed for travelling in a tailored pale-grey suit, blue shirt and grey and blue silk tie. He picked up the telephone and dialled. 'Room service? This is Haydn Powell.' He laughed. 'Thank you for your kind words but I never sing down the telephone. Send up smoked salmon sandwiches for one, please, and mixed sandwiches and a plate of cream cakes and coffee for two. Please note that my niece and her friend will be staying in the suite tonight. They'll be ordering supper and breakfast. Thank you.' He dropped the receiver back on the cradle. 'It'll be here in ten minutes.'

'That gives me time to bag first bath in that royal bathroom.' Kate carried her haggis into the bedroom and closed the door.

'Tactful friend you have there.' Haydn went to the bar and poured himself a whisky.

'Kate's been my best friend since we started grammar school.'

'And you went to the same college?'

'By chance. Kate's main is English and she really wants to be a teacher.' She wrinkled her nose.

'Your mother told me you want to be an artist and only went to teacher training college under sufferance because she nagged you to study for qualifications you could fall back on if you had to. But she's right. It's good to have something in reserve. And, before you tell me I didn't have anything other than my voice, you'd be right. But unlike you and your brothers and sisters, I never had the chance to go to grammar school.'

'Mam told me you started work when you were fourteen.'

'Ten,' he smiled. 'She never found out I mitched off to work the markets and run errands. But your mother started work as a ward maid in the Graig Hospital before her thirteenth birthday. Heavens above, I'm beginning to sound like the old men who bored me witless when I was a kid. Let's settle for your mother and me grew up in different times.' He held up his glass. 'Can I get you anything?'

'No thanks, not on an empty stomach. I've never had much of a head for drink.'

'Then you don't take after the Powell side of your family. Orange juice or water?'

'Water please.'

Haydn poured her a glass of water and added ice and a slice of lemon. He carried the drinks from the bar and sat at the opposite end of the enormous sofa. 'So, you're going to the States?'

'How do you know?'

'Kate told me. That *was* why you were getting visas from the American embassy?' he checked.

'And work permits; we're hoping to find jobs over there.'

'If you want to see the States, why don't you and Kate stay with Poppy and me in Vegas?'

'That's kind of you...'

'You wouldn't be playing gooseberry. Poppy and I are way past the honeymoon stage. Maud put paid to that. You and Kate would be doing me, or rather Poppy, a favour. I work long hours and she loves company. The house has a pool and stables. Last I heard, Poppy had bought two horses and a pony for Maud, and hired a man to take care of them, so you won't even have to muck out,' he coaxed.

'It's not that, Uncle Haydn. I'm hoping to waitress or barmaid in New York so I can see the museums and art galleries. And Kate has already written to a few summer camps.'

'If its jobs you want, I could ask around. I know people–'

'Thank you,' she interrupted. 'But–'

'You want to stand on your own feet,' he guessed.

'I try. But sometimes, like today, I don't always succeed.' She picked up her glass of water.

'You're a stubborn creature, aren't you?' he mused. 'I take back what I said earlier. You're a

Powell after all.' He frowned. 'You've never been to the States, have you?'

'I've never been in a plane. The furthest I've travelled is Italy. And then only with Mam and Dad.'

'Your father likes his culture, and driving around Europe. I've never acquired the taste. It's bad enough driving on the wrong side of the road in the States, and the roads there aren't as crowded as they are here. America's not like Europe, Pen, but you wouldn't be going there if it was.' He sipped his whisky thoughtfully. 'Someone once told me it's a country best seen from the air. They're right.'

She was intrigued. 'What do you mean?'

'Have you seen *West Side Story?*'

'The film, yes, I loved it.'

'I'm glad you agree with the people who voted for the Oscars,' he commented dryly. 'Do you remember the beginning?'

'When the camera pans over New York? Yes. It looked beautiful.'

'It did,' he concurred, 'but they opened with the standard shot of the skyline of Manhattan they always use in movies whenever the producers want to glamorise the city.'

When her uncle said 'movies' she realised how far he'd travelled from Pontypridd, where everyone referred to films as 'pictures'.

'The difference between *West Side Story* and most movies set in New York is the camera zoomed down to street level so the audience could see a little of the reality of the city. The streets came as a shock to me after the skyline of tall,

97

clean, grandiose skyscrapers I saw from the air when I first flew in to Idlewild in the late Forties. The sidewalks are dirtier and seedier than Europe. There's more litter and you're surrounded by tacky advertising, most of it on billboards that block out whatever's behind the sidewalk. Which is why even the country areas look better from a plane, because all you can see of a billboard from the air is the top. And the people...' Haydn hesitated.

She sensed he was choosing his words carefully.

'Americans are the kindest most generous people on earth. But they don't have our sense of humour or understand sarcasm, Pen. A word of warning: never, ever, make jokes about their president, country or flag. Certainly, not in the way *That Was the Week That Was* does about our government and the royal family. Please, be careful what you say to them.'

'Sounds like you're afraid I'll end up in an American police cell.'

'The American police don't mess about when it comes to people protesting against government policy, civil rights or the Vietnam War. You might think you were treated badly in Bow Street. Believe you me, you would have been treated a lot worse if you'd been arrested in the States. And be extra careful if you visit the Southern states. Everyone knows about Martin Luther King's assassination. What hasn't received quite so much press coverage in Europe or America is the treatment of ordinary civil rights protesters in some of those states. Students, housewives and working-class men and women have been beaten, shot, hung and occasionally disappeared from the face of the earth. The Klu Klux Klan isn't history. It's alive and horribly active.'

'They *murder* people?' Her voice dropped to a whisper.

'Probably, and even if the local police departments and authorities aren't directly involved, they occasionally turn a blind eye.'

She started at a knock at the door.

'There's no need to look so serious. Just be more careful there about what you say and do than you are in this country.' Haydn left the sofa to open the door to the waiters who'd brought their sandwiches. 'Keep a low profile, and you'll discover America's a great country for young people. You'll have a wonderful time.'

'If Mam and Dad allow me to go there after today.'

'Today was a mistake. Wasn't it, Pen?'

The waiters rolled in a trolley loaded with covered dishes. Haydn signed the chit they handed him.

'Thank you, we'll serve ourselves.' He slipped the waiters a tip and closed the door. 'You weren't really protesting against America's involvement in the Vietnam War, were you?' he pressed.

'I wasn't. But when I saw the students in the square, I wanted to,' she confessed.

'I understand how you feel,' he sympathised. 'I can't bear the thought of young men being forced to fight far from home and getting killed any more than the next man. Nor do I understand what the war is about. But I've also asked myself what I'd achieve by protesting. Other than earn myself a police record. And, frankly, one of those won't do me or you any good, Pen, when you look for work after you've finished college.'

'I've seen films and photographs of you on civil rights marches with other film stars, writers and entertainers. Weren't you afraid of being arrested or attacked for taking part?' She took the plate of sandwiches he handed her.

'No, because questions would have been asked if a public figure had been beaten or spirited away by the police. And, when it comes to civil rights, I feel it's worth trying to make a difference. You wouldn't believe some of the things I've seen in South Africa and the Deep South of the States. Segregation on any grounds is stupid; on racial or religious grounds it's criminal. Even more so if it's "legalised segregation" by government order. But it remains to be seen whether peaceful protest will achieve anything now Martin Luther King has been murdered.'

'I'd like to make a difference.' Realising she was hungry she bit into a cheese sandwich.

'So, we have another firebrand in the family.'

'Another? Like you?' Penny looked at him quizzically.

'I've been too selfish and concerned with my career to make a serious difference in the world. But you're not the first one in the family to get banged up.'

'I know Dad was a prisoner during the war.'

'Of the Germans, poor man,' Haydn suppressed a smile.

She knew there was tension between her father and uncle but she'd never plucked up the courage to ask her parents why.

'I wasn't talking about him. That was noble imprisonment in a just cause. At least we all knew what we were fighting for in the last war, unlike the poor souls who've been shipped out to Vietnam. Hasn't your mother told you about your Uncle Eddie who was killed at Dunkirk?'

'She said he was a successful boxer.'

'He was, but he also had a foul temper, which he once took out on your father. The police arrested him and he spent quite a few hours in a cell before your father convinced the police not to press charges.'

'Mam's brother beat up Dad?' Penny asked in amazement. 'What on earth did Dad do to him?'

To her annoyance her uncle refused to elaborate. 'If you want to know more ask your mother – or...' he grinned, 'your father, but when you do, don't mention my name.' He glanced at his watch and lifted the covers from the plates. 'I wish I didn't have a plane to catch so I could stay longer with you. But time and planes wait for no man.'

'I can't thank you enough for getting me out of that cell. I was terrified.'

'Anyone but a fool would have been, Penny Piece.' He finished his sandwiches and whisky, brushed crumbs from his jacket and rose to his feet. 'Got a good old Ponty hug for your uncle?' He opened his arms and she embraced him.

'I'll tell Mam what you did. Dad will want to pay you back for this room and the train tickets.'

'I wouldn't hear of it.' He took out a billfold and removed a couple of banknotes. 'I know you're not supposed to take more than fifty pounds in cash out of the country, but call this your mad money. If my wives and daughters are anything to go by, women can always find somewhere to hide money where it can't be found by customs officers.'

'Two hundred dollars,' Penny gasped. 'I can't take this from you. Mam and Dad would be furious.'

'Your Mam and Dad don't have to know about it. And this,' he peeled off another two notes, 'is for Kate. You're lucky to have a friend like her, Pen. Look after her.'

'I will.'

'This,' he gave her ten twenty-pound notes, 'is for both of you to go shopping tomorrow. You'll be backing Britain to the hilt if you buy the latest Mary Quant designs and wear them in the States. Fashion exports will soar.'

'Uncle Haydn...'

'Money is everything to a poor student. When you reach my advanced age you realise how little real value it has. My card – there's an American number on there. It's my agent's. They always know how to reach me. Slightest sign of trouble, telephone. If I can't help, I'll send someone who can. Say goodbye to Kate for me.' He opened the door. The bellboy and a young woman entered. 'The cases are to go to my car, Stephen.' He tipped the boy. 'Anna, make sure that my niece and her friend have everything they need for the night.'

'I will, Mr Powell.'

'Bye, Pen. Love to your mam, and everyone

102

back in Ponty, and yourself and Kate.' He blew her a kiss and left.

That's when she realised that like her, her uncle hated goodbyes.

CHAPTER NINE

Swansea, June 1968

'If you really loved me you wouldn't go to America.' Rich's voice broke the silence. The quietest time in the boys' hostel was between supper and pub closing.

'I'm sick and tired of you trying to blackmail me into not going to the States.'

'It's a joke,' he snapped.

'An unfunny one.' She moved away from him, which wasn't easy in a single bed.

He wrapped his arm around her waist to prevent her from leaving.

She tried to read the expression on his face but he'd pulled his curtains against the sunset glare and the room was shrouded in shadows. Freeing herself from his arm, she swung her legs out of the bed. 'I'm packed and set to leave tomorrow and I'm going.'

'Unpack and cancel your ticket. If you're worried about losing the money I'll take a part-time job.'

'I'm more concerned about you behaving like a two-year-old than money. "If *you* loved *me*",' she

103

mocked, mimicking his Welsh accent which was more pronounced than hers, 'you wouldn't ask me to give up a trip I've been planning for months. You *know* how much time I've spent reading up on the exhibitions in the New York and Boston galleries and museums.'

'Don't tell me you're going to America for art's sake. It's not going to take you four months to walk around galleries and museums,' he scoffed. 'You could see all you want to in a catalogue. You'll be having a good time with Kate and the boys you'll pick up.'

'You make us sound like tarts.'

'I know Kate.'

'No you don't,' she contradicted. 'I told you she's taken a job as a nanny. I'll hardly see her once we're there.' She hadn't admitted it to Kate, but she was disappointed that Kate had accepted a position in Scarsdale, a suburb outside New York. Kate had tried to persuade her to apply to the agency for a nanny's job as well, but she was determined to keep to her original plan and look for a waitressing or barmaiding job in Manhattan or Greenwich Village

The thought of her living alone in New York terrified her parents, especially as she didn't have a job lined up. But she'd consoled them by promising if New York didn't work out she would look for a nanny's job when she was there.

'No doubt Kate will be spending her days off with you,' Rich persisted sourly. 'And in between you'll be alone. Anything could happen. Considering the mess you got yourself into in London–'

'London wasn't my fault.'

'If you say so.'

Furious, she shouted, 'IT WAS A MISTAKE! The police swept up protesters in Grosvenor Square. I didn't move out of their way fast enough. My uncle sorted it in a couple of hours.'

'Your rich influential uncle might not be around to sort out the next lot of trouble you get yourself into.'

She picked up her bra and pants from his bedside locker and began to dress.

He plumped the pillows behind his head, sat up and watched her. 'I mean it, Pen. You go to America, we're through.'

'Then we're through.' She pulled on her jeans. As he was in the bed she lay on the floor to zip them up. She and Kate had each bought two pairs of jeans in London and shrunk them by wearing them while sitting in baths of hot water. As a result, she could only fasten hers when lying on the floor.

'I'm serious.'

'So am I.'

'While you've been gallivanting with Kate in London and going on endless shopping trips, I've been seeing someone.'

She'd caught her head in the polo neck of her skinny-rib sweater. Tugging it viciously down, she yanked her long hair. When she finally disentangled herself and emerged, Rich was grinning.

'Who is she, Rich?'

'What's it to you?'

'I've a right to know who you've been seeing behind my back.'

'So you're saying you have rights over me but I

don't over you?'

'I don't have the right to tell you what to do, any more than you have the right to order me around. But given that we've been going out together for seven years and you've asked me to marry you, I believe I do have the right to know if you're two-timing me. Who is she, Rich?' she reiterated.

He shrugged. 'A girl; one who appreciates having a boyfriend and knows how to treat him,' he taunted.

'I'm glad I found out what you were like before you put a ring on my finger.'

'You're the one leaving me.'

'To work abroad,' she reminded. 'I've never two-timed you.'

'What was I supposed to do when you and Kate went up to London for a couple of days? And all the afternoons and evenings you two spent in your hostel making plans? Did you really think I sat around here twiddling my thumbs, waiting for you to give me five minutes of your precious time?'

'I'm not your court jester, Rich. I assumed you were old enough to amuse yourself.'

'But evidently not to amuse you.'

'You're stifling me, Rich.'

'By loving you, I'm *stifling* you?' he retorted. 'Well, that's not how Judy–' He fell silent after saying more than he'd intended.

'Judy? Judy Brown?' Shoes in hand Penny whirled round and faced him.

'What's wrong with Judy Brown?' he challenged.

'Nothing. I hope you'll be very happy together.'

106

Judy was a first-year student who boasted about her ability to drink any boy under the table. The cattiest girls said that Judy prided herself on her ability to down alcohol because she had no other talents, or looks, to fall back on. But that had been after Judy had won a reputation for stealing other girls' boyfriends.

'If you don't go to America, I'll finish with Judy,' Rich coaxed.

She unlocked the door. 'For Judy's sake, I hope you've been more honest with her than you have with me.'

'What do you mean?'

'You just said you'd finish with her if I stayed.'

'You'll stay?' He sat up eagerly.

'If I wouldn't stay before you told me you were two-timing me, I certainly won't now. You've just given me all the more reason to go. Does Judy know she's your second string?'

'She knows about you. The whole bloody college has known we're an item since the day we arrived.'

'We *were* an item, Rich.' She wrenched the door open.

'Pen.' He jumped out of bed, realised he was naked, and grabbed the sheet to cover himself before following her into the corridor. 'Please, don't go to America...'

'Have a good summer, Rich.' She hit the lift button, the door opened and she stepped into it.

'I've lost count of the number of times you've quarrelled with Rich.' Kate pushed her chair back from her desk and faced her. She was sitting cross-legged on Kate's bed, ostensibly looking through a collection of brochures on New York.

'He's never admitted two-timing me before.'

'He took Carol Howell home from the Regent Ballroom last summer when you were on holiday with your family. You were furious when I told you, but you forgave him afterwards,' Kate reminded.

'He was drunk.'

'Not *that* drunk. I was there, you weren't.'

'Do you think he's gone out with other girls besides Carol and Judy?'

'Why ask me? You're the one who's almost engaged to him.' Kate looked her in the eye. 'You really mean it this time? This is the end for you and Rich?'

'Absolutely.'

'No regrets?'

'None.' She shuffled the brochures into a neat pile.

'No tears?'

Ignoring the burning sensation in her throat she shook her head. 'The only emotion I feel right now is relief. As to whether I cry later, that remains to be seen. We've been going out together for seven years.'

'Out of habit, if you want my opinion. And seven years is longer than some marriages.' Kate ducked when she threw a cushion at her. 'It's true. One of my cousins went home to her mother after the honeymoon and hasn't seen her husband since. She says she doesn't intend to until they're in the divorce court.'

'Rich and I talked about marriage.'

'I know,' Kate murmured in a 'martyr's' voice.

Penny felt guilty. 'I've put upon you over the years with my ups and downs with Rich.'

'You've always been there for me. Although I've never hit anything like the downs you hit with Rich.' Kate screwed the top back on her fountain pen.

'And now I'm stopping you from working.'

'Yes.'

Her guilt didn't prevent her from carrying on the conversation. 'Your love life has always been more straightforward.'

'Straightforward and several degrees colder,' Kate conceded. 'I keep boys at arm's length, except physically when I'm in bed with them. Emotionally, I've always kept my distance.'

'Why? No – forget I asked,' she amended. 'It's obvious when I think of how Rich tried to control my life. You've always been the independent sensible one.'

'It's my mother's influence. She does what she wants, when she wants, and dresses and behaves to suit herself. After seeing the way some of the men on our estate treat their wives it's what I want. Independence and no lord and master to bow and scrape to.'

'You make it sound as though we're living in a feudal society, not the 1960s.'

'The way most men carry on we could be in the Middle Ages. How many times have you heard a woman say "if his dinner's not on the table when he gets in from work, there's ructions"; or "it's his job to bring in the money, mine to keep the house clean. He goes up the wall if he finds a

109

speck of dust"? They even say it proudly.'

'Often enough on Pontypridd market.'

'As for going out, it's not an option for the downtrodden.' Kate had begun to lecture on one of her favourite topics and wasn't about to abandon her tirade halfway through. '"He doesn't like me going out without him and it's more than my life's worth to try",' Kate mocked in a strong Valleys accent. 'Then there's the one that really makes my mother see red. "His mother's never entered a pub in her life and he says no decent woman should". That came at her from all directions when she tried to organise a ladies' night in the social club on the estate. The way some of the men carried on you'd think she'd suggested putting a red light outside the door and running a brothel.'

'I've heard women talk like that but not in our family. My father's never insisted on his meal being on the table when he walks through the door. If no one's in he'll make himself a sandwich or scramble a couple of eggs.'

'I bet your father hasn't had to make himself a meal very often. You've always had help in the house.'

'I suppose we have,' she agreed. 'But my father's never tried to tell my mother, my sisters and I what to do or how to live. He encouraged all of us to take an interest in things outside of our home.'

'Unlike Rich. Given his attitude to our trip to America, I bet he'd expect things to be run his way if you two married.'

She had a vision of Rich's mother, known to everyone in Pontypridd as 'Mrs Evans'. She realised she didn't even know Rich's mother's Christian name. Her husband, like her sons, referred to her as 'Mam'. Mrs Evans dressed in brown and grey tweed skirts and twinsets, thick lisle stockings, low-heeled lace-ups, modest jewellery and shapeless hats on top of unflattering perms, eyes always downcast and manner self-effacing.

Whenever Rich's brother Jack tried to include his mother in the conversation her answers were always soft-spoken and diffident. Was Mrs Evans naturally timid or too terrified of her husband to voice an opinion lest he take offence? Would she end up browbeaten if she married Rich? The last few weeks had proved Rich's character was closer to his father's than his mother's.

For the first time she wondered what Rich's mother had been like at her age? Had all originality, spontaneity and joy been drained from her by marriage to Rich's father?

'You're right, Kate,' she said thoughtfully. 'Rich has been doing his best to control me now. The situation between us would become unbearable for me if we were married.'

'You're well rid of him, Pen.' Kate left her chair and walked to the window. As her room was at the back of the hostel it overlooked the front gates and the road. 'My only concern is that you'll change your mind.'

'There's no fear of that.'

'I don't mean about going to America, but taking Rich back when we return.'

She remembered the boy who had pushed her out of the path of the police horse and smiled.

Kate murmured. 'You're thinking about the

American boy we met in London.'

'How did you know?'

'Because you're wearing the same soppy look now that you were when you talked about him on the train back from London.'

'Am I?'

'You haven't forgotten him?'

'No, I haven't forgotten him.'

'It'll be a tall order to find him among all the Bobbys in America. You didn't get his surname?'

'No.'

'Imagine us let loose among all the Bobbys in America,' Kate said brightly. 'There'll be dozens, if not hundreds, like him and every one of them gorgeous. It'll be a perfect tragedy if your out-moded idea of morality prevents you from having fun with them.'

'What do you mean, "my outmoded idea of morality"?' she demanded indignantly.

'How many boys have you slept with?'

'One.'

'Exactly one – Rich. This is the Sixties, Pen. We've been liberated by the pill. We don't have to stay with the first man to notice us. Time you shopped around and looked for a lover who's funnier, brighter, has more personality and better skills between the sheets than Rich.'

'What do you know about Rich's skill between the sheets?'

'I can tell by looking at him he's lacking in that department.'

'No he isn't.'

'How can you say that when you've only slept with him? You've no one to compare him with,'

Kate argued logically. 'I've been worried about you for years.'

'Me? Why?'

'Since the age of thirteen you've acted the part of handmaiden to Rich. Gone to the parties he wanted you to go to. Seen the films he wanted you to see—'

'As if there's an enormous choice of things to do in Ponty,' she interrupted.

'Face it; you came here because it was the only college to offer him a place with his low-grade A levels. You could have gone to any college in the country.'

'Apart from the fact that my parents wanted me to have qualifications to fall back on, I am my own person, Kate,' she insisted defensively.

'You could be now you've dropped Rich.' Kate looked into her eyes. 'Happy now you're single?'

'Definitely.'

'Scared?'

'No.'

'The truth?'

'Just a little.'

'We're about to have the time of our lives,' Kate declared. 'America, here we come. We're foot-loose, fancy-free and out to have a good time. And, who knows, maybe you'll find another Bobby there.'

She didn't believe she'd find another boy like Bobby. But what chance did she have of tracking him down when all she knew was his first name and he was going to study for a masters in medieval history at one of the Oxford colleges next academic year?

CHAPTER TEN

Pontypridd, 1987

'Hello? Pen? Anyone in?'

Jerked from the past, and resenting the interruption more than she would have believed possible, Penny closed the photograph album, rose from the floor and dusted herself down. She walked out on the landing and called down. 'I'm upstairs. Be down in a minute. Make us coffee.'

'Will do.'

Penny went into the bathroom and looked in the mirror. Her face was smudged with dust. Her hair a mess. A quick wash and brush through later, she walked into the kitchen.

'Hello, sweetheart.' Jack was sitting at the table, two mugs of coffee in front of him. 'I thought you'd need cheering up with Andy away. I'm packed, the car has a full tank of petrol and I'm ready to carry you off to the West Country for a couple of days. There're vacancies in our favourite pub and I've bought a bag of mint creams for the journey. This is yours, by the way.'

She took the mug he handed her and leant against the worktop. 'What about the farm?'

'I've left it in the hands of capable minions.'

She looked at him dispassionately, as though she were seeing him for the first time. The wrong side of forty, his face was rugged, weather-beaten

114

with the healthy glow and colour of a man who spends most of his days out of doors. His thick brown hair was greying at the temples, his face creased with laughter lines and his dark eyes shone with intelligence. Rich's elder brother had been her understanding and undemanding lover for over fifteen years.

He sensed her mood. 'If you don't want to go, we can stay here.' When she failed to answer him, he said, 'What's the matter?'

'Why should something be the matter?'

'Pen, I know you. I love you. I was hoping to marry you when Andy leaves for college.'

'Jack–'

'I sense an argument brewing. It can wait. Whatever's bothering you, can't. Something's wrong. Do you want to talk about it?'

She pulled the envelope she'd received that morning from her back pocket and handed it to him. He read it carefully. 'Brosna Estate. Andy's father is Robert Brosna? *The* Robert Brosna? The recluse?' He stared at her in amazement.

'I thought everyone would have guessed that he was Andy's father after the car crash. There was enough press coverage at the time.'

'Everyone knew Robert Brosna was in the car, badly injured and not expected to live. No one could avoid knowing, given the headlines and TV bulletins. But you were a student. You'd all been to a party. There was nothing about any of you being romantically involved. And Robert Brosna's worth billions...'

The last thing she wanted to talk about was Brosna money, especially as it had all been left to

Andy. 'I spent the whole of the summer of '68 with Bobby Brosna. Did you think Andy was the result of a casual pickup? A one-night stand with a stranger?'

'Knowing you, not for one minute.' He abandoned his coffee and ran his fingers through his hair.

'Then what?' she demanded.

'I assumed Andy's father was a plausible bastard – given Andy's looks, a handsome plausible bastard – who'd spun you a story, got what he wanted and abandoned you both. But this,' he held the letter in the air, 'wasn't written by a man who didn't want you.'

'That's what my father said when I showed him the letter this morning.'

'You have to take Andy to America, Pen. He has a right to know his father.'

'Andy has all the family he needs, including enough father figures. Between my father, you, my brothers–'

'That's not the same as knowing his biological father,' he broke in. 'Heaven only knows, given my relationship with my own father, I've no personal experience to build on but I've always thought that the bond between father and son should be something special.'

She couldn't bring herself to look at Jack. She'd lost count of the number of times he'd asked her to marry him over the last twelve years. She knew how much he longed for a family life and children of his own. So much so, she'd sent him away from her more than once. But somehow, he'd always returned and they invariably picked up where they'd left off. Living a life that wasn't anywhere near the family life he craved.

'Jack, you've been Andy's father in all but name for the last thirteen years,' she argued.

'No, I haven't, because you wouldn't let me,' he countered. 'We've never lived under the same roof, never woken in the morning to share breakfast.'

'You've called in here for breakfast dozens of times.'

'That's not the same as living together twenty-four hours a day, Pen, and I'm not complaining. You made it clear from the outset of our relationship that Andy would always come first with you. I accepted that. Frankly, as you well know, I've accepted whatever you offered, and gladly. If you'd said you could only spare me one day a year I would have taken it, grateful for the crumbs of your time. But this isn't about us. It's about Andy. As the letter says, you've no right to keep him from his father and half his family.'

She went to the window. Clouds obscured the sun. Blue sky of early morning had turned grey.

'And there's the money...'

'The money's the problem, Jack. If you knew what Brosna money had done to Andy's father, you wouldn't want Andy to have a cent of it.'

'You have to tell Andy about it.'

'I will,' she promised. 'Just as soon as he's sat all his exams. And not a minute before.'

He finished his coffee. 'If you need me, you know where to find me.'

'I'm sorry, Jack. A trip would have been lovely, but...'

117

'Not when you have thinking to do.'

She blocked his path and rested her head against his chest. 'Thank you for being so considerate.'

'I'm finding it harder and harder to play the nice guy, Pen.'

'I know.' When she looked up at him her eyelashes glistened with teardrops. 'I'm sorry.'

He kissed her. 'If you need me, I'll be at home.' He opened the door and walked away without a backward glance.

After Jack left, Penny returned upstairs intending to pack away the things she'd brought down from the attic. But the photograph album was too seductive. She picked it up and, minutes later, returned to the floor. As she turned the pages the images came alive. Once recalled they were familiar again – most heart-rendingly so, bringing with them the sights, sounds and scents of the late Sixties. Was it her imagination or could she actually smell Aqua Manda – that long-discontinued perfume she and Kate had loved and used?

A group photograph taken outside Swansea College. Twenty-two students squashed in three rows in front of a coach. Most, smug and smiling – presumably in response to the photographer's 'cheese'.

Joe Hunt was in the centre of the back row, arms extended as if he was the patriarch of the clan assembled around him. Rich was there too, away from and to the side of the group, standing with Judy and the other students who'd gathered to say goodbye to those about to set off. Rich's arm was around Judy but he was looking in her direction.

She was next to Kate who was clutching her haggis to her chest. Penny recalled that Kate had spent the night with Joe in the flat he shared with three other boys. Living out and self-catering were privileges reserved for third-year male students, much to the female students' disgust. Kate had an on-off relationship with Joe. It had begun during Freshers' Week, which was possibly why Joe had given Kate advance notice of the trip.

Penny had never been sure who was using who. Joe made no secret of the fact that he was engaged to a girl in Cardiff College and he and Kate both occasionally went out with other people, yet they managed to remain friends and wouldn't tolerate anyone saying a bad word about the other.

The coach had been the first and easiest part of the journey to New York. The excitement had lasted as long as it took them to pick up the students from the other Swansea colleges. One of the girls from the art college was so overwhelmed by the prospect of trying to earn enough to live independently far from home that she succumbed to hysteria the moment she stepped on to the bus. They drove to Stansted to the accompaniment of her sobs and the boys' rugby songs.

There were a few snaps of the airport. In 1968 Stansted could have doubled as a film set of a Battle of Britain airfield. The terminal was an aircraft hangar, the sole concession to 'modern conveniences' the introduction of benches in the draughty metal-walled area set aside as a 'waiting room'. After the two-hour check-in for international flights, there had been a three-hour delay which had stretched to four hours then five ... and six...

When they finally saw their plane eight hours after arriving at the airport they discovered why their flight tickets had been so cheap. Joe referred to the plane as 'a jet prop engine' which meant nothing to her or Kate. Other than they never wanted to see, hear or enter another plane as rickety, noisy or ancient again.

She, Kate and most of the students on board started vomiting five minutes after take-off and their heads were still immersed in sick bags when they landed in New York, a juddering, shuddering, mind-and-body-numbing twelve hours later.

Every time the boys sitting behind them lowered the trays in front of their seats, the backs of the seats she and Kate were sitting on were pushed forward at a forty-five degree angle. They hadn't been in the air ten minutes when the white-faced girl who was playing 'air hostess' announced that the pilot thought there might be a problem and they would possibly have to land in Dublin.

They didn't – and there were no further threats of landing until after they'd crossed the Atlantic. But if there'd been floating airfields in the ocean, she was certain the pilot would have been tempted because the threats resumed as soon as they were within striking distance of land. Newfoundland and Boston were mentioned, before the plane roughly and finally bumped down in New York.

She wasn't able to compare the airline view of skyscrapers with the one in *West Side Story* because she didn't dare look up from her sick bag. The only consolation was that after twelve hours of retching there was nothing left in her stomach to come up.

Trembling, knees buckling, she'd followed Kate off the plane. None of the students had been happy at being forced to pay in advance for two nights' accommodation as part of their 'orientation and welcome to America', but all she wanted when she walked down the steps from the plane was a bed. If someone had wheeled one towards her she would have curled up on it there and then.

New York, June 1968

'We've been in this queue for two years.'

Kate glanced at her watch. 'Half an hour.'

'It feels like two years. What's this?' She frowned at the sheet of paper Joe Hunt handed her.

'I missed a form,' Joe passed her and walked down the line.

Penny read it. 'I've given all this information ten times over.'

'Make it eleven, or you won't be allowed out of the airport,' Joe advised.

She sat on the floor, straightened her duffel bag and used it to press on. She filled in the form and handed her biro and bag to Kate. Before Kate had finished writing they found themselves at the head of the queue. Their cards were stamped, their visas entered in their passport and the grim-faced clerk told them to 'have a good day'.

'Ladies,' she mouthed to Kate, pointing to the sign as she exited immigration. After washing her hands and face, repairing her lipstick and mascara and disentangling her hair as best she could, she was joined by Kate.

'Joe said hurry up. The coaches are waiting.'

'They can damn well wait. I'll never forgive Joe for that plane.'

'We're here, aren't we? In America!' Kate smiled as the realisation dawned on her. 'Come on, let's get our bags.'

Joe Hunt was waiting for them outside the coach.

'You look healthier than anyone has a right to, considering we drove away from college over twenty-four hours ago,' Penny upbraided him in disgust.

He grinned at her. 'And you look as though you flew here from Swansea without a plane.'

'I wish I had. Fresh air might have kept me from throwing up.'

'I was going to suggest a shower before going out to paint New York as red as we can on our budget. But instead of a taxi, I think I should call an undertaker. You're crawling as if you're at death's door.'

'If there's a door, I've walked through it. If I had the energy I'd slap you for looking so good. All I want is bed,' she yawned.

'Where's your sense of adventure?' Joe teased.

'I left it in a sick bag on the plane.' Penny

climbed on to the bus.

'It's two o'clock in the afternoon. Sleep now and it'll take you days to adjust to the time difference,' Joe warned.

'That would be good advice if we were in a fit state to take it.' Kate slumped beside her.

Joe stood next to the driver, looked down the bus and began counting heads.

'Can you get this bus to drop me off at the docks?' a third-year student from the art college asked.

'Why?' Joe demanded.

'To hell with orientation, getting to know America and mind-broadening experiences. In four months you're going to expect me to get back on that plane, if it hasn't crashed or rusted away.'

'That plane was sound,' Joe insisted. 'The airline wouldn't have allowed it to take off if it hadn't been.'

The student remained unconvinced. 'I want to spend the next twenty or thirty years producing art, not swirling around as disconnected molecules in the Atlantic.'

Joe ignored him, checked the list pinned to his clipboard and nodded to the driver who started the engine.

'You risk your neck if you want to,' the student persevered. 'I'm going to look for a ship bound for Europe so I can work my passage back. From now on it's train and ferry for me.'

'I'll come with you.' Penny wasn't sure whether or not she was joking.

'They don't allow women on merchant ships.'

'Can't stand the competition of superior minds?' It was Kate's standard reply to every misogynist statement.

Penny closed her eyes and the next thing she knew they were in the middle of Manhattan.

Horns were blaring, people shouting, and the boys were offloading the bags. Reluctant to move, she was the last to leave the bus. She reached the pavement to be accosted by a tall familiar young man who looked amazingly, almost shockingly healthy, clean and alert.

'Hello, Penny. I'm so glad you managed to break out from your cell.'

She stared at him, not because she didn't recognise him but because she couldn't understand what he was doing meeting her coach.

'We talked on the bus in London from Grosvenor Square to Bow Street police station. I was the one in handcuffs with a bruise on the side of my head. Remember?'

'Of course I remember, Bobby.'

'Gee, you remembered my name. That's neat.'

'That's what?' The Welsh Valley expression 'tidy and neat' or 'neat and tidy' sprang to mind but it didn't seem to fit.

'I forgot you British were so literal. "Neat" is good. I'll give you a lesson in Americanisms.'

A middle-aged man and woman were watching them.

'Directors in charge of orientation,' Bobby whispered. Raising his voice, he said, 'Welcome to America, Miss John. Here's your orientation schedule,' he handed her a sheaf of papers, 'plan of hotel, complimentary map of New York.' He dumped a file on top of the papers. 'And your room key.' He slipped an outsize keyring beneath her fingers. 'You're in a triple. Room 409 with Miss Katherine Burgess and Miss Anne Holland.'

She pushed the key into her jeans pocket. 'Do you work for the hotel?'

'I'm just one of the many students helping out with orientation, Miss John. I'm delivering the opening lecture at nine o'clock tomorrow morning.' He lowered his voice again. 'How would you like to see something of New York after you've cleaned up?' He didn't wait for her to answer. 'Meet you in the hotel's coffee shop in an hour?'

'Thanks, Bobby, but the only thing I want to see at the moment is bed.'

'You'll have all the time in the universe to sleep when you're dead.' He took her arm and steered her into the hotel foyer. 'Besides, I want to hear how you escaped the clutches of the British police. And,' he raised his eyebrows, 'you haven't heard how I broke out of my cell. It's a fascinating story.'

'It'll have to wait. I really am exhausted,' she insisted.

'Central Park is lovely at this time of year.'

'There's no way I could walk a step further than I have to in order to reach my bed.'

'Then you're in obvious need of food and coffee. I'll buy you both before escorting you along the shortest route to your room.'

'I look a wreck. I need a shower...'

'You look beautiful.' Bobby approached Kate as she entered the hotel with her own and Penny's

125

bags. 'Kate, isn't it? We met in Grosvenor Square but there wasn't much time for conversation. Here's your orientation file, hotel papers and key to 409. You're sharing with Penny and Miss Holland.' He lifted another file and stack of papers from the box under his arm and handed it to Kate. 'That's Miss Holland's pack. Would you give it to her, please? Penny will be along in half an hour, unless you'd like to join us for coffee?'

Kate winked suggestively. 'I wouldn't dream of intruding, Bobby.'

'You remember my name too? This is my lucky day.' Bobby steered her towards the coffee shop.

'Pen?' Kate called out from the lifts.

She turned. 'Yes?'

'Bobby's a definite improvement on the last one. And remember, we're in New York, not Ponty.'

CHAPTER ELEVEN

Pontypridd, 1987

Penny had pasted postcards of the hotel into the album. She remembered the building as a non-descript skyscraper like so many others in New York. One of the postcards was of the interior of a room. She gazed at the brown and orange decor – so dated, two decades later – and tried to recall if the room she'd shared with Kate and Anne had been similar.

She couldn't visualise it but she didn't need the postcard of the coffee shop to jog her memory. She closed her eyes and jetted back to that June afternoon.

The hotel had aimed for economy version gentlemen's club, with mock-leather brown vinyl chairs, fake-wood-grained Formica tables and heavy glass ashtrays. Three walls were covered with woven brown hessian, the fourth gold. All were studded with gold-framed silhouettes of eighteenth-century ladies and gentlemen.

New York, 1968

'Two cappuccinos, two ham sandwiches and two blueberry muffins.' Bobby called their order to the waitress while escorting Penny to a corner table set behind the door. Only two other couples were in the coffee shop. After the bustle of the plane, airport and bus she found the quiet blissful.

'I can't wait to show you America.' Bobby's enthusiasm was palpable. 'As soon as we've eaten we'll go to Central Park. The first thing you *have* to see is the Burnett Memorial Fountain in the Conservatory Garden. There's a statue there of a young girl and boy, characters from her *Secret Garden*. The sculpture's stunning. So stunning I considered studying art when I was younger, until my professor pointed out I have absolutely no talent. You?'

'I don't know yet if I have talent. But I'm attempting to study art.'

'I knew it. With auburn hair and tawny eyes, you couldn't be anything but an artist. And there's so much for an artist to see in the park. So many sculptures and beautiful gardens. From the Burnett memorial we'll go to the *Alice in Wonderland* statue of the Mad Hatter's tea party. It's fabulous, less than ten years old, but it gets a good polishing from the kids who climb on it every day...'

'The park authority allows children to climb on a statue?'

'It's meant to be used as a climbing frame. A beautiful bronze climbing frame that was given to the city for kids to play on. They swarm all over it. I wish the guy who commissioned it thought of it ten years earlier so I could have had fun when I was growing up. People would have looked sideways at a teenage boy climbing on it with four- and five-year-olds.'

'You grew up in New York?'

'I lived here before I went to school.'

'You must know the city inside out.'

'Not that well. I wasn't allowed out on my own until I was ten, and I was sent away to a boarding school in New Hampshire when I was seven.'

'But you must have come back for the holidays?'

'Weekends occasionally, either side of summer and winter camps.'

The waitress brought a tray to their tables, and set glasses of iced water, coffee and plates in front of them.

'Thank you.' Bobby pushed two of the plates in front of her. 'Eat and we'll go to Central Park.'

'I meant what I said about not being able to walk a step further than I need to reach the door of my room. What's this?' She looked down at her plate.

'English, American and Italian comfort food. The Italian is the cappuccino, the American the sandwich and the muffin English. I figured you'd need all three. One of your party said it took you over twelve hours to fly here.'

'Over twenty-four if you add the bus journey from the college and waiting at the airport.' She picked up one of the cupcakes and pulled the top from it. 'A currant bun?'

'An English muffin. I thought you might like a blueberry one, a taste of the old world and the new,' he explained.

'This doesn't look like any muffin I've seen, not that I've ever eaten one.'

'You've never eaten an English muffin?'

'Possibly because I'm Welsh.' She picked up her coffee, smelt the sprinkling of chocolate on top and drank. 'This is heavenly. Just what I need, caffeine.'

'They make great coffee here. A couple of those and you should stay awake until bedtime. By then your body clock will have adjusted to stateside time and you won't suffer from jet lag. Well, less than you would have if I'd allowed you to go straight to bed.'

'*Allowed* me...?'

'Admit it; you're having a good time.'

'I'd have a better one if you'd allowed me to shower and change before coming in here,' she retorted.

'There's no point in rushing to your room, your friends will be using the tub. But you could use mine.'

'What kind of a girl do you think I am?'

'The kind that gets herself arrested.' He smiled when she didn't reply. 'I was joking.'

'I'm tired.'

'You haven't a boyfriend hovering around here, have you?'

'No.'

'You left him back in England?'

'In Wales, with the new girl in his life.' She wondered why she'd told him about Rich.

'He must be mad to let you go.'

'He didn't think so.'

'Why are we talking about him when he's history and three thousand miles away?' He leant close to her. 'Let's swap cell stories.'

Pontypridd, May 1987

Restless, Penny rose from the floor and walked to the picture window that overlooked the garden and the hills beyond littered with scatterings of grubby grey sheep and startlingly white lambs. Blind to the view that had inspired her to choose this corner of the barn for her bedroom she remained lost in memories.

Why were the young the only ones who discussed the important questions life presented – and always late at night? Was it because they were free from responsibility and could afford to sleep their days away? Or did the heady mixture of youth, new-found freedom, camaraderie and too much alcohol lead to a profundity that didn't exist outside of their imaginations.

Andy's arrival had been a watershed for her. Before, there'd been time for philosophy, fun and, occasionally, even boredom. Afterwards there hadn't been enough hours in a day. She'd painted sample pictures to send to agencies in her efforts to forge a career as a jobbing artist, in between cooking, cleaning, washing nappies and feeding Andy. Before he'd begun nursery school there'd been times when she had been so tired by the evening, it had been as much as she could do to crawl into an armchair and watch television, or curl up in bed with a book, praying that Andy would sleep until morning.

Single motherhood had been tough. It would have helped during Andy's early years if she'd had a husband to turn to, but she'd had her parents' unstinting support, and when black moments descended, she'd tried to concentrate on the good memories of Bobby. Later ... there'd been Jack.

Occasionally, during the small hours when sleep eluded her, she was beset by feelings of unease. Despite her parents' and Andy's teachers' assurance that she'd made a competent job of bringing up her son, she'd felt guilty for working long hours. Physically she'd always been there for him. Mentally was something else. And Andy had always known when she hadn't been listening to him when he'd visited her in her studio after school.

She was almost forty but she was no closer to answering the questions that had perplexed her at twenty. But what she did know was, from the very beginning of her relationship with Bobby, she could no more have stopped herself from falling in love with him than she could have stopped breathing.

New York, 1968

Bobby sat back in his chair and said, 'Do I know how to order, or do I know how to order? That was a great ham sandwich and blueberry muffin.'

'Anyone would think you made them yourself,' she countered.

'If I had, they would have been even better. I can cook.'

'Americans class making a ham sandwich as cooking?' She crumbled the last of her enormous blueberry muffin between her fingers before admitting defeat and pushing her plate away.

'Muffins are baked.'

'You bake?'

'If I did, I'd be a champion baker.'

'Is that what you Americans call "bullshit"?'

'"Bullshit"?' he repeated indignantly. 'And there's me thinking I'd found myself a real British lady who wouldn't know the word existed. But I suppose I have to make allowances for your condition.' He watched her yawn.

'I need a bath, a change of clothes and–'

'Don't say sleep,' he warned. 'If you do you'll never adjust to East Coast time.'

'Try telling that to my eyelids. They're weighing heavier by the second.'

'I noticed. They were closed the whole time I was telling you about Central Park.'

'They were not,' she protested.

'What was the last thing I said?'

She looked mutely at him and he laughed.

'I'll carry your bag. Give me your key.'

She handed him her room key and followed him to the lift. He hit the button for the tenth floor. She leant against the wall and closed her eyes for a moment ... the next thing she knew he was helping her out into a corridor.

'Lean there. I'll get your bag.'

'I'm fine.'

Bobby didn't argue. He picked up her bag from the doorway of the elevator, where he'd left it to prop the door open.

'The hotel must have put us the furthest possible point from the lift,' she grumbled when they walked down what appeared to be an endless corridor.

'So would you if you owned the place. The organisers of the orientation course block-book at preferential rates. Discounts never get the best rooms.'

'I thought you were reading medieval history not economics.'

'Who told you I was reading medieval history?'

She recalled the police cell. The memory still had the power to make her shiver. If she told Bobby about Rose, he'd realise she'd been discussing him with his friends and she didn't want him to know how interested she was in him. Not until she could be sure how interested he was in her. 'I'm psychic.'

133

'And I'm Mickey Mouse. You've been asking people about me?'

'Don't flatter yourself.'

The sound of hammering and shouting emanated from her room. Bobby handed her back the key and she tried to unlock the door only to find it open.

The room was tiny. There was barely space to walk between the single and double beds. Kate, dressed in clean jeans, T-shirt, her hair soaking wet, was hammering on the bathroom door.

'Problems?' Bobby asked.

'Anne must have gone to sleep in the bath. I've tried shouting...'

'We heard,' Penny said dryly.

'I tried shouldering the door, but I'm not strong enough to spring it. Don't suppose you'd like to give it a go?' Kate asked Bobby.

'No, I wouldn't,' Bobby refused. 'Hotels overcharge guests for damage. And I doubt the lady would be amused if I broke in on her when she wasn't dressed.'

'Any suggestions?' Kate asked.

'If you don't want to use the bathroom, leave her. She'll wake up when the water gets cold,' he advised.

'Which hopefully won't be too long,' Penny chipped in. 'I'm desperate for a bath or shower and change of clothes.'

'I grabbed first bath because I want to join Joe and the others on their tour of New York. Anne didn't want to come. You coming?' Kate picked up her shoes and slipped them on.

'I need to get out of these clothes.'

'If you're that desperate, use the bathroom in my room,' Bobby offered.

'Quick work, Bobby.' Kate raised her eyebrows.

'How do you know my name? I don't remember introducing myself in Grosvenor Square.'

'You did to Penny and she hasn't stopped talking about you since. In fact, when her uncle eventually managed to get her out of Bow Street police station, it was as much as we could do to stop her from going back in to demand the police release you as well.'

'Really? You wanted to help me?' Bobby smiled.

'You and the other girls in my cell,' she qualified. 'The police were foul to us.'

'They weren't kind to the boys either.' He changed the subject. 'My bathroom's not luxurious but it's fairly clean and has a shower head over the tub.'

'And you in the bedroom to help Penny should she run into difficulties using the facilities?' Kate rifled through the contents of her haggis.

'I don't have to be in my room when Penny uses the shower,' Bobby protested. 'I could go for a walk in Central Park.'

'Brilliant, Bobby,' Kate enthused. 'You can show Joe, me, and the others the sights. I'll phone his room and let him know that you'll be meeting us in reception in five minutes.'

'Make it ten.' Bobby picked up Penny's bag. 'That gives me time to show Penny to my room.'

CHAPTER TWELVE

Bobby's room was on the first floor. Even smaller and dingier than the one allotted to Penny, Kate and Anne, it held two small double beds, a rickety veneer wardrobe and bedside table.

'The bathroom.' Bobby pushed his way between the beds, opened the door and switched on the light.

The tub was stained a greenish brown below the taps, the towels were thin and there was an empty basket devoid of complimentary toiletries. He saw her looking at the basket.

'My apologies, but orientation staff get even worse rooms than the students.'

'I thought it would be better as it was on the first floor.'

'Unlike you Brits, our rich occupy the attics, which they've renamed penthouses to make them sound desirable. The lesser beings are housed below.' He dropped her bag on one of the beds. 'If you want to stretch out after your bath I haven't slept in this one. My robe's hanging on the back of the bathroom door; you're welcome to use it. Help yourself to whatever you need from my toilet bag. Soap, toothpaste, bath salts,' a mischievous smile curved his mouth, 'razor ... shaving cream.'

'Thank you, but I've everything I need.'

He glanced at his watch. 'I'll be back in an hour.'

'No you won't,' she warned. 'Now Kate's organised an unpaid tour guide for the group, they'll keep you for as long as it suits them.'

'And if the guide has better things to do?'

'They'll bribe him.'

'I'm not easily bribed. Lock the door and put on the safety chain.' He raised his eyebrows. 'That means you have to stay until I return.'

'The door locks when you close it.'

'It's more secure double-locked.'

'I doubt anyone will try to break in if I return to my own room.'

'You'll have more privacy in this room, plus a free bathroom,' he pointed out.

'Only until your return.'

'Give me a break,' he pleaded. 'I'm a wonderful guy when you get to know me. And, I promise, as soon as your friends no longer need my services you'll get to know me very well.'

He left, closing the door behind him. She opened her bag and took out clean underclothes, jeans and T-shirt. Forgetting Bobby's advice about the safety chain, she went into the bathroom and started running the bath. The water flowed sluggishly but steamed hot.

A black leather toilet bag stood next to a paper-wrapped glass on a shelf below the mirror. Mindful of Bobby's directive to help herself to his toiletries, she opened it and discovered Bobby's bath salts were French and, judging by their smell, expensive. The pack was three-quarters full but she poured barely a teaspoonful into the water. The room was instantly filled with pine forest fragrance.

It was heaven to strip off the clothes she had put on more than twenty-four hours before and step into hot scented water. There was a bar of soap and a bottle of shampoo in the ceramic dish next to the bath. She picked up the soap. It had the same scent as the water, as did the shampoo when she unscrewed the top.

She lay back, soaked her hair, washed it and closed her eyes... She woke with a start when she heard the bedroom door open.

'Hey, man, you're in danger of turning into a girl, splashing about in the tub this time of day.'

The bathroom door opened. Too late she realised she'd forgotten to lock it or put the chain across the bedroom door as Bobby had advised. She jumped up and grabbed a towel from the rail as a dark-skinned face peered down at her. It could have been Bobby with a heavy tan.

'Wow – I mean, I'm sorry.'

The stranger closed the door quickly, but not quickly enough. She burnt crimson before turning the key in the lock.

'You didn't have to do that. I've been brought up properly. I'll mind my manners and stay this side of the door. Although, I've never been so tempted to jump into a tub fully clothed.' The voice had the same accent as Bobby, but it sounded less cultured.

'Who are you and what are you doing here?' she demanded.

'I could ask you the same question, but knowing Bobby, I don't need to. I'm a friend of his. Name's Sandy. You?'

'An acquaintance.'

'You must know him reasonably well to use his tub.'

'I'm only here because my room-mate has fallen asleep in our bath. Bobby offered me the use of his.'

'Lucky Bobby. "Bath" – you're English?'

'Welsh,' she corrected. She put on her best teaching practice voice. 'What do you mean "lucky Bobby"?' She grabbed another towel and wrapped it around her hair before drying herself.

'Girls have a habit of falling at his feet and into his room. I wish I could persuade someone as gorgeous as you to use my tub. Not that I have a tub to offer.'

'You still haven't told me what you're doing here,' she reminded.

'Bobby and me have been friends since we were kids. I'm in town so I decided to pay him a visit.'

'He didn't know you were coming?'

'No, I thought I'd surprise him.'

She looked around for her clothes. She remembered taking them from her bag. Had she left them on the bed...? To her relief she saw them piled on the window sill.

'Are you sharing his room?'

'Most certainly not,' she retorted indignantly. 'I'm only here–'

'You said – to use his tub. Good, if you're not staying with him, I can. Are you the Brit girl he's chasing?'

'I'm Welsh, remember.'

'You have a Brit accent.'

'I'm still Welsh.'

'What's Welsh?'

139

'Wales is a part of Britain, like Scotland and Ireland.' She pulled on her underclothes.

'I've heard of Scotland and Ireland, but not Wales.'

'You heard of Tom Jones?'

'The "Not Unusual" guy? First time I heard him sing I thought he was black. That's some voice he's got.'

'He's Welsh. From Pontypridd, the same town as me.' She pulled on her jeans but she had to lie on the floor to zip them up and when she did she could scarcely breathe. She looked in the mirror anxiously, wondering if she'd put on weight during the flight. Fluid retention? Did people expand in the air? After all that vomiting she'd expected to be pounds lighter than when she'd left the UK.

'But you're the girl Bobby met in London, right?'

She donned her T-shirt, slipped on her shoes and picked up her toilet bag. 'I met Bobby in London but he's hardly chasing me.'

'Oh yes he is. He just hasn't told you how hard in case he frightens you off. You didn't think he was here by chance, did you?'

Her tired mind groped to make sense of what Sandy was saying. Had Bobby really planned this meeting? Had he tracked her down to this hotel and this orientation course from the short conversation they'd had about her and Kate's planned trip to America after they'd been arrested? It was ridiculous. Or was it? Bobby hadn't seemed surprised when he'd seen her leaving the bus outside the hotel. She slid the bolt back on the door and

140

opened it. Sandy was lying on Bobby's bed, reading the room service menu. He glanced up at her.

'When did you get here?'

'A couple of hours ago.'

'From Swansea College?'

'How do you know what college I'm from?'

'Bobby studied the orientation schedule to see when you'd be arriving. When he discovered the date he checked the staff list until he found someone he knew on it. There was a guy called Arnie who'd been at tennis camp with him. Bobby paid him a hundred dollars to take his place on the staff for forty-eight hours.'

'Why would Bobby pay someone to take his place on the staff?'

'So he could be here to meet you.'

'Then Bobby isn't on the staff of the orientation course?'

'Nope. And it's anyone's guess what he's going to talk about when he gives the "welcome to the states" speech tomorrow. Now you know the effect you've had on him. After seeing you I understand why. I would have raided my piggy bank for a chance to meet a girl like you. Not that there's a hundred dollars in it.' He sat up and held out his hand. 'Sandy Buttons.'

'Penny John.' She shook his hand before bundling her washing into her laundry bag.

'So where's Bobby?'

'Showing my friends around Central Park.'

'Bobby loves that place, he could be gone hours. You hungry?'

'I've just eaten.'

'I'm starving.' He dropped the menu. 'Change your mind. They have great burgers here. We'll stick them on Bobby's bill. Or we could go down to the coffee shop.'

'I've just been there with Bobby, thank you.'

'Then it'll have to be burgers in the room. Sure you don't want anything?'

'Quite sure. But thank you for asking.'

The door opened and Bobby walked in. 'I thought I heard voices. What are you doing here, Sandy?'

'Stealing Penny. Finders keepers, remember.'

'Hands off. I've staked my claim. You should be digging latrines.'

'I *was* digging latrines but our leader–'

'The Bishop or Pill Face?'

'The Bishop,' Sandy answered.

'"The Bishop" is the nickname we give to the guy in charge of our section of the summer camp. Pill Face is his wife, so named because she always looks as though she's swallowed a large one,' Bobby explained.

'Your section of the camp?' She'd tried to keep up with the conversation, but whether it was exhaustion or Sandy and Bobby's bizarre mention of latrines, bishops and pills, she was confused.

'Summer camp – the one we're working in,' Bobby continued. 'It has three sections, one for five-to-ten-year-olds; another for ten-to-fifteen-year-olds and one for sixteen-to-eighteen-year-olds.'

'We're working with the sixteen-to-eighteen group.' Sandy held up his hand, Bobby slapped it. They shouted 'Pioneers' in unison.

142

'And the latrines?'

'It's a camp.'

She knew they were teasing her. She'd seen photographs of American summer camps in the brochures Joe had shown her. They'd all been like Butlin's with tarmac walkways between wooden chalets and plumbed-in bathrooms and kitchens.

'Shouldn't you be somewhere else?' Bobby asked Sandy.

'Nope. I'm staying the night.' Sandy lay back on the bed.

'Who said so?' Bobby demanded.

'The Bishop. He decided we need another female counsellor for the other side of the lake besides the one you told him you'd be bringing back.'

'You've found a counsellor?' she asked.

'I told you on the bus in London I'd help you find a job. Remember?' Bobby was so carried away with his plans, he either didn't notice, or ignored her lack of reply. 'It's a great camp in a beautiful area of Connecticut, you'll love it. It's on the bank of a lake; you can swim, sail, canoe–'

'I can do all those things in Wales,' she interrupted. 'I'm here to see the galleries and museums, not experience the outdoor life.'

'Great, we'll travel into New York and Boston on our days off. You'll have your own personal tour guide – me. I know all the best sights and places culture-wise and fun-wise in both cities. We'll have a ball.'

'This orientation is about finding jobs for us, isn't it?' she checked.

'It is,' Bobby allowed warily.

'Then there's bound to be something going in New York I can do.'

'Low-paid jobs in catering and hotels. Waitressing and chambermaiding for less than fifty cents an hour,' Bobby dismissed.

'I only need to earn enough to keep myself.'

'Have you any idea what it costs to rent a room in this city? It's one of the most expensive places in the world to live,' Bobby informed her.

'Which is why I'm bunking in with Bobby tonight,' Sandy chipped in.

'You said you were staying. I didn't realise you meant my room. Go get your own,' Bobby retorted.

'No cash. Besides, the Bishop told me to bunk in with you.'

'How generous of him to allocate my room space. Don't you have to meet him?' Bobby asked pointedly.

'Not until tomorrow. He's dining at his club and staying the night.' Sandy pulled a face. 'I wasn't invited.'

Bobby burst out laughing. 'Did you expect to be?'

'A man can live in hope. Even a Hispanic. He told me he'd be here for the employers' afternoon seminar tomorrow at three.'

'Aren't there any live-in jobs in the city?' she asked. 'Kate's found one as a nanny in Scarsdale. She's getting twenty dollars a week and her keep.'

'And she'll be expected to work 24–7 for it with no time off,' Bobby warned. 'I know the type you get in Scarsdale. Couples who complain about the influx of illegal immigrants into the States

144

from Mexico, but are first in line to employ one as a domestic. They'll pay her ten cents an hour while proclaiming it doesn't reflect on them as a family because they only took her in "out of charity".'

'Kate's not an illegal immigrant and she's more than capable of looking after herself. If she doesn't like it, she'll leave.'

'They may not let her. Scarsdale people can be vicious.' Sandy spoke as though he'd had personal experience.

'You're letting life pass you by here, Sandy.' Bobby picked up Sandy's arm and tried to pull him off the bed. 'If you go to Central Park you'll meet Penny's friends. Kate's your type. Grey-eyed blonde, delicate features, long legs...'

'I'm too exhausted from all that latrine digging to walk.' Sandy fell back on the pillows.

'What the hell. It's only money. Book yourself a room and put it on my bill.'

'There's no need for Sandy to go anywhere. I'm going to my room.' She picked up her bag.

'I didn't offer to pay for his room so we could be alone.'

'No?' Sandy raised a sceptical eye.

'No,' Bobby repeated. 'Tomorrow's a big day. I'm giving the opening lecture. I need a good night's sleep and you snore.'

'Why don't we all go to Central Park to look for Penny's friends?' Sandy suggested.

'You're too tired to walk, remember?' Bobby emphasised the last word.

'So I am.' Sandy settled back comfortably and closed his eyes.

'And you're exhausted from all that travelling.' Bobby turned to Penny.

'It's odd, but I feel quite awake after that bath. Although given the horrors and length of the journey here I might collapse later.'

'We'll make it a short walk round the park. And if you collapse I'll carry you back.' Bobby took her bag from her. 'Leave this here.'

'No way. Because I'll have to come back here to get it.' She wrenched it from his grasp.

'At least let me carry it for you.' Bobby tried to take it from her.

'Children, stop quarrelling.' Sandy lifted the pillow from beneath his head and punched it into a more conducive shape. 'You're disturbing my beauty sleep.'

CHAPTER THIRTEEN

The early evening air in Central Park was hot and humid and strangely seductive after the 'canned' air in the hotel. But not as seductive as Sandy's assertion that Bobby had paid someone a hundred dollars to take their place at the orientation course so he could see her again.

She stopped and looked around. 'It's lovely here. So green and peaceful. Block out the skyscrapers and you'd never think you were in the middle of a city.'

Bobby reached for her hand as they strolled towards Conservatory Water and the *Alice in*

Wonderland statue. 'This is one of my favourite walks to one of my favourite places. Do you have any?'

'Dozens. There's a beautiful park in Luxembourg and a stunning one in Rome... What's so funny?' she asked when he started to laugh.

'You. Your favourite places aren't even in your own country.'

'Pontypridd – that's the town I come from – has a wonderful park too. It's huge and right in the centre of town. And we're surrounded by mountains. My brothers, sisters and I used to pack a picnic in the morning, take our bikes or horses and roam for miles when we were small.'

'You ride?'

She nodded.

'And have your own horse?'

'My family had a few. My father arranged for them to be stabled at a farm near our home.'

'And you've travelled?'

'That's down to my father. He loves Europe. Especially France and Italy. He used to drive us there every summer when we were children to show us the palaces, cathedrals and museums. Although there never seemed to be enough time to see everything properly. I remember one fortnight–'

'That word is so Shakespeare.'

She looked up at him. 'You don't have fortnights here?'

'No, but we will now you're here to tell us about them.'

'Where did you go on holidays with your parents?' she asked curiously.

147

'Nowhere.'

'You stayed home all summer?'

'All my holidays were spent in camps. Tennis, sailing, chess, riding, skiing in winter – you name it, I was sent there. Which is why I'm an expert on absolutely everything.'

'And modest with it,' she mocked. 'You couldn't have spent much time with your parents.'

'None. I see my grandmother occasionally. But before I went to boarding school it was mainly nannies.'

'You were brought up by nannies?'

'A succession of them, because my grandmother didn't like me getting too close to any particular nanny. She was also always on the lookout for a stricter version of my current one. Why do you find that strange?' he asked. 'Nannies are a British invention.'

'You do have parents?' she checked.

'My mother's dead.'

'I'm sorry. I had no right to pry,' she apologised.

'You don't have to look sad, I can't remember her.'

'She died when you were a baby?'

'Three years ago, but she'd been in and out of nursing homes for years for drink and drug addiction.'

'That must have been dreadful for you and your father. No wonder he sent you away to camps.'

'He didn't send me anywhere. My father's step-mother – who I suppose is my step-grandmother, but I refer to her as my grandmother, to save time – did. I haven't seen my father since I was one –

or so my grandmother tells me. He's just divorced wife number seven and lives in a hippy commune in Mexico. My mother was wife number one. When my father divorced her, my grandmother drew up the settlement. She gave them cash and annuities in exchange for me.'

'Your parents handed you over to your grandmother for money?' She was aghast.

'My grandmother wanted to groom me as her heir. My parents didn't want me for anything in particular.'

'I can't imagine any parent just handing over their child, especially for money.'

'They married too young and I think I did well out of the deal. By all accounts my mother was a career hypochondriac and nymphomaniac. And I don't think I'd enjoy life in a hippy commune in Mexico. No amount of free love can compensate for a lack of electricity and hot and cold running water.'

Fired by her college psychology classes, she asked. 'Is that your way of coping with your parents' rejection, making jokes?'

'Some people are good at bringing up kids, some disastrous. Whenever I see her, my grandmother reminds me that I had a lucky escape. If either of my parents had kept me I would have been dragged around here, there and everywhere and, in all probability, abandoned on the way and left to fend for myself.'

'You're not bitter?'

'No.'

'Well, I would be if my parents had handed me over to a relative when I was born.' She imagined

Bobby's upbringing as cold, lonely and impersonal, filled with nannies, boarding schools, camps...

'You know what it is to have a family. All I've known is life with my grandmother who ensured I received the best money could buy, in education, clothes, toys, food and everything else she could think of. As the saying goes, you don't miss what you never had.'

'Does she live in New York?'

'Occasionally. She travels a lot. She's in Italy at the moment.'

'And your mother and father never contacted you, wrote or telephoned?'

'What for? Both of them knew my grandmother would look after me better than they could.'

'You must be very fond of her.'

'"Fond" – that's a strange word to use in conjunction with my grandmother. She's a martinet of the old school. Terrifying, with fearfully high standards her staff and relatives can never hope to meet.'

'Do you see much of her?'

'No. I was seven when I was sent away to school and, as I said, holidays were spent in camps. But I usually spend Labour Day weekend in her summer place on Cape Cod, and Christmas Day at her New York apartment.' He wrapped his arm around her shoulders. 'There's no need to pity me. I was given all the things I needed and a few luxuries I didn't.'

'Have you any brothers and sisters?'

'Last time I checked, around seventeen half-brothers and -sisters. My mother never reproduced again, but my father couldn't stop. I've never met any of them. Look, there's the statue. Isn't it stunning?'

They'd reached the eleven-foot bronze depiction of the Mad Hatter's tea party. 'They're all here: Alice, the Mad Hatter, the Cheshire Cat, the Dormouse, Alice's cat Dinah, the March Hare and the White Rabbit.' He jumped up on the larger of the toadstool seats. 'That's enough about me. What about you?' He leant his elbow on the toadstool 'table' in front of Alice's arm, propped his head on his hand and gazed at Penny.

'Compared to you I've led a dull life. I lived at home and attended local day schools until I went to college when I was eighteen. I have a sister, two brothers and four adopted sisters.'

'Your parents adopted four girls?' He whistled. 'Brave, brave people.'

'They're years older than me. They were evacuated to Pontypridd from London during the war. Their mother died in the Blitz and their father was killed fighting the Germans. So my mother took them in.'

'Didn't your father have a say?'

'Not at the time, he was a POW in Germany.'

'Large family for him to come home to.'

'He didn't mind. In fact, he's as close to them as he is to us.' She ran her hands over the smooth and shiny surface of the statue, polished by the children who'd climbed on it.

'What would have happened to the girls if your mother hadn't adopted them?'

'They would have had to go into an orphanage.

As they were already living in our house my mother said it was simpler to keep them.'

'But they would have been looked after in an orphanage?'

'Not as well as my mother did, but yes, they would have been looked after. What was it like to spend all your time in boarding school?'

'I told you, I don't know any different. It wasn't bad, but I'd be lying if I said I liked the square-bashing.'

'Square-bashing at a boarding school?'

'It was a military academy. Three generations of Brosnas have been enrolled there. My grandfather loved it – or so my grandmother told me. She thought it would stiffen my back along with my resolve to run the family businesses. Why she thought that, when the academy did no such thing for my father, who absconded from the place every chance he got, I don't know.' He offered her a hand and she sat on the 'table' beside him.

'And will you run the family businesses?'

'Hell no, I intend to do my own thing.'

'Which is?'

'When I've finished at Oxford, music.'

'What kind of music?'

'Every kind,' he said airily. 'Jazz, pop, classical, folk.'

'You play?'

'The piano, guitar and saxophone. I've already played backing at recording sessions. My grandmother approves of it as a hobby.'

'Will she let you follow a career in music?' she probed.

'Not willingly. But I've learnt not to argue with her. It's easier not to tell her my plans. She has people watching me and she approves of my university course. She thinks medieval history will give me risqué stories about ancient royalty to relate at dinner parties while I run the family businesses.'

'What arc the family businesses?'

'Numerous and boring. You're beautiful in this light,' he whispered as the sun began to sink below the trees that surrounded the statue.

She glanced at her watch. 'I'm still on British time.'

'It's coming up to seven. We'll find somewhere to eat on the way back to the hotel. Afterwards I'll allow you to have an early night. Then tomorrow, you should be on eastern seaboard time.'

'You'll *"allow"* me? That's the second time you've used that word.' She thought of Rich. 'I warn you, I don't like bossy men.' She jumped down from the statue.

'That's an improvement.'

'What?'

'Telling me what you don't like in men. One day and already you're trying to change me.'

Dinner was a shared bottle of wine and a plate of pasta in an Italian restaurant. Halfway through the meal, she could barely keep her eyes open. Bobby paid the bill and they left. Night had fallen, warm, sticky and noisy over the city.

Bobby hailed a taxi.

'My room or yours?' he asked when they entered the lobby.

'Yours.'

'Your case is in your room.'

'You said I could use the contents of your toilet bag.'

'Just as well I packed a spare toothbrush.'

They took the lift, rode up one floor and walked down the corridor. He unlocked the door to find a note on the bed. He read it, screwed it up and tossed it into the bin.

'From Sandy?' she asked.

'From Sandy,' he echoed.

'What did he say?'

'You don't want to know.'

'Yes I do.' She dived on the basket and retrieved the piece of paper. Bobby tried to snatch it from her as she smoothed it out but he was too late.

She read it aloud. *'Hope she's worth it and you strike lucky. It's cost you thirty bucks.'*

'Am I worth it?'

He pulled her close. 'Let me find out.'

Slowly, inexorably, his lips pressed down on hers. Warmth permeated from her mouth downwards into her entire body. She lifted her arms and locked them around his neck, pulling him even closer.

He fell backwards on to the bed, taking her with him.

'You're sure?'

'Very sure.' She moved away and stripped off her clothes.

'You're beautiful,' he whispered when she was naked. 'This isn't going to be a one night–'

She laid her fingers over his mouth. 'No talking.'

Taking her fingers from his lips he kissed them

before turning back the bedclothes. She crawled between the sheets and watched him undress.

Thoughts of Rich came to mind when Bobby lay beside her but they were soon dispelled.

During what followed she realised she'd had sex many times with Rich. But this was the first time in her life she'd made love.

She woke with a start. The glare of neon lights penetrated the thin curtains in Bobby's room. Shadows made stick and arrow shapes on the walls and ceiling. The sound of sirens and cars echoed in from the street, mingling with shouts of 'goodnight' and doors banging as guests walked the corridors to their rooms.

She gazed at Bobby lying alongside her, his face relaxed in sleep, his black curls tousled over the pillow. Was it her imagination or were his lips curved in a smile?

Ridiculously wide awake and restless considering it was dark, she moved on to her back. Why had Bobby found it necessary to tell her their relationship would amount to more than one night? Was it a case of protesting too much because that's what it would be?

Would Bobby think less of her for sleeping with him a few hours after meeting her – granted for the second time?

As Kate kept reminding her, the modern world had moved on from the outmoded morality her mother had instilled in her and her sisters. The yardstick of her parents' generation had been made obsolete by the advent of the contraceptive pill.

But outmoded or not – the influence of her mother's teaching persisted in lingering.

Would – did – Bobby regard her as a slut?

She slipped from the bed and reached for Bobby's white towelling robe. It was too long. She wrapped it around herself. It was warm in the cool air that belched from the noisy rickety air-conditioning unit. The collar brushed her cheek and she breathed in the sharp pine fragrance of Bobby's cologne and bath oil.

A siren blasted below her as she pushed aside the curtains. The numbers on the electric clock on the bedside table read three-thirty, yet the street was as crowded as a Saturday morning in Pontypridd market. Although the people looked somewhat different.

A girl was leaning against a building across the road. She pulled her skirt to her waist every time a man walked towards her, and she wasn't wearing underwear.

'Welcome to New York.' Bobby left the bed. Naked, he stood behind her and locked his arms around her waist.

'I can't believe what I'm seeing.'

'The homeless guy bedded down outside that building?'

'I hadn't noticed him. He looks young.'

'Probably is.'

'Don't you have hostels for the homeless in this city?'

'Not enough to accommodate them all. And most of our homeless have drink or drugs problems as well as the biggest problem of all. Poverty.'

'I feel sorry for him.'

'Don't. As you see, he has a brown paper bag that he's lifting to his mouth. My guess is cheap whisky. And while he has oblivion he doesn't need your sympathy.'

'That girl...' Penny watched her lift her dress again. A man walked up to her and stood in front of her, blocking her from view of the street.

'The hooker?' Bobby asked.

'It's public. What about the police...?'

'The police have better things to do than round up hookers at this hour of the morning. Besides, they'd never succeed in running all of them in. If they did they'd have to turn Central Park into a cell. Even then, I doubt it would be big enough to hold every working girl in the city.'

'But that's so blatant.' She watched in disbelief when the man stepped back from the girl and zipped up his trousers.

'You have hookers in London and Oxford. I've seen them operate.'

'Not openly on the streets like that.'

'Yes, openly on the streets like that. But you do have to look for the streets in the UK. You Brits like things neater than us Yanks. We believe in free enterprise and allowing our hookers to operate anywhere.' He brushed her hair aside and kissed the nape of her neck. 'You shock easily. I like that in a woman. Shows your innocence.'

'Innocence...' she summoned her courage. 'We didn't talk about my boyfriend earlier. I want you to know, I've only had one and we were together for seven years. We were almost engaged...'

'He's history. I'm here.' He turned her round

until she faced him.

'I don't want you to think I'm the sort of girl who makes a habit of sleeping with boys the day she meets them.'

'You didn't, we met months ago.' He locked his hands around her waist.

'We haven't seen one another since.'

'Only because we were on different continents. And, as we're in a confessing mood, I haven't lived in a monastery since I returned from Oxford.'

She smiled. 'I'd love to see you in a monk's habit with a tonsure.'

'Kinky. I'll see what I can find.' He bent his head to hers and kissed her slowly and lovingly. 'Why are we standing here, having this conversation in front of a hotel bedroom window with the curtains open in full view of the street at three-thirty in the morning, when we could be doing something far more interesting in bed?'

'I couldn't sleep. I thought I'd see New York by night.'

'I hated waking up and discovering you gone.'

'I was still in the room.'

'But not next to me.' He led her back to the bed and caught sight of the clock. 'Four hours before we have to get up. At least you can sleep while I deliver my talk. I, on the other hand, have to think of something to say that will fill twenty minutes.'

'Do you know what?'

'I haven't a clue.'

'Shouldn't you make some notes?'

'Not now.' He pushed her back on to the bed.

CHAPTER FOURTEEN

Surrounded by jet-lagged students and jet-lagged herself, she couldn't stop yawning the next morning. But exhausted as she was, she couldn't stop looking at Bobby while he delivered his introductory talk. And smiling at the memory of the night – and morning – they'd shared. She flushed in embarrassment when she realised Kate had been watching her while she'd been mentally undressing Bobby.

Kate whispered in her ear. 'You're besotted.'

She saw Bobby watching them. 'Ssh.'

'Admit it.' Kate persevered.

She dug Kate in the ribs with her elbow.

'Jobs in the States aren't that difficult to come by, well-paid ones are.' Dressed casually in jeans and check shirt Bobby concluded his lecture to the students on the orientation course by stating the obvious. 'If you're asked at an interview if you've experience in a particular field, or can operate a specific piece of machinery, the answer you give is a resounding and confident "yes". When you're faced with a machine or the task in hand, you smile,' Bobby bared his teeth in an insincere Hollywood grimace, 'and say, "Ours are different in Europe. Please show me how this one works." You have a question?' Bobby pointed to Joe Hunt who'd raised his hand.

'And if we break the machine or the system or

159

whatever it is we're supposed to be operating?'

'You won't if you don't touch whatever it is until they show you how to manage it.'

'Isn't that somewhat optimistic?' Kate chipped in.

'Not if you insist on being fully briefed before you put a finger on anything that looks complicated or dangerous,' Bobby replied.

'So what if I get a job as a nuclear physicist?' Joe asked.

Bobby waited until the laughter in the room subsided. 'There's a shortage of skilled workers on the eastern seaboard. Possibly that includes nuclear physicists. But I would presume a nuclear physicist's position to be a permanent one. I assumed you were all looking for temporary seasonal work.'

'We are.' Kate made a face at Joe.

'However, if I hear of a vacancy for a nuclear physicist in the city I'll be sure to contact you, Mr...?'

'Hunt. Joe Hunt.'

'And if we can't help you to find a job as a nuclear physicist your second choice would be?'

'Bar work,' Joe conceded.

'You have experience?'

'Only from the customer side,' one of Joe's housemates shouted from the back of the room.

'Then it's bar work with training for you, Mr Hunt, if we can find it.' Bobby declared. 'It's time for a coffee break. Some employers in search of temporary workers are in the suite next door. More will be arriving at three o'clock this afternoon. They'll give you an idea of the type of work on offer in the city and the surrounding areas. They'll also be able to answer any questions you have about working conditions, hours and salaries. If you need assistance finding accommodation our counsellors will be on hand at two-thirty in the green suite. Thank you for listening.'

'Bobby's lecture was as much help as a double open-ended sick bag on a plane.' Kate picked up her haggis. 'You coming next door?'

'I am.' She checked her watch. 'But I'm surprised you are.'

'I've been talking to people. Twenty dollars a week all found as an au pair sounds like slave labour.'

'It is.' Bobby appeared at their side. 'Which is why I've put the two of you down for positions at Camp Resonance. One hundred and twenty dollars a week all found and one day off a week. Does that appeal?' He looked to Kate.

'Where and what is Camp Resonance?' Kate demanded.

'The camp is built on a beautiful wooded spot on the banks of a lake in Connecticut. Ideal for swimming, sailing, canoeing and all water sports. It's a summer camp for children ranging in age from five to eighteen and is designed to build participants' confidence, impart skills, and stretch their imaginations.' Bobby was obviously quoting the prospectus.

'And what would we be doing there?' Kate asked suspiciously.

'You would be working with the eight-to-twelve-year-olds. Organising group activities around your specialities, which are...?' He looked

161

questioningly at Kate.

'I'm studying English main with drama and social studies,' Kate divulged.

'Perfect, you can coach the kids in drama and organise a play for parents' day. The work won't be too onerous,' he added when he saw a sceptical expression cross Kate's face. 'There's a ratio of eight kids to one counsellor.'

'There could be better paid jobs on offer next door.'

'There could,' Bobby allowed, 'but not when you take the cost of food and rent into consideration.'

Penny followed Kate out of the door. Bobby grabbed her arm.

'You'll be working with the fifteen-to-eighteen-year-olds alongside me. So there's absolutely no need for you, or Kate, to talk to anyone. Take it from me, you'll love Resonance.'

She recalled Kate's advice about the Sixties and her resolve to live the free emancipated life of a modern woman. The night had been wonderful, but apart from Bobby's determination to entice her to work alongside him for the duration of the summer, there'd been no promises. Nor did she expect any one day into a relationship. But Bobby had already soothed the emotional bruises Rich had inflicted. And after the few hours they'd spent together, she knew that if she allowed him to get any closer he could easily break, not just bruise, her heart.

'I hope you didn't put yourself out. I really do want to stay in the city,' she explained more coolly than she felt.

'By all means look,' Bobby said as she joined Kate in the room that had been assigned to employers, 'but you won't get a better offer than me and Camp Resonance.'

'We're experienced waitresses and barmaids,' Kate assured the middle-aged woman manning the reception desk in the suite where prospective 'employers' were sitting behind tables stacked with application forms and brochures. Kate was stretching the truth. At fifteen they'd both found Saturday jobs as waitresses in one of the Italian cafés in Pontypridd. But whereas Kate had stuck it out until they'd left for college, Penny'd given up after a few months to take a Saturday job in Marks and Spencer's. Without the tips, it was less money, but it was also easier work and shorter hours.

A middle-aged balding man with a paunch left his table and approached Kate. 'Did you say you were an experienced waitress?' he leered.

'Yes.' She gave him a look that would have frozen a curry.

'I'm Roland Black, the assistant manager of the hotel–'

'Assistant manager?'

Roland ignored Bobby's sceptical interruption. 'If you girls want to stay in the city, you should work here. You've seen first hand the clientele we cater for.' He waved his hand around the room as though he were personally responsible for the decor. 'We need a waitress and a switchboard operator.'

'I can't operate a switchboard. What are the hours and wages for the waitress?' Kate enquired briskly. Early widowhood, coupled with a stunning figure and the blonde hair and grey eyes she'd passed on to her daughter, had taught Kate's mother how to deal with lechers. It was a skill she'd taken care to teach Kate.

'First you should think of the benefits.' The man ran his tongue around his lips. 'You'll be living in the centre of New York city, all meals and accommodation paid. That alone is worth a fortune. And pretty girls like you will have the male members of staff queuing up to show you around New York in your free time. In fact, I may show you around myself when I'm off duty–'

'The hours,' Kate interrupted.

'Six days on, one day off. Forty-eight hours a week.'

'What meals will I be covering?'

'Breakfast, lunch and dinner but you'll have plenty of free time in between.'

'You want me to work split shifts, starting early morning and finishing late evening,' Kate challenged.

'Think of the time you'll have off,' Roland coaxed.

'I know exactly how much free time I'll have. I worked split waitressing shifts last summer in a British holiday camp. By the time I left the dining hall and changed out of my uniform, I had less than an hour before I had to change back and report to the hall to lay the tables for the next meal.'

It was their experience last year in Barry Butlin's that had made both her and Kate determined never to take a live-in job at a holiday camp, where they'd be at the beck, call and mercy of management, again.

'The basic wage is eighty cents an hour but in a place like this you could make a couple of hundred dollars a week in tips,' Roland smiled.

'How much would you deduct for living costs?' Kate asked.

'Thirty-five dollars.'

Kate did a quick calculation in her head. 'So, I'd be working for three dollars forty cents a week plus tips.'

'As I said, smart girl like you could pocket a couple of hundred dollars a week. But I only have a vacancy for one waitress and one switchboard operator. You can operate a switchboard?'

Penny had no idea why Roland Black had singled her out for that job, after Kate's assertion that they were both experienced waitresses and barmaids. But with thoughts of living in the centre of New York and Bobby's inaugural lecture fresh in her mind, she answered confidently. 'Of course.'

'Ninety-five cents an hour, basic forty-eight-hour week, there could be overtime, but no tips and, like your friend, your accommodation and meals will be thirty-five dollars a week.'

Before she could point out that she'd be left with ten dollars sixty cents a week and no prospect of earning tips, Bobby stepped in.

'If they take those jobs the girls will be worked to death. They may live in the centre of New York but they won't be left with a spare minute to see anything.' Bobby turned to her. 'At least in the camp you'll be guaranteed a day off a week and

165

can come into the city to see the sights.'

'And sleep in the street because they won't be able to afford a bed.' Roland smirked. 'I'll give you girls an immediate trial.'

'I'd like to see the restaurant I'd be working in and our accommodation before I make any decision,' Kate said.

Roland Black snapped his fingers and a girl in receptionist's uniform came running from another table. 'Show Miss...'

'Burgess, Kate Burgess,' Kate introduced herself.

'The restaurant and staff accommodation. While I take Miss...'

'John. Penny John.'

'Down to reception to give her a trial on the switchboard.'

While Roland Black's minion led Kate up the corridor towards the public rooms of the hotel, Roland Black steered Penny out of the room and hit the lift button. Before the doors closed Bobby stepped in beside them. As the assistant manager had been eyeing her the same way he'd been eyeing Kate, she was grateful for Bobby's presence.

'Mind if I watch?' As Bobby was already in the tiny cupboard behind the reception area that served as the 'telephone exchange' his question was superfluous.

'I do,' Roland retorted.

'As one of the staff responsible for orientation it would help enormously if we have positive outcomes that we can relate to the next intake of European students.'

'Your presence will make Miss John nervous,' Mr Black snapped.

'She looks a confident girl to me,' Bobby countered. 'You don't mind, do you, Miss John?'

She shook her head because she couldn't trust herself not to laugh.

A sharp-featured middle-aged woman was sitting in front of a switchboard, headphones on, mechanically jamming plugs into various holes, while speaking in a high-pitched robotic voice.

'Good morning, how may I help you?... One moment, sir... I'm connecting you... Connecting you now, madam... Room 652 on the line for you, sir... How may I help you, sir?... Connecting you to room service now, sir... Have a nice day, madam...'

Roland tapped the operator on the shoulder. 'Miss Schumacher, would you mind giving up your seat to Miss John for ten minutes?'

'You're the new relief?' Miss Schumacher looked delighted at the prospect.

'It's only a trial.' She'd watched the operator for less than a minute but it had been long enough for her to determine there was no way she could man a switchboard.

'If it means I won't have to work another double shift, you're welcome to my chair, my headphones and everything else that goes with the job, Miss John.' The operator pushed one more plug home before leaving her seat.

She stood back and pretended to study the board. 'Our European switchboards are nothing like this.'

Bobby covered his mouth with his hand. The

cough he'd intended sounded like a strangulated squeal.

'Surely they can't be that different?' Roland snapped.

'I assure you they are,' she contradicted, trying to sound authoritative, which wasn't easy given that the switchboard was the first she'd seen.

'Give it a try.'

She turned to Bobby. There was a mischievous glint in his eye. If she could have run out of that cubicle and the hotel, she would have. But Bobby and Roland Black were blocking her path. Cornered, she sat in the operator's chair and picked up a plug.

Five panic-stricken plug-pushing minutes later, every telephone in the hotel was ringing, even the ones she could see the receptionists answering through the open door. The noise was deafening. But, even more nerve-racking than the ringing, was the mounting tension in the cubicle.

She knew and Roland Black knew she'd jammed the hotel switchboard.

'You've never sat at a switchboard before.' Roland Black wasn't asking.

'Not an American one, no,' she hedged, in an attempt to save face. She left the chair and backed into Bobby.

'Miss Schumacher, if you could repair the damage.'

She walked away as quickly as she could without running and headed back up the stairs.

'Guess the advice I gave wasn't that sound.' Bobby caught up with her.

'That's the understatement of the century.'

'Don't be mean. I found you a job.'

'One I don't want.'

'How do you know you don't want it until you try it?'

'It's not in New York.'

'It's a couple of hours' train ride away.' He flattened himself against the wall to make room for a waiter who was wheeling a trolley loaded with chafing dishes down the corridor. 'Come to the orientation welcome party with me tonight?'

'I didn't think I had to "go" with anyone. Isn't it part of orientation?'

'You have no idea what the right escort can do to open doors and enhance your social life.'

'Any enhancement of my social life in America would be purely temporary.'

'You're here for four months, aren't you?'

'Bar a few days.'

'With me at your side you'd move up at least three scales on the social barometer.'

'I thought you were studying for a masters in medieval history at Oxford, not comedy.'

'Who told you I was studying for a masters?'

Penny could have kicked herself for letting slip – a second time – that she'd been interested in him enough to question his friends. 'A girl I was locked in a cell with in Bow Street.'

'You met Rose Anne?'

'We were cellmates.'

'I was at school with Mike – her boyfriend,' he explained. 'I know you're studying art, which is probably why you want to stay in the city. But art is all around and there's masses of it in the woods in Connecticut.'

'You're determined to get me and Kate into this camp of yours, aren't you?'

'It's not my camp but yes, I'm determined to get *you* there. And it might be helpful for you to have a good friend around, so you've someone impartial to discuss the wonders that are Bobby Brosna.'

'There you are, Pen.' Kate's mouth twitched and she struggled to contain her laughter as Roland Black walked past. 'I heard your trial didn't work out.'

'You should've seen her in action,' Bobby gushed loudly for the benefit of the students who were leaving the suite. 'I've never seen such courage in the face of total humiliation. Penny walked right up to that telephonist's chair, sat in it, and...' he paused for effect and looked around at the small crowd that had gathered around them '...jammed the entire communications system of the hotel.'

She wanted to be angry with Bobby for making her the butt of the joke, but she was laughing too much.

'How did you fare?' she asked Kate when she could speak.

'It looked all right but I'm not staying here with Roland without you.'

'Then I'll get two travel passes for Camp Resonance the day after tomorrow,' Bobby declared triumphantly.

'Have you heard?' Anne rushed up to them.

'What?' Kate asked.

'They're recruiting Bunny Girls for the New York Playboy Club. A dollar fifty an hour plus tips. I'm going for an interview. You coming?'

CHAPTER FIFTEEN

'Bunny girls! You want to be bunny girls? In those costumes! With ears and fluffy, white, cotton tails old men get a thrill out of tweaking.' Bobby shook his head in disbelief.

'And what's wrong with bunny girls?' Anne demanded, hands on hips.

'Nothing! Absolutely nothing; if that's what you want to do with your summer in the States go ahead. I'm not sure the pioneers of the student exchange movement would approve, given that "bunny girl" can hardly be classed as an educational occupation.'

'No, but it'll give us the money to continue our education,' Kate retorted.

'There are other ways of making money.'

Kate was on a 'burn'. 'You mean more respectable ones?'

'I didn't say that,' Bobby reminded her mildly.

'You think we wouldn't make good bunny girls?' Anne, who was sensitive about her lack of height and waistline, challenged.

Bobby raised his hands in a gesture of surrender. 'All three of you would make stunningly beautiful Playboy bunnies. And, if that's what you want to do, go ahead.'

'Liar,' Anne retorted.

'We would make beautiful Playboy bunnies,' Kate reiterated. 'Really?' She raised her eyebrows. 'I sense a "but" coming.'

She turned to Bobby. 'Is there a "but"?'

'I was going to say this is the era of the emancipated woman,' he ventured. 'Women burning bras on the altar of liberation. I didn't think any educated modern woman would be up for life as a sex object in the Playboy world.'

'I can be a sex object if the pay's right,' Kate answered swiftly. 'Let's go.'

'What about the next lecture?' Bobby asked. 'It's American politics. Something you should know about in an election year.'

'As we have no right to vote in the States it's more important we find jobs. Besides, if the next lecture is as good as yours, we won't miss much,' Kate added.

'Thank you for that, Kate. I'm the forgiving sort. Give me a couple of minutes to get my car from the hotel garage and I'll drive you to the Playboy Club,' Bobby offered.

'Taxi will be quicker. To the loo to repair hair and make-up?' Kate beckoned to her and Anne.

Anne followed Kate but Bobby stepped in front of Penny.

'You'll love Camp Resonance once you get there.'

'So you keep saying.'

'If you're back early enough to play truant this afternoon I'll show you New York.'

'I'd like that.'

'And dinner tonight?'

She suppressed a smile. Sandy was right, Bobby was chasing her. 'If I'm not playing with my new bunny friends.'

'Mother Bunny?' Kate stifled a giggle after the doorman in reception directed them to the lift and sent them to a top-floor office. 'I don't believe we're going to be interviewed by "Mother Bunny".'

'Someone has to look after the bunny girls,' Anne commented. 'It's just a title.'

'I have a feeling she's not going to be your typical Welsh mam in a hairnet and pinny,' Kate murmured.

She noticed the lift buttons. 'Look, there's a little black bunny one-ear-up, one-ear-down symbol on the red lift buttons.'

'And bunnies, ear up and down, were woven into the carpet downstairs,' Anne said. 'I keep pinching myself. I can't believe I'm really in New York's Playboy Club.'

The lift halted, the doors opened to reveal a stunning blonde bunny girl who could have posed for the centrefold in *Playboy* magazine. Penny and Kate stared at the heavily boned skin-tight costume.

'How on earth do you breathe in that?' Kate asked.

'You don't, honey,' the blonde drawled in a Southern accent. She looked from Kate to Penny and Anne. 'You English?'

'Guilty.' The last thing Penny wanted was to get embroiled in another conversation about Wales being part of the UK.

'Is this a good place to work?' Kate, never slow in asking for information, questioned.

'You're applying for jobs?'

'We are.' Anne confirmed.

She beckoned them to a corner of the corridor beside the lift. 'I was so happy when I was invited to become a bunny. My life ... well we'd need hours to go into that, so we'll move on. But I'm the eternal optimist. As I've kept saying all my days, even a blind hog finds an acorn now and then. But believe me, honeys, this job's not all it's cracked up to be. I quit as of five minutes ago.'

'The money's good, isn't it?' Kate checked.

'It's fine, honey, if you only want pin money and you've a man on hand to pay the rent, put food on the table and cover your incidental expenses. All are downright cruel in New York – the rent and expenses I mean. Not the man. And unless your name is Rockefeller you won't be renting around here, so that means getting a taxi when you finish your shift. They don't come cheap in the early hours. Then there are all the bills connected with the job. You have to pay for your own tights – you can get through a dozen pairs a shift – and make-up, perfume ... and whatever you do, don't go cheap on either of those. Mother Bunny can sniff out bargain basement six blocks away.' She looked at Kate. 'If you're not a natural blonde, honey, your stylist's bill will be higher than the Empire State Building. Slightest sign of dark root and Mother Bunny comes down so hard, you'll want to shave your head and join the GIs.'

'Tips?' Kate pressed.

'Can be good if you don't mind where the customer puts the bill – and his hands.'

174

'I thought customers weren't allowed to touch bunnies.'

'What it says in the brochure and what happens in real life are two different things, honey.'

'Marion, to quote your quaint Southern vernacular, your mouth overloading your tail again?'

They all turned. A hatchet-faced blonde with make-up so thick it resembled a mask, wearing an elaborate curled 'beehive' wig, was posing in a doorway in the corridor.

'No, ma'am. I'm doing no such thing, ma'am,' Marion answered.

'No, what?'

'No, Mother Bunny.'

'Are those girls here for interview?'

'We are,' Kate replied.

'I'm sure you were told to go to the office, not stand in the corridor gossiping to a hand who's just been let go. What you doing, girl?' Mother Bunny called out to Kate, who was stepping back into the lift alongside Marion.

'Leaving.'

Penny jumped in beside Kate and Marion. 'You coming, Anne?'

'You girls make your minds up quickly,' Marion commented after Anne joined them and they headed back down to the ground floor.

'Penny and I've already served seven years in an all-girls grammar school without time off for good behaviour,' Kate revealed. 'Apart from the make-up, clothes and accent, Mother Bunny could be our headmistress's twin sister.'

'You got a job to go to?' Anne asked Marion.

'Friend of mine left here two weeks ago and

175

headed for the Cape with her boyfriend. They got jobs the day they arrived. She's waitressing, he's a kitchen hand. Start of the season there's always jobs going on the Cape. Me and my boyfriend thought we'd try our luck there.'

'Cape?' Penny asked quizzically.

'Cape Cod.' The lift reached the ground floor. 'See you around, honeys; good luck with the job hunting.'

Penny looked at Kate. They both started to laugh.

'We can now add the inside of the Playboy Club to our list of New York sights.' Kate led the way to the front door.

'Where do we go from here?' Anne asked plaintively.

'Don't know about you, honey,' Kate mimicked Marion's drawl. 'But I guess I'm heading for twenty dollars a week and living all found in Scarsdale.'

The room set aside for the orientation lectures in the hotel had been transformed into a student common room. People were sitting in groups on the floor and window sills eating sandwiches, cookies and chocolate bars and drinking from soda bottles. The areas around the windows were the most crowded as people fought to look down on the street, a dizzying twenty-two storeys below.

Bobby appeared at their side when they entered. 'Lunch is included in orientation.' He held up four paper bags. 'Chicken, tuna, ham or cheese?'

'I'll take the tuna.' Penny knew Kate preferred cheese.

176

'Cheese,' Kate answered.

'Ham,' Anne held out her hand, took the bag and joined a group in the corner.

'Guess I'm stuck with the chicken.' Bobby handed over their bags.

'If you prefer tuna, take mine,' Penny offered.

'I wouldn't deprive you.' He joined them on the floor. 'Am I talking to bunny girls?'

'No,' Kate replied, 'according to a bunny who was running away, the incidental expenses associated with the job are high.'

Penny started to laugh again. 'You should have seen Mother Bunny. She looked like a waxwork.'

'They have a *mother* bunny?' Bobby picked the lettuce out of his sandwich.

'She could have been Liberace's great grandmother.' Kate finished one sandwich and reached for another.

'I've been to the Playboy Club but I had no idea such a person existed.'

'You can afford to go to the Playboy Club!' Kate exclaimed. 'You must be miles better off than us. Unless I find something in the next twenty-four hours, I'll be left with twenty dollars a week and my keep in Scarsdale.'

'So you're the grey-eyed blonde with the job in Scarsdale Bobby told me about. Hi, and very pleased to meet you.' Lunch bag in hand, Sandy sat next to Bobby.

'Sandy meet Kate. Kate meet Sandy.' Bobby made the introductions.

'Penny told you I have a job in Scarsdale?' Kate asked suspiciously.

'I did,' Penny admitted.

Kate eyed Sandy as she finished her sandwich. 'You spent the night in Bobby's room too?'

'Bobby and I are good friends, but not that good. I was in my own room until eleven this morning, when I had to check out. If I'd met you yesterday, I would have come knocking at your door.'

Kate laughed a deep throaty chuckle that turned the heads of the other boys in the room.

'Tell me about this job of yours.' Sandy screwed the top from his soda bottle and drank.

'I'll be nanny to three children. They're younger than the ones I've worked with on teaching practice and I'm not looking forward to changing nappies. But beggars can't be choosers. One's eighteen months, one three and there's a three-month-old baby.'

'You got a contract for this job in Scarsdale?' Sandy asked.

'A letter. Live-in all found and twenty dollars a week.'

'That's no good. You have to insist on a detailed contract for any job you take in the States. One that gives the exact hours you'll be working and the hourly rate. And, when you're off duty, leave the house so they can't ask you to do anything extra.'

'That wouldn't be polite.'

'"Polite",' Sandy mocked. 'As I said to Penny yesterday, I know the sort of people you'll be working for. They'll have four cars in the garage, a big Mercedes for him, an imported Jaguar convertible to drive to and swank in at the club, a family estate for her to run the kids around and a truck for weekend camping trips. The house will be furnished in mock-European antiques, taste and money no object. But their generosity won't extend to you. Used to illegal Mexican immigrant labour, they'll work you to death from the baby's first feed before dawn until you finish serving coffee and clearing the plates from their dinner party after midnight. In between you'll be expected to scrub, wash and clean up after the family non-stop. You'll be treated and spoken to like a slave, and expected to eat alone in the kitchen.'

'It won't be slavery. The pay is twenty dollars a week all found...'

'For the hours you'll be working, it's exploit-ation,' Sandy argued.

'I've no alternative.'

'Yes, you have,' Sandy said brightly. 'The Bishop...'

Kate looked to Penny for an explanation.

'Their boss. It's a nickname.'

'He's coming over here this afternoon to look for someone to work with the five-to-eight-year-olds at Camp Resonance. You won't be the same side of the lake as me, Bobby and Penny–'

'Hold on a minute. I haven't said yes to the job,' Penny interrupted Sandy.

'After I've worked on you for the rest of the day and night you will.' Bobby gave her his most dazzling smile. 'Forget Pen spoke, Sandy.'

'All Bobby and I have to do is persuade the Bishop you're perfect for the job. And that won't be hard. You're a trainee teacher, Kate?'

'Primary.'

'Primary ... that's like...?' Sandy hesitated.

'Infants five-to-seven-year-olds.' Kate returned her empty sandwich packet to her lunch bag.

'Your first year of study?'

'Third in September. I qualify next year.'

'You couldn't be more perfect. A hundred and twenty dollars a week all found has to be better than twenty, and you'll get a day off a week...'

'In which we can head off to New York,' Bobby said brightly.

'Together? They'll give all of us the same day off?' Kate unscrewed the top from her soda bottle.

'No, but I'll swing it for Pen and me, and when it's your and Sandy's turn I'll loan Sandy my car so he can drive you wherever you want to go.'

'I wrote to the people in Scarsdale accepting the job.'

'A letter's not a contract, but if you've a conscience find someone here to take your place. There are enough girls looking for work,' Sandy looked around the room.

'Say the word and we'll tell the Bishop "mission accomplished" when he arrives,' Bobby offered.

'Your boss listens to you two?' Kate queried.

'He's idle. He'll be grateful we've done the work for him.' Bobby assured her.

'We haven't had an interview yet,' Kate pointed out.

'Yes, you have, I've been interviewing both of you since you arrived,' Bobby countered. 'You're healthy and have stamina. If you hadn't, you wouldn't have survived the horrors of the plane trip your fellow passengers can't stop talking about. So is it "yes"?' He looked at Penny. But it was Kate who answered.

'Yes,' she said decisively.

Penny glared at Kate. 'What about the museums and galleries...?'

'What about sleeping in the street?' Kate retorted.

'How about you leave the camp early at the end of the summer, return to New York with me and I'll show you around,' Bobby coaxed. 'We'll have earned enough to pay for a good hotel room for a week or two by then.'

She thought it odd that Bobby hadn't suggested they stay at his grandmother's apartment, but happy at the prospect of spending time sightseeing with him, she dismissed the thought almost as soon as it came to mind.

The lecture that afternoon was on America, its history, government and customs. Not the best topic to deliver to jet-lagged students. She didn't take in a word after the first five minutes and woke with a start when the students around her started moving to the door of the side room where coffee was being served.

Kate stared wide-eyed at her and she realised she wasn't the only one who'd been sleeping. Bobby and Sandy entered the room by the main door and spotted them.

'Enjoy your nap?' Sandy asked Kate.

'No, because this irritating American droned on and on about the history of the country. After doing the American War of Independence for A level, I knew more than him.'

181

'Do you want the good news or the bad?' Bobby asked.

'Penny and I are sleeping in the streets after tonight?' Kate guessed.

'No, you both have jobs, starting tomorrow. As there's no time to buy your train tickets in advance you'll have to fund them yourselves. Keep the receipt and you'll be reimbursed when you reach Camp Resonance.'

'There's bad news?' Kate looked at him in surprise.

'The Bishop's ordered us back to camp. Apparently the staff shortage is "acute" and I'm driving him and Sandy. We're leaving at ten tonight which means we can't stay till the end of the orientation farewell party with you guys.'

'Odd time to drive,' Penny commented.

'My car's a convertible and I pointed out that in this heat and humidity we'd turn into jelly if we travelled any earlier. So,' Bobby glanced at his watch, 'you – me – seven free hours. What do you want to do, Penny?'

'Go to Harlem,' Kate answered.

'Harlem?' Bobby repeated.

'What the hell do you want to do there?' Sandy demanded. 'It's dangerous even for brown people like me. Lethal for whites.'

'That's why I want to go there. To see why it's lethal.'

'Got medical insurance?' Sandy enquired.

'The best.' Kate left her chair. 'Give us twenty minutes to transform ourselves into stunning dolly birds and we'll meet you in the foyer.'

'"Dolly birds"?' Sandy repeated.

'You'll like them when you see them.' Kate looked at her. 'Bags I the bathroom first.'

'"Bags"?' Bobby asked her quizzically.

'I can see we're going to need an interpreter. British expression that means Kate intends to commandeer the bathroom for eighteen minutes and leave me two.'

'Use mine. The room's paid up until tomorrow morning.'

'Thanks, I will.'

'I'll get your bag from your room.' He winked at Kate. 'Take Sandy with you and make it forty not twenty minutes before we meet in the foyer.'

CHAPTER SIXTEEN

Bobby had barely slammed the door on his hotel room before they began tearing the clothes off one another. Naked they tumbled headlong onto the bed. His mouth sought hers as she guided his erection deep inside her. And for a while nothing existed for either of them outside of one another.

When he finally withdrew, they lay back, exhausted, her head pillowed on his chest, his arm wrapped around her shoulders.

'We're going to have to watch ourselves in the camp,' he warned. 'If we don't, the Bishop and Pill Face will throw us out for corrupting the kids.'

'And then Kate's prophesy of us having to sleep in the streets will come true.' She traced a line down his breastbone with her forefinger.

'It wouldn't be the streets, not in the wilds of Connecticut. But it could be my car and that's not comfortable for one. It would be impossible for two.'

'The voice of experience.' She looked up at him. His blue eyes were bright, sparkling with mischief.

'I confess I've had my homeless moments,' he admitted, 'but rarely more than one night in succession and every one of them down to my own stupidity after drinking more than was good for me.'

'It would be four if Kate and Sandy joined us.'

'They'd have to sleep under the car like pioneers did under wagons in the old West.' He frowned. 'I mean it, about us having to be careful. The Bishop's one of my grandmother's snoops.'

'Your grandmother has snoops?' She buried her fingers in the thick black curly hair on his chest.

'Dozens of them who watch every move I make.'

'You're paranoid.'

'During my boarding school days at least one master if not two used to make weekly and occasionally daily reports to her about me. I cottoned on to what was happening when she knew what punishments I'd received for my misdemeanours when I hadn't mentioned them. I thought I'd get more freedom when I went to junior college. But it was worse. I only had to look at a girl for my grandmother to contact me and tell she was "unsuitable".'

'Your grandmother vets your friends? What on

184

earth will she think of me?'

'If I take care, she won't find out about you.'

Bobby's admission hurt but she concealed her disappointment.

'That's why we have to act cool in front of the Bishop and Pill Face. He and my grandmother are closer than slices of apple in a pie. She supports his church with donations and he treats her like an empress whose wishes are his commands. One of her wishes was that Sandy and I be given jobs in Resonance. She believes clean outdoor summer living with plenty of sport will keep us out of trouble and away from women. I intend for her to keep right on believing that.'

'She approves of Sandy?'

'For two reasons. First guilt. Second practical considerations. My father seduced Sandy's mother, when she was thirteen. My mother was pregnant with me. My grandmother didn't want stories getting out about her newly wed stepson's feckless ways with under-age maids. She paid Sandy's mother to keep quiet and paid her medical bills. When Sandy was born three months after me, my grandmother decided he'd make a suitable companion for me. Sandy and I shared the nannies and the early boarding schools, which left Sandy's mother conveniently free to carry on working for my grandmother. Sandy and I stayed close, although unlike me, he did get to attend a more humane boarding school after the age of eleven. He was also allowed to study the subjects of his choice, music and drama, at an American college.'

'So your childhood wasn't that lonely.'

'Not when Sandy was around. But Grand-mother insisted Sandy and I be housed in different dorms at our prep boarding school because she didn't want me getting "socially reliant" on his company.'

'So you're half-brothers?'

'My grandmother would have a fit if she heard you say that. No Brosna or Buttons would ever admit to it. My grandmother insists on main-taining the master-servant relationship. And, as Harriet's livelihood depends on the status quo, she's just as anxious as my grandmother to pre-tend that Sandy's father was a mysterious unidentified figure.'

'I'm surprised your grandmother told you and Sandy about the relationship.'

'She didn't. Before he left for Mexico, my father used to drink with the gardener at the Cape Cod Estate. He told George, and George told Sandy and me when we were fourteen, after first making us swear to secrecy. But given the similarities between us in height and looks, if not colour, I had wondered before then.'

'Will Sandy go to Oxford with you next term?'

'No,' he answered abruptly, so abruptly she was reminded they barely knew one another. 'You won't forget? Careful around the Bishop and Pill Face.'

She reached up and kissed his lips. 'You're not that irresistibly gorgeous. I can control myself.'

Bobby smiled. A smile that sent the blood coursing headily around her veins. 'You've just proved that's a lie.'

'I may tell little fibs but I never lie.'

'I'll remind you of that next time we're alone together.' He glanced at his watch. 'If we're going to Harlem we'd better dress. This trip is against my better judgement. It's a dangerous place for white people in quiet times. And it's been anything but since Martin Luther King's assassination in April. There were riots then and there've been riots since. The place is a powder keg. All it needs is one spark to set it burning again. Why does Kate want to go there?'

'I've no idea. She never said a word to me about it before she mentioned it just now.'

'Do you want first shower?'

'Yes, and while you're showering, I'll use the mirror above the desk to put on my warpaint.' She kissed him again before leaving the bed. She suddenly realised how easily she and Bobby had slipped into domesticity after only one night together. There was none of the constraints and tensions she'd experienced in her relationship with Rich. But neither were there any promises or plans for the future beyond Camp Resonance.

She remembered Kate's advice. It was the Sixties. The modern age. Women were liberated. No more dependent on men than men were dependent on women. Footloose and fancy-free to live for the day because tomorrow will take care of itself – provided there wasn't a nuclear holocaust.

She had to rid herself of Rich's way of thinking. The more she mulled over their relationship the more she realised just how much time they'd spent planning a future that would never happen.

187

Showered, dried, deodorant and perfume applied, she wrapped herself in a towel and returned to the bedroom. Bobby was still in bed but he'd switched on the television and was watching the news. Bobby Kennedy was on screen addressing a rally.

'My namesake and our next president on the campaign trail.' Bobby adjusted the pillow beneath his head to a more comfortable position.

'You think Bobby Kennedy will win?' She sat on the end of the bed and unzipped her bag.

'He has a good chance.'

'Because of his brother?'

'Do you ask the same question about John F. Kennedy in the UK that we do in the States?'

'Where were you when John F. Kennedy was shot?' she guessed.

'I was playing basketball in school when a guy burst in with the news. That was the end of the game and everything for the day. None of us wanted to believe it.'

'I was clearing out my wardrobe. My younger brother, Evan, shouted upstairs that *Bonanza* had been cancelled because the president had been shot. Like you, I didn't want to believe it. Even when I watched the news broadcasts I still had difficulty believing it. After the Cuban crisis and President Kennedy's *"Ich bin ein Berliner"* speech, I felt with him gone, the world would never be the same again.'

'I thought that too for a long time. But,' Bobby looked at the screen, 'with another Kennedy in the White House, Camelot could rise again.' He flung back the bedclothes and walked naked into

188

the bathroom. He stopped by the door. 'You have finished?'

'Yes, thanks.'

He looked at her as she rummaged through her case. 'No miniskirts, pretty dresses or jewellery for Harlem; jeans and a loose cotton shirt. It's hot out there in every sense of the word.'

It was Sandy, not Bobby, who took charge of the expedition and it was Sandy's idea to travel by bus.

'That car of yours is a magnet for thieves, Bobby. We wouldn't be able to stop anywhere.'

'We won't be stopping for long or walking any distance if we go by bus,' Bobby warned. He turned to Kate. 'Just why do you want to go up there?'

'Because we've heard so much about New York and Harlem in Britain. It's supposed to be dangerous.'

'And instead of taking someone's word for it you want to see it for yourself?' Bobby questioned in amusement.

'I can't imagine people carrying weapons on the streets and on the subway.'

'They do.' Bobby led the way to the stop outside the hotel. 'And forget the subway. That's out of bounds. The streets are bad enough. You want to see a shooting or a knifing?'

'Of course not. But like Penny I'm a social studies student—'

'I thought you were art?' Bobby frowned at her.

'Kate and I are both studying two main subjects,' she explained. 'I want to see what conditions

189

are like there. From what little I've seen of America and the people I've met I can't believe you're an uncaring society.'

'We're not.' Sandy jumped to the defence of his country.

'But although I've only been here one night I've noticed homeless people living on the streets,' Kate continued. 'And I've read articles that say New Yorkers will step over people who are ill and, in extreme cases, even corpses rather than lose time notifying the authorities. They walk on knowing the city will clear away the bodies along with the rubbish in the morning.'

'And bury them in unmarked pits on Hart Island,' Sandy murmured.

'What?' Penny couldn't believe what Sandy had said.

'It's an island off New York. They don't run ferries there but they do ship over all the unclaimed bodies. They're dropped into mass graves.'

'Why so shocked, Penny?' Kate asked. 'There are unmarked graves in Glyntaff cemetery where they buried people from the workhouse, along with those whose families couldn't afford a funeral.'

'That was years ago.'

'Not that many years,' Kate retorted.

'Can't keep bodies hanging around—'

'That's enough, Sandy.' Bobby saw Penny was upset. 'Every society has its alcoholics and addicts who refuse to be helped. Here's the bus. I suggest we sit close to the door and keep our heads down.'

They sat on bench seats opposite one another, Bobby and her one side, facing Kate and Sandy on the other. As the bus headed north, more and more white faces left and more and more dark ones boarded.

She and Kate stared mesmerised out of the windows. The city was so different from any they had seen in Britain and, in her case, Europe.

She had to concede her uncle had been right. At ground level it was very different from the clean clear vista of gleaming skyscrapers she'd seen on so many films and photographs. The billboards her Uncle Haydn had mentioned blocked every vacant lot from view. The streets were littered with rubbish and the deeper they headed into Harlem the more unfamiliar the sights and sounds.

Snatches of jazz and pop music emanated from tenement blocks and fire escapes. Doors hung off hinges and a third of the windows were either broken or boarded over. Signs to 'Beauty Parlours' were pinned above impossibly glamorous posters of models promising 'hair straightening' and 'skin lightening'. Wig shops sported hairpieces of improbable colours and shapes. And overlaying everything was a heavy odour of chicken, potatoes and stale frying fats.

'You white folk come slumming?'

'No, man.' Sandy had given the others a warning look before answering the teenage boy who'd pushed his face dangerously close to Bobby's. His meaning was obvious. Brown skin wasn't the same as black but it was better than white in Harlem. He pointed to Penny and Kate.

191

'English cousins want to meet family.'

Penny took Sandy's cue and held out her hand. 'I'm very pleased to meet you.' She felt even the queen would have been proud of her cut-glass 'BBC' accent.

'Hey, dude. That right. White English cousins for Harlem folk.' The boy shook her hand, watched her through the next three stops and flicked a finger salute at her when he left the bus.

'Can we go back to the hotel now?' Sandy asked Kate. No one else had spoken to them but they were collecting stares from their fellow passengers.

Kate nodded.

They climbed off at the next stop. Bobby hailed a taxi and had it waiting at the kerbside before Kate and Sandy's feet touched the sidewalk.

'Of course I expected poverty,' Kate protested in answer to Sandy's question. 'What I didn't expect was kids wandering around in rags without proper shoes, and buildings without doors and windows marooned in a sea of rubbish.'

'It's called trash here. Pass the salt, please?' Bobby held out his hand. The four of them were eating burgers, fries and salad in a fast-food restaurant around the corner from the hotel.

Bobby had wanted to treat them to silver service dinner in the hotel, but she and Kate wouldn't hear of it. They both knew – Haydn's mad money aside, which they were keeping for emergencies – finances would be tight until they received their first pay cheques. They were determined to pay their own way and keep themselves until it was time to fly home. As Kate had put it, 'Our budget doesn't stretch to linen tablecloths and silverware.'

'The scrap metal and rubbish is down to tenants stripping their apartments of anything they can sell,' Sandy explained.

'People must be destitute to tear their homes apart.'

As they're rented they don't regard them as "homes", only a temporary place to doss before moving on.' Bobby sprinkled salt on his fries.

'What I can't understand is why you two are so accepting,' Kate raged. 'You've seen much more than us. When we were driving here from the airport we passed dozens of posters of slums and cute American Black children looking plaintive under the slogan "Give a Damn". You said you'd lived in New York. Both of you...'

'Not for a long time. And we do "give a damn",' Bobby said quietly.

'We're little more than kids ourselves,' Sandy reminded her. 'This country's not perfect. It needs to change but we've come a long way since black people were enslaved.'

'And you've a long way to go,' Kate snapped.

'Have you seen the slums in London, Kate?' Bobby asked.

'Not close up. But I lived in one in Pontypridd until it was pulled down and we were rehoused on a council estate when I was eleven years old.'

'What's a council estate?' Bobby asked.

'Houses built by the council and rented out to poor people who can't afford to buy their own,' Kate replied.

'Social housing,' Sandy murmured.

'You have a problem with that?' Ever sensitive about her background, Kate stared belligerently at him.

'Hey, my mother is his grandmother's housekeeper. All I've ever had to call home are rooms in servants' quarters.'

'That's only true in New York,' Bobby interposed. 'You and your mother have the use of a guest house in most of my grandmother's houses.'

'Your grandmother has more than one house?' Kate asked.

'She has so many I've lost count.' Sandy opened his burger and spread a thick layer of mustard over the meat.

'Some were rented,' Bobby demurred.

'But she does have more than one house?' Kate checked.

Sensing Bobby didn't want to talk about his grandmother – or her wealth – and knowing how Kate loved a political argument Penny changed the subject. 'Given your benefit of two years' lectures in social studies, Kate, how would you reform Harlem?'

Kate plunged headlong into designing a strategy. 'The first thing is to improve the housing stock and rebuild the entire area. Put in parks and public spaces people can take ownership of and pride in...'

As Sandy argued with Kate that more public spaces would only mean more places for drug dealers and prostitutes to ply their trade, Penny exchanged glances with Bobby. There was gratitude and another expression in his eyes.

194

Something she couldn't quite decipher.

'Quite the firebrand, your Kate,' Bobby commented when they returned to his room.

'That's amusing coming from the man who was arrested by the Metropolitan Police for protesting in Grosvenor Square.'

'I'm young, idealistic, and want to change the world.'

'According to my father it needs changing, but not too quickly or we'll destroy the good along with the bad.'

'He has a point.' Bobby looked at his watch. 'Ten minutes before Sandy and I have to pick up the Bishop. That trip to Harlem and the meal took longer than I intended. See you tomorrow?'

'You'll be picking us up from the train station?'

'If I can wangle it but I might not be able to. You going to the orientation party?'

'I told Kate and Anne I would.'

Bobby rammed his laundry bag into his rucksack and fastened it. 'See you tomorrow, my sweet Penny.' He kissed her and opened the door. 'I'll dream of you tonight. I just have one problem to solve before tomorrow evening.'

'What?'

'How to move your tent and bed as close as I can to mine in Resonance, without anyone suspecting my motive. Keep cool, until tomorrow.' He walked down the corridor. Remembering Sandy's visit the day before, she locked the door, flung herself on the bed and breathed in Bobby's pine scent.

Ridiculous. He hadn't even left the building and she was already missing him.

CHAPTER SEVENTEEN

The following morning she dressed with care in a new lime-green Mary Quant mini-skirted suit she'd bought with the money her uncle had given her. The fitted zipped jacket had a 'stand-up' Chairman Mao collar. Given the heat and humidity, she slipped on a sleeveless white polo neck beneath it. White tights, patent green bar shoes with chunky heels, and chunky green and red plastic earrings; rings and bracelet completed her outfit.

She was brushing her hair when Kate knocked on the door.

'Nice suit, hate the hair. You look like one of the models in the Pre-Raphaelite paintings of damsels at death's door.' Kate hauled her bag into the room and dropped it beside the bed.

'Wish it was tight curly like yours instead of wavy. Then I could cut it short and it would always look tidy.'

'Tidy and boring.'

'I'd settle for boring and neat right now. Nice suit to you too,' she complimented. Kate was wearing a similar Quant suit to hers in cut. But the fabric was patterned. White daisies on a blue background.

'This is hopeless.' She exchanged the brush for a comb. 'I need an iron.'

Kate opened the wardrobe. 'Can't see one.

There's a note in the hotel information folder that says you can get one if you ring house-keeping. Anne almost did until she realised she was running late. She told me to say goodbye to you.'

'She went to Scarsdale?' she guessed.

'She wanted a job. I offered it to her. Mrs "Scarsdale" is picking her up at the train station. Be interesting to see how she gets on. I promised to phone her if there's one we can use in the camp.'

'Do me a favour, ring housekeeping for that iron.' She struggled to run a comb through her tangled hair.

'There's no point in ironing your hair. It'll be wavy again the moment you step outside. It's the humidity. Tie it back or go for the Pre-Raphaelite look.'

'More like the "dragged through a bramble hedge backwards" look.' She tugged at a knot and ripped a clump of hair out by the roots.

'There's always your hat. I intend to wear mine.' Kate indicated the straw hat she'd dumped on top of her bag and haggis.

'I'll dig mine out when I've finished combing this mess.'

'Just as well we don't have to be at the station for two hours.' Kate lay back on the bed. 'Look-ing forward to seeing Bobby again?'

'Looking forward to seeing Sandy?' She turned the question back on Kate.

'He's rather dishy. Pity I won't be in the same area of the camp as you three.'

'According to Bobby you'll only be across the

lake.' She continued to wrestle with her hair.

'You suggesting I swim across every time I feel like a kiss and cuddle – or...' she lifted her eyebrows suggestively '...something more?'

'Depends on how much you want the something more.'

'So what's with you and Bobby? Making plans for an engagement yet?' Kate fished.

'Don't be silly, we've only just met.'

'Met again. Sandy told me Bobby paid a detective to find out when you'd be arriving in the States.'

'That's ridiculous. Bobby didn't even know my second name.'

'But he did know you were Penelope, you were a student at Swansea College and you were coming over on an exchange. Must have been love at first sight. Or,' Kate raised her eyebrows, 'lust.'

She couldn't help smiling but she could hold her tongue.

'Lust, then. But it could turn into more. Bobby's returning to Oxford next term.'

'Oxford is a hundred and fifty miles from Swansea and we've barely talked about summer camp, let alone next term.'

'I wouldn't say no to a rich boyfriend for a summer. But yet again I've drawn the short straw. You get the prince, I get the serving boy.'

'Bobby's grandmother might be rich but Bobby isn't. He's a student...'

'A student with a trust fund. Sandy told me his grandmother's as rich as Croesus. Bobby has an enormous monthly allowance.'

'Really?' She was sceptical.

'Really,' Kate confirmed.

'If he's that rich, maybe he'll pay for Sandy to go to Oxford next term with him. That way you and Sandy will also be in the same country.'

'Sandy's already received his draft papers. He's going to Vietnam.'

She left the comb stuck in her hair and looked at Kate.

'Like thousands of others he has no choice.' Kate shrugged but it was obvious she was upset.

'When did Sandy tell you this?'

'When we were waiting for you and Bobby before going to Harlem yesterday.'

'If Bobby's grandmother is rich enough to pull strings and she's done it for Bobby, surely she can do it for Sandy?'

Kate shook her head. 'Sandy says he feels he should take his chances along with everyone else who's been drafted. His mother came to America from Mexico as an illegal immigrant when she was twelve. He says he feels obligated to pay something back for the life the country's given them.' Kate left the bed and went to the window.

'You like Sandy, don't you?' she ventured.

'I've always been careful to lock my heart away from boys. At most this will be a summer romance. Nothing more.'

'*A summer romance – nothing more.*' Kate was wise beyond her years. It was a sensible attitude and one she knew she should apply to her and Bobby.

But even as she considered Kate's words, she realised it was too late. She was head over heels in love. Her only problem would be to keep the depth and strength of her feelings from Bobby.

The train crawled down the track at slower than walking pace. Kate glanced at her watch for the tenth time in as many minutes.

'It's half past four. We were supposed to reach our stop at three.'

'It's always late,' a middle-aged woman sitting within earshot commented. 'The company that runs this line is losing money. They tried to close it but the government wouldn't let them.'

'Terrific,' Kate said caustically. 'Especially as we're being met. What happens if they don't wait for the train to come in?'

'Are you being met by locals?' the woman asked.

'People from Camp Resonance,' she answered.

'Don't worry; they'll know about this line. Probably will have called ahead to check what time this train's expected in.' Their fellow passenger glanced out of the window. 'Ten minutes and you'll be there.'

The train juddered to a halt. Kate left her seat and opened the door expecting a platform. She managed to steady herself and avoid falling four feet. A frail elderly man in uniform, who looked as though he'd topple in a strong wind, tottered towards them and held out his arms.

'I'll lift you down, miss.'

'There's no need, I can manage.' Kate dropped her bag and haggis and jumped, landing awkwardly and twisting her ankle.

Penny followed. 'I don't see anyone.'

'You expecting someone to meet you, girls?' the old man asked.

She concealed her disappointment at Bobby's absence. 'We're going to Camp Resonance. They said they'd send someone to pick us up.'

'Payphone on the side of the ticket office. You can call them from there.'

She hauled her bag over to the office – a ramshackle shack – opened her shoulder bag and fished around in it for the contact details while Kate limped over with her own bag and haggis.

Although late in the afternoon, the heat and humidity were as unbearable as they had been in the city. While she phoned, Kate looked for somewhere in the shade where they could wait. There were no seats, so she dragged their bags beneath a tree beside the dirt road.

'That was a long phone call,' Kate commented when she joined her.

'It rang for ages before someone answered and gave me an offhand, "Oh, the train's in, someone will be along to pick you up. Thanks for calling, have a nice day."'

'This "have a nice day" is beginning to get me down,' Kate retorted. 'Barely one in a hundred people say it as if they mean it.'

'I could murder a cold drink.'

'How about a warm one.' Kate handed her a bottle of Coca-Cola.

'That's disgusting,' she complained after taking a sip.

'I didn't say it was good.' Exhausted by the heat and still suffering from jet lag, Kate perched on her bag, leant against the tree and pulled her hat

201

down over her eyes. 'Wake me when the boys get here.'

They waited in silence for an hour, by which time the sun had begun to sink in the sky and, although still hot, the temperature had cooled to a more bearable level.

An open-topped truck pulled up alongside them. She and Kate rose to their feet and looked at the boys inside. Both were wearing filthy, sleeveless, khaki vests and khaki Bermuda shorts.

'Camp Resonance?' Kate asked.

They laughed.

'What's funny?' Kate, ever on the defensive, demanded.

'The thought of you two chicks in Resonance,' the driver answered.

'Why?' Kate snapped.

'Dressed like that.'

'You are disgustingly dirty.' Kate wrinkled her nose at their filthy hands, arms and faces.

'That's because we work in a summer camp. Camp as in tents, woods, outdoor faucets, muddy water, the great outdoors...'

'Do you intend to stay here for the remainder of the day laughing at us, or are you going to help us with our luggage?' She picked up her bag.

'I can't wait to see the guys' faces when you two turn up. Name's Ray.' He pointed at his companion. 'Gene.'

'Kate Burgess. And I'm not shaking either of your hands. Not until they've seen soap and water.' Kate lifted her bag into the back of the van.

'Want a leg up?' Ray asked.

'You expect us to get in the back?' she asked.

'Please yourself, but the cab's muddy. We didn't have time to shower after washing down the sailing dinghies.' Gene pulled a dirty scrap of scrunched paper from his pocket. 'If you're Kate, you must be Penny John?'

'I am.' She dropped her tartan bag over the side of the van next to Kate's.

'You're going to the Pioneer camp.' The boy opened the cab, walked round to the back of the truck and dropped the tailgate. 'Kate Burgess is going to the Woodsmen. Sorry the back of the truck's not too clean either. Hold on to your hats. It'll get windy when we start driving.'

Any doubts she had that the boys were exaggerating faded when they drove off a narrow tarmac road on to a dirt lane. After four or five jolting miles that played havoc with her back they halted in a churned-up muddy area adjoining a jetty that jutted into a lake. The sound of children singing came from the woods to their right and smoke rose lazily in the distance, hanging above the treetops.

'This is where we drop you off, Penny John,' Gene announced.

'And me?' Kate asked.

'The Woodsmen's camp is a five-minute drive away.'

They both peered through the trees.

'All I can see is woods.' Kate complained.

'The huts are hidden but the kids are noisy enough.' Ray left the truck and walked on to the jetty. He lifted a tin whistle to his lips. The shrill sound was answered by another whistle across the water. 'They'll be along to pick you up, Penny, as soon as they can paddle across.'

'Paddle?' she asked faintly, conscious of her heels, Quant suit and the hat.

'We dressed for a Buck House garden party to join Robin Hood's merry men,' Kate quipped.

The boys laughed again. 'This is not Sherwood Forest, and whatever else the Woodsmen are, they're not merry.'

'Miserable most of the time.' Ray offloaded her tartan bag. 'Someone's set out to fetch you.' He pointed across the lake where she could just about make out a canoe.

'See you around, Penny John.'

She turned to Kate and realised that, for all her bravado, Kate had as many misgivings about their situation as she did.

'You did understand you were going to a summer camp, not Ascot?' Bobby steered the canoe alongside the jetty.

'I thought it would be like a British holiday camp with wooden buildings and proper paths,' she explained.

'If you look across the lake you'll see tents among the trees.'

'Bathrooms ... kitchens...'

'We have campfires to cook on and plenty of wood to feed them. There are half a dozen cold-water faucets serviced by pipes that come through the lake from this side. And a twenty-gallon water tank fitted with hoses and sprinklers that make a reasonable shower. It's screened off and large enough to accommodate two. With eight counsellors and thirty-two kids you shouldn't have to wait too long to use it provided you pick an unpopular time. And we have hurricane gas lamps for the night.'

'You really did dig latrines?'

'There are toilet seats on the stands above the holes, and huts for privacy.' He tied the canoe to the jetty and joined her. 'You really weren't expecting a camp, were you?'

'Not as primitive as this one, no.'

'I thought everyone liked getting close to nature.' He tied up the canoe, stepped out on to the jetty and picked up her bag.

'I hate camping.'

'You're joking.'

'My idea of getting close to nature is sitting at the table in my parents' garden and watching the birds, squirrels and sheep in the surrounding fields. I wouldn't even go to Brownie camp when I was small, and that was in a church hall with hot and cold running water and plumbed-in toilets.'

'I wasn't around to help you settle in then. Meet the other counsellors and give the place a chance. You'll have a tent to yourself, and tomorrow we have a treat. A trip to Stratford, Connecticut to see Shakespeare's *Androcles and the Lion.*'

'Shakespeare didn't write *Androcles and the Lion.* George Bernard Shaw did.'

'I know and you know but the Bishop doesn't. He's most insistent it was Shakespeare. It'll give you a chance to return to civilisation for the afternoon. You can wear that very fetching suit again.'

'This very fetching suit is filthy after travelling here in a dirty train and truck.' She wasn't in a mood to be mollified.

'It's clean enough to travel to Stratford tomorrow.' He dumped her bag in the canoe and climbed back in before turning to her and holding out his hand. 'Careful stepping in. It might be an idea to take off those high heels.'

'They're not that high and I'd rather not wade into that dirty water sploshing about in the bottom with my white tights.'

'One of the perks of this job is you can send your clothes to the laundry free of charge.'

'And they wash them, how?' She took his hand, and crouching low, slid on to one of the bench seats in the canoe.

'Not very well,' he admitted. 'Everything Sandy and I sent came back grey. The whites were dirty and the black had been bleached. Want a paddle?' He held out a spare one.

'I've never paddled a canoe.'

'Never?'

'Never. I've sailed a dinghy and rowed a rowing boat and ridden a horse. But a canoe is out of my experience.'

'Then sit back, watch my technique and learn. You could be teaching this to the Pioneers tomorrow.'

'That had better be a joke.'

'Let's say Sandy and I might have exaggerated your and Kate's talents a little to get you the jobs.'

CHAPTER EIGHTEEN

'I said that both you and Kate could teach sailing, canoeing, swimming, sculpture, painting, drama, singing, dancing – ballet and tap – judo, karate, and would take callisthenics every morning at six sharp, six days a week,' Bobby replied in reply to her question as to what exactly he'd told the Reverend Howard and his wife about her.

'You're not serious?'

'Not about the callisthenics, judo and karate, no.'

'Why are you paddling so slowly?'

'Because this is about as private as we're going to get until our day off which might not be for a week.'

'So what did you really tell the Reverend and Mrs Howard about me?'

'That you're an art major entering your senior year in September and can teach art and water sports. You can swim?' he checked.

'I can swim and I have the standard – British Standard – life-saving certificates,' she confirmed. 'I've sailed dinghies, but nothing as small as those.' She looked across at the boats clustered on the bank of the lake.

'They're Sunfish, small and unsinkable. Ideal to teach sailing to beginners. There's nothing to canoeing. Sure you wouldn't like a paddle?'

'No, thank you. It's hard enough avoiding the

dribbles from your paddle, without using one.'

Sandy waved to them from the jetty and Bobby quickened his pace. 'A welcoming party's gathered to greet you.'

'One more person on there and the jetty will sink. I suppose they're all laughing at the English girl "dressed for Ascot", as you put it.'

His mouth twitched with suppressed laughter. 'You'll be the first Brit most of them have met and your nation is known for its eccentricities.'

'What are the kids like?'

'Like kids everywhere. Good, bad, intelligent, stupid. The one thing all of them manage to be is annoying.' He stowed the paddle inside the canoe, reached out, grabbed a rope tied to a ring hanging from the jetty and hauled them alongside it.

Sandy held out his hand ready to help her out of the canoe. She took it and found herself in the centre of a noisy group of teenagers who fired questions at her from all directions.

'Give the lady a break, folks,' Sandy shouted.

'This way.' Bobby carried her bag past them.

'We'll escort you to the luxury of your very own tent.' Sandy grabbed her arm as she tripped on the uneven ground.

'The only other counsellor who enjoys the privilege of solitude is Joan. Molly and Doreen share.' Bobby lifted her bag on to a platform that was set a couple of feet above the ground.

'Molly and Doreen are female counsellors from the Midwest, and they're waving to you,' Sandy informed her.

She waved back at the two girls in the neighbouring tent.

'The Midwest's different from the rest of America?' she asked Sandy.

'Very.'

'Be careful,' Bobby warned. 'You're not wearing the best shoes for the woods. I hope you packed sneakers.'

'I have flat shoes.' She climbed up beside Bobby. 'Why the platform?'

'Bugs, raccoons, skunks, snakes,' Sandy grinned, 'wolves, bears, werewolves...'

'Vampires, ghouls and ghosts...' she added.

'Speaking of which, don't forget you're above ground level if you wake in the night.' Bobby ducked into the tent behind her.

'We've had one broken ankle already. Fortunately she was a very ugly counsellor,' Sandy chipped in through the tent flap.

A sonorous masculine voice shouted, 'Bobby? Are you in the new counsellor's quarters?'

'Showing her the tent, and how the lamps work, sir.' Bobby made a face at Penny. He picked up a hurricane lamp from the floor next to a sleeping bag.

She followed Bobby out. Reverend Howard was a large man in every sense of the word. As tall as Bobby, he was as wide as he was long. Fat hung in folds over the waistband of his trousers and the flesh on his arms wobbled when he moved. In contrast, the woman next to him was tiny. Barely five feet, she had a stick insect figure.

'Reverend Howard, Mrs Howard, this is Penelope John, the Pioneer camp's new counsellor.' Bobby made the introduction.

'Pleased to meet you, Reverend Howard, Mrs Howard.' Penny climbed down from the platform and extended her hand. Mrs Howard's handshake was limp and dry. The reverend's strong and damp.

'You're not dressed for camp.' Mrs Howard wrinkled her nose and mouth disapprovingly and Penny understood why she'd acquired the nickname 'Pill Face'. 'I trust you have suitable clothes with you.'

'I have shorts, jeans and T-shirts in my bag, Mrs Howard.'

'I'm glad to hear it. Sandy, introduce Penelope to the female counsellors. Tell them to orientate her to the Camp Resonance and Pioneer way of thinking. And both of you boys – remember the rules. No male counsellor to enter a female counsellor's quarters or that of any female Pioneer under any circumstances.'

'Yes, ma'am,' Bobby and Sandy chorused.

'And no female counsellor to enter a male counsellor's or male Pioneer's quarters.' The reverend stared at her for so long she felt uncomfortable.

'I suggest you change and wash your face, Penelope. We do not allow our female counsellors to wear makeup,' Mrs Howard informed her tartly. 'The Pioneers are here to learn self-sufficiency and enjoy nature in all its bounty, not mimic artifice.'

'It's time you gathered your cook groups together for supper, boys,' Reverend Howard boomed. 'Penelope, you can join Joan's cook group. They meet under the oak tree to the right of your tent.'

Bobby winked at her behind the reverend's back. She went into the tent. It was cramped and too low for her to stand upright. She opened her bag and rummaged around for jeans, T-shirt, canvas shoes, soap and flannel. As soon as she'd changed she went in search of one of the standpipes Bobby had mentioned. It, like the nearest latrine, was a five-minute walk from her tent. After soaking the flannel in the lukewarm water she scrubbed her face and hands.

A pretty girl with short brown hair and brown eyes, carrying an enormous iron cooking pot, joined her while she was rinsing out the flannel.

'I heard Pill Face ordering you to remove your makeup. The woman would make a good prison guard. I'm Joan.' She set the pot on the ground and held out her hand. 'It's my cook group you'll be joining. Not that the food's up to much. I can't cook and neither can any of the kids.'

'Penny John.' She was relieved to see a friendly face besides Sandy and Bobby.

'I've heard your name. Everyone in the camp has. Bobby's talked about you incessantly since we got here. You made quite an impression on him in England.'

She recalled their meeting in Grosvenor Square. 'We made an impression on one another.'

'He said you were protesting against the Vietnam War.'

'Bobby was. I was at the embassy to get a visa to come here.'

'I hate the war,' Joan said vehemently. 'My father sent my two brothers to his cousin in Sweden to avoid the draft. We're a close family

211

and miss them. But my father felt he had no option after what happened to my cousin, Mark. He was drafted last autumn and sent to 'Nam after six weeks' training. One month later he was posted missing. I think the not knowing is even worse than if he'd been killed. My aunt's had a breakdown and my uncle's given up. He can't work, can't eat, can't do anything. He's allowed the business he spent a lifetime building to go bankrupt.'

'I don't know how any family can live with having a son or brother in constant danger, especially so far from home.' She thought of her older brother Ned and younger brother Evan. They'd teased her unmercifully since cradle days, but she loved them and couldn't imagine life without them.

'It's obscene. Forcing fit, healthy, young men to fight in a war hardly anyone in America believes in. And then to see the coffins on television. Being unloaded and sent back to the boys' families... I'm sorry, I'm on a burn. I get angry every time I think about it.'

'That's understandable.' She stepped back so Joan could reach the faucet.

Joan filled the cooking pot. 'Just keep me off the topic of politics, especially when the Bishop and Pill Face are around. If they'd heard me just now they'd have me out of here quicker than I could pack, for spreading anti-American propaganda.'

'It's only natural you feel that way given what's happened to your cousin.'

'The Bishop doesn't think so. He believes young men should consider it an honour to lay down their lives for their country. But words are cheap, especially if you have no children of your own and you're too old to fight, like him. But it's supper time and we have boiled chicken and potatoes to look forward to. It'll be disgusting, but when we tried frying the chicken it didn't cook properly and half the kids were sick.'

'You could boil the chicken to make sure it cooks properly, then fry it to crisp it.'

'Fantastic. You know about cooking, you can take over.' Joan handed her the pot.

Exhausted from travelling, cooking chicken and potatoes for seven people, meeting more Pioneers and counsellors than she would remember and trying to find her way around the camp in total darkness with the aid of a hurricane lamp, the evening seemed interminable.

After cooking, eating and clearing away, simple tasks that seemed to take for ever, there was only an hour left before 'lights out'. The Bishop insisted they spend it together sitting around a campfire. Boys one side, girls the other, as ordered by Pill Face, singing universal songs, most of them wartime favourites like 'It's a Long Way to Tipperary', 'Keep the Home Fires Burning', and ending the evening with 'Auld Lang Syne'.

While they sang, men dressed in what appeared to be spacesuits sprayed clouds of insecticide in a wide circle around the border of the campsite.

'Is that DDT?' she whispered to Joan who was alongside her.

'Insecticide of some kind or other. We've all been bitten. The theory is the bugs inside the

213

circle die and new ones won't fly or crawl in over the area that's been sprayed.'

'Why are the operatives wearing protective clothing and we're not?'

There was a lull in the singing and her voice carried.

'Now you know what it feels like to be an American, Penny,' Sandy quipped. 'We all have too many particles of insecticide in us to be fit for human consumption.'

'And that's enough from you, Alexander,' the Bishop ordered. 'Last song, "God Bless America", then bed.'

She entered her tent at ten o'clock, fell on her sleeping bag and didn't open her eyes until daylight streamed in through the tent flap she'd been too tired to secure. Her arms and face were burning and felt oddly swollen. She lifted her hand. It was covered in raised red welts. Grabbing her robe and toilet bag she crawled out of the tent to see one of Sandy and Bobby's fellow male counsellors standing in front of the assembled Pioneers who were following his lead in performing jumping jacks.

She headed to the nearest latrine. There was a queue outside the only shower. Joan saw her looking at it and gave her a plastic bowl.

'Best time to grab a shower is when everyone's eating. Or disgustingly early in the morning.' She stepped closer. 'You looked in the mirror this morning?'

'No, and I wouldn't be able to see much of myself if I did. I've only a powder compact. I know I'm covered in bites because I'm fighting the urge to claw my skin.'

'Don't. They're mosquito. If you scratch them they could get infected.'

'I know, but I've never been so tempted to do something so stupid.'

'That reaction is way beyond normal. You're obviously allergic. I've some stuff you can rub on – you're welcome to try it but it's not that effective. Nothing is, except DDT. The only consolation is, the bugs generally only bite at dusk and night.'

'I should never have abandoned my dream of living in New York and visiting the museums and galleries.'

'Bobby can be very persuasive.'

'Penelope?' Pill Face stalked up to them. 'From eight-thirty to ten-thirty you'll take a two-hour art class. You'll find all the equipment, paints, brushes and paper you'll need in the storeroom. Joan, show her where that is. The last hour before lunch you'll teach the non-swimmers, while the others have a free swim. Molly's leaving to begin her day off after breakfast, so you'll supervise her cook group at lunch and supper. This afternoon we're going to Stratford to see Shakespeare's *Androcles and the Lion.* You will assume responsibility for Molly's group as well as assist with the Pioneers as a whole. In the meantime I'll sort out your schedule for the week and leave it in your tent.'

Her head was reeling but she managed a 'yes, ma'am'.

'Get a move on, both of you. Breakfast is scheduled to begin in five minutes.'

She waited until Pill Face was out of earshot

215

before turning to Joan. 'Is breathing time scheduled as well?'

'You'll soon learn that all counsellors are expected to do all the breathing necessary for survival on their one day off a week.'

Pill Face was waiting for her when she emerged from her tent after lunch. Forewarned by Joan and Doreen about Pill Face's strict dress code – 'no shorts or trousers of any kind to be worn by students or counsellors on outings' – she'd donned her green Quant suit. It was grubby but as all the Pioneers were travelling to Stratford in trucks she decided Bobby was right. It would be grubbier by the end of the day.

'Your skirt is ridiculously, in fact obscenely short, Penelope. Change it at once.'

'All my skirts are the same length, Mrs Howard.'

'Then wear a coat.'

Penny didn't argue about the heat. She returned to her tent and pulled down the elasticised waist, gaining a couple of inches of extra skirt length by turning it into a hipster.

'Over here.' Bobby waved to her as she jumped down from her tent platform. 'One female, one male counsellor to a truck.'

'Pill Face has allowed us to fraternise?' she joined him.

'The kids persuaded the Bishop,' he whispered. 'I'm driving, so get in the cab. The kids can bang the back window if they need us.'

'So how you coping apart from the mosquitoes using you as a larder?' Bobby asked when they were closed into the relative privacy of the cab.

'The mosquitoes are definitely the worst. I'm considering moving into the lake.'

'You'd have to keep your head above water.'

'Damn, and there's me thinking I'd found a solution.'

'Apart from the mosquitoes?' he reminded.

'You didn't warn me that every second of every minute of every day would be regimented.' She opened the duffel bag she'd packed in her suitcase and filled with valuables and day-to-day things like her purse, passport, comb and make-up. 'Mrs Howard left my schedule on my sleeping bag this morning when I was teaching the kids to make leaf patterns.'

'All the counsellors have learnt to do things slowly. *Very* slowly,' he emphasized. 'We walk at half pace, take half an hour to get the things we need from the storehouse, and extend mealtimes by at least an hour.'

'Pace is one thing, being surrounded by Pioneers every second another. I've always liked a certain amount of alone time.'

'Not too alone, I hope. Tonight, for instance. Half an hour after lights out, slip from the faucet and latrine to the copse of trees behind the canoes. You can't be seen if you hunker down low. Sandy proved that with Molly last week.'

'In the open air, so I can get bitten even more than I am now? No thank you.'

'Then I'll sneak into your tent.'

'Wouldn't that be risky, given that the Reverend and Mrs Howard's accommodation has an overview of the entire camp?'

'They go to sleep early. We're here. Be sure to

sit next to me.' Bobby parked and turned off the engine.

'We're here to watch the play?' she reminded.

'You, maybe. I intend to plot and come up with ideas for more free time – for both of us.'

'Can't we just mooch around Stratford, Bobby?'

'No,' Bobby replied sharply to George, the most vociferous and rebellious of the kids in their group.

'It's hot. None of us want to be here,' Cecile, George's 'girlfriend' of one week, moaned.

'Then where do you want to be?' She knew it was a mistake to have asked when she saw Bobby frown.

'By the lake. It's perfect swimming and sunbathing weather. Theatres are for winter and rainy days.'

'The doors are open. Everyone inside,' Mrs Howard shouted. 'We've block-booked the first two rows in the stalls. Pass out the programmes to everyone, Penelope. Make sure the Pioneers keep them. The parents will want to see them and have a full account of the cultural activities of the Pioneers on parents' day next month.'

'Yes, ma'am. Please!' she shouted above the din of complaining teenagers. 'Take one as you enter the theatre. One at a time,' she reprimanded George when he tried to push past the others.

A man tapped her shoulder. 'Your accent. You're English?'

'Yes.' She fought the temptation to say 'isn't it bloody obvious?'

'How would you like a job in this theatre?'

CHAPTER NINETEEN

'Pen, the play's starting in two minutes, we have to go in.' Bobby took the remaining programmes from her and handed them to George. 'Pass these out.'

George rolled his eyes for the benefit of his fellow Pioneers. 'Wow, the responsibility, man. I can't take it.'

'Shut it, George.' Bobby saw the Bishop looking at him and lowered his voice. 'Just get on with it,' he ordered.

The distinguished-looking man looked from her to Bobby. 'I can see you're busy. I'm Harry Fowler, the manager of this theatre. I'll find you in the intermission, Miss...?'

'John, Penny John.'

'I'll see you then.'

'Yes, thank you.' She had no idea what she was thanking him for. She ushered the remaining Pioneers into the auditorium and followed them in.

'What did that sleazebag want?' Bobby sat next to her at the end of the front row in the stalls.

'He offered me a job.'

'Doing what?'

'He didn't say.'

'I bet he didn't. I saw the way he was looking at you.'

She laughed. 'He's old enough to be my father.'

'He is, but that wouldn't stop him. If you were an ice cream you'd be licked to death by now.'

'Ssh!' Pill Face glared at them from the other end of the row.

'Time to imbibe culture, folks,' Sandy said loudly from the row behind them where he was sitting between Joan and Doreen.

The lights dimmed, the curtain rose. Bobby grabbed her hand, lifted it on his lap and hid it beneath the sweater he'd carried in.

It was good to know he was jealous. Even if it was of a man three times his age.

'You'd be a general dogsbody. Work in the box office, run errands, prompt at rehearsals; go on stage as an extra. Can you act?'

Forgetting Bobby's advice at the orientation to lie when faced with a question about ability she said, 'My only acting experience has been in amateur productions at school and college.'

'No matter, we'll soon find out whether or not you have any ability. As an extra all that would be required of you is to stand onstage and look decorative, and from where I'm standing I can see you're well qualified to do that. Your accent would be an asset in the box office and onstage if you work your way up to speaking roles.' Harry checked his watch. 'The curtain's due to rise. Can we continue this discussion after the performance?'

'We have to get back to Resonance straight after the show.' Bobby hadn't left her side.

'We're camp counsellors,' she explained.

'You've signed a contract with Resonance?'

'I haven't signed anything.'

'Only because you started work there less than twenty-four hours ago,' Bobby intervened.

Harry ignored Bobby. 'That's excellent, Penny. No contract, no rights due to either party. You can leave right away without giving Resonance notice. I suggest you return to the camp after the show with your colleagues, pack up your things and I'll pick you up in an hour. That will give me enough time to get back here for the evening performance. I'll show you around the theatre and you can meet the repertory cast and back-stage workers.'

'I don't know the first thing about the job–' she began.

He interrupted her. 'The wages are a hundred and fifty dollars a week. Ten per cent of all profits to be shared out among cast and backstage workers at the end of the season. We close on the thirty-first of September.'

'Have the cast and backstage workers ever seen a share of profits?' Bobby demanded.

'I only took over the management of this theatre last year. It was run-down. But I'm expecting to turn a profit this year,' Harry replied confidently. 'What do you say to my offer, Penny? I promise you the experience of working in this theatre will be more interesting than counselling in Resonance.'

'At Resonance I live in. If I took this job I'd have to find somewhere to live–'

He interrupted her. 'The actors are all staying in a boarding house, a five-minute walk away. Seventy-five dollars a week including breakfast and evening meal after the last show. At midday we eat cold cuts here, provided by the house.'

'Penny, Bobby...'

Bobby waved to the Reverend Howard. 'We're on our way.'

'I'll pick you up in an hour's time,' Harry pressed her.

'I need to think about it.'

Harry reached for his wallet and removed a business card. 'Call me first thing tomorrow morning. I can pick you up at an hour's notice outside of performance time.'

'Penny! Bobby! The Pioneers!' Reverend Howard shouted impatiently.

'We have to go.' Bobby slipped his arm around her.

'Don't forget to call me,' Harry shouted after her.

'I won't, and thank you for the offer.'

'What offer?' Reverend Howard asked her suspiciously as they exited the foyer.

'It would appear the theatre manager believes Penny has the makings of an actress,' Bobby answered for her as he hustled her out of the building.

'You can't seriously be thinking of working for that dirty old man?' Bobby demanded as soon as they were closeted in the privacy of the cab.

'You're using the wrong adjective. We're the ones with half a ton of Resonance dirt on us. Mr Fowler looked remarkably clean to me.'

'You never said you wanted to work in a theatre.'

'I would love to work in a theatre because it would mean returning to civilisation. Hot and cold running water, loos that flush, paving beneath my feet, lights I can switch on when it gets dark...'

'I get the message,' he interrupted. 'You're not a Pioneer at heart.'

'I was the one who wanted to spend the summer in New York, remember.'

'The city's unbearably hot and humid in summer...'

'The museums and galleries have air conditioning.'

He glanced at her. 'You can't possibly hate Resonance after less than twenty-four hours.'

'I hate the mosquitoes. And I can't say I'm keen on the bathroom and cooking arrangements.'

'You'll get used to them. At the end of the summer you'll be reluctant to return to civilisation,' he prophesied.

'That, I doubt.'

'I don't trust dear old Harry. He's obviously after only one thing.'

'I can take care of myself.'

'And if the lodging house doesn't exist? How are you going to fight him off if he takes you to his house...'

'You've been watching too many horror films.'

'And you're gullible. You know nothing about this man.'

'I know he's the manager of the theatre. He gave me his card.' She waved it in the air.

'He could have stolen it.'

'And the other dozen or more in his wallet?'

'He could have stolen the wallet too.'

When she didn't reply Bobby drove on in silence for the rest of the journey, leaving her to wonder if an affair that had started so promisingly could burn out so quickly.

Bobby parked the truck alongside the ones Sandy and Joan had driven.

'Right, Pioneers, all out,' he shouted.

'No way,' George shouted. 'Pioneers, let the sit-in commence.'

All the teenagers remained in the trucks and began to sing 'We Shall Overcome' loudly and discordantly.

'Quiet, you lot!' Sandy shouted.

'Too late, the Bishop and Pill Face have arrived and are watching,' Doreen whispered.

Reverend Howard left his car and wobbled over to them. 'What's going on?'

'A sit-in,' Bobby explained.

'A what?'

'A sit-in,' Joan reiterated. 'We're not sure what the problem is...'

The Pioneers switched to, 'No no, no more culture, no more shows. You can't tell us where to go.'

'I guess they didn't like the play,' Sandy quipped.

Reverend Howard turned purple. 'Get them out of those trucks.'

'How?' Joan asked.

'Order them out.'

'We tried. They ignored us,' Bobby pointed out.

'They can't sit there for ever. Sooner or later they'll have to leave the trucks to use the latrines.'

'Penny's right. Give them enough time and

they'll get antsy and bored,' Bobby agreed.

Reverend Howard glared at both of them. 'We're here to educate and discipline the Pioneers, not ignore their rebellious streaks.'

'They're exercising their constitutional rights.'

Reverend Howard was incensed by Sandy's remark. 'They're children who need to be taught right from wrong. And you're inciting them to flagrant disobedience.'

'They're teenagers, finding their feet. If we don't encourage them to make decisions based on their own experiences, society will stagnate. We need young people to think for themselves so they can instigate the changes necessary to cope with changing social conditions.' It was only when she saw Bobby and the others staring at her, Penny realised she'd repeated an argument from one of her social studies essays that had earned her a straight A. 'Sorry,' she murmured in embarrassment. 'I allowed myself to get carried away.'

'That's the first time I've agreed with you since you arrived here, Miss John,' Reverend Howard bellowed. 'You certainly did allow yourself "to get carried away" as you put it. Your misguided liberal attitude will only incite these childish miscreants into more flagrant shows of rebellion.'

Penny considered her reply. There was no way she was going to abandon her principles to accommodate the demands of a job she didn't want, especially when there was a better one on offer. 'I apologise for lecturing, sir, but I won't apologise for approving the actions of the Pioneers. I believe that in thinking for themselves, some of those sitting in the trucks will

225

become caring and life-changing members of American society.'

'They'll become idle wastrels and Communists,' he spat out the last word with venom, 'who'll demolish and eradicate everything America stands for.' Reverend Howard's face turned purple. 'Seduced by the likes of Bob Dylan and your Commie-loving John Lennon, they blindly follow Marxism with the aim of overthrowing the work, ideals and principles of the forefathers of our great country. Instead of laying down their lives, and gladly, for their country and liberty, as their fathers did in the Second World War, all the present generation can do is grow their hair long and organise illegal marches and sit-ins to protest against a right and just war to stop the spread of the Communist poison that is already infecting this country. Burn their draft cards and demand rights for the Blacks who are happy with a segregation that protects them as much as it does the white population...'

Although Bobby had warned Penny about the reverend's political views she simply couldn't believe what she was hearing. Nor could she stand idly by and listen.

'You really think it's right for a government – any government,' she added, mindful of her uncle's directive to tread carefully where American national pride and sensibilities were concerned, 'to order its young men to face death fighting in a third-world country to uphold a capitalist creed that none of the native population support or want? I couldn't bear the thought of my brothers dying for a lost cause–'

Reverend Howard finally exploded. 'You are an extremely dangerous young woman. I order you off Resonance. Now!'

'I'll pack.' She clutched the bag containing Harry Fowler's telephone number and walked to her tent.

She heard Bobby, Joan and the reverend arguing behind her. The reverend was shouting, the others remonstrating. But they were speaking too fast for her to follow the conversation.

It didn't take her long to pack. After changing out of her Mary Quant suit into jeans and T-shirt she rammed the rest of her belongings into her tartan bag. The overflow she pushed into her duffel bag. She emerged from her tent to see the Pioneers continuing their sit-in, only now they were chanting.

'Reverend Howard's a big fat coward. Penny stay. Penny stay.'

Bobby was waiting for her in front of her tent. 'Ready?'

'I have Harry Fowler's telephone number.' She held it up.

'To hell with Harry Fowler. Sandy's calling Kate from the supply hut. She can be packed by the time we drive to the other side of the lake. We're going on a road trip.'

'To where?'

'People tell me it's a big country.'

'What'll we do for money?'

'Work. There's always kitchen work and waitressing jobs. You game?'

She looked at the piece of paper with Harry Fowler's telephone number.

'Where's your sense of adventure?' Bobby asked.

'It moved to make room for my sense of self-preservation.'

Sandy waved to them from the supply hut doorway. 'Kate's packing,' he shouted in a momentary lull from the singers.

Bobby looked at her. 'It's up to you, Pen.'

CHAPTER TWENTY

While she hesitated, Bobby picked up her bag.

'I haven't said I'd go with you.' She ran after him. He tossed her bag to Sandy who stowed it next to theirs in the trunk of Bobby's convertible.

'You want to walk to Stratford, or hitch a ride with us?' Bobby asked.

'Hitch a ride.'

'Robert Brosna, have you thought what your grandmother will say about this?' Reverend Howard raged. 'Make no mistake she will find out. I'll call her office before you've had time to drive off Resonance land. I'll tell her you've run off with Sandy and a–'

Bobby glared at him. 'Be very careful how you describe Miss John, Reverend Howard.'

Something in Bobby's voice caused the Bishop to hesitate, but only momentarily.

'You know your grandmother is particular about the company you keep. The last thing she would want is for you to get entangled with a girl.

Especially a foreigner.'

'The entanglement and I are very happy, Reverend.'

'I *will* call her office.'

'Do whatever you think right, Reverend Howard.'

'They'll wire her right away.'

'I'm sure they will.'

The Bishop couldn't have been more furious if Bobby had argued rather than calmly agreed with him.

'Where are you going?' the Bishop raged. 'And you, Alexander. Mrs Brosna is your benefactor. Is this the way to show your gratitude to the lady who sponsored your education?'

'Sorry, Reverend, but your talk about dying for your country reminded me that this may be my last summer, if not permanently, then in the States for a while. I figure I'll enjoy it better doing my own thing.'

'And the Pioneers ... who's going to look after the Pioneers?' the Bishop screeched as realisation dawned that Bobby and Sandy were really leaving. His colour heightened. 'You'll leave me three counsellors down. If you won't think of me or the Pioneers think of your fellow counsellors. Five will have to do the work of eight!'

Unperturbed, Bobby opened the car doors.

'You take the front passenger seat, Pen.' Sandy jumped over the side into the back of the car.

Bobby waited until she'd climbed in and stowed her duffel bag on the floor next to her feet.

'Contact the orientation programme in New

229

York, Reverend Howard, and ask them to send replacements.' Bobby pushed the key into the ignition. 'I've no doubt the British and European students here for the summer have been cleared by the FBI or CIA or whichever government department is responsible for snooping into private lives.'

'Don't forget to ask for four counsellors,' Sandy advised. 'We're taking Kate Burgess from the Woodsmen with us.'

'So, now we've made our escape, where we going?' Sandy asked as they bumped down the dirt track away from Resonance to the sound of booming remonstrations from the reverend and cheers from the Pioneers, who were still in the back of the trucks. They'd changed the words to their chant, yet again.

'Bobby, Sandy go, go, go.
Take Penny with you
Damn good show.'

'The Bishop's so upset he's let the "damn" go unpunished.' Bobby laughed.

'Only until he calms down and it sinks in. Then he'll explode again.'

'As for where we're going, I'm open to suggestions.' Bobby turned the car off the dirt track on to a tarmac road and picked up speed.

'How about California?' Sandy suggested.

'You got enough money to pay for gas to get us there?' Bobby countered.

Sandy dug his hand in his pocket. 'Sixteen dollars and forty-three cents.'

'Anything in your bank account?'

'Fifty cents to keep it open. But that's probably gone in charges by now. I was relying on Resonance money to keep me until I report to the military in September.'

'We'll drive by Stratford. The town will be closed by the time we pick up Kate and get there but I'll go to the bank first thing, hopefully before the reverend's wire reaches my grandmother and she freezes my account. If I clean it out, we'll have enough to buy gas to get to California and keep all four of us until the end of the summer.'

'And if she's frozen it?' Sandy played Devil's Advocate.

'Our motto has always been "don't meet trouble before it hits".'

'We replaced that when we were six years old with "never underestimate Charlotte Brosna's reach or powers",' Sandy countered.

'My uncle gave me some mad money,' Penny ventured.

'I thought you were taking the job in Stratford.' Bobby turned off the road and back on to the dirt track that circled the lake.

'It would have been preferable to staying at Resonance and being consumed by mosquitoes or poisoned by DDT.' She recalled the space-suited operators.

'And now?' He looked enquiringly at her as he slowed the car.

'I've always liked the idea of the great unknown.' At that moment she meant it. If Bobby had suggested flying to the moon for the summer she would have climbed into the space capsule alongside him.

231

Kate was waiting at the gate, her bag at her feet. She started talking as soon as Bobby stopped the car.

'Thank heaven you rang. If you hadn't I would have run away tonight, although I didn't have anywhere to run to. I simply couldn't have stayed another minute in that cross between Dotheboys Hall and a Salvation Army citadel.' She handed her bag to Sandy who loaded it into the trunk before sitting alongside her in the back seat.

'A cross between a what and what?' Sandy asked.

'A bad Victorian boarding school and an evangelical militaristic-based church,' she explained for his and Bobby's benefit.

'Yep, that about sums up the Woodsmen,' Sandy said laconically. 'The counsellors that side of the lake always struck me as having a bad dose of religious fervour and a burning need to pass it on.'

'And you dumped me there to be converted.' Kate looked accusingly at Sandy.

'Did you convert?' Sandy asked.

'No. My beliefs are my own and not up for discussion.'

'Good girl, we knew you wouldn't let them get to you, and you can stop complaining now we've rescued you.'

Bobby drove slowly down the track that led back to the road.

'So where we going?' Kate asked brightly.

'First, to a motel in Stratford for the night, if Sandy and I can scrape enough together to pay the bill,' Bobby declared. 'Tomorrow I'll go to the bank and empty my checking account. That should bankroll us for a while. I'm not sure how much is in it. We'll make plans when we actually have it and know how far it's going to take us.'

Kate tapped her shoulder.

Knowing what Kate was about to say, she said, 'Like me, Kate has some mad money.'

'We don't need it,' Bobby said firmly.

'So, it's all right for us to live off you for the summer but not the other way round?' she challenged.

'That's right.'

'Well I have news for you, both of you.' She was as firm as Bobby had been. 'Kate and I came here for the summer with the intention of keeping ourselves by working.'

'And that's exactly what we'll do,' Kate echoed. 'They have a word for girls who live off men where I come from and it's not a very nice one.'

'We're not touching your money,' Bobby reiterated.

'Don't be so chivalrous,' Sandy chipped in from the back where he was wrapped around Kate. 'I have no scruples about living off the girls as long as it keeps us away from digging latrines, looking after spoilt Pioneers and gets us far far away from the Bishop and Pill Face.'

Bobby stopped at a motel a couple of miles outside Stratford. From a distance it appeared to be in dire need of a coat of paint. Close up it looked as though it was ripe for demolition. Two windows at the front of the building were boarded with cardboard and an insect screen in front of the door was hanging off its hinges. But Bobby had seen a sign, ROOMS $7.50 A NIGHT, and wasn't to be dissuaded. He and Sandy went into the office and emerged with two keys.

'Gee, Kate, our first home.' Sandy unlocked the door of his unit, threw his and Kate's bags inside, swung Kate off her feet and carried her over the threshold.

Penny stepped inside and wished she hadn't. The stench of damp and decay was overwhelming. The linoleum was cracked and pockmarked with black gaping holes edged in green mould, and alive with things that crawled.

'Beetles, ants or bugs?' she asked Bobby.

'Ants. They don't look the biting kind to me. Close the door.'

'I'm not sure I can stand the smell with it shut.' She stepped further into the room and Bobby slammed the door.

The bathroom door was open. The linoleum there was in a worse state than in the bedroom. The walls were missing most of the tiles, the washbasin and shower base cracked and stained, and the WC stank.

'I wish you'd let Kate and me pay for better rooms.'

'Granted this place needs a bit of maintenance but there's not much wrong with it for one night. It has a shower, basin, john – or what you English so quaintly call a "loo"...'

'The best way to give this place the "maintenance" it needs is with a hammer.'

234

They were disturbed by a banging on the wall.

Sandy shouted. 'We sending for takeout or walking to McDonald's?'

'McDonald's in an hour,' Bobby answered.

'Make it two.' Sandy's reply was followed by Kate's giggles.

'Is there a wall or a sheet of paper between the rooms?'

'Probably a sheet of paper, but there are no other cars in the parking lot and all the keys were on the board before the clerk removed ours.'

'I'm not surprised.'

Bobby pointed to the phone. 'You going to call sleaze bag?'

'Not until morning.'

'Still debating whether or not to take him up on his offer?'

She looked at her watch. 'The evening performance started an hour ago.'

'So it did.'

Bobby threw himself on the bed. 'We've two hours.'

'To unpack?'

'What's the point?' He grabbed her waist. 'We're not staying.'

After the Reverend Howard's ranting and reference to her as a 'foreign entanglement', their lovemaking had a delicious sense of illicit pleasure, even in the tawdry surroundings of the dismal motel with the murmur of Sandy and Kate's conversation echoing through the walls.

She and Bobby braved the shower afterwards together, although only after Bobby used the rags the motel called towels to line the shower base. 'Dinner' in McDonald's was an experience. The closest she and Kate had come to fast food in Pontypridd was egg and chips and a cup of hot Oxo in one of the Italian cafés.

Bobby and Sandy began to plan an elaborate summer on the basis of Bobby's checking account. 'We'll head west,' Bobby declared between bites of his triple cheeseburger. 'You girls will love the Rockies.'

'We ought to go by way of Florida,' Sandy insisted. 'The Keys are wonderful. I bussed tables there last Christmas. Pelicans everywhere, dolphins in the sea, and there's the Red Barn Theatre where Tennessee Williams worked, and Hemingway's house...'

'Don't forget Hollywood. And Nevada, so we can call in on the Cartwrights' Ponderosa.'

Bobby and Sandy stared at Kate. She had a disconcerting habit of saying the most outrageous things with a straight face.

'She's not being serious.'

'For a moment there you had me worried.' Sandy grabbed Kate's hand and kissed her fingertips. 'I thought you believed the Cartwrights were real.'

'You mean to say they're not?'

Bobby cut in the laughter that followed. 'We might not be able to show you girls the Ponderosa but we will be able to show you one big beautiful country.'

Bobby left early the next morning while she was in the shower.

She was talking to Harry Fowler on the motel phone when he returned. She finished apologising and hung up. One look at Bobby's face told her everything she needed to know. He was speechless, so she said it for him.

'Your grandmother's frozen your checking account.'

CHAPTER TWENTY-ONE

'Eight dollars and sixty cents.' Sandy looked at the small pile of notes and coins on the bed in the room he and Kate had occupied. It represented the sum total of his and Bobby's cash after they'd paid for the motel rooms. Penny opened her purse and tipped it out.

'Seventy-eight dollars and forty-three cents,' Sandy counted, 'making a grand total of eighty-seven dollars and three cents. Getting better – we can cover some miles with the gas that will buy. To where is the question.'

'Eighty dollars and ninety cents.' Kate also emptied her purse. There was no need for her to check it. Kate always knew down to the last small coin how much money she had.

'That should put a roof over our heads and keep us in hamburgers for a few days, then what?' Bobby asked.

'Beginning to wish we hadn't walked out of Resonance?' Sandy asked.

Kate opened her haggis, took out a manicure

set, removed the nail scissors and unzipped her jeans.

'Hey, we're not desperate enough to turn you into working girls,' Sandy joked.

'This is as far as it goes.' Kate snipped a thread on the inside of the zip plaque.

When Kate finished Penny took the scissors and used them to cut a thread on her own pair. 'Two hundred dollars mad money my uncle gave me.' She pulled out the two one-hundred-dollar bills and tossed them on top of the others on the bed.

'We had to hide it well, because you're only allowed to take fifty pounds cash out of Britain.' Kate added hers to the pile.

'You girls are darlings.' Sandy kissed Kate, but as she was intent on zipping up her jeans the kiss missed her mouth and landed on her chin.

'That will buy us more than enough gas and food to get us to the Cape,' Bobby said thoughtfully.

'And when we get there?' Sandy asked.

'We'll bribe old George. A hundred dollars should be enough to buy his silence. If he doesn't tell my grandmother's office where we are, we'll live rent-free at the Beach House. She hasn't been to the Brosna Estate in years and never rents it out. There are too many valuable pieces in the main house. The rent she'd get wouldn't cover the extra insurance.'

'That doesn't mean she won't think of looking for us there,' Sandy warned.

'My last room-mate was from Wisconsin. I'll write him a letter and enclose one to Grandmother that he can post. I'll tell her we're fine and enjoying summering at the lakes. She might send someone to look for us, but she won't come herself. Not when she's busy setting up the new foundation in Venice.' Bobby saw her looking quizzically at him. 'The Brosna Foundation,' he explained.

'The art foundation. You're one of *those* Brosnas?' She couldn't believe she'd been so naive. The Brosna Foundation was world-famous in the arts world but she'd never connected Bobby with that Brosna family. Not even when Sandy had told them that Bobby's grandmother had money and Bobby had admitted Charlotte Brosna was rich. She'd assumed they meant his grandmother was well heeled – and soled – not on a par with the Rockefellers and the Guggenheims.

'We told you,' Sandy said in amusement.

'People like us just don't move in the same circles as people like the Brosnas.' Her voice was hoarse from shock.

'Oh yes you do,' Bobby contradicted. 'And I'm not my grandmother. She's ruthless when it comes to business but she enjoys spending the profits on causes. This week it's prop Venice up to stop it from sinking. Last year it was to fund a dig and a museum in Egypt. The year before that, the unearthing of an ancient lost city in Albania. Next year...' Bobby shrugged. 'Who knows?'

'About the Cape, Bobby.' Sandy steered the conversation back to the practical. 'Old George died two months ago.'

'George is dead?' Bobby paled.

'My mother wrote and told me. I assumed you knew.'

'So who's caretaking the estate now?'

'No idea.'

Bobby was shocked. 'Grandmother didn't tell me old George died,' he murmured incredulously.

'Presumably because she knew you were fond of the guy. Remember him teaching us to play cricket?'

'I remember we never mastered the rules.'

'The best days were the ones he took us sailing and deep-sea fishing, and the best nights the ones we slept on board the *Day Dream* and cooked our catch.'

'He was one all-right guy.' Bobby clenched his fists. 'If she'd told me I would have gone to his funeral. Damn her, I should know what she's like by now. My dogs disappeared when I went to school. She told me she'd sent them to a farm that had plenty of space for them to run around in outside of the city. I believed her until her chauffeur let slip that he'd taken them to the vet to be put down because she didn't want them around the apartment anymore. The woman's been lying to me all my life–'

'Old George wasn't a lie, just an omission.' Sandy cut Bobby short. He knew once Bobby started railing against his grandmother he wouldn't stop until he was in a foul mood.

Penny helped Kate gather up the cash. Bobby took fifty dollars and gave the rest to Kate. 'You girls can take care of it.' He frowned. 'I hope the new caretaker of the Brosna Estate, whoever he is, can be bribed.'

'This money, tidy sum that it is, won't keep the four of us all summer,' Kate observed.

'It won't,' Sandy agreed. 'But it's early in the season. Everyone will be hiring on the Cape, especially the motels and restaurants.'

'Cape?' Kate asked.

'Cape Cod.'

Penny and Kate recalled the Southern girl, Marion.

'There's always work on the Cape in the summer,' they chanted in unison.

It was Bobby and Sandy's turn to look quizzical.

'The runaway bunny,' Kate explained.

Sandy looked at his watch. 'We have ten minutes to pack and get out of here, guys, before we're charged for another day. Let's go.'

The ride to Cape Cod took the rest of the day. The police stopped them twice. Once when Bobby ran a red light. After a grovelling apology they were allowed to drive on. The second time the police pulled them over because Sandy and Kate were drinking out of Coca Cola bottles in the back of the car. The officer informed them it was illegal to drink in a car in Connecticut – even soft drinks.

Kate protested ignorance in her best 'British' accent. A few smiles and a mild flirtation later she and Sandy were let off with a caution. The boys hadn't said a word.

They reached Hyannisport shortly after midnight. She and Kate couldn't believe how many places were open, or the number of people on the streets. With promises of 'showing you around tomorrow' Bobby drove straight through.

The Brosna Estate was a few miles out of town on the beach side. The entrance was marked by high metal gates and a high fence. Bobby parked in front of the gates and pressed an intercom. He had to press it twice more before a voice answered.

'What do you want at this time of night?'

'Admittance,' Bobby replied curtly.

'Go away until morning.'

'You're obviously new,' Bobby replied.

'Been here a year.'

'I'm Robert Brosna and I resent being kept waiting, so get up here.'

That was the first time she realised Bobby could be imperious.

Five minutes later an enormous black man rode up to the gate on a bicycle.

'Can I help you, sir?'

Sandy left the car and went to the gate. 'You're young George, old George's son.'

The man smiled. 'Sandy, good to see you.'

'It's good to see you too, George. This is Bobby Brosna.'

'Sorry, sir,' the man apologised to Bobby, 'I didn't recognise you.'

'That's understandable,' Bobby allowed. 'I haven't seen you in what – must be ten years.'

'Probably more, sir. Mrs Brosna never did like the staff's kids hanging around, except for Sandy here. And talking about kids. That's what I thought you were when you hit the intercom. Kids messing around.'

'You often get kids messing around with the intercom on the gate?' Bobby questioned.

'Sometimes, sir.' Young George blustered.

'We're here to spend the summer, so open the gate please, George.'

'Mrs Brosna said nothing to me about you or anyone else spending the summer here, sir. The main house is shut up. I'm the only full-time staff. The rest are all with Mrs Brosna...'

'We know that, George. And we've no intention of staying in the main house. There are four of us, so two of the guest houses or the Beach House will suit us fine.'

'I don't know, sir...'

'What the hell's the matter with you, George?' Bobby snapped. Although he and Sandy had shared the driving he was tired and irritable. 'It's my grandmother's place and I'm ordering you to let us in.'

Slowly, and clearly reluctantly, George activated the control that opened the gates. Sandy climbed back into the car, Bobby drove through and down the drive. The moon was full. It illuminated a dozen houses, some with lights on, and the largest swimming pool Penny and Kate had ever seen. It could have swallowed the one in Pontypridd Park ten times over.

Bobby jammed on the brakes.

'You trying to kill us?' Kate cried out.

Bobby's only answer was to reverse at speed until he drew back alongside George who was relocking the gates.

'Sir ... there's something you should know–' George began.

'Too damned right. I know you have permission to live in one of the guest houses. But I counted lights on in ten. What the hell's going on?' Bobby demanded.

'They're homeless.'

'Homeless what?'

'People, sir. Some of the Southern states are giving black folk twenty dollars and a one-way ticket north.'

'I heard about that,' Sandy said. 'It's a national scandal.'

'They heard there was work going in Hyannisport. They turned up with no money left and some had kids...'

'So you took them in?' Bobby guessed.

'They're all working. The women cleaning hotel rooms, the men doing whatever they can get. A couple of the grandmothers are looking after the kids. As soon as they get enough money together to rent somewhere they'll leave.'

'You're not charging them rent?'

'No, sir, Mr Bobby. I told you they have no money. If they did they'd rent a place elsewhere.'

'You haven't said a word about this to my grandmother?' Bobby guessed.

'No, sir. Knowing Mrs Brosna, she'd flay me alive if she found out what I done. My father always said she was a charitable lady as long as her charity didn't impose on her comfort.'

Bobby snorted with laughter. 'Your father was right, George. Anyone in the Beach House?'

'No, sir, just ten of the guest houses.'

Bobby thought for a moment. 'This is what I'm going to do, George. I won't tell my grandmother about your charitable enterprise, provided you don't tell her, or anyone she sends, that we're here. If anyone telephones, wires or asks, you haven't seen us. Understood?'

'Yes, Mr Bobby, sir.'

'Plain "Bobby" will do, George. Got a spare key for the gates?'

'I can give you the code, sir, and the key to the Beach House. Cleaners come in once a week to check it out.'

'Keep them away. Tell them Mrs Brosna's rented it to friends and they need privacy.'

'Will do, sir. I'll get it and meet you down there.' George gave Sandy the code, and Sandy wrote it on his arm in biro. Bobby waited for George to cycle back to the guest houses then drove on down towards the beach.

The white clapboard Beach House shone silver in the moonlight. The small garden, separated from the rest of the grounds by a picket fence, was pristine, as was the outside of the house. As soon as Bobby parked in the driveway, Sandy opened the trunk and deposited their bags by the door.

Feeling stiff after sitting in the car for so many hours, and unaccountably tired considering all she'd done was be chauffeured around the countryside, Penny left the car, turned and stared, mesmerised.

'Impressive, isn't it?' Sandy saw what she was looking at and joined her.

'It's a mansion.'

'Turn of the century, financed by the first Bobby Brosna and expanded by the second who

245

was hellbent on spending his daddy's millions, so no expense spared,' Bobby explained. 'It's full of priceless antiques and expensive works of art, which is why I hate living there. You feel as though you're in a bloody museum.'

'Showing off your English cursing,' Sandy ribbed.

Bobby smiled self-consciously. 'I picked up a few odd words.'

George cycled up and Bobby took the key he handed him. 'Thanks, George. There's just one?'

'The cleaner has another. I'll ask her for it when I warn her off the place. If there's more they'll be in the main house.'

'We'll manage with this one until I can get more cut.'

'If you need anything–'

'You'll be in number one guest house,' Bobby guessed.

'That's it, Mr Bobby. See you around and have a good summer.'

'You too, George,' Sandy called after him.

The Beach House was furnished simply but someone had arranged the pieces with flair. It had a warm, lived-in, Bohemian look and Penny was relieved when she saw the bathroom had a spotlessly clean tub and shower and clean un-stained floor and walls. The simple place appeared luxurious after the horrors of the motel the night before.

'You girls hungry?' Sandy asked. 'If you are we can send out for pizza.'

'All I want is a shower and bed.'

'Me too,' Kate agreed.

'Up bright and early tomorrow,' Bobby warned. 'We need to go job hunting.'

'We'll find something.' Sandy sat on an easy chair and propped his feet on a driftwood table.

'We'll just have to,' Kate the worrier said. 'Rent-free is good. But I was hoping to earn enough this summer to supplement my grant next term.'

They started at a knock on the door.

'Who's there?' Bobby called out tentatively. Penny realised that despite his assurance that his grandmother would remain in Europe for the summer, he was not only wary of her but feared her.

'It's me – George, Mr Bobby. I realised when I got back to my guest house you have no bed linen or towels.'

Bobby opened the door and took the bundle George handed him.

'There's six bed sets and a dozen towels there, Mr Bobby. Give them back to me when you want them laundered.'

'You get them laundered on my grandmother's account?' Bobby asked.

'My sister manages a laundromat. She does them for free.'

'Thanks, George. Goodnight.' Bobby closed the door. Kate took the bundle from him and handed Penny two towels. 'You have first shower, I'll make up the beds.'

'I'll give you a hand.' Sandy disappeared into the bedroom after her and she and Bobby heard them giggling.

Bobby raised his eyebrows. 'The sooner you

shower, the sooner we can get to bed.' He switched on an ancient-looking TV.

'Ten seconds, I'll be with you.'

'I'd be happier with two,' he smiled.

That smile sent her heart racing again. She'd never felt that urgent need and obsession with another person when she'd been with Rich.

It took six minutes to shower and wash her hair, two to clean the bathroom after she'd finished and gather her dirty clothes. Swathed in an enormous bath towel, her hair wrapped in a hand towel, she returned to the living room. She knew something was wrong from the muted tones of the newscaster. She didn't know how wrong until she looked at Bobby and Sandy's faces. They were both numb with shock.

Sandy said what Bobby couldn't bring himself to put into words. 'Bobby Kennedy's been shot.'

CHAPTER TWENTY-TWO

Pontypridd, May 1987

Penny looked up from the album. She rose from the floor and walked over to the window but she didn't see the blossom on the apple and cherry trees, or the bulbs flowering amongst the perennials in the flower beds her father and mother tended. She was back in the Beach House on the Brosna Estate in 1968.

That night Bobby had set a pattern to their

248

lovemaking. Passionate, urgent, all consuming, he had lived as though they were running out of time.

Which, with hindsight, they had been.

Hyannisport, June 1968

Their bodies had been damp from the shower because they hadn't delayed long enough to dry themselves properly. Her orange-based perfume had vied with the scent of his pine until they mingled, creating a new fragrance that blended the alpine north and tropical south.

His skin tasted of soap, his lips of toothpaste. Their wet hair soaked the pillows and the dampness coupled with the murmur of the waves breaking on the shore outside the window lent the feeling that they'd become part of the ocean.

They moved over the bed in an erotic ballet, roused, exhilarated, revelling in the pleasure they gave and accepted. Passion crested, climaxed and fell in waves as mouths, lips, tongues, hands came into play until finally they lay spent, too exhausted to move.

It was then she made the mistake. The beach wasn't overlooked and Bobby had left the curtains open so they could see the ocean. Moonlight streamed in, silvering a vista of foam-topped dark sea outside and plain white walls and bed-linen inside. She looked across at Bobby and saw that he was staring at her. But she misread his mood. Because his face was dark with sorrow she offered solace.

'I've never felt this way about anyone before. I

249

love you, Bobby Brosna, and I always will.'

He turned his back on her. Refusing to accept his rejection, she moved with him, snuggling close to his shoulders, wrapping her hand around his waist. He gripped it and caressed her fingers but didn't turn back.

He whispered, *'I love you now. Isn't that enough?'*

She recognised the quote. 'Scott Fitzgerald, *The Great Gatsby.*'

'He was right.' Bobby's voice was harsh. 'It's no use making plans or talking of "always". The "now" is all we have.'

She learnt her lesson. She never told him she'd love him 'for ever' again.

Had Bobby made a conscious decision that there would be no tomorrows? Not for them. Or, knowing the power his grandmother could wield, had he simply sensed that he wouldn't be allowed to stay with her?

Despite her exhaustion, sleep eluded her for hours that first night on the Cape. And, although Bobby was also awake, they lay in silence. Each locked into their own thoughts.

George brought boxes of crockery and cutlery the next morning, along with brown paper bags filled with groceries: bagels, butter, cream cheese, lox, coffee, orange juice, melons, apples and grapes.

Sandy and Kate set out breakfast on a wooden table in the 'garden' that was a fenced off area of the beach. She sat with them and watched the giant horseshoe crabs crawl along the shoreline as she drank coffee. Bobby joined them after watching the news. He told them the only news about Bobby Kennedy's condition was 'he was gravely ill'.

She and Kate were hungry but neither of the boys had much appetite. She poured Bobby coffee, he sat next to her and it was obvious that he was spoiling for a fight.

'If Bobby Kennedy doesn't run for president, that snake Nixon will get in and then you can forget America pulling out of the Vietnam War,' Bobby predicted. 'Nixon will send more conscripts there to die, or – if they're "lucky" – survive and be maimed, mentally and physically, for life.'

'If Bobby Kennedy makes a full recovery and carries on campaigning – and that's unlikely if the reports of his condition are accurate – he won't be able to stop the war right away, even if he gets into the White House,' Sandy argued.

'Of course he will–'

'The hell he won't,' Sandy cut in fiercely. 'We're in too deep. Too many Americans have been killed there for any president, Republican or Democrat, to stand up and say, "Sorry people, we made a mistake, we're pulling out. All those dead and crippled boys – well it was for nothing."'

'That's bullshit and you know it.' Bobby's anger escalated. 'If Bobby Kennedy gets in, the first thing he'll do is stop sending conscripts into a war everyone on the ground says we can't win. You know what that means. It means that you won't have to go overseas. You can sit out your National Service in a military camp in the good old U S of A, polishing your boots and buttons and saluting officers.'

251

'That's what you and all the other draft dodgers want, isn't it, Bobby?' Sandy taunted. 'A guarantee that while you're sitting on your butts pretending to study in Europe half of our generation aren't getting killed in 'Nam. Well I have news for you, buddy. Some wars are worth fighting. The Communists have to be stopped just as Hitler had to be stopped...'

'In Vietnam? In God's name, it's on a different continent.' Bobby thumped the table and sent the crockery and cutlery rattling. 'You think Ho Chi Minh is going to march his forces up Main Street in Hyannis, or invade Washington. Your problem is you've swallowed the propaganda–'

'You looked at a world map lately and seen how many countries are red? Russia's gobbled up all of Eastern Europe. China is following suit with Korea and Vietnam ... there's even one on our doorstep. The Cubans–'

'The Cubans are too busy foraging for enough food to live on to concern themselves with us.'

'And you, of course, have been there lately, rich boy?' Sandy gibed. 'It wasn't enough for you to slum it in Harlem...'

The argument tennis-balled back and forth, raging ever uglier. She wanted to stop it but she didn't know how, and from the expression on Kate's face she knew her friend felt equally impotent.

Bobby raised his fist, but before he could thump the table again, or Sandy – and Sandy's face was the direction it was flying in – Penny moved between them.

Bobby only just managed to stop his fist from

252

connecting with her cheek.

'I don't know much about politics, but I do know that no argument between students ever changed the world,' she said firmly. 'I also know that political arguments don't put food on the table. We need jobs, remember?'

Bobby stood back and unclenched his fists. 'Now I suppose you're going to ask the two of us to shake hands.'

'That seems like a good idea.'

Neither Bobby nor Sandy made a move.

Kate did what she always did in a volatile situation. Turned to the practical. 'You boys can wash the dishes while Pen and I give the house a quick once-over.'

'It's clean,' Bobby protested.

'It's what I call "unsupervised cleaner keep the dust down" clean, but it's been a while since someone washed out the inside of the fridge, kitchen cupboards and the wardrobes. I'm not putting my food or clothes inside any of them until they're Pontypridd clean.'

'What's "Pontypridd clean"?' Sandy asked.

'My mother's idea of clean. Go on, off with you, sort out the dishes.'

The boys went. Kate had succeeded in diffusing the argument – for the moment. But they could feel it simmering beneath the surface. Penny understood Sandy's conviction that the Vietnam War was a just one. He had to believe it because he had no option other than to fight. She could also understand the guilt that lay behind Bobby's anger. His grandmother's money had bought him an escape that would safeguard his

253

life but not Sandy's.

It was a situation that would blight their summer and their lives. At the time, she didn't realise how much.

When the house was clean enough to meet even Kate's exacting standards, they showered and dressed in job-hunting clothes.

'Tarrah!' Kate twirled in front of Sandy who frowned.

'You girls can't go out like that,' Sandy declared as he eyed their miniskirts and skinny-rib sweaters.

'What's up, they look great.' Bobby was buttoning a white cotton shirt he'd teamed with black pants. A tie was hanging out of his pocket.

'Their outfits might tempt the Playboy Club into hiring them, but this is a conservative town. How many miniskirted waitresses or chambermaids have you seen around here?'

'I've spent most of the last three years in England, remember.'

'I've spent the last two Easter, fall and summer breaks working here. Every restaurant manager will want to hire the girls, but none will, because they're afraid of what their female customers will say when they catch their husbands and teenage sons ogling their legs.'

'Sandy's right,' Bobby conceded. 'Much as I hate to say it, you'd better put on longer skirts.'

'This is my longest,' Kate protested.

'Mine too.'

'In that case, first stop uniform shop, unless you girls hope to find something in a retail store.'

'Uniform?' Penny asked blankly.

'Waitresses and chambermaids wear white dresses in the States.'

'Knee-length dresses?' Kate had exceptionally good legs, long, slim and suntanned, courtesy of a particularly warm May when she'd spent every available minute between lectures sunbathing on Swansea beach.

'Over the knee, would be better,' Sandy advised. 'And you'll need white shoes. And stockings.'

'Stockings in this heat?' Kate pleaded. 'Please tell me you're joking.'

'Unfortunately not. But if you turn up dressed for the part, you're more likely to find work.' Sandy, expert job hunter on the Cape, turned to Bobby. 'Kitchen work suit you?'

'No, but I have to eat.'

'We have enough to cover chefs' whites if we have to. Let's go.'

'What do I look like?'

The changing room in the uniform store was the size of a broom cupboard. She flattened herself against the wall and studied Kate. 'Like you're auditioning for a role as an extra in a film about novice nuns.'

'It's not only long and shapeless; it's horrible stiff nylon. The seams are scratchy and these flat white lace-ups make my legs and ankles look like tree trunks.' Kate stared miserably into the full-length mirror.

'How you girls doing?' The sales assistant bustled in carrying a second uniform dress over her arm. 'That's perfect. You'll soon get a job. The restaurant will probably want you to wear their own hat, but you'd better pick up half a dozen hairnets...'

'Hairnets!' Kate exclaimed in horror.

'Can't drop hairs in the customers' food, or if you're chambermaiding, in their beds or bathrooms. I picked out an identical uniform for your friend. I thought with your accents you could sell yourself as a team.'

Kate smiled maliciously at her. 'It will suit you better than it suits me.'

'You girls will want to buy stockings as well. Restaurants don't like their staff wearing tights.'

'They *look?*' Kate was horrified.

'Every restaurant and fast-food eatery carries out an inspection check of their staff's clothing for tears, stains and general untidiness before the start of a shift. Howard Johnson's chain is the worst. But I'm doing myself no favours. If you get taken on by them, you'll have to wear the full house uniform supplied by management. Long gingham dress, gingham mob caps and apron.'

Penny took the white uniform from the assistant. It suddenly seemed the lesser evil.

CHAPTER TWENTY-THREE

They left the uniform store and walked down Main Street. A muted 'hush' had descended over the town. The streets were crowded, but when people spoke it was in whispers, as if they were in church. The name 'Bobby Kennedy' hung in the air. It was as though everyone was holding their breath waiting for the next news announcement.

'People who live on the Cape consider the Kennedys as part of their family because they've summered in the Kennedy compound outside Hyannis for two generations,' Bobby explained after they passed a group of matrons, damp handkerchiefs pressed to their eyes, who were discussing the tragedy.

Neither Bobby nor Sandy mentioned their argument. She and Kate did their best to distract them by asking questions about the town. It was certainly different from anything in Britain.

A few of the restaurants sported names they'd seen in New York and off the freeway on their journey through Connecticut into Massachusetts. There'd been other 'Frankie Frankfurters' with signs declaring that all their 'franks' were cooked in beer, and the smell that came from Dunkin' Donuts was seductive, sugary and identical to the one next to their hotel in New York. There was the inevitable McDonald's, and when she and Kate saw Howard Johnson's, they edged towards the restaurant to check if the waitresses' uniforms were as hideous as the assistant in the uniform shop had told them.

They were worse. But what they weren't prepared for was the young woman who catapulted out of the door and ran towards them.

'So, you Brits took my advice and found your way to the Cape.'

'Marion?' Penny barely recognised the bunny girl as the waitress dressed in a long-skirted blue gingham dress that almost touched the floor. Marion's face was scrubbed, free from make-up, her blonde hair was screwed into a tight bun covered by a hairnet, and her lace-up white shoes, identical to the ones Penny and Kate had just bought, made her feet look enormous.

'Marion!' A grim-faced man appeared in the doorway.

'That's the manager. He's a real slave-driver and furious with me for leaving my station to come out here. But I couldn't let you pass without a word. Lord, what must you think of me? Every time you see me, I'm in trouble,' she breathed headily. 'We must get together. There's a party here every night. Come and see me and we'll set a date. I'm here six days a week.'

'Marion!'

'Must go.'

She ran back inside.

'How come you two know a Southern girl who looks like an extra from *Wagon Train?*' Bobby asked.

'She's wearing a standard Ho Jo uniform,' Sandy explained for Bobby's benefit.

'Remind me never to eat there.'

'Given their prices and your present situation, you can't afford to,' Sandy observed.

'She's an escaped bunny,' Kate informed the boys.

Bobby whistled. 'So that's the lady I have to thank for you turning down the Playboy job.'

'She put us off,' Kate agreed.

'We should go back to Ho Jo's, order four coffees, and leave her an enormous tip as a thank you,' Bobby suggested.

'That would be a good idea if we had your checking account to draw on.' Sandy reminded him, yet again, that they were unemployed.

'We've just passed Dunkin' Donuts and Frankie's. Want to go back?' Bobby asked.

'Money and tips are better in the specialist seafood places. Last few holidays I worked for Cosmo.' Sandy frowned as he looked up the street and into the sun.

'In the Mayflower?'

'The ship?' she asked.

'Doesn't exist anymore. Although I believe there are as many splinters left of it as the true cross,' Bobby replied flippantly.

'I thought maybe someone had built a replica and turned it into a restaurant.'

'Now there's a business idea,' Bobby mused.

'If we had capital, which we don't.' Sandy stopped to retie the lace on his sneakers.

'So, if you're not referring to the ship that almost sank under the weight of immigrants from the nobility of England ...' Kate was referring to all the people at the orientation party in New York who'd insisted their ancestors came over on the ship and they'd inherited a claim to a title '...what are you talking about?'

'The Mayflower is a restaurant, owned by third- or possibly fourth- generation Greek immigrants. It has frontages on two different streets with a kitchen that covers both back lots in between. An upmarket frontage is in a quiet street behind Main Street. Every table has two dollars thirty cents worth of disposable fake paper linen to give the impression of luxury. The other frontage is here on Main Street, just ahead of us. It's a bar and fast-food joint. And here's Cosmo.'

'Hey, Sandy. Saw you coming.' An enormous plump Greek with a full head of tousled black hair grabbed Sandy, lifted him off his feet and squeezed him in a bear hug. 'Please tell me you're looking for work?'

'I will when I get my breath back,' Sandy said when Cosmo released him. 'You know me. I'm always looking for work when I'm on the Cape.'

'You can have your old job back with a ten-dollar-a-week pay rise.'

'You must have missed me. Short-order chef?'

'Short-order chef,' Cosmo reiterated. 'One twenty a week plus meals on shift, but it'll be two till ten, afternoon and evening shift. My nephew's taken the six-till-two morning shift and I've moved Leroy on the ten-till-six night shift. It's the quietest. He's slowing down and has insomnia, so it suits him on both counts.'

'When do I start?'

'Today. Clean chef's whites and hat in the store-room.' Cosmo smiled at her and Kate. 'Pretty ladies you have there. They looking for work too?'

'They are.' Sandy winked at us. 'Speak, girls.'

'Like performing monkeys,' Kate mocked.

She held out her hand. 'I'm pleased to meet you, sir. I'm Penny John.'

'Kate Burgess.' Kate introduced herself.

'British?' Cosmo beamed.

'Welsh, not that Americans can tell the difference.' Penny returned Cosmo's smile. The Greek positively radiated welcoming warmth.

'Two-till-ten shift, like Sandy. Fifty dollars a week in training, seventy afterwards, plus meals. The other girls make up to thirty dollars a shift in tips. With those looks and those accents you two should do even better. We supply aprons, you'll need uniforms.' He gazed at the length of leg they were displaying beneath their minis. 'For the sake of the peace of mind of my male customers, but not me, with skirts.'

Sandy took the parcel from Kate. 'Already bought.'

'And we'll only need training in the location of everything in the restaurant, sir,' Kate interrupted. 'We're both silver service trained,' she lied.

'Just what I need for outside catering jobs. We're booked solid for the summer. Can you start this afternoon?'

'We can,' Penny and Kate assured him.

'Anything for me, Cosmo?' Bobby asked.

'You?' Cosmo looked at him in surprise. 'Your grandmother would have me flogged out of town if I gave a Brosna a menial job.'

'She's frozen my checking account.'

Cosmo laughed, a huge deep booming that shook his entire body. 'And what sin did you commit to receive that punishment, Bobby Brosna?'

'Annoying her,' Bobby replied evasively.

'You should know better than to do that with a lady who controls your purse strings.'

'I should, but didn't.'

Cosmo slapped Bobby across the shoulders. 'I can always do with an extra kitchen hand. How are you at mixing salads and cooking vegetables, fries and rice?'

'I've never tried but I'm a quick learner, clean and honest,' Bobby answered.

'Kitchen hands are the lowest of the low. At the beck and call of all the chefs, even the short-order chef,' Cosmo warned with an arch look at Sandy.

'I'll manage.'

'It won't all be preparation and cooking. You'll be given the filthy jobs no one else wants. Scrubbing pans, unblocking sinks, taking out the trash, cleaning trash cans, and all for eighty dollars a week plus meals on shift. Uniform provided. But like Sandy you wash your own. And you girls will have to wash your aprons as well as your own uniforms.'

'Sandy will be getting one twenty a week,' Bobby remonstrated.

'Sandy's an experienced short-order chef and they are as rare as gold lobsters. Kitchen hands are two a dime.' Cosmo stepped back into the restaurant and glanced at the clock above the bar. 'If you're sure you're up for it, I'll see you guys in four hours.'

'We'll be back sooner for a coffee if we can afford one, to see if we can pick up any tips from the rest of your staff,' Bobby said.

Cosmo dropped his smile. 'You can have a coffee on the house but I warn you now, Bobby Brosna – as Sandy knows, when we're busy you'll be worked as you never were before.'

Cosmo wasn't exaggerating. Penny and Kate had to learn a bewildering array of locations. The clean-crockery station – the clean-cutlery station

– the napkin station – the iced-water-machine and glasses station. Every potential customer to be given a free glass of iced water on arrival, even if they didn't order anything.

A novel idea for her and Kate but they'd never lived in a climate as warm and humid as the Cape in June. There was a hot drawer for bread rolls and another for cornbread. Prices were on the menus, the specials on a board, cocktail, spirit and beer prices affixed to the bar.

The ice cream station had photographs of what the house ice creams should look like when decorated with chocolate curls, nuts, swirls of cream and pieces of fruit. Penny studied the pictures and dreaded being asked to make one.

Sandy disappeared into a small alcove off the kitchen and reappeared in chef's whites and hat behind a hatch in the fast-food restaurant. Penny watched in amazement as he began to flip burgers, eggs, bacon and chicken as though he'd been doing it all his life.

Bobby went into the kitchen and that was the last she and Kate saw of him that shift, although they heard his name being yelled intermittently by the chefs – and not politely.

She and Kate had been left in the care of a middle-aged waitress, who'd travelled to America as a GI bride. Betty showed them the layout of the Mayflower in between regaling them with details of her life and that of the 'waste of space worse than useless' sergeant husband she'd walked out on after only two weeks of marriage.

'He promised me I'd live the Hollywood high life when we were courting in Britain. But when the boat carrying the GI brides docked, he took me to a four-roomed New York apartment and expected me to set up home alongside his parents, grandmother, two sisters and brother.'

'I'm amazed you stayed with him two weeks,' Kate said.

'Took me that long to find another fellow.'

Twenty minutes after Betty had begun their 'orientation' Penny and Kate were taking orders, ferrying food, glasses, cutlery, and serving customers.

'This is a doddle,' Kate declared during their twenty minute break at a counter in the kitchen to eat chicken burgers and fries. 'In Ponty we had to clear our own tables. Here you have bus boys to do the dirty work, leaving us clean and free to lay up the next lot of cutlery and crockery.'

Halfway through the shift, Penny's feet didn't feel like it was a 'doddle', and after spending twenty minutes trying to please an irritable family of six who didn't want to be pleased and complained about every dish she served them – and left no tip – she felt that waitressing was a hard, very hard, way to make a living.

It was a warm, dark, velvet night when they left the restaurant by the kitchen door. She and Kate leant against the wall in the alleyway, looked at one another and started to laugh.

'Exhaustion, hysteria or relief at the thought of not having to take another order for sixteen hours?' Sandy appeared behind them.

'Combination of all three,' Kate answered.

'Want to see the result of the kitchen initiation rites?' He pushed the door wide.

Bobby was crawling out of the centre of the massive dishwasher. His hair was festooned with leftover spaghetti and meat sauce that dripped down over his forehead and nose.

Kate and Sandy started laughing. Penny held back, unsure of Bobby's reaction. She needn't have worried.

'It's good to know my first attempt at a full day's work in the real world has amused my colleagues.' Bobby turned back to the long table where the chefs were cutting, chopping and mixing and gave them a theatrical bow. 'See you guys tomorrow.'

'Your family may be filthy wealthy, Bobby Brosna, but you're a sport,' the senior chef called back.

'May I take that comment as an accolade?'

'You may.' The chef saluted him.

'You're not going to drive your car like that, are you? You'll stick to the leather upholstery,' Sandy protested.

'One moment.' Bobby returned to the kitchen and reappeared less than a minute later, clean but dripping wet. 'There's a shower. The car upholstery will dry.' He wrapped a soggy arm around her shoulders. 'Home, woman, for some tender loving care and comfort. I deserve it.'

CHAPTER TWENTY-FOUR

'Beer and chill in the garden,' Sandy suggested when Bobby parked the car outside the Beach House.

'Shower and bed,' she corrected.

'I'm right behind you.' Bobby unlocked the door.

'The trouble with you two is, you have absolutely no stamina,' Sandy declared.

'I'll buy some with my first wages' cheque, until then I'll have to do without it.' Bobby went into their bedroom. She followed.

He closed the door. 'Do you want first shower?'

'You should, you're wet.'

'We'll share.'

'I have to wash my uniform.'

'Buy another tomorrow.'

She was too tired to argue with the profligacy.

They went into the bathroom and climbed into the shower. They sponged one another down, rinsed off and tumbled into bed, too exhausted for anything more than short-lived, almost perfunctory sex.

They fell asleep to the murmur of Sandy and Kate's voices. Accustomed to the long hours and hard work of restaurants, they'd taken a couple of chilled beers they'd bought from Cosmo into the garden. Neither appeared to be in a hurry to go to bed.

She woke with a start, uncertain of her surroundings. She looked around, saw the sea through the undraped window, remembered they were in Bobby's Beach House and relaxed back on the pillows. Unaccustomed to being on her feet for long hours, her leg muscles ached unbearably. The luminous hands on her travelling clock pointed to three.

She turned. Bobby's eyes were open.

He smiled. 'You're awake?'

'I wasn't until I dreamt someone was stalking me,' she reproached.

'Come for a swim?'

'It's three in the morning.'

He leant over and kissed her. 'I hate swimming alone.'

'We have to be in work...'

'In eleven hours. Swim for one to cool down in this damned heat and back to sleep for the regulation eight, then breakfast and work.' He left the bed and pulled on his shorts. 'I'd forgotten how much I love the Cape. But this house desperately needs air conditioning. When I'm talking to my grandmother again I must ask her to put it in.'

'You're confident you'll talk to her again?' she asked in surprise.

'This isn't the first time she's frozen my account. But she'll come round. I'm her link to immortality – the mirror image of the only man she ever loved – my grandfather. Or so she keeps telling me. She refuses to recognise any of my father's other children – even the legitimate ones, because their mothers weren't high society enough for her. And, as she's cast my father off with somewhat more than the proverbial penny because he's no interest in the business and would squander every Brosna penny given the chance, that only leaves me.'

'So you'll inherit the entire Brosna fortune?' That was the moment she realised that one day Bobby would be rich with wealth beyond her imaginings.

'Unless my grandmother leaves it to a cats' home, but as she hates animals, that's not likely.'

'I had no idea.' She slumped back into the bed and saw him in a new light. One she didn't like. He'd tracked her down, wooed and won her. But was that simply indicative of the spoilt rich kid getting his own way? Sandy had certainly dropped enough hints that she'd ignored at the time.

'Don't hold it against me.'

She felt as though he'd read her thoughts.

'If you'd prefer me poor, I could give the money away.'

'You'd forgo the Brosna inheritance for me?'

'No, but the offer sounded good, didn't it?'

'Only until you said the word "no".'

'The sea's getting warmer by the minute.'

'Can't we just lie here and look at it through the window.' She snuggled under the sheet.

'Lazybones.'

'That's me.'

'I'll tickle you.' He reached for her foot.

'I'm tired.'

'Too tired for moonlight bathing?' He stood in front of the window and looked out. 'It's beautiful out there. As an artist you should never turn down an opportunity to admire beauty.'

She reluctantly left the bed and opened the drawer she'd used to stow away everything that couldn't be hung in the wardrobe.

'You don't need a bikini,' Bobby urged when he saw her rummaging through her clothes.

'And if there's someone on the beach?'

'Who'd be lurking on a private beach at this time of night?'

'You own this beach!'

'It's part of the Brosna Estate. Surely you didn't think someone else owned the beach when it's surrounded by Brosna land.'

'I assumed the States were like the UK. No one can own a beach there. At least not between tide-lines – it all belongs to the Crown and is accessible to everyone.'

'Unless your queen takes it into her head to roll out barbed wire and fence it off.'

'Now that's an image to conjure with.' She laughed at the idea of the royal family going out en masse from Buckingham Palace to hammer stakes into sand and roll out wire.

'Here,' Bobby threw her one of his T-shirts. 'If you're worried about your modesty, wear this until you're in the water. Though why you should give a damn what I see after what we've been doing is beyond me.'

'It's not you I'm concerned about.'

'The seagulls should be asleep. Not too sure about the horseshoe crabs, though. They might be looking.'

She pulled on the T-shirt, which smelt of Bobby

and was half a dozen sizes too large. They crept past Sandy and Kate's room, which was silent, out of the house and on to the sand.

The horseshoe crabs were moving erratically over the sand. She stopped to watch them.

'Enormous, aren't they?' Bobby reached for her hand.

'Gigantic compared to the ones on Welsh beaches and positively prehistoric. It doesn't take much imagination to visualise them crawling around the feet of dinosaurs.'

Stepping between them they walked hand in hand to the edge of the sea. The waves were small, and they broke softly, foam-crested rivulets dissipating into silver streaks over the sand.

Bobby pulled off his shorts, flung them behind him and raced in, diving down and swimming as soon as he was waist-deep.

Feeling strangely self-conscious, although the beach was devoid of human life just as Bobby had promised, she stripped off his T-shirt and followed him.

Pontypridd, 1987

Penny left the house and returned to her studio. She opened the drawer she had dropped the photograph into and retrieved it, but she didn't need an image of Bobby to recall the sensations of that night.

The silk-smooth water, the satin feel of Bobby's skin against hers as he had embraced her underwater. His firm, unyielding erection when he'd pressed his body along the length of hers. Their failed attempt to make love underwater.

Their laughter had been their downfall. If they hadn't been making so much noise they would have heard the vehicle approaching before the spotlight was switched on, embarrassing them both.

She still thought the law she and Bobby had broken that night a ridiculous one. Especially for a country that proudly hailed itself 'the land of the free'.

Taking the photograph, she carried it back to her living room, propped it against the lamp on her desk, sat back – and remembered.

Hyannisport, 1968

The first indication they weren't alone was a blinding white light. A metallic voice boomed through a loudspeaker.

'Leave the sea slowly. Don't run. Keep your hands above your heads.'

'Not bloody likely,' Bobby shouted back. 'We're naked.'

'Naked in a public place is a felony. And you don't sound British, so why are you using a British swear word?' the uniformed officer demanded, moving the light so it shone full on Bobby who was standing waist-deep in the water next to Penny.

'Because I've been living in Britain for the last three years. And this isn't a public place. It's a private beach, I'm Bobby Brosna...'

'I'm Doris Day and he's Charlton Heston,' the officer mocked. 'You're American. You know it's illegal to be on a beach after six o'clock at night.'

'This is a private beach,' Bobby repeated stubbornly.

'There's no fence up.'

'Because my grandmother is away...'

'Everyone in Hyannis knows the old lady hasn't been here in years. You,' the officer motioned to Penny with his gun. 'Hands in the air now.'

'Turn your back,' Bobby whispered.

She did as Bobby suggested. But the disembodied voice boomed out of the darkness again. 'Turn around. Keep your hands in the air.'

Bobby shouted, 'My girlfriend's shy. How about I come out first and throw her the T-shirt?'

'Here, catch.' One of the officers took pity on them and tossed them Bobby's shorts and the T-shirt she'd worn. Both landed in the sea and both were soaking wet, but keeping her back turned, she pulled on the shirt.

'Now out, both of you.'

Bobby slipped and fell when putting on his shorts, but he didn't argue. She waded on to the sand, he crawled.

'Hands high against the side of the vehicle. What are you doing here at this time in the morning?'

'Swimming,' Bobby answered.

The single word earned him a cuff across the head. Terrified, she fought panic. It was Grosvenor Square all over again, only this time there was no Uncle Haydn on hand to solve the problem. She tried to calculate how many miles

away Las Vegas was.

'We were swimming,' Bobby repeated, his voice cracked from the effects of the blow.

An overweight officer opened the back of the vehicle. 'Inside the cage, both of you. We'll sort this in the morning.'

For the second time she found herself shivering next to Bobby in a police vehicle. Both of them were soaked, and wearing only a thin, wet T-shirt she felt naked and vulnerable.

When they reached the police station she was handed over to a female officer who body-searched her even more roughly than the police-woman had in London. When she'd finished humiliating her, she handed her a filthy, grey, greasy, nylon blanket, opened a door and walked her to a cage in the middle of a large room.

Sitting in it were two of the thinnest women she'd ever seen. The only large thing about them were their breasts, which as they were unevenly placed were obviously false. They were wearing enough make-up between them to grease a boat engine; their skirts were even shorter than Kate's and the expression on their faces a mixture of terror and misery behind the paint.

Opposite them sat a beautiful girl, dark-skinned with long black hair and dark eyes. She was holding the hand of a blue-eyed blonde boy who also looked frightened. In the furthest corner from the others a black woman cowered Two toddlers were sleeping on her lap and she clutched them tightly as if she was afraid the were going to be torn from her arms.

Stretched out on the floor beneath a bench was an old man. Stinking of alcohol, covered in vomit, the crutch of his pants wet, he twitched and mumbled in a drunken stupor.

The female officer waited for one of her colleagues to leave the desk in the room and open the cage. A thump between Penny's shoulder blades propelled her inside. She stumbled over the outstretched hand of the drunk and reached for the cage bars to steady herself. She slipped; the blonde boy caught her.

'Hi, I'm Paul. You can sit next to my girlfriend, Mary, if you like,' he offered.

'You're Irish.'

'Guilty.'

Relief flooded through her at the sound of an accent, which if not exactly home, was familiar. She suppressed the impulse to kiss him.

'I'm Welsh.'

He looked at her wet T-shirt visible above the dirty blanket she was reluctant to use. 'They caught you swimming?'

'Yes.'

'Were you hoping to reach Martha's Vineyard or Nantucket?'

For the first time she saw humour in the situation.

'I didn't know it was illegal to be on a beach after six o'clock at night.'

'Strange law. But perhaps they want to leave the sands free for leprechauns and witches to dance on.'

'Shut up,' the officer behind the desk bellowed.

The door opened. Bobby stumbled in escorted

by two of the officers who'd taken them into custody. He was wearing his boxer shorts and carrying an identical but even dirtier blanket than the one they'd given her. One of his eyes was swollen and there was blood on his mouth.

He gave her a lopsided grin. 'This is getting to be a habit.'

Mary moved along the bench to make room and Bobby sat next to her on the wooden bench. He reached for her hand.

'Look on the sunny side, Pen. At least this time we're together.'

CHAPTER TWENTY-FIVE

'Should we sing to keep up our spirits?' Paul gave the officer at the desk a sideways look.

'I wouldn't. The stateside police are not renowned for their sense of humour, particularly at this time in the morning.' Bobby rubbed her hands between his in an effort to warm his own as well as hers.

'Anyone any idea of the time?' Paul asked.

The two girls held up their bare wrists.

'So, they took your watches too,' Paul commented.

'Shut up!' the officer behind the desk bellowed a second time. He rifled through a box of cookies and picked out half a dozen.

'We were driven here sometime after three; it must be about four by now,' Bobby whispered.

The duty officer left the desk and waddled to the cage. He shook his fist, but as it was with the hand holding the cookies the gesture was more ridiculous than terrifying.

'If you know what's good for you, you'll shut it,' he reiterated when he saw Bobby and Paul suppressing smiles.

The door banged open. A pale-faced officer walked in. 'Bobby Kennedy died a couple of hours ago.'

The duty officer stopped chewing his cookies. His mouth opened, his lips fell slack and he dribbled crumbs. 'Oh no! God no!'

Penny looked from the officers to Bobby. The only indication he'd heard the conversation was the increased pressure of his fingers on hers.

Silence reigned in the holding cage and the room beyond. Bobby's arm lay heavy on Penny's shoulders, but she found the pressure too comforting to shrug it off. She closed her eyes but the fierce light from the single electric bulb burnt through her eyelids. The foul smell of the drunk lying on the floor, coupled with the stench of the blanket wrapped around her shoulders, was making her nauseous. Without a watch she felt as though time had frozen.

As there were no windows in the room it was impossible to gauge whether dawn had broken or not. The two children on the woman's lap woke. Their eyes opened but they didn't make a sound. Only clutched her dress tighter.

Footsteps echoed. They stopped outside the door. It opened. An officer stood, dwarfed by the massive figure of George.

Bobby moved his arm, rose from the bench and went to the door of the cage. 'George?'

'Mr Bobby, what are you doing in there?' George walked over to him.

'Researching a thesis on life in a Hyannisport holding cell,' Bobby answered sourly.

The officer at the desk joined George and the officer who'd escorted him in. 'You know that man?'

'I sure do. He's Bobby Brosna the Fourth.'

'He's *really* Bobby Brosna?' The officer clearly didn't want to believe it.

'Sure is,' George confirmed.

'We picked him and the girl up skinny-dipping on the beach in the early hours.'

'I told you it was a private beach,' Bobby reminded.

'You were breaking the law on two counts. You were on a beach after 6.00 p.m. and you were in a state of indecency.'

'You want me to apologise after you locked me and my girlfriend in here all night?' Bobby's voice had changed to imperious. Yet again Penny was reminded how little she knew him.

'I suppose we could let you go with a caution,' one of the officers demurred.

'And, I suppose if I felt magnanimous, I could decide not to complain about the treatment we received.'

Bobby's threat was enough. The officer manning the desk fetched the keys and unlocked the cell. Bobby offered her his hand. She took it and moved slowly upright waiting for the circulation to return to her limbs.

'You here to fetch us, George?' Bobby asked.

'No, Mr Bobby. I didn't know you were here until I walked in.' George drew closer to where the woman with the children was sitting behind bars. 'You called your cousin last night, ma'am?'

'I did,' she answered.

'She sent me to get you and the children.'

A tear rolled down her cheek.

'Here, let me help you with the little ones.' George stepped inside the cage and took one of the children from her lap. Paul lifted the other.

'Don't suppose there's any chance of you getting Mary out of here, Bobby?' Paul asked. 'I don't mind for myself but this is no place for a lady.'

'Why did they pick you up?'

'Vagrancy. We could only raise three bucks between us. We came to town hoping to find live-in jobs.'

'There's a couple of cottages free, isn't there?' Bobby turned to George.

'Only one, Mr Bobby sir, after this lady and her little ones move in.'

'One is all they need.' Bobby looked at Paul. 'We can help you with accommodation.'

'I just said we have no money...'

Bobby lowered his voice to a whisper. 'Neither have we. What the owner doesn't know isn't going to upset her. Just keep the place clean.' He turned back to the officer. 'Can we take...?'

'Paul Smith and Mary Night,' Paul said.

'Can we take them to the Brosna Estate?'

'You'll vouch for them, sir?'

The elevation to 'sir' surprised Penny but not Bobby.

'I'll vouch for them,' Bobby answered.

'Although the girl is Native American?'

'Makes no difference to me,' Bobby said coldly. 'Take them away.'

'We should arrest you every night, Mr Brosna,' the overweight officer joked. 'You have a way of cleaning up the holding cell in the morning.'

'What about us?' one of the thin girls asked.

'Transsexual soliciting. You need more than a Brosna to get you out of that one. You need a good lawyer,' the officer barked.

She was dreaming that she was rocking in a boat on the sea. The rocking grew wilder, more violent...

'Wake up, sleepyhead.'

She opened her eyes. Bobby was shaking her.

'Don't you dare suggest another swim,' she warned.

'We have to be at work in an hour. I thought you'd want time for a shower and a meal.'

'No, I don't.' She snuggled back down in the bed and held out her arms.

'If I get down there with you, I won't get up again this side of sunset.'

'Good.'

'If it wasn't our second day in the job, I'd agree with you and spend the afternoon sleeping on the beach.'

'Don't mention the word "beach" to me ever again.'

'Not until after our shift,' he joked. 'Come on,

279

sleepy. We can't let Cosmo down.'

She reluctantly forced herself to sit up in the bed. 'Five minutes I'll be with you.'

'I'll be in the garden with Sandy and Kate.'

When she emerged freshly showered with wet hair, dressed in jeans and T-shirt, Kate pointed to the washing line. 'I washed your uniform and apron.'

'Thank you, but how did you know I hadn't done them?'

'Because we saw them on the floor of your bedroom when we looked for you this morning. They should be dry.'

She felt them. 'Thank you. They are.'

'Hi, Brits.' Marion opened the gate and walked into the garden with a handsome young Hispanic in tow.

'Joe. You're looking good. Great to see you.' Sandy left his chair and hugged the young man.

'I don't know who you are but put the love of my life down,' Marion ordered Sandy.

'Nice to meet you guys.' Joe shook hands all round.

Like Sandy, Joe was tall, dark and very handsome, with a Clark Gable moustache and long dark hair.

Marion hugged Penny and Kate.

'How did you know where to find us?' Kate asked.

'We didn't. We came here to see George. He told us Sandy was staying here with Bobby and two Brit girls,' Marion divulged.

'Are you in one of the cottages?' Bobby asked.

'No freebies for us, unfortunately. We're renting

a room the other side of town. Joe has a friend who works at the Melody Tent and can get half-price tickets for concerts that aren't sold out and hard-to-get tickets for those that are. We brought round two for the Joan Bacz concert that George ordered. He offered us a cup of coffee and we got to talking. He told Joe that Sandy was here. I mentioned the Brits I'd met yesterday in town and he said two Brits were staying here. I wondered if you were the same ones. And you are.'

'Can you get us half-price tickets for the Joan Baez concert?' Sandy asked eagerly.

'I might be able to get tickets, but not half price, not for Joan Baez,' Joe warned. 'Last time my friend looked there were only half a dozen left.'

'Before you buy any tickets we have to square time off with Cosmo,' Bobby reminded, 'and speaking of Cosmo, we have to leave for work in five minutes.'

Penny took her uniform and apron from the line, dived indoors and changed. When she came out Sandy and Kate were making arrangements to visit Marion and Joe when they came off shift.

'We'll know then when we'll have our evening off and will let you know about the tickets,' Sandy told Joe.

Joe noticed Bobby's guitar propped against a chair. 'You play as well as Sandy?'

'He thinks he's better than me,' Sandy winked at Joe.

'Bring them. Marion has a good voice and we have music most evenings.'

'Thanks, we will.' Bobby walked them to the gate.

'That should keep you and Bobby off the beach and out of mischief in the early hours.' Sandy waved Marion and Joe off as they left on Joe's motorcycle.

'And there was me looking forward to another swim.' Bobby opened his car door. 'Work everyone.'

'Not until we've packed a change of clothes. There's no way I'm going to any party in a waitress uniform.' Kate ran back into the house and Penny followed.

None of them expected a gathering the size of the one outside the white clapboard house where Joe and Marion were renting a room. The yard was crowded. More than a dozen people were roasting franks and marshmallows on sticks over a campfire. Even more were clustered around a makeshift bar set up on crates from which Joe and Marion were dispensing drinks. A sign pinned to the tree above it, said ALL DONATIONS GRATEFULLY IMBIDED.

'Glad you could come.' Marion handed Penny and Kate glasses as soon as they walked through the gate. 'Cold white wine, the only way to drink it.'

'Sandy, Bobby, you've brought your guitars, great. Over here with them.' Mark, the sous-chef from Cosmo's waved to them.

A few moments later the sound of Bob Dylan's 'I Shall Be Released' was being belted out by an improvised choir and half a dozen guitars.

Penny and Kate sat between Bobby and Sandy. Someone handed her a hot dog. Every time she set her paper cup on the ground it was refilled, so she clung on to it.

Six Dylan songs in, Bobby started playing 'The Times They Are a-Changin'. Penny left the circle round the campfire and went in search of a bathroom. She was leaving the house when she noticed a man sitting apart from the others. He looked lost and lonely, although she couldn't have said with any certainty why.

She walked over to where he was sitting, leaning against a tree, brown paper bag in hand, and offered a tentative, 'Hi.'

He lifted his hand in acknowledgement but didn't say anything.

'You OK?' she asked.

'Nope, but I'll be better when they stop playing that,' he muttered. The song had changed to 'With God on Our Side'.

She opened her bag, took out a pencil and artist's block and sat on the grass. 'Mind if I sketch you?'

'What do you want to do that for?'

'I'm studying art. And there's something about your face...'

She was already making broad outline strokes on the paper.

Joe brought her a fresh cup of wine and looked over her shoulder. 'That's good.'

She glanced up. 'It's very rough, but thank you.'

'You've met my brother, Eric?'

'We haven't been formally introduced.' She smiled at Eric. 'Hi again, Eric.'

Eric nodded.

'Eric, this is Penny, she's a Brit and a friend of

Marion and Sandy. He worked with us last season, remember?'

Eric lifted his hand again and gave another perfunctory wave.

'Eric's back from his first tour in 'Nam,' Joe confided loud enough for Eric to hear.

'And returning as soon as I've had the regulation dose of R&R prescribed by the shrink.'

'I'm sorry,' she sympathised.

'Why? You didn't send me there.'

'I'm sorry that anyone has to fight a war. It's such a horrible concept. Two armies of men lined up and ordered to kill one another.'

'It's not a concept when you're there. And the armies aren't facing one another. It would be a cleaner fight if they were. We're fighting the whole goddamn population.' He looked at her. 'You really are sorry, aren't you?'

'Yes.'

'Wish I'd met you before I got my draft papers.'

'I have a boyfriend...'

'I've a girlfriend. She's a nurse in Mexico City. I didn't mean it that way. If you'd invited me to stay with you in England, I could have become a draft dodger like the rich kids.'

She carried on sketching. 'What's it like over there?'

'You don't want to know.'

She longed to reach out to Eric, offer him more than sympathy, but as she couldn't even begin to imagine what he'd experienced, she didn't know where to start.

'I have to talk about it soon,' Eric murmured. She had the feeling he was talking more to himself than her. 'I promised to visit my buddy's wife.'

'You OK, Pen?' Bobby joined them. There was a suspicious look on his face that she would have liked to interpret as jealousy.

'This is Joe's brother, Eric. He's a soldier, back from Vietnam.'

'Is it as bad as they say over there?' Bobby sat beside them.

'As I don't know what they're saying I can't answer that.'

Eric was so offhand she said, 'Eric was telling me he has to visit his buddy's wife.'

'You have a message for her?' Bobby lifted his guitar from the grass on to his lap.

'The kind no one wants to deliver.' Eric flipped open a pack of cigarettes and pushed one between his teeth. 'He gave me his last letter.'

'He was killed?'

'Drowned along with everyone in our platoon, except me. We were in a waterlogged paddy field for a week. There was nothing to cling to. Lost six the last day. The lucky ones went sooner. I watched them go under. When they fished me out they thought I'd gone the same way as the others. But,' he grimaced, 'as you see, I made it.'

She was too shocked to say a word.

'Where does your buddy's wife live?'

'About sixty miles from here. Figure I'll be spending most of tomorrow hitch-hiking there and back.'

'I'll give you a lift. But it would have to be early. I have to be in town at two o'clock for work.'

Eric narrowed his eyes. 'Why would you do that?'

Bobby shrugged. 'Giving you a ride is no big deal.'

'You want to watch her pain?'

'I'm not a voyeur.'

'Then it's guilt. You won't be going to 'Nam yourself.'

'Do you want the ride or not?' Bobby countered.

'Hell, yes. I'm not too proud to take it and not dumb enough to turn you down. Pick me up here at seven.'

'I'll be here.'

'Bring your girlfriend, she talks real pretty.' Eric took another swig from the bottle in the brown paper bag before passing it to Bobby.

'No thanks,' Bobby refused. 'I have to drive in a couple of hours.'

CHAPTER TWENTY-SIX

Dawn had broken; the light was grey and clear when Penny and Bobby left the Beach House early the next morning and drove through the town. Assistants from the twenty-four-hour bars and restaurants were cleaning windows and clearing litter from outside their premises. Store workers were sweeping the sidewalks in front of their doors and hauling out their stands.

Eric was waiting for them. He dropped his bag into the back seat of the car, climbed over the side and sat beside it.

Bobby turned his head and said, 'Good morning, Eric.'

'Morning,' Eric growled, as taciturn as he'd been the night before.

'I'm happy to drive you but I'd like to know where we're going.'

Eric delved into the pocket of his jeans and produced a crumpled piece of paper. He handed it to Bobby.

Bobby looked at it. 'I know the town. Can you direct me from the centre?'

'Never been there. Gerry told me if you enter from the south side and head up Main Street towards the shopping mall, turn right at the mall and follow the road for five miles, you'll come to his house on the left. He said you can't miss it. It's the only house on that road for two miles and it's painted yellow.'

'Gerry gave you directions to his house while you were in Vietnam?' she asked in surprise.

'We talked about home.' Eric pulled his cap down even lower and closed his eyes, ending the conversation.

After they left the interstate, their progress was slow because they were frequently delayed by slow-moving agricultural vehicles. The directions Eric had given Bobby were good, but when they reached the house, she suspected Eric's buddy hadn't really looked at his home in years. The only evidence of yellow paint was in the shreds of faded colour under the eaves and the shards below the rotting window frames.

The house was massive, its clapboard walls weathered a dull grey. Three storeys high, the dozen windows at the front were hung with curtains so faded it was impossible to determine their original colour. All were laced with cobwebs. The building and barn behind it were marooned in an undulating sea of scrap metal. Abandoned cars, refrigerators with their doors removed, broken stoves, battered kitchen appliances and pieces of rusting agricultural machinery were piled high, spilling over on to what might have once been a drive.

A woman dressed in a calico overall was pegging washing, one-handed, on to a line while cradling a baby in the other. Her face was lined, her grey-streaked black hair tied back with twine. Two toddlers were playing in the dirt at her feet. She watched the car approach. As soon as Bobby parked in the road, Eric picked up his bag and climbed out of the back.

'Mrs Buckley? Mrs Gerry Buckley?'

She dropped the washing she was holding back into her basket and moved tentatively forward. 'You're Eric, Gerry's buddy from 'Nam.'

'Yes, ma'am.'

'Gerry sent me a photograph. There were six of you in a bar.'

'Gerry gave me a letter. He asked me to give it to you if anything happened to him.'

'And you brought it all this way. That is kind.' She remembered her manners and dropped the peg she was holding into her pocket. She wiped her free hand on her overall, shifted her baby and held out her right hand to Eric. He shook it.

'Bring your friends inside. I'll put coffee on.'

Bobby left the car and stretched. 'Pleased to meet you, Mrs Buckley. I'm Bobby, this is my friend Penny. We'd like to walk around for ten minutes or so after being cooped up driving.'

'We'll see you later, Bobby, Penny. Come on, kids, let's go in the house.' She pushed open the side door and revealed a room as chaotic as the yard, with dirty dishes heaped on every surface and trash scattered over the floor.

Bobby looked beyond the yard. 'Pretty country-side around here.'

'As long as you don't look in the direction of the cemetery.' She left the car and joined him.

'What cemetery?'

She pointed to the wall that ran alongside the side yard of the house. The head and wing tips of a marble angel were visible above a mountain of rusting ploughs.

'Let's go and read the epitaphs. There should be some good ones. Place like that should be at least a century old and a hundred years in America is equivalent to a thousand years in Europe.'

'And after you've completed your masters in Oxford you'll return here and start a course in medieval American history,' she joked.

'Now that's an idea I can take to my old Harvard professors. I even have an examination question. Compare the colonisation of the American West by white settlers to William the Conqueror's in-vasion of England.'

They walked to a gate set in the wall that separ-ated the cemetery from the road. Bobby opened it and they entered. The marble angel dominated what looked like the oldest part of the cemetery. It was laid out in large plots, each bearing the name of a single family. The most startling thing was how well kept the graves were, even the old ones. The stonework was scrubbed, although the letters carved on some of the monuments were too weather-worn to be decipherable.

A path separated the cemetery into two halves. At the back on the right, in a large area partitioned from the main part by a low hedge, identically sized tombstones were set out, twelve to a row. The ones at the front were white marble that glittered and gleamed in the sunlight, those behind them, weather-beaten stone. An old man was scrubbing a marble headstone halfway along the front row. He saw them, sat back on his heels and eyed them warily from beneath bushy grey eyebrows.

'You come to gawp?' he challenged as they drew close.

'No, sir,' Bobby replied.

'We've had nothing but goddamned reporters and news people here. Turning our boys' deaths and our grief into entertainment–'

'We're not reporters, sir,' Bobby broke in.

'Then you're pacifists, damn you to hell. Taking pictures of the graves. Making propaganda out of our boys' sacrifice–'

'We're not pacifists, sir. We're here to visit a local family. The Buckleys,' Penny interrupted.

'You are, are you?' The old man's eyes narrowed in suspicion.

'We've brought a friend of their son Gerry to visit them,' Bobby explained.

'Gerry Buckley Junior is dead.' The old man moved slightly so she and Bobby could read the name on the headstone. It was Gerry Buckley.

'We know, sir. Eric...' she faltered when she realised she didn't know Eric's surname. 'Eric served with Gerry in Vietnam.'

'Why didn't you say so earlier?' the old man snapped.

She was tempted to say because they hadn't been able to get a word in edgeways.

'These graves are beautifully kept, sir,' Bobby observed.

'Least a town can do is look after those who died for their country.' The old man indicated the back row of stones. 'Those are from the War of Independence, although the lettering on most is so worn you can't read the names. But they're all recorded in a book in the town library. In front of them are the graves of the boys who fell in the Mexican War. Then there are fifty boys from hereabouts who died in the Civil War. Most from the town that got killed in any war, until now, although some believe that number will be overtaken by those killed in 'Nam. After them come the boys who were killed in the Spanish American War, then there's those who made the ultimate sacrifice in the First and Second World Wars. Between those and the Vietnam dead are those who died in Korea. I've heard people say that wasn't a real war, although it felt like it to those who fought there. I can say that because I was one of them.' He struggled to rise but fell back on his knees.

Bobby extended his hand to help the old man up. The man checked his fingers were clean before taking Bobby's.

'There are twenty-two young men here who

291

died in Vietnam and there'll be four more head-stones by the end of the week. The first four belong to kids from the class of '64 who volunteered the day after they graduated from high school. There's not much in the way of work around here and the army promised them college scholarships. They were killed in '65. Alongside them are boys from the class of 1965. Five were killed in '66, three in '67 and two this year. Then there's the class of '66, eight killed so far, one of them Gerry. The four new headstones will be for boys from the class of '67. Gerry's commanding officer wrote Gerry's wife and said Gerry was officially posted missing presumed dead and there was no hope. She wouldn't believe it and didn't until Eric Moran wrote and said he'd watched Gerry drown in a paddy field along with the rest of Gerry's platoon. Pam had to give up hope then.'

'I'm so sorry, Mr Buckley.' The words sounded trite but she couldn't think of anything else to say.

'I'm Gerry Buckley senior, Gerry junior's father. I know he's not in that grave, but the town decided back during the War of Independence that every soldier in this parish who died fighting for his country deserved a grave, even if the body couldn't be shipped home. Town's seen no reason to change that decision since. Over half of the military graves here are empty but it gives folks somewhere to come and pay their respects and do their mourning.' He picked up his tin bucket and threw in the sponge and brush he'd been using to clean the graves.

'See that grave over there,' he pointed to a freshly dug mound covered with flowers. 'That's my Mayleen, Gerry junior's Mom. She died last week. Doctor said it was pneumonia but Pam and me know different. Gerry was our only boy, and after we had the news from Eric that he'd gone she gave up. Simply didn't want to live anymore. Not even for Gerry's babies. We had two girls as well as Gerry but they couldn't wait to get out of here. They're somewhere in New York. Hardly bothered to visit after they left; now Mayleen's gone don't suppose I'll see hide or hair of them again. Gerry's passing's been hard on all of us. But it's hardest on Pam. Girl her age shouldn't be shut up here with an old man and three babies. She should be out enjoying herself.'

'How old is Pam?' she asked.

'Nineteen last birthday.'

She was shocked. She'd assumed Pam Buckley was at least forty.

'Pam and Gerry were childhood sweethearts. They married after Gerry received his draft papers. Mayleen and me tried to talk them out of it but you know what kids are. What am I saying? You two are kids.'

'We promised Pam we'd be back for coffee in ten minutes,' Bobby reminded her. 'It must be more than that now.'

'I'll walk with you.' The old man led the way to the gate. He opened it, watched them walk through, then leant on it for a moment.

'The military graves are beautifully kept.' Bobby looked back at the section.

'As I said, the least a town can do is look after

the last resting place of its heroes,' the old man said gruffly.

Eric was sitting on a rough wooden bench outside the kitchen door, holding the baby. The other two small children were sitting at his feet, grubby fingers in mouths, staring up at him.

'Any good with kids?' Eric didn't wait for Penny to answer. He thrust the baby into her arms as soon as she and Bobby joined him.

'I've had some practice with my nieces and nephews.' She sat down and settled the baby into the crook of her arm. 'What's his name?'

'Mayleen. It's a girl.' Pam carried four mugs out of the kitchen. 'Never got round to buying girls' clothes. Seemed a waste with the boys' things going begging. Besides, even without a father, with two older brothers she's bound to grow up a tomboy.' She handed out the mugs, giving the last one to Gerry. 'Here you are, Dad, I'll get another for myself.'

Despite the warmth and sunshine the day took on a grey tinge. The tragedy of Gerry's early death cast a long shadow and Penny was grateful when Eric left the bench and picked up his bag.

'We have to leave if we're going to get back to the Cape in time for you and Penny to work your shift.'

Pam took the baby from her. 'Thank you for coming, Eric. I appreciate it.'

'It was good of you to spend time with us that you could have given to your folks,' Gerry senior allowed.

'I could spare it. They gave me a month's leave.

Gerry and me were closer than brothers. But that's what it's like in 'Nam. Everyone looks out for his buddies. It's what we fight for.'

'Where are your family?' Gerry walked with them as they picked their way through the scrap to the road.

'Boston. But I'm heading for Mexico City. My girlfriend's a nurse there.' Eric turned left at the road. 'I'll pay my respects, Bobby. See you at the car in a couple of minutes.'

Penny turned to Pam. She wanted to give her something that would give her hope for the future but she couldn't think of a single thing to say. As for practical help, she had little money and she sensed Gerry and Pamela would regard it as an insult if she gave them any. She opened her purse and took out three of the Kennedy half dollars she'd been collecting to give to her own nieces and nephews as souvenirs of her trip. She handed them to the oldest boy. 'For your money box.'

He looked up at his mother. 'Can I, Mom?'

Pamela nodded. 'What do you say?'

'Thank you, lady,' he murmured shyly.

'Sorry we had to meet like this.' She kissed Pam's cheek.

'Thank you for bringing Eric.'

'If we hadn't he would have hitch-hiked.' Bobby opened the car door.

'Way out here, it would have taken him a long time.' Gerry senior waved his hand and returned up the drive. 'You take care,' he shouted before disappearing into the house.

Penny and Bobby sat in the car. Pam returned to her washing basket and continued to peg clothes on the line.

'Strange when you think of all those empty graves and people shedding tears over them,' Bobby commented. 'I wouldn't want anyone crying over an empty grave for me.'

'I can understand people wanting one if that's all they have to remember someone by.'

'I wouldn't want to be remembered as a headstone on an empty plot.'

'How would you want to be remembered?' she asked.

He forced a smile that didn't quite reach his eyes. 'If my grandmother had her way she'd name a medieval museum after me. But only because my name is the same as my grandfather's.'

'The Bobby Brosna the Fourth museum of medieval American West history.'

'That joke's wearing thin but yes. Complete with life-size Bobby Brosna bust in the foyer.'

'Very grand.'

'Grand, maybe, but it doesn't alter the fact that when you're dead, you're dead. That's it, nothing left except rotting meat. And that's what Gerry Buckley junior is. Meat rotting in a Vietnam paddy field for all that he has a headstone.'

'There is something left of Gerry,' she contradicted. 'His children, wife and his father.'

'Living sad lives. Those kids will be blighted by their father's death.'

'You'd rather Gerry Buckley was forgotten?'

'I didn't know Gerry Buckley and I have no idea what he'd want. But the last thing I'd want after my death is to make people unhappy. That's why I don't want to get too close to anyone.

Sentiment interferes with living.'

His words hurt. She knew he was aware how much. But she also knew him well enough not to try to change his mind by trying to argue with him.

He loved her now and that had to be enough.

CHAPTER TWENTY-SEVEN

Eric returned to the car and climbed into the back. 'Thanks for the ride. Can you drop me off at the interstate?'

'We can take you back to the Cape,' Bobby offered.

'I've decided to fly to Mexico City a day early and surprise my girl.'

'But your ticket—'

'Haven't bought one yet. Bound to be some freight heading for Boston airport from the freeway. I'll hitchhike.'

She glanced at Eric's face as he sat in the back. His lips were tight, compressed. His fists clenched. She couldn't see his eyes. His baseball cap was pulled too low. The atmosphere was tense and she sensed that now Eric had fulfilled his buddy's request he couldn't wait to be rid of them.

'It's your choice.' Bobby accelerated to overtake a hay waggon.

'You got to get back for your shift anyway.'

'We can spare a couple of hours to take you to the airport.'

'No!' Eric's reply was terse. Finite.

'Have it your way.'

Bobby pulled in on the approach road to the interstate. Eric picked up his bag and climbed out. 'Thanks for the ride.'

'My pleasure,' Bobby said, automatically resorting to the manners that had been drilled into him during childhood.

'But it wasn't, was it?'

Bobby looked at Eric.

'A pleasure. Not for you, Penny, me, Pam, Gerry Buckley or Gerry Junior. Be seeing you.' He grabbed his bag and ran.

Pontypridd, May 1987

Penny moved restlessly from the desk. Clouds had darkened the sky, greying the atmosphere. The day was threatening to end in rain. She checked the time. Three o'clock on a dismal afternoon in May in Pontypridd. But mentally she still remained in that burning hot Cape Cod summer of 1968.

The visit to the Buckleys had been a watershed for Bobby, although she hadn't realised it at the time and she doubted he had. It was the closest either of them had come to the tragedy that was Vietnam.

Even then, she couldn't imagine anything further from the experience in Grosvenor Square where the anti-war rally had, for so many, like the girl who'd gone out of her way to antagonise the police, been little more than an excuse to flout authority. She'd wanted to join the protest because of her pacifist ideals, but she hadn't really given any thought to the effect the war was having on the conscripts who had no choice but to obey orders and fight.

The sombre atmosphere generated by the grief that had so devastated Gerry Buckley's family hadn't carried over into the subsequent weeks, or if it had, she'd been too in love with Bobby to be aware of it. But with hindsight, she could see that the knowledge of one conscript's life and tragic death had lurked in the shadows waiting to resurface as it had done that final fatal night.

And in between the visit to the Buckleys and that last night? The restaurant had been incredibly busy. She, Kate, Sandy and Bobby barely had time to take a deep breath in between serving and cooking for customers. It was hardly surprising that tempers had frayed.

Cape Cod, July 1968

'Outside catering job. Hyannisport Yacht Club. Six o'clock. I need seven more waitresses urgently. Anyone know where I can find them?' Cosmo glanced up from the counter where he was scribbling notes and looked directly at Penny and Kate.

'We're strangers here, remember,' Kate said.

'You girls go out, meet people. I saw you with that Southern girl who works in Ho Jo's in the Melody Tent.'

'Exactly, she works in Ho Jo's,' Penny answered.

'There's Mary,' Sandy answered from behind

299

the short-order counter. 'She only works mornings in the motel.'

'Great, that's one. Call her, Sandy.'

'She's Native American.'

'Then don't call her,' Cosmo continued writing.

'What?'

Penny and Kate stared at Cosmo in disbelief.

'Welcome to America, land of the free except for the natives. They have to stay locked up on reservations as if they're zoo animals.' Betty bustled past with a double order of franks and beans.

'You're not serious?' she challenged Cosmo.

'It's the yacht club. You can't get a more conservative place.'

'All the more reason to employ her. She's stunning,' Kate argued.

'No.'

Betty intervened. 'I have friends–'

'I know your friends, Betty, and the answer's no,' Cosmo said firmly.

'Why don't you come right out and say it, Cosmo? You only want pretty white girls like Penny and Kate to serve the stuck-up snobs in the yacht club.'

'I want experienced waitresses who know how to serve food with a smile and be a credit to my establishment.'

'You saying I don't?' Betty challenged.

'You've a big mouth on you, Betty.'

'I've put up with as much as I can take from you, Cosmo. You ... you bastard...' Betty tore off her apron, flung it at Cosmo and stormed out. A hush descended over the restaurant.

Cosmo continued to sit at the counter adding to his notes. After a minute the customers gradually began to speak to one another again. Penny picked up her order and served four police officers spaghetti with meat sauce.

An hour later Cosmo went into the kitchen and checked the yacht club's menu with the chefs. Then he left. When he returned, he had Betty in tow.

'You came back?' Kate said incredulously.

Betty shrugged. 'Cosmo and I yell at one another all the time. Phone your friend Mary and offer her the job. Cosmo pays two bucks an hour for outside catering and much as I hate the old farts in the yacht club they tip well.'

Penny and Kate came to prefer the outside catering jobs to working in the restaurant. The smaller jobs in people's homes were serviced by just the two of them and a chef. The larger, club catering jobs warranted two chefs and they were usually joined by two Southern waitresses, who resented them because, as one of the girls put it, 'Your British accents have killed our Southern ones dead.'

They served ex-servicemen at the motor yacht club, where two men, so old and decrepit they appeared to be in imminent danger of collapse, had insisted on taking her and Kate out in their speedboats and racing against one another. Kate's old codger won. There'd been catering jobs and drops at the Kennedy compound, where journalists, cameramen and television news companies had erected lights on the lawn while waiting

301

impatiently and hopefully for an announcement from the one remaining Kennedy brother, Edward.

Every Democrat in America, including Bobby Brosna, wanted him to take over his brother's campaign and run for president.

Outside of work, there'd been deliciously happy times. Late nights, or rather early mornings, after their shifts in the restaurant spent in the garden of the Beach House or Joe and Marion's; groups of them singing to the accompaniment of Sandy and Bobby's guitars while drinking more cheap wine and beer than was good for them. Lazy mornings spent in bed with Bobby, followed by an hour or two swimming and lazing on the private Brosna Beach before their shifts.

Days off were spent exploring the Cape: road trips to Provincetown and places with English names – Truro, South Yarmouth, North Falmouth, Sandwich, Chatham, Harwich ... unforgettable concerts in the Melody Tent – Joan Baez, Bob Dylan, The Doors...

And, best of all, sailing trips with George, Marion, Joe, Paul and Mary on board the *Day Dream*.

'There she is, folks. The *Day Dream*.' Bobby couldn't have been prouder if he'd built her himself.

'She's beautiful,' Marion sighed enviously. 'Why don't you own something like that?' she berated Joe.

'Because I'm not a multimillionaire. She's really yours?' Joe asked Bobby.

'A family possession. Commissioned by my

302

great-grandfather.'

'And the first time she's been out of dry dock and in the water for ten years,' George chipped in. 'My father said it was a waste. He'd be real pleased to see her now, all gleaming, shipshape and ready to go. Want to see if she can still out-race everything around here?'

'You as good a sailor as your father?' Bobby teased.

'No one was as good as him, but even if I have to say it myself, I know my way around a deck.'

'Let's go before we miss the best part of the day.' Sandy picked up one of the baskets of food they'd packed. Paul took a box of wine.

'If only people in Ponty could see us now.' Penny carried a bundle of towels on board.

'You thinking of Rich?' Kate followed with a bag of suntan creams and oils.

'I'm thinking of the girls in school. It's like we've landed on a Hollywood film set.'

'Or fallen into a dream.' Marion joined them with Mary.

'George, Sandy and I'll take her out.' Bobby went to the tiller.

'Sailing lessons will be given to anyone who's interested when we reach open water,' George offered.

'After working six days straight, the only lesson I intend to take is in sunbathing.' Kate looked around. 'We won't be in the way here, will we?' she called to Bobby as she headed for a spot near the rail.

'No, but you might get wet when we're under way.'

'Good, it'll cool me down.' Kate spread a towel and lay face down before slipping her bikini straps from her shoulders. 'No marks,' she explained to Mary and Marion.

Marion handed the bag she'd brought on board to Joe. 'The wine should go in the cabin. It's hot out here.'

'There's an icebox in the galley,' George advised.

'When you've done stowing everything away, Joe, can you and Paul give us a hand with the sails?' Sandy shouted from the other side of the deck.

Penny sat next to Kate. 'I can't believe all of us have managed to get the same day off.'

'Sundays are generally quiet in the restaurant. People have either packed and gone home or are still travelling and haven't arrived.' Marion stripped off her shirt and lay next to Kate.

'This is absolute bliss.' Kate closed her eyes. 'Sea lapping, gulls crying, warm sun on my back, the smell of salt in the air. No customers screaming their food is late, no children howling because they don't like their parents' choice of a meal. No ugly spotty boys saying, "Gee, you're a Brit. Come out for a drink with me when you get off shift?" And best of all, no smell of burgers and fries.'

'You want to work with difficult customers and an impossible boss, try my place,' Marion said.

'What's it like in the motel, Mary?' Penny asked. Mary was diffident and self-effacing to the point where it was easy to forget she was sitting with them.

'Good. The owners are kind and the work's not

too bad unless teenagers are in. They can be messy, especially in the bathrooms.'

'Do you realise we're moving?' Kate called out.

They all turned and watched the coastline receding behind them.

'It feels like we're flying over water.' Penny moved away from the side to avoid the spray.

'Wine anyone?' Marion asked.

'Coffee maybe,' Penny amended. 'Eight o'clock is a little early for me.'

'Me too,' Kate added. 'I'm not awake yet.'

Bobby appeared. 'George has taken over the tiller, want a tour?'

'Is that a general invitation, or one just meant for Penny?' Kate winked at Marion and Mary.

'All of you. You need to know where the bathroom and heads are, and the kitchen. On board men sail, women make food.'

Kate almost flung a sandal at him until she remembered she'd slipped down the straps of her bikini.

The yacht was crafted out of oak. The living area was sumptuous, with three sofas, unfortunately bare bookshelves, a desk and table. The galley was beautifully fitted, the crockery porcelain, the cutlery silver and glasses crystal. The three staterooms had double beds and there was an amazing amount of closet space.

George joined them as Bobby showed them around.

'Everything's been cleaned, Mr Bobby, right down to the knives and forks. The shipyard asked my permission to throw the books. They were mildewed.'

'Adventure books?' Bobby asked.

'The best – *Rob Roy*, *Treasure Island*...'

'My family's taste in literature was never high-brow,' Bobby explained. 'There you have it, girls. Three staterooms, two showers, two heads; we'll drop anchor soon and go swimming.'

'And the staterooms?' Kate asked.

'Are yours for the day.' Bobby raised his eye-brows. 'All except this one.' He opened the door to the largest. 'This is mine and Pen's and I'm about to get changed.' He stepped in and pulled Penny in after him before catching the back of the door with his heel and closing it.

The girls' giggles echoed through the walls.

'That was ill mannered of you,' she reproached.

'Much as I enjoy the company of our friends I enjoy yours more, and with both of us working eight hours a day there never seems to be enough time to–'

'Make love.'

'I was going to suggest, to get to know you properly. I'm tired.' He flung himself on the bed. 'Do you realise we went to bed at five this morn-ing and were up two hours later?'

'We have all afternoon to sleep.'

'You want to swim?'

'Absolutely.'

'Pen, come down here, just for a minute...'

She left the stateroom before he had time to get off the bed. George had dropped anchor. He was sitting on the deck eating one of the hot dogs Mary and Paul had prepared. Sandy and Kate were already in the water. She stripped off her shirt and shorts, climbed over the rail and dived in.

Before she'd surfaced Bobby was alongside her.

CHAPTER TWENTY-EIGHT

Pontypridd, 1987

The sensation of swimming in a warm sea with Bobby was so real – so acute – she felt his fingers caress her breasts, his legs brush against hers, the sting of the salt sea on her skin.

'If only'.. The saddest two words in the English language. If only she could reach out and tear down the veil that separated the present from the past and return to that time ... and Bobby.

The clock chimed her back into the present. But her yearning for Bobby remained; an intense physical desire that neither time nor distance had diminished.

She looked out of the window. The threatened rain was finally falling, dense and heavy. She had never felt more alone. The house she loved was suddenly oppressive. She had to get out, talk to someone. The last people she wanted to burden were her parents. They had helped her through so many traumas already.

But there was always Jack. He'd provided the shoulder she'd cried on for the last twelve years. She'd treated him badly earlier. Spurning his offer to take her away for a few days break, even when she knew he'd put time and effort into organising the surprise.

She went into the hall, opened the cupboard and took out her boots and raincoat. It was barely a mile from her house to Jack's farmhouse but walking it in this weather would be a muddy and wet experience.

She locked her front door and, despite the weather, passed her car. She wanted to feel the rain on her face and breathe in cold fresh air. She walked quickly up the road and turned on to the track that led to the farm. The view from the approach to the farmhouse was usually spectacular with the wooded valley spread out below like a living map. It was rumoured that the old oaks, beech, sycamore and elm trees that grew around the small lake on the valley floor were the last remnants of the ancient forest that had once covered Wales. But all she could see of the woods in the downpour were the tops of the trees. Mist lay thick and deep, obscuring the surface of the water and the undergrowth around it.

The rain was so heavy it soaked through her coat in minutes. Her hair was plastered close to her head and she could feel cold droplets dripping down inside her collar.

Jack's two sheepdogs came bounding out of the barn as soon as they saw her. Not wanting to get covered in mud she shouted sharply to them and they retreated, tails between their legs.

She knocked on the kitchen door before opening it. A welcoming warm belched out from the range that was kept alight day and night and there was a pleasant smell of cooking. Disappointed at her refusal to accompany him on a trip, Jack had already prepared his evening meal.

She pulled her muddy boots off, stood them on newspaper and hung her dripping raincoat on a hook on the back of the door. Padding across the flagstone floor in her socks, she opened the door to the range and looked inside. There was a huge cottage pie, enough to feed Jack for two or even three days.

She walked through the inner door to the passage that led to the dining and living rooms. Both had been freshly vacuumed and the old oak furniture smelt of beeswax polish. Jack rarely used either room. The little time he remained indoors was spent in the kitchen. He'd even moved his desk, bookshelves, books, TV and music centre in there when he'd taken over the farm after his grandfather's death.

She went to the foot of the stairs and called out, 'Jack?'

An answering shout came from the attic. She walked up the stairs past the four bedroom doors to the narrow staircase that led to the top floor of the house.

'Whatever are you doing up there?'

'Checking for leaks.'

'You've just had the house re-roofed.'

'That's why I'm checking.'

She joined him and looked around at the dust-covered, mildewed, old trunks, packing cases, wooden chests and mounds of broken furniture that had been deemed 'too good to be thrown out'.

'Your grandfather wasn't one for throwing things

309

away, was he?'

'Nor his grandfather and probably all my fore-fathers back to the eighteenth century, when one of them built this place. I've been meaning to clear this rubbish out and put electricity on this floor since I moved in. Fifteen years and I haven't found the time.'

'Perhaps you never wanted to.'

'Possibly because I was afraid of what I might find. My father wasn't exactly a charmer and he must have got his personality from someone. There could be papers among this lot that prove my suspicions that my ancestors were evil.'

'I could help you make a start now?' she offered.

'No thanks. I haven't the energy to tackle the job and you didn't come here to muck out my family's rubbish.'

'I don't mind, really.'

'The answer's still no. You look pale. Are you all right?'

'Absolutely fine.'

'You're soaked through.' He felt the collar of her sweater. 'Don't tell me you walked over in this.'

'I wanted fresh air.'

'Come downstairs, I'll find you a towel and dry clothes.'

'Please don't fuss.'

'That's not fussing, it's saving you from pneumonia and me the trouble of driving you to East Glamorgan Hospital.' He led the way down the stairs, went into his bedroom, took a clean sweater from his wardrobe, a towel from his en suite bathroom and handed them to her. 'Want coffee?'

'Please. I'm sorry I was so foul to you this morning.'

'You had a shock. I'll get over it. After all, it's not the first time you've turned down one of my offers. I'll make the coffee. Dry your hair, before you change. It's dripping down your back.'

With her hair wrapped in a towel, and wearing his clothes, she followed him downstairs. She watched for a moment from the doorway of the kitchen as he filled the kettle and put it on the range to boil, just as his forefathers had done for generations.

Jack had made a few changes and concessions to modernity when he had moved into the house. With his large circle of friends and four godchildren in mind, he'd installed en suite bathrooms in each of the four bedrooms. But apart from a new and more efficient range, and laying new flagstones, the kitchen remained untouched. His family had probably been boiling kettles on ranges similar to the present one for centuries and he'd seen no reason to replace the enormous oak Welsh dresser, 'stand-alone' cupboards and scrubdown table with modern fitted units and worktop simply to accommodate modern gadgets like electric kettles and toasters.

He took two mugs and a tin of ground coffee from the dresser. 'Have you made any decisions about Andy and America?'

'No. It wasn't for the want of trying. I started remembering.'

'I know it's none of my business but I have to ask. Did you love Bobby Brosna? Or were you on the rebound from Rich when you met him?'

311

'Definitely not on the rebound. Rich and I were over before I climbed on to the bus that took us to the airport.' Still cold, she moved nearer the stove. 'Rich and I were a huge mistake. I only have to look at what he's become to realise that.'

He smiled. 'A clone of our father.'

'He and Judy seem happy enough,' she murmured absently.

'When she's not threatening to divorce him,' Jack said dryly.

'About Bobby. When I met him I realised I'd gone out for years with your brother out of habit. Looking back, I think I stayed with Rich so long because he was the first boy I'd slept with and I was in love with the fairy tale of being in love.'

'And Bobby?'

'If he'd told me to walk on hot coals I would have done it if I thought it would please him. I was besotted. Gone ... hopeless. All I wanted was him to be happy.'

'Did he love you?'

She hesitated.

'I'm sorry. I had no right to ask.'

'You have more right than anyone else to ask, Jack. Yes, Bobby loved me. As much as he was capable of loving anyone.'

Bobby's voice echoed through her mind. *'I love you now, isn't that enough?'* If he'd been in the room with them, she would have screamed, 'No, it was never enough!'

'Would it help to talk about Bobby?' When she didn't answer, he added, 'I'd be happy to listen if it would. But if you don't want to talk, I'd be just as happy to sit in companionable silence.'

"Companionable silence",' she reiterated. 'You make it sound as though we're in our dotage.'

He raised his eyebrows. 'We're not getting any younger.'

'No, we're not,' she agreed automatically without thinking what she was saying. Her eyes grew dark as long-suppressed memories surfaced. 'Goddamn it! I wish I could forget the past – and Bobby Brosna.'

He allowed the Americanism to pass without comment. 'Given the letter you received this morning, that's impossible.'

'It's unfair that Andy has to pay for our mistakes.'

'"Our mistakes"?' he repeated. 'Yours and Bobby's?'

'Andy being here may be down to my carelessness but he's the best thing that ever happened to me,' she insisted fiercely. 'But now he has to face up to the mess caused by mine and Bobby's faults. It's so unfair on him.' She bit her lip. 'We were so stupid.'

'You loved Bobby, you were besotted with him, yet you were realistic enough to know he had faults?' He looked surprised.

She sat in one of the armchairs placed either side of the range. 'Bobby could be imperious, demanding, egotistical, self-centred, wilful, and because of his upbringing, with nannies and boarding schools, emotionally cold. The only constants in his life before me were his friend Sandy and grandmother, Charlotte, and he rarely saw Charlotte more than twice a year and then only for a few hours.'

'Poor little rich kid.'

'Bobby lived the cliché. Charlotte did her damnedest to separate him from Sandy when they reached college age.' She looked across at Jack. 'That summer was wonderful but Bobby was far from perfect. When it ended, I couldn't even talk to my parents about what had happened. Just after my physical injuries healed, I discovered I was pregnant. I insisted on finishing my college course because I didn't want to leave myself any time to think about what had happened. And after Andy was born there was no more time to think. I put Bobby Brosna out of my mind for nineteen years and I resent being forced to think about him now. But most of all I resent the Brosnas interfering in Andy's and my life.'

'Some people would welcome the interference if it meant inheriting a fortune.' The water began to boil. Jack spooned ground coffee into a percolator, filled it and left it on a hotplate while he fetched milk from the fridge, and sugar. He poured the coffee and handed her a cup, the way she liked it, black with no sugar. Taking his own mug he returned to his seat opposite hers.

She looked at him. 'Bobby was the second man I made love to. Your brother was the first. You were the third and last...'

'Penny, I've never asked you any personal questions about your love life because I have no right to. I love you. Your past doesn't concern me and frankly is none of my business.'

'Kate used to say my morality was out of the dark ages. It probably goes back to my upbringing, not that either of my parents ever looked down on

314

unmarried mothers. In fact, my mother told me once that she was pregnant before she married.'

'You're kidding.'

'No.'

'But your parents –'

'Weren't always upright members of the community. I've thought a great deal about the Sixties. Kate used to say the pill emancipated women. That, for the first time in history, we could behave the way that men had for centuries and sleep around with a different boy every night if we chose to. I don't think it was like that for most girls. I believe we were simply the first generation of women to sleep openly outside of marriage with our boyfriends. What worries me about Andrew is most girls now seem to think no more of having full sex with a boy they've just met and moving on to another than we did of exchanging kisses with boys when I was young.'

'You sound a hundred and ten years old,' he teased.

'There are days when I feel a hundred and ten.'

'Promise me you won't lecture Andy about girls. You brought him up to think for himself. He's a sensible lad. He'll make the right choices.'

'I wish I was as convinced as you.'

'You're worried he'll make the same mistakes you did?' he asked perceptively.

'In what way?'

'I know you, Pen. You wouldn't have slept with Bobby if you thought he wasn't serious about you.'

'I admit, I didn't know Bobby well in the early stages of our relationship – that came later – but

I knew I loved him and I knew he cared for me. I didn't love him any the less later, when I discovered his faults. If anything I loved him more because of them. He'd been given everything money could buy except love and affection. If I excused his shortcomings, it was because of the things he confided about his childhood. What I'm not sure is how much I should tell Andy.'

'In what way?'

'If I tell him about Bobby and me, will it encourage him to be as wild as his father was? If he accepts the inheritance, he'll have enough money to do whatever he wants. Will it go to his head?'

'No one can answer those questions, Pen,' he said seriously.

'You know how everyone has one special summer in their life. Well, for me, until it ended in the car crash, it was that one. We had to work hard but we played hard too, and we had the Brosna toys.'

'Toys?' he was bemused.

'The Brosna Estate; it had a mansion that we dared not go near, twelve guest houses the caretaker, George, filled with homeless people, a two-bedroomed Beach House where Bobby, Sandy, Kate and me lived. There was the largest swimming pool I'd ever seen. George kept it immaculate. And we had the Brosna private beach and the Brosna yacht, *Day Dream*. For the first month we lived there, Bobby, Sandy, Kate and me used to wangle the same day off and go sailing or driving around the Cape together. Then Cosmo – he owned the restaurant we worked in – said the schedules wouldn't allow it. Cosmo was lying;

Bobby told me afterwards that he'd asked Cosmo to give us a different day off to Sandy and Kate so we could be alone. The night before our day off we used to drop Kate and Sandy off at the Beach House and drive on to the marina and the yacht. We'd sleep on board and sail out in the morning. Just far enough to be away from everyone and everything. It was as though we were the only two people in the world.'

She looked inward to that time and her younger self. 'I loved the friendships we made that summer. I loved the new experiences. The cookouts, the parties, the visits to the Melody Tent to hear musicians I'd only heard on radio, but most of all I loved the times when it was only Bobby, me and the sea.'

'When I fell in love with you I knew I was up against a ghost. But I didn't know he was still alive.' He asked the question she hadn't answered in nineteen years. 'What happened to end it, Penny?'

CHAPTER TWENTY-NINE

Penny sat back and stared at the flames flickering around the coals in the fire set in the range while Jack waited patiently for her to continue.

'Kate and I saved a fair sum of money that summer.' The commonplace opening revealed she was bracing herself for what was to come. 'We had no rent to pay and Cosmo was generous with his leftovers. Sometimes he gave us burgers and franks to take back to the Beach House or down to Marion and Joe's. Not just enough for us, but for twenty – thirty people. A few nights he even insisted he had spare lobsters. We didn't believe him but we took them.'

'So you didn't starve.' It was a banal comment but she'd fallen silent again.

'No.' She looked across at him before turning back to the fire. 'Then, Kate and I realised we had barely two weeks left before our return flight home. For all my talk of wanting to see the galleries and museums in New York and Boston, I'd only been to two in Boston. Bobby had driven me there on one of our days off. It made me all the more determined to spend my last week sightseeing in New York.

'Bobby made a couple of calls and arranged to borrow an apartment from a friend in the Village who'd be away for our last week in the States. Sandy and Kate decided to go with us and we told Cosmo we were quitting.

'Cosmo didn't mind; the season was winding down and there were times when Kate and I could actually sit at the counter for ten minutes at a time instead of scurrying around like demented ants. Three days before we were due to leave the Cape, we went to work and from there on to Marion and Joe's for a party. We didn't get back to the Beach House until dawn. And, when we did, every light was on in the main house.'

'Charlotte Brosna?' Jack guessed.

'Bobby had been optimistic about laying a false trail in Wisconsin. I found out later that Charlotte knew exactly where he was the day we reached the Cape. She'd paid people to watch him – and us.'

'Who told her?'

She shrugged. 'Possibly one of the "snoops" Bobby had referred to. The people she'd hired to report his movements to her when he'd been younger. When I was in the hospital after the accident I heard rumours that it was a local solicitor hoping for Brosna business. Someone else suggested it could have been one of the homeless people George had housed. I never tried to find out.'

'You're very forgiving.'

'More forgiving to whoever sold us out than I was to Charlotte Brosna. Presumably they desperately needed Charlotte's money and were prepared to do whatever it took to get it. I suspect Charlotte simply enjoyed interfering in people's lives because it gave her pleasure to exercise the power she wielded.' She set her empty cup on the floor beside her chair. 'Bobby saw the lights on in the main house, turned his back on them and went into the Beach House. George was waiting for us in the living room.

'He said, "Your grandmother's back, Mr Bobby, and there's hell to pay. Everyone's been ordered to leave the guest houses by midday."

'Bobby's first thought was for George. "You?" he asked.

'George replied that he'd been "let go." A horrible American expression. At least the English, "you're fired" is honest.

'Bobby was furious. George's father and grandfather had worked for the Brosnas. If anyone had a right to expect lifetime employment, it was George junior. But George took his dismissal better than Bobby. Charlotte had offered George a thousand dollars if he went quietly. A lot of money now, but even more in 1968. George told Bobby he couldn't afford to turn it down and he'd soon find himself another job.

'Bobby knew the likelihood of George finding a job that paid as much or came with halfway decent accommodation was slim, but George was insistent that he would be fine and Bobby should worry about himself. But George, like Sandy, knew all about Bobby's fraught relationship with his grandmother.

'George's parting shot as he left the Beach House to pack was that Charlotte wanted to see Bobby "right away."

'Bobby's response was his grandmother could damn well wait.

'George turned back and advised caution, but Bobby was in no mood to take advice. Sandy offered to accompany Bobby to the main house. Bobby refused and stormed out without looking at me, Kate or Sandy.

'Sandy tried to be philosophical. He kissed Kate and said, "It was great while it lasted. Sorry the summer had to end, sweetheart, but in my experience they always do."

'Like Sandy, Kate tried to make light of the situation; she announced she was going to pack and went into the bedroom she'd shared with Sandy. Sandy called after her and asked her to pack his things too.

'I tried to be practical and suggested that if we had to get out by midday we'd better get motel rooms for the next couple of days.

'Sandy said he'd borrow George's bike after breakfast and return to Marion and Joe's house to see if there were any empty rooms. Quite a few people had already left the Cape to spend the final days of the holidays with their families. And we only needed a place for a couple more nights.

'I couldn't bear the thought of staying on for any length of time and asked Sandy if he thought Cosmo would allow us to leave earlier than we'd arranged. Sandy said he'd talk to him, but even as we discussed it, I wasn't thinking of galleries and museums. Only Bobby. Every minute that passed seemed like a week, and I thought it unlikely he'd return to the Beach House. I assumed the grand-mother he'd spoken of so often, and never fondly, would send one of her minions to collect Bobby's things and order us out of the Beach House. And that, as Sandy had said, would be the end of the summer – and Bobby and me.'

She sat back in the chair but didn't look at Jack.

'We were close to the main house but didn't have a clue what was happening there and not one of us dared knock on the door. Now it seems ridiculous that three young people well able to take care of themselves were frightened of a cantankerous selfish old woman.'

'A rich powerful old woman who had total control over a grandson you all loved,' Jack reminded. 'Wealth brings power and I doubt many people ever stood up to Charlotte Brosna.'

She thought of Andy and how Charlotte had

tried to take him from her.

'So what happened then?' Jack prompted.

'Sandy made coffee and breakfast although I don't think any of us ate anything. After he washed the dishes, Sandy opened the front door. Shadows were moving in front of one of the windows in an upstairs room. But we were too far away to hear anything. There were so many questions I'd wanted to ask Bobby and never had. I couldn't wait any longer and I asked Sandy why Bobby was so frightened of his grandmother.

'His answer was short and to the point. "Because she's controlled his life since the day he was born and she has all the money."

'I tried arguing with Sandy that there had to be more. We'd lived all summer on our earnings from the restaurant, which were good but not as much as Kate and I could expect to earn once we'd qualified. And we'd lived well. When Sandy pointed out that we hadn't had to pay rent or service charges I reminded him that we'd saved more than enough to cover those expenses and had intended to travel to New York on it.

'That's when he said that I had no idea what it was like living with the kind of money the Brosnas had. What it was to have a limo at your disposal, twenty-four hours, seven days a week, and all the yachts, cars, houses and luxuries money could buy.

'I asked him if he thought Bobby would give up his lifestyle for me. It was only after I asked the question I realised Bobby had already given me his answer. He'd never made me any promises about a future together.'

'*I love you now, isn't that enough?*' She didn't repeat the words to Jack; some things were too personal, even for him. But Bobby's voice echoed through her mind.

'Sandy was honest, disconcertingly so. He didn't answer my question because he said there was no point in him telling me what I already knew. He said he was sorry, sorry about the way the summer had ended. Sorry to be leaving Kate and me, but, most of all, sorry to be losing his freedom and having to ship out to Vietnam.

'He also tried to console me by telling me it was easier on him and Kate and even Bobby, than it was on me because all three of them had accepted there would only be the one summer for us from the beginning.

'I said the first thing that came into my head, "You don't think Bobby loves me?"

'Sandy gave me an answer I didn't want to hear. He reminded me that he'd known Bobby all his life and assured me, honestly and sincerely that as far as he could tell, Bobby loved me as much as he was capable of loving anyone. Before he left he suggested that if I wanted to know any more about Bobby or Bobby's thoughts I should ask Bobby, not him.

'I went into the bedroom I'd shared with Bobby, packed my things and tidied up Bobby's clothes. I showered and changed into a clean shirt and jeans. When I'd done all I could, I knocked on the door of Kate and Sandy's room. Kate was lying dressed on the bed. Her own and Sandy's bags and her haggis were packed on the floor beside her.

323

'She looked at me and said, "We can't do anything until Sandy gets back so we may as well sleep."

'I lay beside her. Two hours later Sandy returned. He told us two rooms would be vacant in Marion and Joe's house from four o'clock that afternoon and he'd taken them for the night. He also warned us that the landlady was a stickler for propriety and he'd taken one room for himself and another for Kate and me.

'The landlady must have either never gone near the place or been blind because everyone in that house was sharing a room with a girl or boyfriend. Joe and Marion had also agreed we could drop our cases into their room before we worked our shift.

'Sandy had returned George's bike and suggested we call a cab. There was no sign of Bobby and we could hardly take his car without his permission. The homeless people had started moving out of the guest houses at eight. Most, including Mary and Paul, called in the Beach House to say goodbye on their way.

'Not one of the three of us had the courage to ask them, or George, where they were going. The cab came at midday and Sandy was helping the driver load our bags into it when Bobby finally emerged from the main house. He grabbed my arm, took me to one side and asked me to stay.

'At first I said I couldn't. That we were moving our things into Marion and Joe's place and we had to work.

'Sandy reminded him we owed Cosmo and couldn't let him down. Not after he'd given us jobs when we'd needed them. Bobby continued to plead with me and my resistance crumbled.

'I handed my duffel bag, which held my uniform, waitressing shoes and apron, to Kate and told her and Sandy I'd see them at the restaurant at the beginning of our shift.

'Bobby waited until Kate and Sandy left in the cab before telling me that his grandmother wanted to see me. He also warned me that the meeting wouldn't be pleasant. An understatement if ever there was one.

'I asked him if she disapproved of me.

'He looked up at the main house and I knew Charlotte Brosna was watching every move Bobby made. He said, "She disapproves of everyone, Penny. She's given me an hour to talk to you first. Can we walk on the beach?"

'I don't know what the weather on Cape Cod is usually like in the summer because I've only been there that once. The summer of 1968 was certainly glorious. But walking on the beach with Bobby that early September morning I felt an autumn chill in the air. The sun shone as bright as it had in July but it was as though someone had turned down the temperature. The sea, the scenery were still beautiful, still idyllic and I recall trying to imprint every view, every sensation on my mind so it could become a memory I could refer to later. Even then, I sensed that one day I'd want to relive even the unhappy moments I'd spent with Bobby.

'For a while we just walked along the shoreline, avoiding the debris. The broken fishing lines, the dead crabs, the shells. We kicked up sand with our bare toes because we'd taken off our shoes. I didn't want to be the one to begin the conversation because I didn't want to be seen as too clinging – too needy.

'Finally Bobby said, "I love you." It was the declaration I'd been waiting for all summer, but the way he said it made my blood run cold.'

CHAPTER THIRTY

Pontypridd, 1987

A cloudburst of rain thundered down, smashing against the farmhouse windows in a staccato drumbeat. Although it was only five o'clock, the light that filtered through the deep-set windows had darkened to twilight-grey.

Jack left his chair and switched on the side lamps. 'If your parents don't see the lights on in your house they'll be worried. Phone them and tell them you're staying over. I'll open a bottle of wine and you can help me eat my cottage pie.'

'It's tempting but I should go back.'

'With Andy away you've no reason.'

'Except work,' she demurred.

'If you were able to concentrate on your painting you wouldn't be here.'

She went into the hall, picked up the phone and spoke to her mother. As she'd expected, her father had told her mother about the letter she'd received from America.

'Andy's only eighteen, darling. To inherit a fortune at that age–'

'I know it's not going to be easy for him,' she interrupted. The last thing she wanted to do was discuss the implications of her son inheriting the Brosna fortune over the telephone. 'I promise you, I won't do anything without talking it over with you and Daddy first. He did tell you that I don't want Andy to know about it until after his exams?'

'Yes, darling.'

'Please don't worry, Mam. As Jack keeps reminding me, Andy's a sensible boy.'

'He is.' Her mother said it as if she was trying to convince herself. 'Have a good evening and don't hurry back. Stay a few days. You've been working too hard lately.'

'Perhaps I will stay over if Jack can put up with me. Love you.'

'Love you too, Penny.'

She rang off and returned to the kitchen. Jack had been to the barn to retrieve the dogs. They were both wet from the hosing down he'd given them before allowing them into the house. He'd also closed the curtains and poured the wine.

'This looks cosy.' She returned to her chair, curled up in it and picked up the glass of wine.

'This could be us every night after Andy goes to college.'

She took a deep breath. 'Jack–'

'I'm sorry. I shouldn't have brought up the subject of us. Not when you have other things to think about.' He patted one of the dogs who went to him looking for affection. Reassured, the dog

327

stretched out alongside his brother on the rug in front of the range.

'So, did you meet Charlotte Brosna?' he questioned.

'Yes. But to go back to Bobby and me on the beach, I knew he would only admit that he loved me if he was leaving me.'

'Because he found it difficult to express his feelings?'

'That, and because for the entire summer he'd lived for the moment. He'd never once talked in depth about the future. The past occasionally – but never what he intended to do in the next couple of years other than rather nebulous plans to "make music".'

'The young live for the moment,' Jack the philosopher observed.

'They may live for the moment but they also think and talk about the future. The jobs they hope to get once they qualify, the people they'd like to stay in touch with. Sandy talked of visiting Europe and looking up Kate as soon as he was discharged from the army. And most of the friends we made that summer had plans. Two couples, Marion and Joe and Paul and Mary, decided to marry.'

'Did they?'

'Paul and Mary in 1970. Joe and Marion in 1974.'

'You stayed in touch with them?' He was surprised.

'Obviously. After Vietnam, Joe went to college on a veteran's scholarship and became a Methodist minister. The one-time bunny girl, Marion, now runs church socials and a kindergarten group. They have five children and live in Atlanta, Georgia. Paul and Mary settled in Canada after he completed his arts degree. He works as a photographer and they have two children. Both couples have a standing invitation to visit me and me them. One day we'll amaze one another.'

'But Bobby never mentioned the future?' He steered the conversation back on course.

'Not until that day on the beach when he told me his grandmother had picked out his future wife when he was fourteen. Her name was Victoria Jefferson Hamilton, she was two years younger than him and her family were bankers. The Brosna Empire accounts were with the Jefferson Hamilton firm and his grandmother had decided to announce their engagement at Christmas.'

'Did Bobby or the girl have a say in it?'

'Apparently not. I remember being shocked. I told him arranged marriages were medieval in concept and had no place in civilised society. He said he barely knew Victoria and had only met her a couple of times, but his grandmother was determined their marriage should go ahead as she'd planned. And she'd done that down to the last detail; a two-year engagement followed by a society wedding to which everyone who was anyone in eastern seaboard society would be invited, along with Hollywood actors, writers and European royalty. His grandmother had even planned their honeymoon. Two weeks on a Brosna-owned Caribbean island followed by a six-month tour of Europe. Afterwards he would begin working in one of the Brosna businesses and he and his bride would live in whichever of the Brosna properties they chose.

'The way Bobby talked about his grandmother's plans for him was bizarre. As if he was talking about Charlotte Brosna's plans for someone else. But despite his tone I knew he was serious. When he finished I asked if Charlotte was very angry with him for leaving Resonance and taking me with him. He said it was impossible to say as she was an expert at concealing her feelings.'

'The question is, were *you* very angry with Bobby for keeping quiet about his prospective fiancée?' Jack asked.

'I was shocked more than angry. I asked Bobby why he'd never mentioned Victoria. He said she was nothing to do with us. I pointed out that as we'd lived together all summer I thought he was something to do with me, and as Victoria was going to be his wife he could at least have mentioned her.

'He insisted he had no intention of living with her after they were married. He even said it was common for married couples in their social circle to lead separate lives. I asked if he would have told me about Victoria if his grandmother hadn't returned. Or if he would have simply allowed me to fly home and never contact me again.'

'What was his reply?'

'That it was time to go and see his grandmother. It was then I lost my temper. I was furious with him for trying to avoid an argument with me by forcing me to meet his grandmother. I should have left then. But I loved Bobby so much; a small optimistic part of me hoped he'd disobey Charlotte and run away from her estate and influence just as he had done in Resonance. We left the beach, brushed the sand from our feet, put on our shoes and walked up to the house. A butler must have been looking out for us because he opened the door as soon as we climbed on to the veranda. We went into the hall. It was enormous and had a vast staircase. I remember thinking all that was needed was a couple of dozen girls in crinolines to re-enact the ball scene in the hall of Twelve Oaks in *Gone with the Wind*.

'I took my time over wiping my feet before following Bobby up the stairs and along a gal-leried landing. He knocked at a door at the end. I heard footsteps and a dark-skinned woman opened the door.

'She bobbed a curtsey to Bobby before saying, "Your grandmother is waiting, Mr Bobby."

'Charlotte Brosna was sitting behind a desk. Bobby had mentioned that she was in her eighties but she looked no older than fifty – slim and frighteningly elegant to a girl dressed in cheap jeans and T-shirt. She was wearing a tailored suit even my inexperienced eye could see was Chanel. Diamonds circled her neck, fingers and wrists and her hair and make-up were immaculate.

'Her voice was clipped, harsh. She didn't waste a word and it was obvious she was used to being obeyed. She dismissed the woman with a "that will be all, Harriet".

'Eyes downcast, the housekeeper left the room and closed the door behind her. It was only after she'd left that I realised she was Sandy's mother.

'Charlotte proceeded to look me up and down as if I was a candidate for a maid's position. Finally she said, "So you're the girl Robert spent the summer with."

'I didn't answer her because the comment seemed superfluous. Nonplussed by my silence, she continued to study me and added, "Well?"

'I have no idea where I found the courage but I said, "It appears you know as much about the time I've spent with Bobby this summer as Bobby and I do, Mrs Brosna."

'She turned from me to Bobby and said, "So you've finally found yourself a girl who can answer back, Robert?" Bobby didn't say a word. She looked at me again and said, "Robert says he loves you and you love him."

'I didn't flinch but met her eye.

'She sat back in her chair and said, "Has he told you that he's engaged to Victoria Jefferson Hamilton?"

'I replied, "Yes, a few minutes ago."

'She turned away from me and looked at Robert. "You didn't tell this girl about Victoria before?"

'Bobby walked to the window, and turned his back on both of us so he could look out at the view. "No, I didn't."

'Charlotte turned her attention back to me. "If Robert had told you about Victoria, would the knowledge have dissuaded you from moving into the Beach House with him?" she demanded.

'I remembered Bobby's assertion that he didn't love Victoria and answered, "only if I thought he loved her."

'She glared at me. Her voice was cold, iced with

frost, just like my old headmistress, and just like my old headmistress I recognised Charlotte Brosna for what she was. A lonely old interfering bully who'd made it her mission in life to blight the lives of everyone unfortunate enough to find themselves within the boundaries of her control. Pity help me, at that moment I even felt sorry for her.

'"I will allow nothing to interfere with my plans for my grandson's future. Nothing!" she warned. "And certainly not a small-town doctor's daughter from Wales." That was when I realised she'd not only paid people to watch Bobby and me that summer, but also paid someone to research my background. She pushed an envelope across the desk towards me. A large fat envelope and ordered me to take it but I didn't pick it up.

'She held it out to me. "Inside this is five thousand dollars in cash. It's yours on condition you never see my grandson again." She smiled, confident she'd already bought me.

'I stared at her for a moment, then walked to the door. She shouted after me, "Isn't it enough?"

'When I didn't answer she called out, "I'll make it ten thousand dollars."

'I kept walking. A heavily built man blocked my path. Charlotte shouted from inside the room. "Don't let the girl leave the house."

'He said, "Mrs Brosna wants you to return to her drawing room, miss."

'I answered, "And if I don't want to go?"

'He stood his ground. There was no way I could pass him so I returned to Charlotte's room. Bobby was standing in front of the window with his back to Charlotte and me.

'Charlotte had an open chequebook in front of her. "A cheque made out to cash for twenty thousand dollars." She held a pen poised over the book.

'I told her I couldn't be bought.

'She countered with, "In my experience, Penelope John, everyone has a price, especially soiled goods."

'I called to Bobby. He didn't turn around.

'Charlotte watched me appealing to him and laughed. "Surprised?" she crowed. "My grandson knows where his dollars come from and how easily they can be cut off." She wrote the cheque and held it out in front of me.

'The room began to spin around me. I looked from Charlotte to the man who was blocking the door.

'I was determined that Charlotte wouldn't get the better of me. I noticed French doors in the room, moved quickly past Bobby and wrenched them open. George was loading a truck outside one of the guest houses. I screamed down to him. Told him to get the police because Charlotte was imprisoning me.

'Charlotte laughed and said, "George won't get the police. Not if he wants his money. Everyone always wants money. First they argue and, pretend to take the moral high ground, but in the end everyone has a price.

'It was then I realised just how malevolent Charlotte could be. How she controlled everyone around her with threats, not just against them but their friends. I finally understood why Bobby was so frightened of her. He, like me, couldn't appeal to anyone for help because he knew Charlotte could hurt them.

'I returned to the room. Charlotte had left her chair. I finally took the cheque from her. The man blocking the door moved away. I walked out, tore the cheque in two and threw the pieces behind me as I charged down the stairs. I heard footsteps but I didn't look to see if it was Bobby because I was afraid it wouldn't be.

'I ran down the drive and through the gates. George caught up with me on the road. His truck was loaded with boxes. He stopped alongside me and asked if I was all right. Two women with small children on their laps were sitting in the cab alongside him. I told him I didn't want to get him into trouble and I'd rather hitch a lift with strangers. He nodded and drove on.

'A couple of soldiers on leave picked me up outside the gates and dropped me in town. I went straight to the restaurant. Sandy and Kate were eating lunch before the shift started. I sat in the staffroom with them and drank coffee. They could see I was upset but they didn't press me. That shift was the last and longest I worked in Cosmo's.

'Cosmo knew something was wrong because Bobby didn't turn up for work. He reluctantly agreed to pay us off that evening and gave each of us a twenty-dollar bonus. He tried to give Sandy Bobby's wages but Sandy wouldn't take them. We told Cosmo that Charlotte had returned to the estate and Cosmo said he'd post Bobby a cheque.

'We picked up some beer and walked down to

335

Joe and Marion's. As usual there was a party in the yard. Sandy started asking around for recommendations for cheap hotels in New York and car rental as we intended to set off early in the morning. The apartment Bobby had mentioned in the Village was out of the question, even if we'd known where it was.'

She held out her glass and Jack refilled it.

'But the accident … you did see Bobby Brosna again?' he checked.

'Yes, I saw him again. But I wish with all my heart I hadn't.'

CHAPTER THIRTY-ONE

Pontypridd, 1987

Rain continued to hammer down on the window panes. Jack didn't prompt her. He simply waited for her to continue while she struggled to find the words to describe what had happened that night.

'Because we were leaving the Cape early the next morning for New York, Sandy, Kate and I decided to forgo Marion's donation bar and stick to our beer. Sandy had volunteered to drive but Kate and I had both applied for international driving licences and were prepared to take over if Sandy was tired. As usual, there was music and a bonfire in the yard and we joined Marion, Joe and Paul and Mary, who'd also taken a room in the house, and the others.

'Bobby arrived in his car shortly after midnight. I could smell brandy on his breath. I'd never seen him drunk before. None of us had more than two or three glasses of wine or beer after our shifts. And, usually after Bobby had a drink, he started yawning and became mellow. Sandy told me he always knew when Bobby had been drinking because he smiled more. But when Bobby joined us that night he was excited. As wound up as a clockwork toy with a tensed spring.

'He'd abandoned his car a couple of feet from the kerb. Sandy saw a police officer examining it. The officer came into the yard looking for the driver. A crowd gathered around him when he accused Bobby of stealing it and driving erratically.

'There were angry murmurs from Joe about police harassment and brutality. Sandy tried to diffuse the tension. He apologised and told the officer Bobby was celebrating his last day at work before returning to college. He also mentioned Bobby was a Brosna. That was when the officer told him Charlotte Brosna's butler was the one who'd reported the car stolen.

'Fortunately Sandy knew Bobby kept his licence and ownership documents in the glove compartment. He showed them to the officer and promised to drive the car back to the Brosna Estate so the misunderstanding could be cleared up.

'If there had been fewer people in the yard I think the officer would have arrested Bobby. But Joe was heavily built and all of us were incensed by a police presence at a peaceful gathering. After ordering Sandy to return the car to the Brosna Estate immediately, and sort out the situation with Charlotte Brosna's butler, the officer cautioned Bobby and warned him not to drive again until he'd sobered up. After the policeman left, Bobby grabbed my arm and dragged me away from the others.

'He said he'd told his grandmother he was leaving the Cape with me and no longer cared whether she disinherited him or not.

'Sandy and Kate overheard him. Sandy tried to calm Bobby; he told him we'd taken rooms in the house and suggested Bobby went to bed while he returned the car. Bobby point-blank refused and insisted the car was his and Charlotte had no right to take it. He took a paper bag from inside his jacket. There was a bottle in it.

'Sandy asked Bobby where he'd got the liquor. Bobby said he'd bought it with the wages he'd picked up from Cosmo.

'Bobby tried to punch Sandy's arm playfully, missed and hit air but he wasn't too drunk to outline his plans. He intended to drive to New York with us, sell his car and use the proceeds to buy flight tickets to Europe for him and Sandy so they could travel back with Kate and me. When Sandy pointed out that unlike Bobby he didn't have a place at Oxford, Bobby announced he had no intention of returning to university.

'It was then Bobby started shouting and swearing. "To hell with Oxford and to hell with my grandmother's plans. From this moment on I'm living the life *I* want."

'When Sandy reminded him that he had to

report to the army in a week, Bobby shouted "and you can tell the draft board to go to hell too."

'Unfortunately Joe had also been drinking and he was looking for the fight the police officer had denied him. He called Bobby "a spoilt rich boy" and "spineless Brosna bastard" among other things, and suggested Bobby join all the other rich draft dodgers in Europe while the real Americans like him and Sandy faced the Commie menace.

'You can imagine the argument?' Penny looked at Jack.

'The Commie menace and the draft dodgers?' Jack suggested.

'Exactly. When Bobby pointed out there were no Commies in Hyannisport, Joe retorted that he was looking at one. Bobby lurched forward. Sandy assumed Bobby was about to punch Joe and stepped between them. But Joe wouldn't let it drop. Joe's two brothers were fighting in Vietnam, and like Sandy, Joe would be out there as soon as he'd finished his training. He reminded Bobby that while the recruits like him and Sandy were fighting and dying the rich American kids like Bobby would be sitting in Europe living it up.

'The argument escalated. Paul who was a Pacifist joined in and argued that if everyone refused to go to 'Nam, there wouldn't be a war.

'Joe challenged Paul and asked if he wanted the Commies to take America.

'It was then Bobby broke down. He shouted, "Don't you understand, boys our age are dying over there. And when you die, that's it! The end! Black! Nothing! No feeling! No thoughts!

Nothing! I've seen their graves and so has she." He pointed at me. "Some of them aren't even in their graves. All they have is an empty plot of earth and a headstone with a name. The army told their relatives they were missing. But given what's happening in Vietnam, I don't believe there was enough left to send home and bury. Tell them, Pen. Tell them we saw the class of '64 buried next to the class of '65 buried next to the class of '66, and now the class of '67 and '68 are being shipped home in boxes."

'Even then Joe wouldn't let it go. He taunted Bobby calling him "rich boy" again and said the real men knew what they were fighting for in Vietnam even if Bobby didn't.

'It ended with Joe and Bobby fighting. Joe hit Bobby on the chin. Bobby fell over and Paul and Marion pulled Joe off before he could close in with another punch.

'Sandy helped Bobby to his feet. Bobby moved towards his car. Sandy snatched Bobby's car keys from his hand.

'Bobby protested and said he had to fetch his clothes from the Beach House. Sandy said that as he had to take the car back and straighten things out with Charlotte Brosna's butler he may as well take Bobby with him so Bobby could pick up his things.

'Sandy saw I was worried and reassured me that he wouldn't let Charlotte see her grandson in the state he was in. He'd drop Bobby off at the Beach House so he could pack, then, after he'd left the car with Charlotte's butler, he'd walk down from the main house and pick up Bobby.

He asked Marion to ring a cab company and ask them to send a driver to pick him and Bobby up at the entrance to the Brosna Estate in an hour.

'Marion agreed. Bobby staggered to the car and climbed into the driving seat. Sandy heaved him out of it, dropped him into the back and fastened him in with a seat belt.

'Bobby was shouting for me so I climbed into the back and sat beside him. Kate refused to be left behind so she took the front passenger seat.

'Sandy turned the ignition and we drove up the road.

'Bobby passed out before we left Main Street. Sandy drove quickly but he was careful to observe the speed limit because he suspected the police would be on the lookout for Bobby's distinctive car.

'We were about a mile from the Brosna Estate when Bobby woke up. He sat up with a start, and although it was dark I could see his eyes wide, staring. He was obviously disorientated. He looked around, saw the back of Sandy's head, un-buckled his seat belt and shouted, "Damn car thief!" He leaned forward and tried to wrest the wheel from Sandy. They fought for control. I wrapped my arms around Bobby's waist, and using all the strength I could muster, tried to pull him back into the seat. The car was swerving from side to side. The headlights swept round in arcs, illuminating undergrowth one minute, tarmac the next. I saw a tree looming closer and closer ... there was an enormous bang, a flash of light, an explosion ... then nothing.'

The rainstorm had quietened to a soft patter of drops on the window panes and sills. It was so still in the kitchen Penny could hear the dogs breathing.

'You were unconscious?' Jack asked.

'I came round in hospital the following afternoon. As to what happened after I was knocked out, if you've read the press reports you know as much as me.'

'It was nineteen years ago, Penny. And I didn't know you that well then.'

'The police were at my bedside. They told me the car had hit a tree and burst into flames. I didn't remember the fire, presumably because it didn't start until after I was out of it. They asked where I'd been sitting in the car. I told them I'd been sitting behind Sandy who'd been driving. Kate was sitting beside Sandy in front of Bobby. Neither Bobby nor I were wearing seat belts. The officers said it looked as though Bobby and I had been flung out of the car on impact. They didn't tell me that Bobby had been catapulted headlong into the fire. When I asked, the police admitted that they were on the scene within seconds. They had, as Sandy suspected, been following us.

'The doctor arrived and sent the police away. He informed me I'd broken both my legs, three ribs and my left arm. I asked about Sandy, Kate – and Bobby. He tried to fob me off with platitudes. When I became agitated, he gave me a shot of morphine.

'The next time I came round my father, mother and Uncle Haydn were in the room. Anything a Brosna did was news in the States and one of the local reporters had asked around Hyannis for the name of Bobby's girlfriend. It hadn't taken him long to find out. As soon as Uncle Haydn heard about the accident he cancelled his show in Las Vegas. He and my parents arrived at Boston airport at the same time.

'They told me Bobby was badly burnt and not expected to live. Kate had been killed and Sandy had disappeared. No one knew where he was and not even the police could find him.

'I felt as though my world had come to an end. The man I loved was dying, my best friend was dead. I would never ever see them again. I also felt desperately sorry for Sandy. I knew how guilty he'd be feeling, although the accident wasn't his fault but Bobby's.

'Charlotte Brosna walked into my room before my father finished telling me about Kate. We found out afterwards that she'd paid one of the nurses to inform her of my progress.

'She tried to give my father a cheque to cover my medical expenses, the cost of flying Kate's body home and Kate's funeral. My father refused to take it. Then she demanded I sign an undertaking that I would never try to see or contact Bobby again.

'Uncle Haydn called a doctor and demanded he remove Charlotte Brosna from my room. I believe it was the first time Charlotte Brosna had met her match. The staff were reluctant to order a Brosna to do anything but Haydn was insistent. Three days later, when the doctors agreed I could be moved, Uncle Haydn arranged to have me flown home by air ambulance.

'I thought the worst thing that could happen to me in life had. But that was before I faced Kate's mother. She was more than grief-stricken; she was broken, distraught. She and Kate had been very close. But you know she died of cancer not long afterwards.

'After Kate's funeral, which I went to in a wheelchair – but you were there with Rich so you know – I tried to pick up the pieces of my life. I began by going back to college. A week after I returned I fainted and was taken to hospital. The doctors in Swansea thought it was down to trauma and stress from the accident.

'They ran a battery of tests and discovered I was pregnant. I shouldn't have been surprised. I hadn't taken my birth control pills since the night of the accident.'

CHAPTER THIRTY-TWO

'Did you ever find out what had happened to Sandy?' Jack's voice sounded unnaturally loud in the silence that had fallen over the kitchen.

'Not for months. The first police officers on the scene saw him. In fact, one of the officers insisted that he couldn't have pulled Bobby from the burning wreckage without Sandy's help. But, by the time Bobby and me had been loaded into the ambulances he'd gone.'

'Did the police look for him?'

'At first – because they believed he was respon-

sible for the crash. After I told them it had been
Bobby's attempt to wrest the steering wheel from
Sandy that had caused the accident they
appealed for him to come forward as a witness.
Marion, Joe, Paul and Mary visited me in hospital. They told me the police had searched their
house the morning after the crash and taken
Kate's and my bags for safekeeping. They hadn't
found Sandy's. Bobby had never moved any of
his things out of the Beach House so I presumed
they were still there.'

'Your things were returned to you?'

She thought of the rusted tartan bag in the attic
of her barn conversion, the sketch books she'd
filled that summer. Somehow they were more evo-
cative than the photographs she'd taken. Sketches
she hadn't been able to look at for years.

'The police brought my bag to the hospital.'

'Didn't you think it odd that Sandy didn't come
to see you?' he asked.

'Yes. I was worried about him. As I said, I knew
he'd be guilt-stricken and devastated over Kate's
death and Bobby's and my injuries. Before I left
the hospital a nurse told me that a man telephoned several times a day enquiring about Bobby
and me but he wouldn't leave his name. Later,
Uncle Haydn discovered that the police had att-
empted to track the calls, but they'd all been made
from payphones in different states. Charlotte
Brosna issued a statement through her solicitor
asking Sandy to come forward. She stated that she
knew he was in no way to blame for the accident.
Sandy's mother, Harriet, filmed a television
appeal. It was heartbreaking to see her crying, beg-

ging Sandy to get in touch and reassure her that he was all right. With Kate dead and Bobby close to death I think the police and Harriet believed Sandy to be a suicide risk.'

'I recall that Bobby Brosna wasn't expected to live.' Jack stirred the fire into life and placed another log on the flames.

'He hovered on the brink of death for months. Charlotte Brosna had the best and most experienced burn injury surgeons flown into the States from Europe to treat him. As soon as he was pronounced medically stable she had him transferred to a Boston hospital, but that was four months after I'd flown home. And by then the police had discovered Sandy's whereabouts. He'd joined the army as a volunteer and told the officers all his personal papers had been destroyed in a fire – which I suppose in retrospect they had been. He gave his real name, Alexander Buttons, but no one made the connection between him and the man wanted after a car accident on Cape Cod.'

'So he did serve in Vietnam.'

'As a volunteer not a conscript,' she confirmed. 'After six weeks' basic training he was shipped out. I don't know if he expected to die, but I thought it ironic that he'd named Charlotte Brosna as his next of kin. Possibly he thought the news of his death would be easier for his mother to bear if Charlotte broke it to her.'

'How long was he in Vietnam?'

'Less than two weeks. Marion sent me a newspaper cutting from the Cape's local paper. *Alexander "Sandy" Buttons died in a helicopter crash on November 2nd 1968 in South Vietnam.* She was worried sick because Joe was out there and she expected him to get killed at any moment. Marion told me in a later letter that Sandy's body was shipped home and Harriet Buttons buried him in a cemetery on the Cape. He was only twenty-two. Just one of sixteen thousand, five hundred and eighty-nine Western casualties of the Vietnam War in 1968.'

'I'm so sorry, Penny.' The fact that she could recall the exact figure indicated how much Sandy's death had affected her. 'Did you have much contact with Bobby after the accident?'

'No. Charlotte must have set snoops to watch me because when my pregnancy became notice-able she sent a solicitor's letter asking if the child I was expecting was her grandson's. Bobby was in the Boston hospital at that time but as I didn't know anything about his condition other than the official bulletin which stated "he was gravely ill" I asked my father to answer the letter for me. I told him to tell Charlotte the child was Bobby's but I intended to bring him or her up alone. And I didn't need or want help from anyone, espe-cially her.'

'And she never came back to you?' Jack said in surprise.

'She persisted, offering me money to give up my child, but I was adamant that after the way she'd treated Bobby she was not going to get her hands on his son or daughter.'

'A lot of money?' Jack fished.

'Millions – dollars not pounds,' she said quickly. 'But I remembered what Bobby had said about being brought up by nannies and sent to expensive boarding schools and summer camps. There was no way I wanted that kind of childhood for my child. But even after I refused, Charlotte kept writing and even sent an American lawyer to my parents' house. About a month before Andy was born I wrote to Cosmo and asked him to find out how Bobby really was and if he was still in the hospital that had issued the bulletins. Cosmo, bless him, phoned me as soon as he received my letter. He told me Bobby's injuries were severe but the doctor's believed, no longer life-threatening and he had years of corrective surgery in front of him. I sent a letter to the hospital in Boston where Bobby was being treated and marked it urgent and personal. A nurse wrote a reply for him as he didn't have the use of his hands at the time. He promised to speak to Charlotte and respect my wishes regarding our child's upbringing, which he did and has done since – apart from sending me an obscene cheque after Andy was born. I returned it and told him I would never take his money.'

'Andy was his son too, Pen. Money means nothing to the Brosnas...'

'That's the point, Jack. The Brosnas have so much, they believe, really believe, money can buy them anything they want, even people. I didn't want Andy beholden, especially financially, to anyone with that philosophy.'

'Bobby's written since?'

'Several times and always offering money. I returned his letters with my refusals.'

'You haven't wanted to see him again?'

'So we could relive that awful night when Kate

died?' she shivered. 'No.'

'You said there were happy times.'

'There were, but after Andy arrived I had to move on, make a life for both of us.'

'You succeeded,' he complimented. 'You say you sent Bobby's letters back. Will you return the one you received this morning?'

'No, because Andy has to read it.'

Jack left his chair. 'Tragic,' he mused. 'Sandy may have died in Vietnam anyway, as he was intent on going there. But the rest of you. Three young lives ruined—'

'Two lives ruined,' she interrupted. 'I came out of that crash comparatively unscathed. When I was carried away from that car wreck on a stretcher I had my life, I was able to regain my health and had Andy the following year. I've never stopped grieving for Kate or regretting her loss. She was my best friend. We had no secrets from one another. And her memory has made me grateful for every day I've lived since that night. If Andy had been a girl I would have called her Kate.'

'I remember her as a pretty girl, full of life.'

'She was.' Penny smiled unconsciously as she recalled Kate bouncing into the common room with the news about America. 'As for Sandy, you're right. He may well have died in Vietnam as a conscript. 1968 was the worst year of the war for casualties. Bobby's life was certainly ruined that night. Not because he was maimed and crippled by the fire but because his injuries enabled Charlotte to regain control of his life. I wonder if they became reconciled. Knowing the way Bobby felt about her, I doubt it. I think that's why he chose to live on the Brosna Estate. It's easier to become a recluse when you have several houses to choose from. I doubt he ever lived in the main house with her.'

'Bobby never wanted to see Andy?'

'He never asked. I never offered. Possibly he was afraid how Andy would react to his disfigurement. Bobby respected my decision to bring up Andy as a John. He never caved in to the pressure I knew Charlotte brought on him to claim a father's rights, but he did ask me to name him as the father on the birth certificate in return for relinquishing all claims on the child. After checking with my father and his solicitor that the declaration Bobby sent me giving up his father's rights to Andy would hold up in court, I did. I felt it was little enough. The one thing I wasn't prepared for was how I'd feel about Andy after he was born.'

'I can imagine.'

'No you can't, Jack. You think you can, but no one knows how emotional they'll be about their own child until they're holding it.'

He looked back at the fire.

'I'm sorry,' she apologised when she realised how cruel her words must have sounded. 'There was another casualty that night only he wasn't affected until years later.'

'There was?' he asked in surprise.

'You. I know how much you wanted a family of your own.'

'I accepted a long time ago that I couldn't have you and a family of my own.'

350

'It was selfish of me. I should have sent you packing.'

He smiled. 'You did, several times, but I kept coming back. The proverbial bad penny.'

'And I was weak and selfish enough to take everything you offered and give you nothing in return.'

'You gave me the time you could spare, Pen. It was enough, although I always sensed the ghost of Andy's father hovering between us. Thank you for explaining about Bobby. You must have missed him when you were bringing up Andy. Does he look like Bobby?'

'A mirror image. I'll show you photographs some time. As for missing Bobby. I did for years. And sometimes, late at night, I still regret the "might have been". But I've you and Andy, my parents and a lot to be grateful for. The worst was just after I returned to college. My parents supported my decision to return there as soon as my legs healed. I worked hard on my portfolio, crammed in as much as I could before Andy was born, and afterwards my parents paid for a rented house and a full-time nanny while I sat my finals. But it was dreadful. Because I'd lost Bobby, Kate and Sandy I didn't want to leave Andy for a minute. As soon as I qualified I gave the nanny notice, returned here with Andy and the rest you know.'

'Andy has to make a tough decision. I don't know what I'd do if someone handed me the Brosna millions.' Jack opened the oven door and checked the cottage pie.

'Since he was old enough to steal my father's

351

and brother's stethoscopes and play with them he's wanted to be a doctor like his grandfather and uncle. I hope for his sake he makes the right decision.'

'And for you that would be medical college and a place in your father's practice.'

'Would that be so awful, Jack?' She looked up at him through misty eyes.

'It's a decision you have no say in. Andy's a grown man. It's time you allowed him to act like one. But this conversation is getting too serious and too full of imponderables. The pie's ready, it's time we ate and afterwards we can do whatever you want. Listen to music, watch television, play chess, or you can choose something to watch from my magnificent video collection.'

The last offer was a joke. The only videos Jack owned were the cartoons he bought for his god-children.

She left her chair. 'I'll set the table.'

She fetched plates, knives, forks and place mats from the dresser. Jack went into the pantry and brought out salt and pepper. When everything was ready he lifted the cottage pie from the oven and placed it on the table.

'You've never been back to America?' He served her a portion of pie.

'You know I haven't.'

'Would you like to?'

She thought before answering. 'I don't honestly know,' she said truthfully.

'Not even to see the museums and galleries?'

'That I didn't get around to visiting in 1968?' She sat at the table.

'A lot of things will have changed in the last nineteen years.'

'Not much on the Brosna Estate, knowing Charlotte Brosna. We had some good times and made good memories. But they've been overshadowed by the way the summer ended.'

'And Bobby Brosna? Do you want to see him again?'

She knew the reply she was about to give Jack would hurt him, but she couldn't lie.

'Yes, I want to see him. Especially as Charlotte saw fit to disinherit him and leave everything to Andy.'

'So tell me about this latest book jacket of yours.'

She was grateful to him for changing the subject and they talked about trivia, Pontypridd gossip, the touring productions that were coming to the New Theatre in Cardiff, the last film they'd seen in the cinema. He refrained from reminding her that it had been her who'd made the decision to see the Australian comedy, *Crocodile Dundee*, instead of the Vietnam War film *Platoon*.

After they'd eaten she helped him clear the table and wash the dishes. He opened a second bottle of wine and they played three games of chess, all of which he won because she couldn't concentrate.

They went to bed early and he made love to her slowly, surely. They were practised lovers and he knew her body and her reactions. Afterwards, she lay on her side and he curled around her back. But despite his comforting presence she found it difficult to sleep.

She listened to the patter of raindrops on the

windows, and thought about Andy. She couldn't even begin to guess what his reaction would be when she told him he'd inherited a fortune. And then there was the question of travelling to America.

Should she write to Bobby and demand he come to them? Or should she take Andrew to Cape Cod and show him the places where she'd lived with his father almost twenty years before?

CHAPTER THIRTY-THREE

20th May 1987

Dear Bobby,
I received your letter – that's a stupid thing to write when I'm answering it. Did Charlotte Brosna leave the Brosna Estate to Andy instead of you out of spite? You were never close, but then I don't believe she could have been close to a human being in her life, not even her husband. After meeting her twice, I'm convinced the only person she loved was herself. To me she will always be the epitome of the selfish, self-centred, wealthy American matriarch, accustomed to getting her own way in all things.
People say you shouldn't speak ill of the dead. Although after what Charlotte Brosna did to you and her attempts to 'buy' me and, after he was born, Andy, I cannot be magnanimous.
I have discussed Andy's inheritance with my parents and we've agreed Andy shouldn't be told about it until

after he's sat his A levels – the examinations he needs to pass to go to medical college. Given Charlotte's propensity for hiring 'snoops' I'm certain she knew what Andy's plans for his future were. If you've found the file she kept on him I don't need to explain the UK educational system to you.

Andy's ambition is, and has been for a few years, to follow in his grandfather's and uncle's footsteps and become a doctor. I have no idea how he'll react when he receives the news of the Brosna inheritance, whether or not he will accept it, or allow it to change the plans he has made.

I don't want anything to distract him before he takes his examinations. I trust you will respect this, the final decision I hope I have to make on Andy's behalf without discussing it with him beforehand.

After his examinations I will show him your letter and tell him about his great-grandmother and the Brosnas. I will leave it to Andy to decide whether or not we accept your invitation to arrange flights for us, but should he want to see you, I want to meet you – alone – before you speak to Andy.

I don't think I could bear to return to the Brosna Estate or Cape Cod. If Andy wants to see the place where we spent a happy summer before the night that ended it, perhaps he could go with you. I am, however, certain that he will want to see New York and I would like to revisit the Alice in Wonderland statue in Central Park and see if the passage of time has been kind to it.

As soon as I have spoken to Andy, and know his reaction to your letter, I will write to you again.

With warm wishes and remembrance of that summer,
Penny

Pontypridd, July 1987

Penny kept reminding herself that it was ridiculous to feel nervous but to no avail. Andy was
sitting his last examination but that wasn't the
reason. Like her father and Andy's teachers she
was quietly confident he would gain the coveted
place at medical school.

It was the letter she'd received from America.
Was she right in insisting she should show it to
Andy when they were alone? Would it have been
better to have had the support of her parents?

Restless, unable to paint, she'd cleaned the
entire house from the front door to the attic and
when she finished she took her dusters, vacuum
cleaner and mop into the studio. The windows
sparkled, the furniture had been beeswaxed, the
bathrooms and kitchen shone, the tiled walls and
floor freshly bleached.

At four o'clock she laid the tea table, although
she knew Andy's examination wouldn't finish
until four sharp and he'd want to spend at least
half an hour discussing the questions with his
friends before driving home.

She set it out in the breakfast nook in the
kitchen that overlooked the fields. It was where
she and Andy ate most of their meals because
they preferred the view there to the dining room
which overlooked the courtyard between her
barn conversion and her parents' house.

Because Andy enjoyed what he called 'children's
tea parties teas' she laid out ham and cheese salad

356

sandwiches, cheese and fruit scones, gingerbread and fruit trifle, all of which she'd made that morning. She watched the clock and boiled the kettle at four-thirty in case he'd want tea instead of his customary coffee. At a quarter to five she checked her reflection in the hall mirror. She was wearing one of her favourite dresses, the exact same shade of green as the long-discarded Mary Quant suit. She brushed her hair and checked the clock again.

Had Andy flunked the examination? It was chemistry. He'd been dreading it because it was his weakest subject. She walked to the front door, opened it and looked out in the yard. When she saw her father and mother sitting in the conservatory watching her, she self-consciously waved back and closed the door.

She left the house by the back door and went to her studio. The painting of the girl in harem dress she'd been working on when the letter had arrived had been despatched. She'd even been paid for it which was a miracle, considering how long it usually took her agency to pay for work she'd completed.

There was a very different painting on her easel. One she was doing for love, not money

Four young people were standing on the deck of the *Day Dream*.

It would have been easy to have copied the photograph, but she had deliberately set it aside and not looked at it again after the day she'd received it. Instead she'd sketched out and painted the figures from memory.

Bobby and Sandy, so alike in many ways, so

different in others: both the same height and build; muscles rippling beneath the exposed skin on their bare arms, legs and chests. Bobby's fair skin burnt blush red by the sun, Sandy's darker skin tanned the colour of milk chocolate. Bobby's hair a rich brown-black, Sandy's a Hispanic blue-black. Bobby's deep-blue Irish eyes command-ing, assured, secure with the confidence that he could make the world dance to whatever tune he chose. Sandy's blue eyes paler, diffident because she suspected Charlotte Brosna had taken care that her housekeeper's son knew his place in the social order that governed the Brosna world and that of their minions.

Kate, blonde, beautiful, and a little sad because she'd imagined her that way. She'd caught the exact shade of grey in Kate's eyes and she'd painted them misty with dreams that would never come to fruition. And her? Her tawny eyes gleamed with love as she looked uncritically, ador-ingly at Bobby. Should she have forced him to talk to her about his feelings for his grandmother?

Could she have exercised more control over him? Prevented him from getting drunk and causing tragedy?

It was a canvas she'd intended to take to America as a gift. But looking at it she wondered if anyone involved in the events of that summer's night could accept something so poignant, and to her at least, heart-rending.

The clock chimed six before she heard the crunch of car tyres on gravel that she'd been wait-ing for. She left the studio and went out to meet Andy.

'I know I promised to be home early for tea, Mam. I'm sorry–'

'The exam,' she interrupted Andy.

'Oh that,' he said airily.

'Yes, that?' she snapped, nerves tensed to breaking point.

'It was a doddle,' he grinned. 'I went to see Jack. You know I said I'd work for him this summer, helping him expand the riding school at the farm?'

'Yes.' She spoke to fill the silence while he moulded his features into an 'I want something my mother might not agree with' expression. 'Well, I talked to a few of the boys after the exam and they're thinking of going to Majorca. I thought I might raid my bank account and go with them.'

'When?'

'Next week. There's a special offer on in one of the travel agents in town. It's really cheap because we'll be returning before the school holidays even start.'

'What did Jack say?'

'Something odd. He said I'd have to talk it over with you but he hadn't been counting on me to work for him this summer and he could cope without me.' He frowned. 'There's nothing wrong is there? You and Jack haven't quarrelled...?'

'No, we haven't quarrelled,' she assured him.

He followed her into the kitchen and watched her remove the foil wrapping she had used to cover the sandwiches and cakes to prevent them from drying out. 'I feel guilty. While I've been driving around you've made this wonderful old-fashioned tea. We're not going to eat all this ourselves, are we? You have invited Granny and

Granddad to help us out?'

'No,' she steeled herself. 'I need to talk to you alone.'

'That sounds ominous.'

'Do you want tea or coffee?'

'Coffee, please.'

She busied herself making coffee, waiting for the percolator to finish before carrying it across to the table where Andy was already sitting, eating sandwiches while looking out over the fields. Her desk was in the living room. She left the kitchen and fetched the letter she'd received in May. She opened it and placed the photograph Bobby had enclosed on top. Then she handed both letter and photograph to Andy.

'What's this?'

'Wipe your fingers and look at the picture.'

He rubbed his hands in a paper napkin. 'Nice bikinis. Nice girls; not the sort of picture I thought a mother would want to show her son.'

'Look again.'

'That's not you, is it?' His eyes widened as he stared at her.

'Me in 1968 with my friend Kate, taken when we went on the student exchange to America. The boys with us are Alexander Buttons...' she pointed to Sandy '...he was besotted with my friend Kate. The other boy is Robert Grayson Brosna the Fourth, your father. But you've probably guessed that. You look just like him.'

'You said you didn't have any photographs of him,' he said accusingly.

'I didn't have this one until he sent it to me. But I did have others. I lied about them.'

360

'Why?'

'Because I would have found it painful to have shown them to you.'

'Because my father's disfigured now?' Andy asked.

'Because the photographs would have made me cry. And, I didn't want you to associate your father with my tears.'

'This is the first time you've brought up the subject of my father without me asking about him first. Why now?' Andy's blue eyes were dark, mysterious. For the first time in his life she couldn't determine his thoughts.

'Because I have to.' She handed him the letter from America. 'Read this. There are some newspaper clippings in the envelope as well, American ones. Your father, Kate, Sandy and I shared a wonderful summer until the accident. It's all in the clippings and the letter. After you've read them come into the studio and we'll talk.'

She left the room quickly, closing the door behind her. She rubbed her arms with her hands, although it wasn't cold, then she went into the studio, sat on a stool and stared at the picture.

She was still looking at it when Andy walked in an hour later.

'Why didn't you show me my father's letters before now?' he demanded.

'Several reasons, principally because Robert – Bobby's – grandmother, your great-grandmother Charlotte, who's just died, wanted me to hand you over when you were born so she could bring you up. When she found out she had no legal recourse she offered me money...' She almost said 'as if any mother would sell her child', before remembering that's exactly what Bobby's mother had done. 'But most of all because of the Brosna billions. Your father hated the way his grand-mother had brought him up, with a succession of nannies and boarding schools. He had everything a child could possibly want except love. Another reason was your father was very ill for years.'

'I looked up the Brosna businesses and foun-dation.'

'You never told me.'

'I suppose I always sensed you didn't like talk-ing about my father.'

'The inheritance will be vast. Sandy – your father's friend Alexander once told me the Brosna annual income was larger than half a dozen of the poorer African countries combined.'

'I had a right to know my father,' Andy re-proached.

For the second time that day she failed to decipher the expression on her son's face. 'Yes, you did. But he never asked to see you and I never offered. He – and I may have made the wrong decision, Andy, but I did what I thought best at the time. I wanted you to grow up secure, rooted in a family, and the only way I thought I could do that was to bring you up alongside my own parents. Charlotte Brosna would never have allowed that to happen if I'd given your father any rights over you, simply because he was too ill when you were a child to fight her.'

'Did you love my father?'

'Very much.'

'What was he like?'

'When I knew him, good-looking, confident, charming, sure of himself, used to getting his own way. Like many overconfident people, he could be arrogant, selfish, opinionated and high-handed, but he had a way of making you forget his faults. You must also remember the Bobby Brosna I knew was nineteen years younger than he is now, and before he suffered his terrible injuries in the accident. Would you like me to get plane tickets to New York?'

'Yes, please.' He hesitated for a moment. 'You will come with me?'

She smiled; she'd told her son the truth and she hadn't lost him. She felt like dancing. 'Of course, darling.'

11th July 1987

Dear Bobby,

I've booked flights to New York. We'll be landing at JFK airport on Wednesday, 17th July at three in the afternoon. Will you please ask your office to arrange transport and rooms for Andy and myself? I insist on paying mine and Andy's bills.

Warmest wishes,
Penny

CHAPTER THIRTY-FOUR

New York, July 1987

'Mr Andrew John, Ms Penelope John, this way please.' The uniformed official met them at the steps of the plane. He took them into a small comfortably furnished lounge just inside the building.

A man dressed in a chauffeur's uniform and cap rose to his feet when they entered. His face was heavily scarred, and Penny noticed he had a pronounced limp when he stepped forward to meet them.

'Ms John, Mr John, I'm Tim Garber, Mr Brosna's chauffeur. He sent me to fetch you.'

'Our luggage?' Penny asked.

'They're getting it for you now, ma'am.'

Irritated by the man's subservience, which reminded her of the way Charlotte Brosna's staff had behaved when she'd visited the main house on Cape Cod, she held out her hand. 'I'm Penny, not ma'am. You said your name is Tim?'

'Yes, Penny.' He shook Penny's hand, then Andy's.

'Nice to meet you, Tim, I'm Andy.'

'We didn't expect five-star treatment on landing and we certainly didn't expect to be upgraded to first class on the plane,' Penny commented suspiciously.

'Airlines are always looking for people to up-grade because they oversell the cheap tickets and inflate the price of first-class tickets beyond most people's pockets.'

'You think so?' Penny looked sceptically at Tim.

There was a discreet knock at the door. Tim opened it. An airport official and a porter were outside.

'We're here to check Ms and Mr John's visas, sir. We've retrieved their luggage. A porter is waiting to wheel it out for you.'

'Thank you, Mr Brosna will be most grateful.' Tim discreetly slipped the official and porter tips.

Penny and Andy handed Tim their passports. As soon as they had been stamped, Tim led the way out of the airport. A black limousine with darkened windows was parked outside the 'arrivals' gate. Tim opened the back door and the trunk for the porter. Penny and Andy climbed into the back.

'There are refreshments, drinks and cham-pagne in the fridge. Please, help yourself. If you need to talk to me, use the intercom. Enjoy the ride.' Tim closed the inside window.

Andy was gazing intently out the window, straining his neck to catch his first glimpse of America. Penny was reminded of how she had done the self-same thing when she'd landed in New York in 1968.

'Don't try to take it all in at once,' she advised. 'It's impossible, especially around the airport.'

'It's not what I expected.'

'I remember saying the same thing to Kate.

Your Great-Uncle Haydn once told me that New York is best seen from the air at a distance. His words certainly rang true for me nineteen years ago.'

'You tired?' Andy asked.

'I can barely keep my eyes open. I'd forgotten how exhausting a long flight can be.'

'It was more tiring than flying to Spain, or Italy,' Andy agreed.

'It took me days to get over jet lag the last time I was here. Right now I feel as though I should be going to bed, not thinking about afternoon tea.' She recalled the meal Bobby had bought her in the coffee shop just after she'd arrived at the hotel and realised she'd landed at practically the same time.

'Part of our exhaustion could be down to travelling to the airport the day before we flew, the night noise in the airport hotel and having to get up at some ghastly hour this morning so we could sit around for hours before we flew out.' Andy opened the fridge and inspected the contents.

'I hope I stay awake until we get to the hotel. I fell asleep on the bus last time.'

'How about a glass of champagne?' Andy removed the bottle.

'Forget the champagne. I could murder a glass of water.'

Andy took a bottle of water, opened it and filled two glasses. He handed her one, then continued to look out of the window as they drove into the city.

Penny opened her eyes what seemed like only

minutes later to discover Tim had pulled up outside the canopied entrance to a hotel. He opened the panel that separated driver from passengers.

'Mr Brosna's arranged for you and Andy to have one of the penthouses here, Penny.'

'Won't that be expensive?'

'Mr Brosna told me to inform you that this hotel is a Brosna business enterprise. The suite and all your expenses during your stay will be met by the company.' Tim reached into his inside pocket and withdrew a letter. 'He also asked me to give you this.'

'Thank you.' She took the letter and slipped it into her handbag. 'Have you known Mr Brosna long?'

'I've been working for Mr Brosna since August 1969.'

'Then you know him well.'

'I have reason to be grateful to Mr Brosna. It wasn't easy for Vietnam veterans to find work when they returned to the States, particularly those disabled as a result of their service.'

'How long were you in Vietnam?' She wondered if he had known Sandy and acquired the job through personal recommendation.

'Too long, Penny.' Tim left the car and opened the trunk.

A top-hatted, uniformed doorman stepped out from beneath the canopy and opened the car door. Penny climbed out of the limousine and looked around. The sidewalks were more crowded than she remembered, but the streets were cleaner and the people appeared more prosperous.

'I'll arrange to have your luggage delivered to your suite,' Tim assured her.

'Thank you and thank you for the ride. I'll see you again?'

'Almost certainly, Penny.'

Penny shook hands with Tim again before entering the foyer.

The receptionist excused herself from the people she was dealing with and walked over to Penny and Andy.

'Ms John, Mr John, welcome. This is your welcome pack and the keys to your suite.' She handed them to a bellboy. 'Gary will accompany you. I hope you enjoy your stay with us, ma'am, sir.'

'Thank you.' Penny and Andy followed Gary to a discreet corner of the foyer.

'This private elevator takes you directly to the penthouse floor, ma'am,' Gary explained. He opened the door and when they entered she saw there was only one button. He waited until Penny and Andy stood alongside him, pressed it and the elevator slid effortlessly upwards.

The doors opened in a wood-panelled hall floored with ceramic tiles. There were only two doors.

'You and Mr John are in the Emperor Suite, ma'am.' Gary opened the door and stood aside to allow them to enter ahead of him.

Penny noted the other door was labelled 'Royal Suite'.

She walked into an enormous, light, spacious living area. One wall was glass.

'This is the door to the terrace, ma'am.' Gary

pressed a button and part of the glass wall slid back. Penny stepped into a conservatory furnished with wooden-framed chairs and a matching table. Gary opened a second door that allowed access on to an outside balcony. She stepped outside and breathed in a lungful of warm humid air.

'Fresh air is rare in New York,' she said to Gary.

'It certainly is, ma'am.'

She returned to the living area. The sofas and chairs were cream leather, the carpet cream, the furniture good-quality reproduction antique French.

Gary opened two doors that led out of the rooms. 'There are two bedrooms, ma'am, with en suite bathrooms. The room service menu and house telephone numbers are in the desk.' He rolled back the top. 'If you should need anything, room service and reception are manned 24-7.'

'Thank you, Gary.' Penny opened her handbag and removed a five-dollar bill. She handed it to the boy.

'Thank you, ma'am. Your keys are on the desk.' He left the suite, closing the door quietly behind him.

'You have to see the bathrooms, they're fantastic. Both have walk-in multi-jet showers and there are separate whirlpool tubs, double sinks...'

Andy was so excited that Penny followed him into one of the bedrooms. Before she reached the bathroom she was transfixed by the size of the bed. It was the largest she'd seen. Opposite it was an enormous television and a glass-fronted fridge filled with soft drinks, beer, wine and liquor.

'I thought we lived well and our house was luxurious. I had no idea people lived like this.' Andy's voice echoed from the bathroom.

She followed him. 'We do live well, Andy.' She suppressed her irritation and tried to modify her lecturing tone. 'Our house is fine. The only people who can afford to live like this are extremely wealthy.'

'Which I suppose I will be, if I accept the Brosna inheritance.'

'Yes, I suppose you will,' she conceded as the implications of Charlotte Brosna's will hit her anew.

'I can't wait to try the shower and whirlpool bath.'

'Why don't you?'

'Water would wake me up and make me feel more human.'

'Don't fall asleep in the bath,' she warned.

'I'm not likely to do that.'

'You wouldn't be the first jet-lagged traveller to do just that,' she smiled, thinking of her and Kate's roommate. 'Are you hungry?'

'I prefer to have a shower first. If I'm peckish afterwards I might raid the fruit basket I saw in the living room.'

'I'll unpack and shower as well. Get together in an hour or so?'

'Sounds good to me. Which bedroom do you want?'

'As you're here, you can keep this one.'

She left him and went into the conservatory. The air was warm. Too warm. Something else she'd forgotten about – the heat and humidity of a New York summer. She closed the door to the outside terrace, turned up the air conditioning, retrieved the letter from her handbag and opened it.

Dear Penny,

I find it difficult to believe that you will be reading this letter a few hours from now in the suite next to mine. I have given you and Andy the two-bedroomed Emperor Suite because I thought you would like Andy close to you. Mine – the Royal – only has one bedroom.

My direct-dial telephone number is at the foot of the page. Telephone or visit me any time. It might be best if you telephone first. I would appreciate a few moments to prepare myself.

May I invite you and Andy to an early dinner – early because I assume you'll be jet-lagged. I agree; it would be better if we met one another without Andy before we eat.

I know the years have been kind to you because I have seen recent photographs of you. I also know that you are aware of my disfigurement. So there shouldn't be any unwelcome surprises on either side.

In my dreams the four of us haven't changed since that magical summer of 1968. I relive those days and take strength and comfort from them constantly. Possibly because it feels as though my life ended when that season changed.

See you soon, Penny.

R

Penny folded the letter and returned it to her handbag. She checked that the bundle of letters she had taken from her desk at home were still there.

Only then did she open her suitcase and remove the simply cut, short-sleeved, crinkle silk dress that was one of her favourites. She'd packed it because it was impossible to crease. She went into the bathroom, showered and washed her hair and applied body lotion, perfume, deodorant and cosmetics with more care than she'd taken in years.

She dried her long hair and twisted it into a simple knot at the nape of her neck. Her underclothes were silk, as were her stockings. She slipped on the dress and cinched it in at the waist with a leather belt.

She checked her reflection in the cheval mirror and added simple black-pearl earrings, a plain silver watch and the final touch: a black and white silk striped scarf.

Her court shoes were plain with two-inch heels. Did she look too severe? Like an applicant for a job interview?

Deciding she'd spent enough time on her appearance, she picked up the telephone receiver in her bedroom with a shaking hand and dialled the number at the foot of the page of Bobby's letter.

It was answered immediately and she visualised Bobby sitting in a chair next to the phone, waiting for it to ring.

'Hello?'

Whatever else had changed during the last nineteen years, his voice certainly hadn't.

'It's Penny.'

'I'll open the door and wait for you. Do you still drink beer?'

'I prefer dry white wine.'

'I'll open a bottle and pour you a glass.'

She picked up her handbag, left her bedroom and knocked on the door of the adjoining bedroom.

'I'm not asleep.' Andy's voice sounded distant as it echoed from behind the closed door of the bathroom through the empty bedroom.

'I'm going out for half an hour or so.'

'Wait.' There was the sound of water splashing. 'I'll come with you.'

'No, we've been invited out to dinner. I'll be back in good time. Enjoy the suite and order anything you want from room service.'

She didn't wait for him to reply. Picking up one of the sets of keys she left the suite, closed the door behind her and walked to the second door off the hall. It was ajar.

She knocked and entered. The luxury and layout of the suite were similar to the one she and Andy occupied.

He was sitting waiting for her in the conservatory. He left his chair and turned towards her. He was wearing a silk hood over his face, with slits at eye and mouth level. The slits were large enough for her to see his painfully familiar blue eyes. He wore a Panama on his head; his suit was lightweight beige linen, his white cotton shirt fastened at the neck by a beige silk tie.

He lifted a glass of wine and held it out to her.

She walked across the room, opened the door and joined him in the conservatory.

'Penny, before we go any further, there is something you should know–'

She interrupted him. 'I already know. I've known for years, Sandy.'

CHAPTER THIRTY-FIVE

Penny took the glass of wine Sandy handed her and sat facing him in the conservatory.

He sipped his own wine before setting his glass on the table. 'How did you find out?'

Her answer was brief. 'Bobby.'

'You saw him after the accident?'

'I never saw him again after that night. Charlotte made sure I couldn't go near the room that Bobby – you – were taken to in the hospital. She hired security guards to keep everyone, especially his friends and the press, away. The doctors endorsed her decision because you weren't expected to live. At the time I assumed she gave the order because she wanted to regain control of Bobby's life. Now it's obvious. She didn't want to risk anyone discovering that you weren't Bobby.'

'Charlotte believed I was Bobby after the accident and for weeks afterwards. It was an understandable mistake. I was burnt and bandaged beyond recognition. Bobby and I were the same height and build. Both of us had blue eyes.'

'But your hair was different. Yours was blue-black, Bobby's a brown-black.'

'My hair had burnt off.'

374

'I'm sorry. I didn't know.' She looked into his eyes. Imagined the scars he was concealing beneath the silk hood. 'I'm so sorry, Sandy. You must have been in excruciating pain.'

'You didn't see me at all after the accident?' He reached for his wine glass and cradled it.

'No. I was unconscious for hours. When I came round and asked to see you, the doctors – and Charlotte – said you were too weak to receive visitors.'

'The doctors kept me on morphine for months. My first memory – and it's a hazy one after the accident – is Charlotte informing me that Sandy had been killed in Vietnam. That was in late November or early December. I told Charlotte I was Sandy and she was furious. She ordered me not to talk to the medical staff. On her next visit she said if she couldn't have one grandson she'd have another. I needed the best care money could buy. She promised if I impersonated Bobby she'd buy it for me – and take care of my mother. If I didn't go along with her plan she'd throw us both out on the street. I was past caring what happened to me but my mother...

'Charlotte always was good at blackmail. Your love for your mother made you vulnerable. And, she was an expert at picking people's weak spots. But what possible reason could she have for asking you to pretend to be Bobby?'

'The first was money, the only thing that ever mattered to Charlotte. But I'll come back to that later. The second was the accident. A change of identity would have led to a reopening of the police enquiry and more newspaper reports and

375

scandal. It was months before I remembered some of the things that happened that night and over a year before I discovered Charlotte had managed to keep your statement that Bobby was responsible for the accident out of the press. I've had nearly twenty years to piece together the events. But there are still a few things I don't understand.'

She took two letters from her handbag. 'Perhaps I can help you.'

He looked at the airmail stamp on the envelope and recognised the handwriting. 'Bobby wrote to you?'

'Twice, once from the States and once from Vietnam. The second letter was sent on to me after he'd been killed.'

Sandy made no attempt to take them from her. 'I can tell you how the mix-up happened. The police officer who asked me to drive Bobby back to the Brosna Estate that night in Marion and Joe's yard went to their house the following morning to inform them about the accident. Marion told him that I'd woken her in the night collecting my things. My bag was missing; your bag and Kate's were still there. Bobby's bags were at the Beach House. The officer accepted Marion's story. He had no reason not to. He'd told me to drive Bobby's car the night before and I was seen driving it away. A driver who causes an accident will often panic and run from the scene, particularly if people are killed or injured. For the first day or so the police believed the accident was down to my bad driving. They didn't change their opinion until you gave your statement. But even then they believed that Sandy had collected his belongings from the house and disappeared and the survivor dragged from the wreck was Bobby.'

She thought about what he'd said. 'Now I can see why Charlotte didn't realise who you were at first.'

'And now we come to the money. Charlotte had set up a tax avoidance trust fund in Bobby's name. I have no idea how much was in it, but Charlotte had attached all sorts of conditions. Bobby wouldn't have been able to access any of the money or property until he was thirty-five. She contacted her lawyers to find out if Bobby had made a will. She was fairly certain he hadn't and she was right. As Bobby had no wife or known children at the time of his death, under Massachusetts law, his estate would have been divided between his parents. His mother was dead, so that left his father and Bobby's vast brood of half-brothers and -sisters. Charlotte was determined her stepson and his offspring wouldn't get a penny more than she'd already given him. So the moment the doctors cut the bandages from my hands in February 1969, she brought lawyers to my hospital bedside, pushed a pen between my fingers and made me sign document after document. The trust must have been difficult to dismantle. I was still signing papers two years later.'

'But your signature...'

'My right hand had been burnt to the bone. I was undergoing skin graft operations. But most significant of all, I was simply too damned weak to fight Charlotte. It was easier to go along with what she demanded of me, especially when she reminded me that although my mother had been resident in the States for years, she'd entered as an illegal immigrant. I didn't know if my mother had ever taken citizenship but I had more sense, even in my confused state than to ask Charlotte if Harriet had or hadn't. And, Charlotte gave me a letter from my mother – you met Harriet?'

'I did,' she confirmed.

'Charlotte allowed me to read it once before burning it in front of me. In it, my mother said she was pleased that I was getting the expensive medical care I needed, and being unable to acknowledge me as her son was a small price to pay for the treatment Charlotte was arranging.'

'Did you see your mother after the accident?'

'Not until Easter 1969 when Charlotte had me conveyed to the Brosna Estate on the Cape to recuperate between operations. She wouldn't allow Harriet to visit me before then in case either of us failed to control ourselves in front of the hospital staff. She warned that at the faintest flicker of recognition from either of us she'd stop funding my treatment and throw us both out.'

'She was a hard woman.'

'I'd rather not talk about her,' Sandy said decisively. 'After the accident she destroyed what little relationship she'd allowed me, as Bobby's childhood companion, to have with my mother.'

She offered him the letters. 'These explain why Bobby acted the way he did.'

'Aren't they personal?'

'Very,' she concurred. 'Which is why I've never

shown them to a soul.'

'Not even Andy?'

'Especially Andy.'

'Wasn't he curious about his father?'

'Yes. And, I always tried to answer his questions about Bobby as honestly as I could without mentioning you. Given Charlotte's – personality – I thought it best to keep the secret of "Bobby Brosna's" identity to myself.'

'Wise move.'

'I'm more grateful than you can know for signing the document that relinquished your paternal rights to Andy.'

'Like you, I too was afraid of Charlotte and with good cause. I saw what she was capable of when I was growing up. Saw just how cruel she could be, especially to Bobby.'

'Bobby told me some of it.'

'Whenever Bobby showed affection, she'd punish him. To her love and affection were weaknesses.'

'She's dead and gone, Sandy,' she reminded him softly.

'But her legacy lives on,' he said bitterly.

'When Andy was small I told him his father was someone I'd met before he was born and didn't want to stay with because I preferred living with just him. He grew up happy,' she insisted defensively. 'We live close to my parents. My brothers and sisters all live in the same town...'

'I know.' He reached down to the floor beside his chair and handed her the file he'd taken from Charlotte's room.

Stunned, she leafed through the pages. 'Bobby

said Charlotte employed snoops but this...'

'It's Charlotte's copy of one I commissioned. I wanted to ensure that you and Bobby's son wanted for nothing. She simply wanted to watch you. Are you sure you want me to read these letters?'

'Read them in the order they were written. The dates are on the envelopes. Although they were written weeks apart and one was sent from the States and the other Vietnam, I received both in January 1969. They had bounced around Swansea University, Art College and College of Further Education for weeks before they reached me.'

He removed the first letter and unfolded it.

Wednesday, 9th October 1968

Dearest, darling Penny,
I hope you get this letter. The only place I could think of to send it is your college. We never did ex-change addresses. It didn't seem important when we were living together. After all the arguments I had with Joe and Sandy about fighting a war no one believes in or wants, I'm a GI.

In between training I've had time to think about what Joe and Sandy said about caring enough for your country to fight in defence of decisions our leaders have made, because that's democracy. I disagree with the war, most of my fellow GIs disagree with it too but, unlike me, they had no choice but to fight.

Now comes the difficult bit.
I can't even begin to tell you how much I regret getting drunk. The sour taste of guilt is with me every

380

minute of every day. When I think of that night now, it's almost as though it happened to someone else. Or else I'm watching it on film. Especially when I recall how I tried to wrench the wheel from Sandy's hands.

I killed Kate, and from what the hospital told me this morning, almost certainly Sandy. When I telephoned they said the prognosis wasn't good. They only admitted that much because I pretended to be Sandy's father.

The sight of you unconscious in the road haunts me, as does the last image of Kate. She was on the verge, her body badly burnt, her neck broken. Drunk, shocked, not knowing what the hell I was doing, I tried to help a police officer drag Sandy from the wreckage. When we finally got Sandy away from the fire I thought he was dead too. His skin was blackened and peeling, his hair reduced to ashes on his head.

Horrified at what I'd done, I ran. It was a cowardly thing to do. The police shouted after me. I knew they wouldn't follow because the ambulances had arrived and they were busy loading you and Sandy into them.

I had no idea where I was running to, but I took the road towards the town and saw a taxi. I flagged it down.

The driver opened his window and said, 'Sandy Buttons?'

I told him I was and asked him to take me to Marion and Joe's house. It was the only place I could think of. I could hardly return to the Beach House and I wanted to get as far away from the site of the crash and the Brosna Estate as I could.

In my shocked alcoholic state, and I'm not making excuses, simply trying to explain why I acted the way

I did, I decided to atone for what I'd done by joining the army in Sandy's place.

I know it doesn't make sense. A brave man would have gone to the police and told them what he'd done. I lacked the courage.

I paid the driver. Marion and Joe's house was in darkness. I went in – you know they never lock the door. I meant to go upstairs to look for Sandy's room and find his draft papers because I didn't know where he was supposed to report. It was only when I reached the top of the stairs that I realised I didn't have a clue where Sandy's room was. I opened the first door I came to. A figure sat up in the bed and Marion mumbled sleepily, 'What is it?' I said, 'I'm looking for my room.' She said, 'It's on the right.'

I took Sandy's bag and crept downstairs; someone was in the kitchen so I left the house, walked out of town, hitched a ride and kept on hitching until I reached the army base a few days later. I used Sandy's name and said I'd lost my ID in a fire. They didn't question my story because I had the letter from the draft board. They said they'd put me down as a volunteer instead of conscript to make the paperwork easier.

I watched the news after I arrived and heard an announcement that Bobby Brosna was close to death. I saw a police appeal for Alexander Buttons to come forward. The officers were joined by Sandy's mother and Charlotte's lawyer who stated that they knew the accident wasn't caused by Alexander Buttons. It was only then I realised that the police, and presumably everyone else, including you, thought I was the one in hospital.

If Sandy recovers, as I hope and pray he will, it's

inevitable that Charlotte will find out about the identity switch. But I have a feeling that she'll consider a grandson on the brink of death easier to control. After all, Sandy is also her grandson. My father may never have acknowledged him as his son but we have the same blood running through our veins, and as neither of us is related to Charlotte by blood, she'll probably consider him a fair swap for me. People – especially family – have always been regarded by her as playthings.

I've telephoned the hospital every day. They told me you'd returned to Britain. I hope you make a full recovery, darling. I'm finding it very difficult to live with the tragedy and misery I've caused. Kate dead, Sandy in his Bobby guise seriously ill and not expected to recover, and you with broken bones and in pain...

I finished my training a week ago. Tomorrow we fly out to Vietnam. My fellow GIs are a friendly bunch. No one talks much about where we're going, only about family and friends and where we've been. All I talk about is you (I don't mention your name) and the summer we shared on the Cape.

I think if we were truthful we'd all admit we're terrified at the thought of fighting the Vietcong. There are stories, horrible stories, being bandied around the camp by some of the boys who've been out there.

I'm sorry for all the times I quoted Scott Fitzgerald and told you 'I love you now'. I don't know why I kept doing it. Perhaps in an immature way I thought life would be sweeter if I lived more on the edge.

I couldn't have been more wrong, Penny. 'I love you now' isn't enough and never will be. My country owns me body and soul for the next two years. I carry a dream that at the end of that time I'll come and find you, and when I do, I'll discover that you've found it in your heart to forgive me.

I imagine us living together in a small house like the Beach House, you painting, me making music. Having children, sharing our lives. Nothing out of the ordinary, just simple day-to-day living – and loving.

It must be the army that is making me this sentimental because all the boys are writing exactly the same sort of letter to their girls. Imagining their future as part of an ordinary family life. For most of them it will be a continuation of the life they've already lived. For me, an exotic new experience.

I love you, Penny, and I'll keep writing to you until you reply. My army number is at the top. Please, please write, my darling. I know I'm asking too much of you to forgive me, especially when I consider Kate and Sandy.

If you have any feelings left for me at all try to think only of the good times.

I know now I will love you until the day I die – and afterwards, if there is an afterlife.

Your Bobby, who was too wrong-headed and stupid to realise what he had with you and won't forgive himself for being stupid that night, and for what he did to Kate and Sandy, if he lives to be a hundred.

CHAPTER THIRTY-SIX

'Bobby was drunk that night.' Sandy finally folded the letter and returned it to the envelope.

'Being drunk isn't a defence. Bobby chose to buy the brandy. Kate died horribly. You–'

'You're still angry with him.' There was resignation in Sandy's voice.

'I thought that you, of all people, would understand why.'

'Spending months in hospital while doctors struggled to rebuild my face and body has taught me patience. What happened, Penny, happened. Kate's dead, Bobby's dead. No amount of anger or resentment can change the past.'

'I wish I could be as forgiving.'

'You would have forgiven Bobby and taken him back if he'd survived Vietnam.' It was a statement, not a question.

She thought about what he'd said. 'Yes, I would,' she conceded.

'Charlotte turning up the way she did, issuing orders, letting George go, throwing people out of the guest houses although she had no use for the houses and they had nowhere else to go, drove Bobby mad. He'd had a taste of freedom that summer; working with ordinary people in the restaurant, making music in his spare time and most of all being with you. Charlotte stepped back into his life and tried to force him to live the life she'd chosen for him yet again – just as she'd done since the day she'd paid his parents to hand him over to her. She turned back the clock for him and he hated it. You've no idea what he had to put up with, growing up with her as his legal guardian. If he liked a nanny when he was small, she'd let her go and employ another who wouldn't get too close to Bobby. If he made a friend in school, she'd ring the headmaster and ask him to move the boy out of Bobby's dorm.'

'He told me a little.'

'Such a waste of a life.' Sandy's eyes grew damp behind the slits in the hood.

'Read the second letter.'

He opened the envelope and carefully removed the letter that had grown brittle with age – and constant reading.

Friday, 1st November 1968

Dearest Penny,

I suppose it was too much to expect you to answer my first letter. Ever the optimist I hope, although I don't entirely believe, your silence is down to the time it takes mail to cross the Atlantic.

No matter how much you may hate me you cannot hate me as much as I hate myself for killing Kate and Sandy and ruining your life. I feel guilty for living when Kate is dead and Sandy hovering on the brink of death.

It's small consolation, but if there's a punishment that fits the crime, it's the hell that's Vietnam. I understand why I have to suffer, what I can't understand is why so many innocent boys are being punished alongside me.

I've been here two weeks and can't begin to describe the conditions to you. Someone as sweet, gentle and loving as you shouldn't be made aware of horrors. No film, training or lecture could possibly prepare for the reality. The smells and sounds are the worst. Gunfire, bombs, shells, grenades and human screams shatter our nerves daily. Not only because of the noise but because we know that somewhere close by a healthy body is being smashed, broken and torn apart. Possibly one we were talking to minutes earlier.

I find myself wondering if the next shell has my name on it. Silence is even more terrifying because we're all waiting for an explosion to end it.

We've been told we're being flown out tomorrow. We don't know to where or for how long, but we can be sure that wherever it is, it will be Vietcong-occupied. As a result everyone in my platoon is writing letters to be sent on to their folks 'in case' of non-return or return in a body bag.

I now understand why some families insist on having an empty grave. It means their husband, son, father or brother's name is recorded in stone. Proof they existed, and as the saying goes, 'once walked this way'.

On to practical things before I get any more maudlin. I've named Charlotte as my next of kin. I was the one who got drunk. She was the one who drove me to it and I want her to know right away if I'm killed. Although I doubt she'll shed a tear. I never meant as much to her as one of her pet dogs. But I'm not sending her a last letter. I've reserved that dubious privilege for you.

Even if you hate me, this letter will close the episode

387

of your life we shared. If our story was a Hollywood film I'd write a lot of platitudes about you living on for both of us, remembering only the good times we shared and finding another man worthy of you. But this isn't a film, and as you already know, I'm all too fallible.

I hate the thought of dying but most of all not being around to grow old with you. If there is an afterlife in which you can look down on people on earth, I'll resent everyone who is able to see you, talk to you and, most of all, touch you.

The strange thing is at this precise moment I believe I'm immortal. In a few minutes I know I'll feel different, but for now I believe – really believe – you'll never read this letter.

Thank you forgiving me the happiest days of my life. I'm desperately sorry for getting drunk and behaving like an idiot. I can't bear to think of the pain I've caused Kate's family and friends and Sandy. Or how much I regret dismissing the love you offered as if it wasn't the most precious gift I'd ever been given.

I love you, Penny. I have from the very first moment I saw you. Sandy said he'd told you how hard I chased you after we met in Grosvenor Square. I knew then you were the only girl for me but I was afraid you'd take my love and reject it as Charlotte did when I was a child. I imagine us meeting again when this is over and I cling to the hope that we'll have a future together.

Not goodbye, Penny, but goodnight. I will see you again, my dearest darling girl who I love now and will love always. I carry you in my heart.

Bobby

Sandy stared at the letter for a long time after he read it. Finally he lifted his head and looked at her. 'You've really never shown these letters to anyone? Never told anyone it was Bobby Brosna who died in Vietnam and Sandy Buttons who has been impersonating him for the last nineteen years?'

'No.'

'Not even your parents or Andy?'

'Especially my parents and Andy. Given Charlotte's wealth and power and insistence on keeping Bobby alive to the world, I thought the knowledge Bobby was dead, dangerous. She's not a woman I would have ever wanted to cross.'

'You knew me. Did you regard me as dangerous?'

'Of course not. But very few people had seen you since the accident and then only when you were covered by a hood. I couldn't even be sure that you were you, if that makes sense.'

'It makes perfect sense.'

'You appear to have been lucky with your parents.'

'Very,' she agreed. 'I hid the letters and kept them in reserve as a trump card I would have been loath to use. Charlotte's lawyers contacted me often about Andy when he was small, trying to get me to hand him over to her the way Bobby's parents had Bobby. But your insistence on not claiming parental rights reassured me and I was grateful for it. Although I did wonder why you wanted Bobby's name on the birth certificate.'

'I knew Bobby was dead. That was my trump card. If Charlotte had pushed too hard I would have told the world I had no claim to Andy because I wasn't Bobby Brosna.'

'You would have done that for me?'

'For you and Bobby's son. Thank you for keeping these.' He returned the last letter to the envelope. 'And thank you for showing them to me.'

'Apart from Andy they were all I had left of Bobby. Did Tim Garber know him?'

'Yes, but in Vietnam and as Sandy Buttons.'

'Bobby never told him who he was?'

'No, but I did one night when I was drunk. It's difficult being lonely and having no one to talk to. Which is probably one of the reasons I find it easy to forgive Bobby for what he did. Given Charlotte's habit of employing "snoops", I realise now he thought he couldn't trust anyone. Not even me. For all he knew I could have taken Charlotte's money.'

'You didn't?'

'I'm surprised you feel the need to ask. Not that Charlotte didn't offer. She did, several times.'

'That last afternoon she offered me money to leave Bobby alone.'

'Charlotte told me she'd tried to buy you. In fact her last words were "stupid girl, how dare she refuse me".'

'I annoyed her?' Penny smiled.

'Everyone who refused to dance to her tune annoyed her. When I returned to the Cape to re-cuperate, Charlotte wouldn't allow Harriet and I to meet without a witness present. Generally her. As I couldn't speak to Harriet about my change of identity, that left Tim. He survived the helicopter crash that killed Bobby and wrote to me when he was invalided out of the army, telling me he'd been Sandy Buttons' buddy in 'Nam and was in desperate need of a job. I wanted to help him for Bobby's sake. He accepted my invitation to visit and I discovered he knew almost as much about Bobby, or Sandy, as I did. Bobby had talked to Tim about the grandmother who brought him up and the English girl he was in love with and was going to search for when he was discharged from the army. Tim's a good man, I'm glad Bobby suggested he look me up.'

'And now we've found one another again,' she murmured.

'Have we, Penny? Do you really want to be part of my life in the future?' Sandy asked seriously.

'Yes. I would like to have your friendship.' She took the letters he handed her.

'That, you've always had.'

'How much do you want to tell Andy?'

He left his chair and walked slowly and awkwardly to the glass door and looked over the veranda before turning back to her. 'I think it's time I stopped living a lie and told, not only Andy, but the world the truth about his father, don't you? That way we can arrange to have Bobby's name added to the Vietnam War Memorial in Washington.'

'But the Brosna inheritance. If Andy turns it down...'

'He won't.'

'You're very sure of my son's reaction.'

'If Andy rejects it, it will all go to the Republican Party.'

For the first time she detected a trace of humour in his voice. 'It's an obscene amount of money, Penny. Miracles can be conjured with millions of dollars. Research centres given funding so they can find and test cures for diseases. Children's education programmes can be sponsored which will enable bright kids to go to college. And I haven't even started on the Third World. Wells can be dug in drought-stricken villages, starving people given the means to farm land...'

'Charity needs organising.'

'Tim has overseen our military veteran programme for years. I work on the charity side of the Brosna Foundation. We have some good people on our payroll.'

'And Andy's medical studies?'

'The Brosna Foundation funds a medical school in Harvard.'

'He was hoping to go to Guy's.'

'He's Bobby's son. He'll make his own decisions. Charlotte did stipulate that he has to take the name Robert Brosna the Fifth to inherit. But he doesn't have to use it except on legal documents. Or, he could be Bobby Brosna here in the States and Andy John in Wales.'

'That's for Andy to decide. But I'll never call him Bobby.'

'Do you want to eat here or in your suite?'

'Which would you prefer?'

'Here.'

'I'll fetch Andy.'

'Before you go, I'd like your opinion on this.' He removed his hat and pulled off his silk hood.

She stared at the ravages of the face she had often sketched and admired.

'It's horrendous, isn't it?' He lifted the hood intending to replace it.

She walked over to him, took it from between his fingers, tossed it on to the chair and kissed him lightly on the lips. 'You could never be horrendous, Sandy.'

'But, Andy—'

'Is a grown man who wants to be a doctor. He'll admire your courage in allowing us to see your face.'

CHAPTER THIRTY-SEVEN

Penny left Sandy's suite and walked along to her own. She unlocked the door. As she entered, Andy rose from the sofa where he'd been sitting, flicking through the channels on the TV set.

'You've been gone ages.'

'I'm sorry—'

'Does my father want to see me?'

She went to the bar and poured herself a vodka. Taking a glass and a can of beer for Andy she handed them to him. 'Your father died in Vietnam in November 1968.'

'Before I was born?' Andy took the beer but

made no attempt to open it. 'You told me Bobby Brosna was my father...'

'And so he was, darling. The man who's passed himself off as Bobby Brosna for the last nineteen years is your father's friend Sandy Buttons. He and I have a lot of explaining to do but I think it's best done together. He's waiting for us. Shall we go to dinner?'

Sandy had left the door to his suite open. He was sitting in the conservatory with his back to them. When he turned to face them, Penny saw that he was watching Andy's face intently to gauge her son's reaction to his damaged face but the surprise was his.

Andy walked forward and offered him his hand. His movements, his gesture, were all Bobby. Sandy was too stunned to even shake Andy's hand.

'He's–'

'His father all over again,' Penny said.

Tim brought in Czar after walking the dog in the park. He served them dinner and, at Sandy's invitation, joined them.

'Tim is the only person who can tell you about your father's time in Vietnam,' Sandy assured Andy.

The explanations began with the cocktails, continued through the first course of mussels, and steaks grew as cold as the salads on their plates as Sandy and Penny answered Andy's questions. By the time Tim served the fresh-fruit and sorbet dessert, Andy, Sandy and Tim were making plans to return to the Brosna Estate so Sandy could show Andy the place where his father had been happy and talk through the implications of his acceptance or rejection of the Brosna inheritance.

'I really don't have to run the businesses? I can study medicine just as I planned?' Andy checked.

'I think what Sandy is trying to tell you, darling, is the decision is yours to make. You're the boss,' Penny reminded her son.

'You have no idea how good it is to hear someone use my real name again.' Sandy nodded as Tim held up a fresh bottle of wine. 'If your great-grandmother heard you say that you still wanted to be a doctor, she'd no doubt tell you that you're in serious danger of running the businesses into the ground and frittering away the Brosna millions. But there's so much money it wouldn't be a bad idea to fritter some of it, in the right places. Now, about this medical school in Harvard that Brosna money built. It's absolutely the best...'

Penny took her coffee and walked to the window.

'Mam, you're coming to the Cape with us, aren't you?' Andy left the table and joined her.

'No.'

'It's changed out of all recognition since 1968. Cosmo's is closed, Pen–' Sandy began.

'It's not that, Sandy,' Penny interrupted. 'I think it's a good idea for Andy to get to know Bobby through his closest friends. You'll have a wonderful time, Andy, and while you're with Sandy I won't feel guilty for abandoning you and making other plans.'

'Other plans?' Sandy reiterated.

'I need to make a telephone call.'

'There's one in the conservatory. Shut the door if you want privacy.'

'Thank you.' She did as Sandy suggested, dialled 'nine' for an outside line followed by a UK number. It was answered on the sixth ring. Only then did she think to check her watch. Nine o'clock in New York, two in the morning in the UK.

'Jack Evans.'

'I'm sorry, Jack, did I wake you?'

'Pen, what's wrong?'

'Nothing.'

'You rang me at two in the morning to tell me nothing's wrong.'

'I forgot the time difference.'

'Have you and Andy seen Bobby Brosna?'

'Yes.'

'And?'

'Andy's going to Cape Cod with Sandy...'

'Who's Sandy?'

She looked through the glass wall at Sandy, Tim and Andy, talking animatedly. 'Bobby's closest and best friend. It's a long story, Jack. Andy's going to discuss the inheritance with the Brosna executives and see some of the places his father lived in when he was young. But I didn't phone about Andy. He's fine. Do you remember that short break you wanted to take...'

'To Dunster?'

'I wondered if you could hand over your farm to one of your minions, as you call them, for a few weeks and make it the States. I never did see

396

the galleries and museums in '68 and I'd love to show you the *Alice in Wonderland* statue in Central Park. Afterwards we could go to Washington and see the Vietnam Memorial.'

'To lay your ghosts?'

'They're laid and have been laid a long time. You can find someone to take care of the farm, can't you?'

'Might be possible if you add Las Vegas to the itinerary,' he ventured. 'I've always fancied one of their quickie, tacky weddings.'

'I'll look for an Elvis suit you can wear. Do you want me to look like Dolly Parton?'

She heard a sharp intake of breath.

'Do you mean that?'

'Yes.' She thought of Bobby's last letter. Of his assertion *I love you now isn't enough...*

Seconds ticked past.

'You're very quiet. You're regretting your answer?' Jack asked in concern.

'No. Just thinking.'

'About what?'

'The future.'

'When we return from the States you will move in here, won't you? It would be difficult to run this place from your house.'

'Yes, I'll move in with you but I'll keep my studio.'

'I could build you one here.'

'No point when I've one less than five minutes away by car.'

'I'll concede your studio. What will you do with your house?'

'My parents can use it for a guest house for my

sisters, brothers and their children. That way they'll have no excuse not to clear up their own mess when they come to visit. But I do have one question.'

'Fire away.'

'Do you think we're too old to have children?'

The publishers hope that this book has given you enjoyable reading. Large Print Books are especially designed to be as easy to see and hold as possible. If you wish a complete list of our books please ask at your local library or write directly to:

Magna Large Print Books
Magna House, Long Preston,
Skipton, North Yorkshire.
BD23 4ND

This Large Print Book for the partially sighted, who cannot read normal print, is published under the auspices of

THE ULVERSCROFT FOUNDATION